KU-432-205

From

The Women's Press Ltd
34 Great Sutton Street, London EC1V 0DX

Gillian Slovo *Photo by Andy Metcalf*

Gillian Slovo was born in Johannesburg, South Africa in 1952, and came to England in 1964. Over the last eight years she has worked as a journalist and film producer. Her first novel, *Morbid Symptoms*, was published in 1984. She has recently completed a third Kate Baeier thriller.

GILLIAN SLOVO

Death by Analysis

The Women's Press

First published by The Women's Press Limited 1986
A member of the Namara Group
34 Great Sutton Street, London EC1V 0DX

Copyright © Gillian Slovo 1986

All rights reserved. This is a work of fiction and any resemblance to persons living or dead is purely coincidental.

British Library Cataloguing in Publication Data

Slovo, Gillian
Death by Analysis.
I. Title
823[F] PR6069.L/

ISBN 0-7043-5008-4
ISBN 0-7043-4018-6 Pbk

Photoset by MC Typeset Limited, Chatham, Kent
Printed in Great Britain

For Andy

One

'I've got a feeling that this is our lucky try,' Daniel said.

Encouraged by his optimism, I edged forward and looked into the distance.

'Forget it,' I said. 'Another dead end.'

Daniel grimaced. 'I don't want to be here any more.'

'So move out of the way,' the irate man behind him snapped, 'you're blocking my view.'

We sighed and turned back.

The crowd seemed to stretch forever. It was a waiting crowd, and a bad-tempered one at that. People had come in family groups with the apparent purpose of quarrelling in the open. Fathers administered random slaps at whining children, grandparents complained about the view and mothers worked overtime to keep order. Unity within the family only seemed possible when an unwary stranger stepped too close. Then they would fix the outsider with glares that could reduce the strongest to pulp. Stay longer, and abuse would be thrown. Heaven help anybody who unwittingly steps into the charmed circle of the English family at celebration.

For this was supposed to be a celebration. We had come *en masse* to crane our heads at fireworks we could have better seen on television. We had ended up getting a better view of each other's dandruff than of the famous, and the restricted breathing space was leading to rising tempers. I suppose all of this was predictable since we were all playing our minor parts in a pre-wedding event, played out on a cosmic scale. It was 28 July 1981, the night before the wedding of Charles, heir to the throne, to Lady Diana Spencer.

The people had come to celebrate but there was an air of desperation in their attempt. While unemployment rocketed, while disorder spread to the streets, while more men followed Bobby Sands in lingering deaths, while, in Liverpool, the police used a landrover to kill a boy who could never have got away, the English were celebrating the fact that there was one thing they could still do: organise a pageant.

I was beginning to hate myself for being part of it. For the twentieth time that evening someone stepped hard on my foot. For the twentieth time that evening I cursed Daniel for ever persuading me to join the throng. He was ahead of me, pushing and prodding, trying to find a way out. I took a step towards him and then attempted another. I was out of luck. A hand had grabbed my ankle and was holding on to it. I looked down in irritation. And did a double take.

I hadn't seen her for almost a year and it was an odd angle from which to take in the once familiar face. She smiled up at me from where she was sitting on the ground.

'How are you, Kate?' she said.

'Fine.' I wished the stiffness would go from my voice. 'And you?'

'I'm well.'

While we looked and smiled at each other, the crowd around us started to push towards the wooden dais that had been constructed in the centre of the park. I looked up just in time to catch a glimpse of Nancy Reagan's light blue dress as she mounted the platform. When I looked down again, Franca's eyes were still on me. For a moment the crowd seemed to recede into the distance. I felt an uneasy stillness descend on me. I was used to silence with her, but this was different.

'Not the sort of place I expected to see you,' I stuttered.

'No, it isn't. But I'm glad we met like this,' she replied.

'Me too.'

'Because I was about to get in touch with you,' she continued in a rush. I saw that she too was nervous. It was the first time I could remember noticing that about her.

She talked over my surprise. 'I'd like to ask you something,' she said.

'That would make a change.'

She threw me a quick glance. 'Would you be free to visit me on Tuesday?' she asked. I nodded my head.

'At eleven?' she said.

Again I nodded. 'Same place?' I asked.

'If you could,' she said. 'I'd be grateful. My schedule, you know.'

'Don't I,' I said. 'See you there.'

The background of noise that I'd managed to shut out invaded again. I turned to go. I bumped straight into Daniel, who had pushed his way back to see what had kept me. He was standing surprised at the awkwardness of the encounter. His eyes held a question. I brushed past him and he followed.

It took another twenty minutes before we made it to the road. Twenty minutes of concentrated work to fight our claustrophobia and the resistance of the crowd, who were pushing the other way. It took us a further two minutes to get our breath back. Daniel was the first to make it.

'That was odd,' he said. 'Who is she?'

'Franca,' I answered.

'No shit. How did it feel?'

'Weird,' I said, 'very weird. Had to happen one day, but what a place for it.'

In contrast to Hyde Park, Cardozo Road seemed peaceful. Sam was at the desk, rooting through a stack of photographs, muttering to himself. It was hard to tell whether he was going to succeed in finding illustrations for his article on geometric forms in modern landscaping. Anna was on the floor surrounded by open suitcases and half-folded clothes. She took one look at our faces and got up.

'This seems to call for a drink,' she said. 'Don't say I didn't warn you.'

'Wasn't all that bad,' Daniel protested. 'I had to get a glimpse of that aspect of English life. Specially now . . .' He stopped himself and looked at me.

'Oh, go ahead,' I snapped. 'Say it. It's no secret to us that you're leaving the country. We have accepted it. Just don't think we'll ever forgive you.'

Anna pulled a face. 'She's starting again,' she said.

'Ignore her,' said Daniel. 'How about some wine? We could try that Dão Kate and Sam brought.'

He went out of the room and up the stairs. Anna knelt down again, intent on sorting her scattered belongings. Sam was on his last pictures and didn't lift his head. I sat on the bed and looked around.

I looked at my friend packing on the floor and felt a wave of sadness. Anna and Daniel had taken so long deciding whether to return to the States that I'd almost begun to believe they'd never go. But now it was inevitable. And soon.

I had met Anna and Daniel four years previously and could no longer imagine life without their presence. They were both from

New York but had seemed indefinitely settled in London. They'd got together when she'd just extracted herself from the BBC and a painful marriage and he was on the loose and trying to turn from academic to journalist. It was a whirlwind romance that was never meant to last. They were supposed to act like two strangers in transition.

It hadn't worked out like that. They'd stayed together, and in London. But they'd always had an ambivalent attitude to English life. They liked the environment and the left: they weren't so keen on the food and social relations. And now they were packing up. Back to New York in what looked like a permanent move.

Daniel came back into the room as I was in the middle of depressing myself about life in the future without them. He poured us each a glass of wine and sat down on the floor, his back to the glass doors which led to the garden.

'Did you tell them about Franca?' he asked.

Sam lifted his head. 'What about her?'

'I got to meet her,' said Daniel. 'Or at least to see what she looked like.'

'She was there?' Sam asked. 'Among the millions?'

'Yup. And she wants to see me,' I replied.

'That's odd. Did she say why?' Anna said.

'No she didn't. I guess she just misses me too much,' I joked.

'And wants to pay you to come back,' Sam finished.

'No need to be jealous,' I said. 'Anyway, we have to go home soon. I've only got six days to decide what I'm going to wear.'

Two

The road and the outside of her house were painfully familiar. I stood there to remember the times I'd walked along the pavement; sometimes fast, sometimes slow, often confused, but always on time. Some things never change, I thought, as I double-pressed her bell at precisely eleven o'clock.

She was waiting for me at the top of the stairs. The same style, the same smile, the same open hello, but everything was different. I followed her into the room. When I was inside I stopped.

'You changed the chairs,' I said.

She was still closing the door. She smiled. 'Did you think it would remain unaltered without you?' she asked.

'There's always hope,' I said.

I crossed the room, taking in the details I'd never quite forgotten. It was a bare space, furnished for utility. At one end of the white room, in front of the french doors which led to the small garden, stood the two chairs. They looked as if they had been stranded there. They were placed at angles to each other so that the eyes of their occupants would only meet at some point in the middle of the varnished floorboards. Between them stood a glass table, sparkling and metallic. It held the two familiar objects: a transparent vase, filled this time with small pink roses, and a box of tissues. There were only two other pieces of furniture in the room: the desk, small and wooden, and the couch, large and leather.

I sat down in the place that had once seemed like mine. I stared at the spot on the floor.

'How are things?' she said, her voice pulling me into the present. She was sitting upright on the second chair.

'Not bad,' I said. 'Same indetermination with work but otherwise content.'

'I'm pleased,' she said.

'Except I'm very nervous now. Maybe you should tell me why you asked to see me.'

I turned my head to look at her, but she avoided my gaze. She'd never done that before. Something was wrong.

'I thought a lot about inviting you here,' she said.

She was sitting straight. I saw that she wasn't comfortable. She leaned forward slightly, one hand holding the other. I noticed that the gold ring she'd often twisted was no longer there.

'Before we start,' she continued, 'I want to say that you must feel free to say no. I think it is the right thing for me to do to ask you, but equally you must be able to refuse.'

She left her words in the air for a while before she moved back in her chair. I nodded.

'Somebody I know, somebody I have been seeing, has died.'

'A client?'

'No, somebody I saw for supervision.'

She got up abruptly and went to stand by the window, her back to the room. I had to crane my head round to see her. Her voice, when she spoke, seemed to be coming from far inside her as if the effort was almost too much for her.

'I'm not altogether satisfied that his death was an accident,' she said. 'I'd like you to investigate it for me.'

'You think he was murdered?'

'I do.'

'Why?'

She shook her head as if to toss off an unbearable thought. She moved from the window and sat down again, crossing her arms.

'I'm not at liberty to say. I am by no means certain. It's just a feeling I have. A feeling combined with certain information.'

'That you got in supervision?' I asked.

'I cannot reveal my sources,' she said.

'Have you told the police?'

'I'm not in a position to. They wouldn't believe me unless I gave them more.'

'Which you won't give me?'

'No,' she said, 'I cannot.'

'Who was he?'

'His name was Paul Holland. Two weeks ago he was found dead in the street. The police say it was a hit-and-run accident.'

'Did you know him well?' I asked.

'I told you,' she said. 'He came to me for supervision.'

I looked at her. Her face gave nothing away but it seemed like an effort.

'Why me?' I asked.

'Because of your skills,' she said. 'And understanding. You have the experience gained from your investigation of Tim Nicholson's death and you have a knowledge, an inner knowledge, of psychotherapy.'

'Do you think I could do it?'

'I am not certain that anybody can,' she said, 'or that there is an answer to Paul's death. But you have the ability and if you want to use it I would trust you above many others.'

I sank into my chair while the years came back to me. I thought about the times, three hours a week, that I had been in this room, in this position, if not in this chair. I thought about the silences there had been, the understanding and the words. And I thought about the way I had grown up here.

'You want me to investigate the death of this man but you won't tell me why you suspect it's murder. Is that right?' I asked.

'Yes.'

'What happens if I find out?' I said. 'Will you go to the police?'

'We will deal with that when, and if, it happens.'

'And if we disagree as to the course of action?'

'You have to do what you think necessary,' she said, 'and I will be able to cope with it. It is better to know the truth than hide in the dark.'

'The truth is not always comfortable,' I said.

She smiled with me as we both remembered the time when our positions were reversed: when I had done battle with my fears while she had sat by me.

After a while she spoke again. 'There is one other thing. I don't want anybody to know that I hired you.'

'I see.'

'Will you do it?' she asked.

I tried to think about it but I found that I'd already made up my mind. Reflecting on it later, I don't think there was any way I could have refused her request.

'I'll try it one week at a time,' I said. 'If it doesn't work out, I'll stop. I'll give you one day's notice.'

'That seems right,' she said.

'I'll charge £40 a day. Plus expenses. But I won't charge you for hours I don't work.'

'Don't cheat yourself,' she said.

She got up and went to the desk. She opened the drawer and took out a piece of paper. She handed it to me. I glanced at it and saw that on it was written the name Paul Holland, followed by an address.

'This is where he lived. His daughter Regina is still there. That's all I can tell you.'

I folded the paper and put it in my bag.

'You were very sure,' I said. 'Writing this out before I came.'

'Not really,' she said. 'Just a belief.'

'Like Paul Holland was murdered.'

'Along those lines,' she answered.

I got up and so did she. We walked to the door. She opened it for me and I stepped through.

'Keep in touch,' she said.

I nodded.

Paul Holland's house wasn't far away. I decided to leave my car and walk to it. On the way I tried to concentrate on how I felt about working for Franca. I didn't get far. My mind kept turning instead to the time when I'd first played detective. Hired to look into the death of Tim Nicholson by a group of journalists called African Economic Reports, I'd embarked on an investigation that had proved to be both fascinating and, in the end, painful. I wondered whether this would be the same.

The thought sent a shiver to my neck. In the back of my mind I heard Franca's voice, an echo from the past. 'Nobody ever said it would be easy,' she was saying. But neither is freelance journalism, I thought, as I rang the bottom bell that bore Holland's name. His house was still in shrink territory: in one of those roads which join Primrose Hill to Swiss Cottage and where every building has a garden, at least three apartments and one shared consulting room.

It took a very long time for the woman to answer my ring, and when she did, she seemed in doubt as to what had brought her to the door. She stared at me with big brown eyes. She was dressed in faded jeans and a pink sweater that had seen better days, but she looked like she'd just got up. Her brown hair hung limp down the sides of her long, pale face.

'Regina Holland?' I asked.

She nodded.

'Could I come in?'

She stepped backwards and let me pass into the cavernous entrance hall.

‘I suppose you’re another of them,’ she said. ‘You all look alike.’
‘Of whom?’ I asked.
‘His patients. The ghouls. Come to display their agony to me now he’s dead.’
‘No, I’m not . . .’ I started and then stopped myself. I realised that I couldn’t come up with a single reason for visiting Paul Holland’s house. I realised that I was more shaken up by Franca’s request than I’d thought.
My lack of words didn’t matter to Regina. She was acting like she was in a world of her own. I don’t think she would have heard me whatever I’d said. She walked to the stairs, gripped on to the ornate banisters, and almost hauled herself up a flight. I followed.
Paul had lived on the first floor in a flat whose proportions were spectacular. A huge entrance hall, with its high ceilings and intricate wall mouldings, led to an even bigger living room. This was a room that should have reeked of comfort and of wealth, furnished as it was in soft leather, and thick pile. Dark blue velvet curtains hung by the grand windows through which could be seen the calm of Primrose Hill. Solid objects, heavy glass ashtrays and decorative shapes, dotted the place and soothed the eye.
Altogether it should have been an elegant room. There was just one major problem: it had been devastated. Books and papers scattered the floors, sofas sat without cushions, bureaux without drawers.
‘What happened?’ I asked.
‘We . . . I was burgled,’ she said. ‘Last night.’
Abruptly she picked up one of the brown cushions that lay on the carpet and threw it on to the sofa. She sat down on top of it. I went and sat next to her.
‘Have the police been?’ I asked.
She nodded.
‘Was much taken?’
‘Our video,’ she said. ‘And his notes.’
‘The notes on his clients?’ I asked.
‘Patients.’ She looked at me with an expression I couldn’t quite fathom. I wasn’t sure I liked it.
‘Were there a lot of notes?’ I asked.
‘Worried now, are you? Scared that somebody’s going to blackmail you? What grimy secrets did you reveal in the inner sanctum?’
‘I’ve never been here before,’ I said.

'They all say that. I wasn't born yesterday. Why are you interested in his notes then?'

'They do seem like an odd choice for a burglar.'

'The police said thieves take stuff that looks interesting just for a laugh. Best thing that could happen to them in my opinion. At least somebody would get some joy out of them.'

'I gather you didn't like your father's profession,' I said.

'It's hard to live with a god,' she said. 'You only had to take him in fifty-minute doses.'

'Were you jealous?' I asked.

'Jealous? Of attention from that . . . that . . .'

She tried to spit the words out but they wouldn't come. She tried to stop shaking but that didn't work either. She buried her head in her hands. I noticed how big-boned they were. I wondered how long she'd been that thin.

She sat there a while before looking up. When she did I saw that her face was wet with silent tears.

'Is there somebody you'd like with you?' I asked. 'I could ring them.'

'I'm all right,' she said. 'My friend's coming back.' She gave a sudden smile that sparked a bit of life in her passive face.

'You must think I'm crazy,' she said. 'I'm not, you know.'

'It's been a shock.'

'He had so much time for everybody else. And so little for me. I was beginning to feel I'd never known him. And now I never will.' She stood up and glowered at me.

'I suppose you too would like a last look at the sacred room,' she said.

'If I could.'

She turned on her heel and walked out of the room. I followed her down the corridor. We ended up by the last room on the left. We went in.

It was a therapy room of a different genre to Franca's. Instead of the two statutory chairs there were large cushions lining the heavy pink pile carpet. The walls were cosy; covered in brightly coloured rugs and blankets that made the room feel padded. It looked like Paul Holland had gone out of his way to create a womb, a man-made womb, for his clients.

The effect was so cloying and somehow unworldly that the open filing cabinet seemed incongruously efficient. I went up to it and looked inside. It was empty. Only a few scraps of paper on the floor beneath it showed that it had ever been used.

I leaned down, picked them up and looked through them. They were mostly odd notes, taken at seemingly random times and interspersed with doodles so intense that they belied the calm of the room.

The doodles were all variations on a theme, except for one. On a scrap of paper, criss-crossing lines intersected names which seemed placed at random on the page. I turned to Regina, who was standing listlessly by the door.

'Was Paul into genealogy?' I asked.

'He was open to anything, so he boasted,' she answered.

I held up the piece of paper. 'Can I keep this?'

She shrugged in a gesture I took for consent.

'Didn't he keep his filing cabinet locked?' I asked.

'Sure he did. Just like I kept the flat locked, and you can see how solid the doors are. The police say this was done by a professional. Some professional.'

She stared in the direction of the corner of the room. I followed her gaze. For the first time I saw that somebody had attacked one of the cushions. It was ripped apart, slaughtered by a sharp knife, its foam sticking out in protest. I turned to say something, but Regina got there first.

'Let's end this little pilgrimage, shall we?' she said.

She stepped aside and made a sweeping gesture with her hand. I was escorted to the door.

Just before I was out, I turned to her. 'I'm sorry this happened.'

She gave me a weak smile. 'And I, that I'm like this.'

The door closed behind me.

I walked back to Franca's house to pick up my car. It crossed my mind to tell her about the missing notes. I decided this was a bad move when I arrived outside her house. There was a woman at the door. She rang the bell twice before the door clicked open. I watched her going inside and thought I understood Regina's jealousy. Then the feeling went, replaced by something more solid. I got into my car and drove to the *Street Times* office.

Tony was sitting behind his desk in his third-floor cubicle. It was a small office, dingy but homely. He didn't look occupied and he didn't look happy. On the wall above him a blow-up of Humphrey Bogart pointed his finger accusingly, instructing people to join the National Union of Journalists.

Tony looked up and saw me.

'Brought any stories with you?' he asked.

'Afraid not. I'm after some information,' I said.

'That's typical,' he grumbled. 'There once was a time when I thought all a good journalist had to do was to sit in the pub and the news would come to him. Then I learned that good journalism was a result of sheer hard work. Now I've done the work, everybody and her mother comes to me to find out things the easy way.'

'What's the matter, Tony?' I asked. 'Caroline still pushing for a baby?'

Tony laughed. He got back the boyish look that he usually carried around with him.

'I blame you, you know,' he said. 'You started it. Want a coffee?'

I sat down in front of his paper-filled desk and watched as he poured from the full percolator. Coffee dripped from its side on to the stained surface. I wondered whether Tony lived in so much mess at home and if he did, how Caroline could stand it. He turned round and saw me wondering. He made a helpless grab for a dry J-cloth which had been abandoned there. I smiled at his gesture and he went all wide-eyed and innocent. I took in the rest of his appearance.

'You're looking good,' I said. 'Domestication agrees with you.'

It was true. Tony looked better, more contented, than I'd ever seen him. He'd got involved with Caroline while I was investigating the death of Tim Nicholson. In fact, co-operating with her to help me had been what had brought them together.

From the beginning of their affair it had been obvious that Tony had finally found what he wanted. He had changed, albeit gradually, from an inveterate bachelor, scared of women and himself, into somebody with roots and the confidence to show them.

It hadn't all been easy and now they were going through a rough patch. Caroline's wish to have a baby seemed to have shaken Tony out of his contentment. He was thrown back into his pre-Caroline days when security seemed a threat, and settling down a betrayal of his individuality. I thought he was scared and told him so while he handed me a cup.

'Thanks for the analysis,' he said. 'How much do I owe you?'

'Funnily enough, I'm interested in a therapist,' I said. 'Paul Holland. Ever heard of him?'

'The groping groupie. Yeah, I heard he was run over. In Finsbury

Park. Bit down market for him, wasn't it?'

'Watch it. Some day somebody will begin to suspect your antipathy to therapy. They'll begin to wonder why you're so resistant.'

Tony sat back in his chair and put his feet on the desk. It all looked a bit forced.

'Seriously, Kate,' he said, 'this guy was a creep. I'll show you what he wrote.'

He got up again and went out of the room.

He wasn't gone long. When he returned, he was holding five cuttings.

'I thought we had more,' he said. 'There's something I'm trying to remember but can't. I'll have to think about it. Never forget a story, you know.'

I smiled at the bravado behind the words and looked at the first cutting. It was a full page from a two-year-old *Street Times* issue. It was an article written by Paul Holland. As I read it, I saw what Tony meant by a creep.

The article was ostensibly a summary of differing schools of therapy ranging from the analytic to the orange. In fact, it was more like an espousal of a kind of personal growth which would have gone down well at an after-dinner speech at the Monday Club. The stress was on the individual's capacities which entirely ignored any forces outside the psyche. As a theoretical piece it wasn't very interesting; as a guide to therapy it was downright misleading.

I finished it and turned to the other cuttings. They were various letters written in response to the piece. Paul's article had aroused strong passions from different groups—some who saw this as an opportunity to launch an attack on therapy, others who were selling their own brand of personal growth. All in all, an undistinguished bunch. Only one letter got my sympathy and that was from a woman asking where the collectivity of the sixties had gone.

With a grimace, I handed the cuttings back to Tony.

'See what I mean?' he said.

I nodded. 'Has anybody from *Street Times* asked the police about Paul Holland's death?'

'Not that I know of. Should they have?' Tony leaned forward. He had that look about him, that investigative look.

'I'd like to approach the police,' I said. 'Do you think it's all right if I say I'm from the *Street Times*?'

'Why?' he asked. 'Give it to me.'

It was then that I remembered why it was that I'd never taken a job like Tony's. It was that look when friendship went overboard for a story. It was the constant probing for information that knew no boundaries. I didn't like it, and I didn't like it when my friends tried it on me.

'Why were you looking so gloomy when I came in?' I said, to change the subject.

Tony sighed. 'Deadline half an hour ago and I still haven't filled the column that Stephen palmed off on me while he writes the Great English Novel. And don't think I haven't noticed you didn't answer my question. Why are you interested in impersonating a *Street Times* hack? Thought it wasn't your style.'

'Well . . .' I said.

'Go on, tell,' Tony urged, 'Don't be so coy.'

'Off the record.'

'For the moment,' he agreed.

'Somebody thought it might be worth investigating Paul Holland's death.'

'Why?' Tony asked.

Good question, I thought. 'That's private,' I answered.

'Are they paying you to investigate?'

'Something like that.'

'That means yes,' Tony said. 'So what else is there to it?'

'Nothing at the moment,' I said.

'Not a bad story though,' he mused. 'Woman detective. Bring in some of the Tim Nicholson case. Threats of death, murder in Finsbury Park.'

'Can't get any sex in it, can you?' I asked.

'That's for later,' he said. 'And don't push it. How come you can be so cocksure—do you have so much information that a bit of publicity wouldn't help?'

'No,' I admitted.

'Let me run it, then.'

'Well . . .'

'I'll protect your sources,' he cut in.

'I haven't given them to you,' I said.

'So what you got to lose?'

That seemed right, so I agreed. Tony's eyes lit up. I could see him working out the headline already. He nodded absently when I asked if he'd back me up if the police checked my *Street Times* credentials. He wanted me to leave so he could start writing. I complied. Before

I was out of the door his typewriter was making fast action along the blank page.

It was one-thirty and I was hungry. I tried to come up with somewhere creative to eat but I failed. Halfway to Finsbury Park I stopped and ended up eating a crust with topping at the Pizza Hut on Upper Street.

I was feeling full, if unsatisfied, when I drove to the police station. Three hours later I walked out feeling very, very tired. I had waited on one official, been put off by a second and insulted by a third. I had watched youth being booked and youth being released. They always came out looking worse than when they went in.

I had tried to talk to the officer on duty the night Paul Holland was killed and had been fobbed off with the community policeman whose expertise was burglar-proofing and sealing images. While I listened to him enthusing about the success of police forays into primary schools, I drank three cups of tea. They were all stewed.

Eventually I left, having discovered that the police thought Paul Holland had been killed by a hit-and-run driver who would never be found. They didn't seem to care. They had other things on their minds.

I knew what these were as I drove to Dalston. I gambled on Mildmay Road as the smoothest route. I couldn't have made a worse choice. I'd only driven down fifty yards of it when I felt I was back in the police station. The police were out there in force, standing beside a roughly constructed road block. Inside their cars, on the back seats, sat the subdued arrested. They were almost without exception young and black.

Across from the road block a crowd had gathered. It carried with it the sense of excitement that had spread through so many parts of London that summer. It was a sense of liberation and of anger. Defiance was in the air and it was for defiance that the police were searching.

'Bristol, then Brixton. Dalston is next,' was shouted from the crowd.

The police pretended not to hear.

My car was given a cursory glance. I drove round the barricades, past Kingsland Road with its hastily boarded shop windows, and parked outside my house.

Sam was sitting in the middle of the bedroom when I arrived. He was surrounded by sheets of paper that I recognised only too well. He gave a theatrical groan which I returned in sympathy.

'Incredible, these prices,' he said.

'Any more trouble in the streets, and they'll start going down,' I replied.

'Wishful thinking,' he muttered and then looked at me. 'Or is it? I've been meaning to ask you. Are you having doubts about our living together?'

'Not exactly,' I said. 'Are you going to cook supper?'

He got up and gave me a hug.

'Not exactly,' he said. 'In the same sense of the words.'

I made us a chef salad which we ate with French bread and a cold white wine that was more cold than tasty. While we ate, I told him about Franca and my re-entry into the detective business. Sam approved. He always approved of everything that took me away from freelance journalism which he thought made me unhappy. Of course he was right about that, but finances usually got in the way, so I didn't like to think about it.

'So did one of Paul Holland's clients bump him off?' Sam asked.

'I guess so. Franca must have learned something in supervision that worries her.'

'And how does it feel to be employed by your ex-therapist?'

I got up. 'Who can tell yet? I'm going to blow off some steam.'

I spent the next twenty-three minutes with my alto. I know it was twenty-three minutes because after the first ten it was an effort to keep myself at it. My concentration kept going and half way through a particularly difficult riff I would find that I'd lost the thread, the breath and the will. But I stuck at it, gambling on improvement. At twenty-two minutes, things were getting better. I began to feel part of the sounds I was making. At twenty-three minutes I was stopped by an insistent banging from outside.

I stuck my head round the kitchen door where Sam was sitting at the table reading.

'Is it bad enough to cause a protest from the streets?' I asked.

Sam smiled. 'Sounded good, as if you just got going. I don't know what that noise is. I was trying to ignore it but it's not going away. Let's take a look.'

We went down the stairs. The banging persisted. It was a steady constant thud. As we got lower we could hear the sounds of instructions, ringing out in the night.

I got down first and opened the door. I stepped outside. And was so surprised at what I saw that I involuntarily stepped backwards, catapulting into Sam who was following closely.

The street, or at least the section of the street two doors down from me, was flooded with police. When I recovered my balance I took in the six police cars and two Black Marias. As we stood there on the steps a plain-clothes policeman came running past, gun drawn. He ran to one of the cars and got in.

Two doors down was the source of the banging. Five policemen, one behind the other, were thudding rhythmically at the door of number 47, using a strong beam of wood to push their way through. Behind them stood a senior policeman with his peaked hat and confident air. And in the ranks behind him stood a group of young constables, riot shields in hand.

I looked up to my left and saw the next-door neighbours all hanging out of their windows. They were exhibiting that air of excitement that so often goes with tragedy.

'What's going on?' I called.

A policeman, who had stationed himself outside my house stared at me. He didn't answer.

'There's someone in that abandoned building,' the woman from number 45 shouted. 'He was making a noise, wrecking the place with a hammer they think, so they've come to get him out.'

I couldn't believe it. I counted up and down the street. I reckoned there were forty uniformed policemen at various places. To get one man?

Just after I'd finished counting them, they broke through. Six of them piled into the house.

It didn't take long to bring him out. When he came, he was being dragged, his hands bound behind him: one rasta surrounded by six burly policemen. As they pushed him into the van the woman from number 45 shouted again.

'Serve you right, squatter,' she said.

I felt sick. I looked at Sam. He shrugged. Silently we went indoors.

The rest of the evening wasn't much of an improvement. We spent a couple of hours at Anna and Daniel's watching the debris disappear into the last of the suitcases. Nobody had much conversation. Friends dropped in and out, wishing them *bon voyage*. Everybody started a variety of drinks but nobody seemed to have the energy to finish them with the result that half-empty glasses littered surfaces and landings.

It was when I set myself to clearing up some of the debris that I realised that I was having a strange reaction. These were my closest friends, who were taking off, perhaps for ever, and yet I wasn't feeling anything. Nothing, that is, except a vague watchfulness and the intrusion of a few memories from the time when I had moved from Portugal to London seven years ago. But apart from this it was as if I wasn't really there, not really concerned with what was going on around me.

I tried to conceal my curious detachment, but I'd reckoned without Anna. She took me aside during a lull in the activity and stood in front of me so that I couldn't sidle away.

'It's rough,' she said.

I nodded. I felt uneasy. For the first time since I'd known her, Anna seemed to be standing too close. It felt almost as though any contact seemed intrusive because, in my mind, she had already left.

'Don't blame you for not speaking to me,' she said.

I laughed and the distance between us didn't seem quite so troublesome.

'But is that all that's worrying you?' she asked.

I didn't know what she was getting at. 'Not every day your friends leave you,' I joked, 'and then ask you if that's all.'

Anna didn't smile. Her face was solemn, her cheeks, reddened by the activity of the last few days, paled.

'I have to say it,' she started. 'Even though it's a bad time. But what's happening to you and Sam?'

'What do you mean?' I asked.

I frowned and thought about it. I didn't like it. Another first this was, to have Anna come up with the completely unexpected. Usually what she said fitted in—an initial surprise it might be, but it always made sense. But this came from somewhere I'd never anticipated.

'What do you mean?' I repeated. I heard the confusion in my voice turn to hostility and there was nothing I could do to stop it.

'Something doesn't feel right between you. Perhaps I'm imagining it . . .'

'Worried that you're leaving me in a total mess?'

Anna laughed. 'Probably my overwhelming ego at work.' And then doubt crept back into her voice. 'It must be strange working for Franca,' she said. 'Is it bringing up old memories?'

'Not really,' I said and watched as the lie stood there between us. It was then I knew that Anna was right, that something was not okay. But I couldn't help myself. I pushed the doubt away and exchanged it for a big grin.

Anna didn't look convinced but she moved a shade closer and hugged me. For an instant I let the barrier dissolve and the love I felt for her became mixed with the loss I'd already taken on board. And then the feelings went and we parted, sadly but without words.

They had different styles, these two women, sitting together in the room. One looked like she'd been there a long time: her back was straight but her body was relaxed. The other looked like she'd just arrived: and she was ready to leave at a moment's notice. Her eyes kept flickering across the space, moving over the pictures on the wall without seeing them, and then glancing across at her companion. She had an air of alertness which was imbued with a restlessness that she was trying to hide behind her apparently carefree front.

'Tell me why you thought of consulting me,' Franca said. She had a soft voice but it was firm and rounded, unmistakably confident.

I can't survive this, Kate thought, even as she heard herself instantly and brightly responding. 'It's the fashion. Going to therapy. I can't be left out, can I?'

She regretted the words as soon as she'd said them and she looked to the other chair to see if they had condemned her. Franca nodded.

'I don't feel happy in myself,' Kate continued, her voice a shade softer, 'not happy enough.'

'How would you measure that?'

Kate smiled brightly, hoping her fear didn't show through.

'I don't feel in control,' she said. 'Everything happens to me. My friends, my work, my life. I don't feel that I really, deeply care for anything.'

'And you think I could help?'

'Can't you?' Kate asked, and hoped that her companion couldn't read the disappointment in her voice.

'Perhaps we could work on it together,' Franca said. 'But it isn't easy, this kind of exploration. It can go very deep and bring up all types of painful feelings you might better wish hidden.'

'Trying to put me off,' Kate quipped.

'Just to be honest,' Franca said. Kate thought she noticed reproof in the statement but Franca's face had not changed.

'I'd like to try,' Kate said.

'I suggest we both think about it. We have met each other and we should take a week to think if we are right for each other.'

Kate looked upset, tearful even. She used a smile to disguise it. She nodded her agreement. And found herself smiling as she left the room.

Three

Wednesday morning was an extension of the evening before—full of activity whose main purpose was to drive the sadness away. Sam and I got up early and went to Cardozo Road. We picked Anna and Daniel up and then I chose a roundabout route to Heathrow. I kept away from the main roads. I wanted them to remember London at its best: to be able to compare it with the glass and metal of New York.

It was a strange London we saw that day. The sun was shining bright—bright enough to harden the colours we passed. We drove through areas solid in their wealth which had survived centuries and were set to survive more. They looked like nothing could touch them. But we also journeyed through places which had become suddenly uncertain—caught in the uproar on the streets and not knowing what the rest of the summer would bring them. The uncertainty was reflected in the presence of police vans on every corner and in the boarded-up windows and graffiti-covered walls. It showed in the gait of the people, the way they watched each other, and more than that it showed in the way that, even in daylight, the youth moved with a confidence of power, an acknowledgment of the small victories of the night before.

Despite the sightseeing we arrived at the airport hours too soon. Anna and Daniel checked in and then we went upstairs to endure the uneasy atmosphere of waiting. We tried to talk but the words floated into the air to join with the mish-mash of pleasantries and half-finished sentences that congregate in airports. After a while we lapsed into dislocated sentences which had no purpose and only hinted at the pain behind our parting. I began to feel like I was sitting with strangers.

So it was a relief when their plane was called. We all got up quickly and walked to passport control. Sam and I stood and watched while they moved towards the no-man's-land of the boarding lounge. Just before she rounded the corner, Anna turned to me. 'If you need me, just call,' she said. And then she was gone.

'And I'll be there,' I muttered to myself cynically.

Sam put an arm around my shoulder. Instinctively I shrugged it off. I don't know why I did that and when I looked into his eyes I saw the hurt in them. I tried to apologise but I couldn't find the words. So we drove back to London not touching, not speaking.

It wasn't an altogether uncomfortable silence. When I dropped Sam off at work I found that the smile that I threw him was unstrained. He returned the smile but there was still a question in his face as he got out the car. It was a question that I left unanswered.

The flat seemed empty when I got back. Down in the street, life was in full swing as people took advantage of the sunshine to exchange gossip from their front doors. The activity only helped to make my sense of isolation more acute. I felt a kind of hollowness inside that nothing would fill.

I sat at my desk and tried to goad myself into action by sorting through the pile of papers that I'd put aside to file. It didn't help. Halfway through I found a picture of Anna and Daniel smiling at the camera against the background of their patio of geraniums. I stuck the picture above my desk and stared at it. Ten minutes later I shook myself alert. My eyes had glazed over and I'd gone into a sort of reverie where my thoughts could not be put in words. I forced myself to concentrate on Paul Holland.

I spent the first half of the afternoon trying to get a better idea about Paul Holland's life. I phoned Regina for a list of his friends but she said he didn't have any. She sounded terrible but she hid her pain behind hostility. She made it clear that she considered my enquiry unwanted and unfeeling. By the time we said goodbye I knew what it was to feel like a snoop.

I carried on telephoning—putting out feelers to the world of therapy. It wasn't very productive. A few people said they'd ask around; a few even expressed regret at Paul's death. But most of them seemed reluctant to talk about him. By the end of the session I was tired, hoarse, and still in the dark, although I had managed to sketch out a picture of Paul's past.

He'd started his professional life as a social worker and had seemed set to carve out an ordered existence within a local council hierarchy. He married, had one child, and gained a reputation for being something of a liberal who was prepared to put himself out for people in distress. He played by the rules though: eager as he was to help, he never did anything to threaten his position at work, or his lifestyle at home.

And then the sixties had intervened. Paul became filled with ideas of personal liberation and disillusioned with his own lifestyle. He tried to interest his wife, who was just emerging from a welter of nappies and broken nights, in the new promiscuity. When this didn't appeal, he left her. There didn't seem to be many hard feelings on either side about the split.

Paul began to spend less and less time at work and he started to bend the rules. He experimented with hallucinogenic drugs, and getting up in the morning became more difficult each day. In the end he dropped his job like many others were doing. He'd managed to save some money and he used it to go on a visit to California.

He went for a few months and ending up staying for years as he shed the last remnants of the social worker in himself. Growth was what he was into and at first he'd chosen the extreme options. He lived in a community which ate, slept and shouted EST and for a while he was just one of many in a self-abusing crowd. But that didn't last long. He'd soon had enough of public humiliation. He decided to channel his search into the milder routes to personality change.

He'd come back to Britain a guru, trained in therapies that were just becoming fashionable. His ex-wife demanded that he take responsibility for his daughter so he'd set up home with Regina. There was no shortage of willing women to help this lone man bring up his cute little girl, and so he had time for the development of his new career. He started a series of bio-energetic groups with a bit of gestalt and encounter thrown in on the side. His way of being suited a particular mood and he attracted a large clientele. He had energy, he had power, and he felt no guilt at using both. Not for him the slow twists and turns of analysis, nor the safeguards of the therapy room. In Paul's groups anything went: he was everywhere and nowhere, encouraging his favourites, baiting those that annoyed him, and keeping himself always invincible.

After a while, the strain began to tell. Paul withdrew from the groups, concentrating instead on one-to-one sessions. One cynic I spoke to said he thought Holland had done this with his usual business acumen: he'd moved to individual therapy at a time when it was becoming the vogue and people were ready to pay exorbitant sums to be alone with the great Paul.

Whatever his reasons, Paul had seemed to turn away from the

growth movement. He attended part-time analytic training and got himself a supervisor. He practised quietly for a few years and then began to take a more active part in theoretical developments in the alternative analytical field. He'd specialised in the psychic construction of masculinity and was regarded as something of an expert. People said that in the process he'd found some humility and that he seemed more likeable. And then he'd died, run over in Finsbury Park.

It's hard work talking to the profession about a fellow therapist. For a start I had to overcome the prejudices of those at the top of the hierarchy who saw no reason to equate Paul's work with their own. In their eyes, he didn't have enough training, enough publications and, in some cases, enough courtesy. Not that any of them came out and said this outright. Instead they were masters of discretion. None of them would utter anything that, written down, could be remotely derogatory. Instead their judgments were contained in the nuances of their voices, the pauses between sentences and the silences which followed some of my questions. It was like negotiating my way through a minefield where I couldn't tell whether the mines were capable of damaging. But I ended up walking carefully anyway—just in case.

It took a few hours to obtain the sketchiest of biographies. I got the impression that Paul wasn't very much liked by the profession but then I'm not sure that some of the people I'd spoken to were capable of liking anyone. It had been a long, hard haul for almost nothing. But I had managed to find the names of two therapists who had agreed to see me. They were very different people but they had in common an eagerness to talk to me, although neither would say why they were keen.

The first, Dr Edgar Greenleaf, had instructed me how to get to his offices at the back of Baker Street. The facade of the building was on a grand scale and spoke of money and so I was taken aback when he answered the door himself, dressed in a three-piece pin-striped suit. He would have looked more like a successful businessman than an analyst if his thick grey hair hadn't been a shade too long and his opening gaze a shade too direct.

He led me into his consulting room, pointed to a chair which stood in one corner of it, and sat himself down on the only other chair. He let me look around while he watched me with an inviting smile on his face. It was an elegant house and an elegant room, but it had been furnished for intimidation. Edgar Greenleaf was a large man and he liked his furniture to match. Everything, that is, except the chair I'd been allocated. It was small and shaky and made the couch which lay parallel to Greenleaf's chair look safe and attractive in comparison.

Greenleaf himself exuded confidence. He settled himself in his high-backed chair as if he were ready to listen to me forever, even though a look on his genial face said that he'd take it all with a pinch of salt.

'You wanted to consult me, Miss Baeier.'

'About Paul Holland,' I said.

'Ah yes.' The two words carried with them a meaning that I couldn't quite decipher.

'I understand that you taught him,' I said.

'He attended certain of my classes, yes. Although he never received anything near a complete training.'

'I'm investigating his death.'

'An unusual task for a woman. I don't remember hearing about you from Paul.'

'I never knew him,' I said.

For the first time since I arrived Edgar Greenleaf looked like I'd said something unexpected. Confusion showed in his face. I didn't think it was an emotion he often experienced. He leaned forward in his chair.

'Why are you consulting me?' he asked.

'I've been hired to investigate his death,' I said.

'And by whom, may I ask?'

'I'm afraid I can't tell you that. All I want is some background on Paul Holland.'

There was a long silence before he spoke again. It hung heavy in a room which was used to silence. When he spoke it was as if something was troubling him.

'Have you ever been in psychoanalysis or psychotherapy?' he asked.

'Yes,' I said.

'And who did you consult?'

I told him. He grinned. Relaxation returned to his face.

'Ah yes,' he said. 'I have come across her in certain of my capacities. She was connected to Paul Holland, I understand.'

I looked at him and didn't say anything.

He didn't need me to. He stood up and I followed suit.

'Franca was trained at one of the minor institutions,' he said. 'Well-meaning but hardly . . . Anyhow, I don't think I can be of help to you.'

The force of his personality propelled me across the room and towards the door. It was with an effort that I stopped myself.

'Why did you agree to see me?' I asked.

'I thought it my duty. I'm afraid that I supposed you were a distressed client of Paul Holland. We at the Institute often have reason to pick up pieces of, how shall I call it, misguided attempts at analysis.'

'And there's nothing you can do to help me find out about Paul Holland's death?'

We were standing by the door. He put his arm around me in an attempt to get me through it. It was done with style, as if he were merely offering guidance, but the gesture contained a threat.

'My dear Miss Baeier,' he said. 'Training to be an analyst takes years. Even after formal training is complete we are still learning. Experience counts for so much. I cannot expect a layman, or should I say lay person, to understand the intricacies of the process, the nuances of transference.'

He looked down at me and chuckled before he continued.

'You feel that you have been out of psychotherapy for a long time. But time is relative. It is hard to understand the influence your psychotherapist may still have on you. I don't ascribe the blame to you. But we have to be careful. Paul Holland was a misguided young man and I'm afraid that your own psychotherapist may have been unduly influenced by him. I advise you to let the matter rest.'

And with that, he gave my back a final push. I found myself outside the door.

I stood there a while, regaining my bearings and thinking about Greenleaf. He was a man with power, no doubt about it. But one thing I didn't understand was why he'd acted so trapped. True, he'd done a good job of concealing it, but what did I expect? The man had been trained for confidence. But he'd given himself away—he'd been a shade too off-putting—with his reputation he'd no need for that. And I also thought I'd detected an edge of relief in his actions: relief that I hadn't confronted him with a secret fear. Yes, I thought to myself, Greenleaf is definitely hiding something. The only trouble is, I've no idea what.

There was silence in the room. It wasn't a comfortable or an understated silence, but a silence that intruded. Outside, light was sparkling on the newly moist plants; inside, it felt as if no light would ever penetrate. It was almost as if the silence was poised to attack, bringing with it darkness and despair.

Kate didn't like it, and she didn't like the fact that it was affecting her. She sat back in the brown chair, attempting at least a semblance of calm. But her body would not relax and she kept her hands tied to her lap, knotted together in their stillness.

Franca glanced across at her. She too felt the silence and the weight of it. But in her case it came to her almost as a puzzle, a mystery suddenly launched into the stillness of the room. Her face showed concern, but it also showed something more—an attempt to cross the divide, to break the intimidating silence, but to do so without words. She frowned as she saw the position of Kate's fingers and the tension in her body. Then she looked down at her own hands which she'd placed loosely on her skirt: at the lines of the skin, the brown spots that had come with age and were now part of her identity, at the softness of her skin. As she looked, a glimmer of comprehension dawned.

She looked up again at Kate and at the way she had fixed her eyes angrily on the white wall opposite.

'I am perfectly well,' said Franca. Her soft voice floated across the abyss between them.

Kate shook her head. She looked crossly at Franca over the gap between the two of them.

'I don't know what you mean,' she said. 'Why are you being so difficult today?'

'We were talking of aloneness,' Franca answered, 'and it occurs to me that you fear for my safety. I have had a cold and you're not used to me being ill. I wonder whether you think I might be about to leave you.'

'Don't be silly,' Kate snapped. Her voice was tinny, hardly denting the silence that seemed to threaten to invade again.

But the silence was muted this time: still there but not so heavy. Both women noticed it and, in their own ways, both understood it.

'Why be so scared of something that you're used to?' Kate asked. 'Sometimes I think you make all this up. I never even thought aloneness was a problem before I met you.'

'You have had many people come and go in your life,' Franca answered. 'It hasn't been easy but you have found ways to function within the loss. The question is whether you can now give up those

ways, and replace them with something truer to yourself—and more secure.'

Kate nodded almost imperceptibly. She kept her face still but not still enough to prevent the tears from slowly welling in her eyes, and then trickling down her cheeks. Not for the first time Franca saw how only one side of her face seemed affected by the softness of the tears: the other staying stern as if to move would be a betrayal.

'Which ways?' Kate asked. 'The old ones, I mean?'

'I think you know the answer to that,' Franca said.

'Cutting off, you mean? Not caring? Doing without? A kind of fuck you, you're not going to be around but I don't need you anyway?'

Franca smiled. Kate caught the smile and almost echoed it. But she couldn't quite make it and her face froze once more.

'We should discuss this next time,' Franca said, shifting slightly in her seat.

Kate nodded. Wearily she got to her feet and walked towards the door, followed by her companion. She glanced at her before she stepped out of the door, taking care not to touch the other woman.

Edgar Greenleaf had represented psychoanalysis at its most established. The person I saw next was of a different genre.

She operated out of a centre in Islington's Canonbury. It was a fancy building, once a club for the rich. In the last two years the space had been transformed into a meeting place for the followers of Bhagwan. I'd been to the club before its takeover, when it had seemed like a backwater of polite upper-middle-class conversation. But its clientele had faded and the young of its class were no longer interested in the solidity of the establishment, preferring discos to coffee lounges. The club had gone into a slow decline, to be finally bought by the new capitalists of eastern religion.

The place still looked the same but the atmosphere had completely changed. It positively hummed with surface energy. Women and men dressed in their various shades of purples and pinks bristled around, connected to each other but each carrying a feeling of self-contained self-satisfaction. When I asked at the desk for Maya I was greeted with a sympathetic smile and an intense eye-lock. When I bought a cup of coffee I got the same treatment. It was as if everybody was willing to register my presence with one long lingering look to invite me to join them, but then, if I resisted, they would ignore me.

Everything associated with these people in their colours of the rising sun was bright and cheerful. The coffee bar was no exception. The lighting was concealed strip but arranged so that no corner of the room was left either too dazzling or too gloomy. Groups of people sat at round tables, each of which held a shining carafe of water, a lone flower in a small glass vase and a menu handwritten in the finest italic.

The bar had been arranged for maximum order as if to offset the constant movements of its occupants. Conversation flowed rapidly over tables and between groups, but cunning insulation kept the noise level down.

It was like sitting in a self-contained world where contact and friendliness were the norm. As I waited for Maya, I reflected on how much this community echoed the hippy world of the sixties. Echoed it in some ways, that is: the rejection of the outside, the creation of a life-style which functioned in and of itself were both there. But in this milieu, behind the constant physical contact there was a strict order that hippies would never have accepted. People looked like they belonged. They also looked like someone had told them where they belonged and how they should stay there.

Maya bounced into the room, identified me by my irregular clothes, and made straight for me. She was wearing the colours, in her case in the form of a pale mauve sweater on top of a dark purple skirt. She walked with a spring in her step and a smile on her face. She greeted me with open friendliness and then led me through the labyrinth of corridors.

We ended up in a small whitewashed room whose pale pink carpet was scattered with soft cushions. There was no other furniture in the room. Bhagwan, a benign smile on his face, stared down at us from one of the walls. With his grey hair and twinkling eyes, he looked as if he were trying to share a joke with us but didn't quite expect us to get it.

Without bending, Maya sat down on the floor and crossed her legs. Her back stayed poker straight. I joined her on the floor.

'As I told you,' I said, 'I'm investigating the death of Paul Holland.'

She nodded and continued to gaze at me as if trying to decipher something in my face.

'I understand that you trained with him,' I said.

She smiled but she kept silent.

'Did you see much of him?'

'We had a parting of the ways.'

'Over what?'

'He felt threatened by my life-style,' she said, and gestured to the heavy chains of beads that hung around her neck and carried her grey-bearded hero with her. 'And I couldn't get through to him any more.'

'Paul didn't strike me as the type,' I said, 'to disapprove of your faith. After all, he'd been around . . .'

My voice slowed to a fade as I realised I hadn't a single idea how to finish the sentence without sounding insulting. It didn't bother Maya. She smiled at me, a direct, open, unthreatened smile. It looked like she'd had a lot of practice with smiles like that.

'Paul changed,' she said. 'He went after respectability. He dissociated himself from anything he saw as being on the fringes. He wanted establishment recognition.'

'He once had it,' I said, 'when he was a social worker.'

'And he never quite got over the fact that he gave it all up. He acted like he'd sacrificed himself for the good of others instead of what he did which was to go with the flow. And he felt he was over forty and deserved to be among the big boys. So he tried to go analytic. Not that it worked.'

Maya sounded almost bitter. It didn't suit her. I looked closely at her face. She made no attempt to flinch away from my gaze. For a few seconds we stayed that way, and in those seconds I thought I understood something about her. She'd chosen what could be seen as conformity to a closed life-style, but it was also a conformity which society scoffed at. So for her, a Paul Holland who was trying hard to get back into the fold was a man who'd given up on the struggle to build an alternative. I began to feel that Paul often let people down: his daughter, his colleagues, and, in all likelihood, his clients.

I shook the thoughts out of my head and got back to the conversation.

'Why didn't he succeed,' I asked, 'in going analytic?'

'I never thought I'd hear myself say this,' Maya said slowly, and she formed each word separately and distinctly. 'It feels like going over to the enemy camp. But I think Paul would never make it because he wasn't rigorous enough. He wanted power too much. He wanted to meddle. He didn't stop to think. He was heading for trouble.'

She heard her last words as they filled the bare room and she smiled. 'He sure found it,' she said.

'Do you think he was murdered?' I asked.

She twisted her locket in front of her as if searching for something.

'That's a heavy thing to say about anybody. Life isn't bad but you have to learn to sometimes go with it instead of struggling against it.' She let the locket drop back on her chest.

'Do you mean that Paul was creating trouble for himself?' I asked.

'Paul had difficulty in being,' she said. 'I gave him a massage once and I noticed how stiff his left side was: that's his female side, his ability to accept and to go with the flow. Paul could never leave anything just to be.'

'What specifically wouldn't he leave?'

'He worried too much about fitting pieces together. He hadn't learned that understanding comes from acceptance. He was too concerned with discovering the answer and too little involved in the real search.'

'I'm afraid you've lost me,' I said. 'Are you talking in general or about something Paul was investigating?'

She leaned forward and put her elbows and palms straight down on the carpet. Her knees stayed touching it as if her body was made of rubber. Her back kept perfectly straight.

When she sat up it was as if she'd made a decision.

'I did see Paul before he died,' she said. 'He seemed more than usually tense. He said he'd come across some interesting connections. I tried to warn him about his curiosity, but he was too far involved.'

'Was it to do with his clients?' I asked.

'It might have been.' In one flowing movement she got up. 'I'm afraid that's all I'm at liberty to say. Thank you for coming to share your investigation with me.'

I almost got up with her and left the room like the good girl she thought I would be. But I didn't—I decided I'd had enough. First Greenleaf and his power trip and now Maya with her half answers. Greenleaf, I could understand—he'd been trained to keep aloof, to hold back from us ordinary mortals. But I couldn't believe that Maya's ethics would prevent her from telling me more. I gazed up at her where she stood above me, and then I got it.

'You don't know,' I said, 'what Paul was up to. Do you?'

Maya's mouth half opened in surprise but she had good control over it. She shut it quick and threw me another one of her smiles.

'Have it your own way. There's nothing more I can contribute.'

I didn't reply. I carried on looking up at her. And saw the discomfort spreading.

'I have work to do,' she said.

'Do you?' I asked.

Abruptly she moved away. She went to her cushion and sat down, heavily.

'No,' she said. 'You're right. I don't know what he was up to—he wouldn't tell me. But I had a feeling.'

'What sort?'

'That something was very wrong. He was into something corrupt. I could smell it. He was abusing his position. It was just a feeling but I've learned to trust my instincts.'

'Why did you pretend it was more than that?' I asked.

I got up as she replied, 'I didn't think you'd believe me.'

It was her turn to look up at me. She shot me a glance that was full of pleading.

'I feel you are in danger,' she said. 'Be careful.'

I smiled at her. 'I will. Thanks for seeing me.'

I thought about them all, Maya, Greenleaf and Holland, on my way home. However much I tried to avoid it, I found myself comparing them to Franca—and finding them all wanting. But even as I was doing this something was bugging me. I realised that I felt bad that Franca had been involved with Paul—giving supervision to a man who, by all accounts, used his position as a means to power.

I knew my reaction was childish—wanting Franca to be perfect—and I wondered why I was doing it. I wasn't sure that even three months previously I would have been thinking this way.

My mind went back to the conversation with Anna when she'd asked me what was wrong. I'd pretended nothing was but now I wasn't so sure.

And now Anna was three thousand miles away, Franca was my employer, Sam was fed up with the way I was behaving, and I was stuck with a murder enquiry.

As the gloom piled up, I did what I should have known would never work: I just resolved to be better, to treat Sam more openly, to take control of myself and stop being so cut off. I should have known better.

Sam was waiting for me when I arrived at his flat. In his hand he held a sheaf of papers. He thrust them at me. I took a quick glance and then I groaned. They were descriptions of houses, taken from six different estate agents. Sam had selected a few that sounded slightly less run down and slightly less expensive than the main and he dragged me round them. I tried to concentrate on the expedition but my mind kept wandering away: first to my day's work and then to mentally check the progress of Anna and Daniel's flight. They must have been arriving at the point when Sam's words penetrated my reverie.

'And you can tell me,' he was saying '. . . even if you are the most aggravating and distracted person I could hope to spend time with.'

'Sorry,' I said. 'It's with them going.'

Sam parked the car. I saw he'd driven us to Brick Lane. We got out and walked into the Akbar. When the waiter had taken our order, Sam returned to the offensive.

'We have to talk about it,' he said.

'We do?'

'Yes. And don't think I haven't noticed your reluctance. It's not good you know. What's going on?'

'You what?' I asked.

Sam leaned across the table and gently touched my cheek. It was a controlled movement and I wondered whether aggression was hiding behind it.

'You're hopeless,' he said. 'You don't know what I'm talking about, do you?'

'Not really,' I admitted.

'It's about us living together.'

'Oh that!'

'That's what I mean. We both agreed we wanted to do it and now you avoid the subject. If you've changed your mind okay, but we've got to discuss it.'

At that point the waiter returned with the food.

'Let's eat,' I said. 'I'm starving.'

Sam grimaced but he didn't say anything.

The meal was almost very good—a delicious cauliflower bhajee on the same table as a bhindi dish which was obviously tinned; dhal with chilis so hot I gasped to eat them and a chicken tikka that came sizzling with subtle spices to the table.

I took the edge off my hunger while I thought about what Sam had said.

'I think it's about freedom,' was what I came up with.

'What about it?' Sam asked. He didn't look pleased.

'I'm scared I'll lose mine,' I said.

Sam stopped eating and looked at me. His face changed expression and he couldn't hide the look of hurt coming through.

'I'm not saying I don't want to live with you . . .' I started.

'Not in so many words,' he said, 'but . . .'

'Not at all. You did ask what was going on and I'm trying to tell you. I think you should listen.'

He stayed silent.

'I do want to live with you,' I said, 'and at the same time I feel ambivalent. Not so long ago life-style was all important: now we seem to be building the nuclear family.'

'But so much of that was ideology,' Sam said. 'And you know it.'

'Some of it was,' I said, 'but not all. And you know it.'

Sam nodded. He had that vague look on his face, that look of times remembered. I knew he had a lot to remember. Sam had come from a family of lawyers and in 1967 he was three-quarters of the way to the bar. He never finished his training. To the horror of his father and the delight of himself he threw it up and spent three years caught up in a whirl of student and left-wing politics. When things died down a bit he took himself back to school and turned to the subject that his family had always regarded as utterly impractical: mathematics.

He'd got himself a degree in it and was now teaching in London while finishing his thesis. And although the attraction of algebraic typology and the like had begun to wane, and he'd turned instead to economics when he wasn't writing poetry, Sam never regretted the change he'd made, nor forgot the lessons he'd learned. So many of us had thought we could change society; we hadn't succeeded but we still carried the ideas and the hopes with us.

We also had to carry with us the mechanisms to deal with the changes the years, and the recession, had wrought. Sam and I got on to talking about them, by tacit agreement dropping the subject of the house. It didn't really matter. We hadn't said much but in a way we'd gone as far as we could. Nobody ever said buying a house was easy, anyway.

We left the restaurant, each in a much better mood than when we'd entered, had a momentary panic when we tried to work out what to do next and then solved the problem by going to bed together. It was only when I was on the point of sleep that I remembered Paul Holland, and the fact that I wasn't sure what I would do tomorrow.

Four

Thursday's edition of *Street Times* solved the problem. I opened it as soon as it arrived and searched through for Tony's piece. It took some time to find. I had been expecting at least a column: what I got was three sentences in the middle of an article about weird happenings in London.

> Plucky female detective, Kate Baeier, is on the path of a murderer again. She is investigating the suspicious death of shrink Paul Holland, who was run over in Finsbury Park two weeks ago. Ms Baeier refused to spill all to *Street Times* but rest assured, if murderer there be, then she is the woman to search him out.

That was all. And to make matters worse it was buried between a description of an Esperanto convention in Hyde Park and a side swipe at a conference for greater freedom in advertising at the Mayfair Hotel.

I was just contemplating the form my revenge against Tony would take when the phone rang. I picked it up and said hello.

'Kate Baeier?' said the voice at the other end. It was a gruff voice, almost strained in its lowness.

'Yes?'

'I need you.'

'Excuse me?'

'I have a problem,' he said.

'Who is this?' I asked.

'You're a detective, aren't you?'

'In a manner of speaking.'

'Well I need help. I've lost my marbles,' he said before bursting into a fit of giggles. More childish laughs echoed in the background before they ended the call.

The second caller was more advanced in years if not in psyche.

He wanted me to come right over and help him with a deeply personal mystery. I got him off the phone as quick as I could but the sour taste lingered for a while after.

Calls three and four were probably from the same person—or else there were two self-confessed murderers of Paul Holland wandering about London. After I'd dealt with number four I was just considering getting my calls forwarded to Tony's *Street Times* office when the phone rang again. I picked it up.

'Yes?' I shouted.

'Is that Kate Baeier?' The man's voice on the other end was hesitant.

'Have you phoned to persecute me too?'

There was a pause.

'Did I call at a bad time?' he asked.

'Depends on what you want,' I said.

'My name's James Stanford. I knew Paul Holland and would like to talk to you. Only if it's convenient of course.'

I told him it was and apologised for the way I'd answered. I tried to get some clue from him but he said he was about to go into rehearsal and couldn't talk. I arranged to meet him later in the day.

That done, I decided to give the phone a rest. It was a glorious day, bright sun which even managed to carry some heat with it, so I took my latest detective novel down to the garden and lay on the grass with it.

Laura Maxwell knew how to get attention.

'So you're the people's dick,' was the first thing I heard her say.

I blinked myself awake and tried to work out who she was. It wasn't easy. She was standing with her back to the sun so all I really saw was a halo of bright yellow around her hennaed hair. I lowered my gaze and ended up focusing on her red shoes.

'I said are you the people's . . .'

'I heard you. Hold on a second, I'll just get up.'

I stood, and tried to overcome the dizziness that hit me. I glanced at my watch and saw that I'd only been asleep for half an hour. I was dehydrated and still only half-conscious.

'Your neighbour told me you were down here,' Laura said. 'I'm a busy woman, you know.'

I nodded and picked up my book. 'Come upstairs,' I said. 'I have to have a drink.'

She complained constantly while she followed me out of the

garden, up the side entrance and into the house. She complained about how difficult it was to find Dalston, how difficult it was to get hold of me and how she hated people who slept on the job. She complained when I let her in and she complained while I ran myself a glass of cold water. She refused a cup of coffee because she was temporarily off caffeine, a cup of tea because she hated tannin and a fruit juice because she didn't believe in overloading on the vitamins.

'So what do you do?' I asked.

'I run a health shop,' she said.

I sat down and looked at her. Even when she was not complaining, she gave off an atmosphere of suppressed and angry energy. She had dressed herself to be noticed and was in some danger of overdoing it. The skirt of her pink suit would have been so tight as to make walking hazardous if it hadn't been slit all the way up one side. The matching jacket hugged her waist close but fell away from her chest. The red shirt underneath it seemed to have been put on more to tone with her shoes than to hide her breasts.

'I wasn't aware I was part of a fashion show,' she said.

'How can I help you?'

Abruptly she sat down opposite me. She used her long red nail to shift a rose-filled vase away from her. She sniffed.

'I'm not sure you can,' she said. 'Not sure at all. Do you get much work of this nature?'

'There you have me,' I said. 'We don't seem to be understanding each other. What exactly do you want?'

'Information. Confidentially. Can you keep a secret?'

I stayed silent. She looked at me as if she wanted to ask something but then she changed her mind.

'I'm the owner of a health food business,' she said. 'I also run a restaurant. Someone is ripping me off. I want him caught.'

'For what?' I asked.

She used her finger nails to tap an impatient tune on the glass-covered table.

'That's my affair. Will you do it or not?'

'Not,' I said. 'Store detective's not my thing. So if that's all?'

I got up and gestured towards the door. She didn't budge. I stood watching while she did some thinking, her head bent so she could study the floor. Time passed. I was getting impatient and it was my turn to tap with my feet. She looked up.

'For God's sake don't be so prim,' she said. 'Let me explain.' I sat down.

'It's an alternative business,' she said. 'I still have my principles. But I can't afford to lose that much money. The only avenues open to me are the police, a private detective firm, and you. I heard about you from someone I know who reads the *Street Times*.'

She sounded unconvincing and I stayed unconvinced. She saw this and went into another gear, her voice becoming louder, more bullying.

'I can give you a guarantee,' she said, 'if you deign to work for me.'

'What sort of guarantee?'

'That I won't prosecute. I run a friendly operation and all I want to do is find out who's doing it and plug the loophole. I'll just give the person a warning. That's why I've come to you. Other investigators push for prosecution.'

She threw me a smile that almost lit up her stiff face. I say almost because there was something reserved in the smile: something bordering on the malicious.

'I'll pay well,' she said.

'I charge £50 a day.'

'That's far too much.'

'Plus expenses,' I finished.

'Well, I suppose I have no choice. Come to "Grains", that's my restaurant, tomorrow.'

'I'll need a cover.'

'Anything you want.'

'Tell them I'm an economics student doing a thesis on small businesses,' I said. 'And I want your guarantee in writing.'

'Anything you say.' She got up and tweaked her skirt back into place.

'I'll expect you,' she said.

She walked towards the door. I followed her. Just as she was about to go, she turned.

'This won't be full-time,' she said, 'so it won't interfere with any other investigation. Feel free to fit the two together.'

'Thanks,' I said.

'But don't expect me to pay for their time.'

She went, leaving a trail of Ma Griffe behind her.

I waited until I heard the street door slam. Then I turned back to the kitchen and prepared myself some lunch. I was in the middle of finely slicing two spring onions to go with a tomato and avocado salad when the phone rang.

I picked it up. There was a slight pause, a transatlantic pip and then Anna's voice sounded through the static.

'Bit early for you, isn't it?' I asked.

'Jet lag,' she said. 'Can't sleep and I don't know what I'm doing here.'

'That makes two of us. They fly planes the other way, you know.'

Anna laughed.

'How's it going?' I said.

'Confused, but Monika was here to meet us and I realised how many friends we have in this place. How's with you?'

'Fine,' I said.

'Really?'

'Lonely,' I said.

'It's rough on you,' Anna said. 'I phoned to say I love you.'

'Me too, you.' I said. My voice cracked. Anna heard it and hers followed suit. We tried to find the words to fill the 6000-mile gap but we didn't get far. She rang off. I went back to my salad.

It was three o'clock by the time I'd eaten it, along with a piece of flash-fried entrecôte and four new potatoes. I cleared the lot away. I had two hours before meeting James Stanford so I checked the contents of the kitchen cupboards, made myself a list and hit the streets.

When the sun shines, Dalston has two sides: the first of life and the second of dirt. That Thursday, both were in evidence. Leftovers from the market competed with common street dust to litter the place. On the Kingsland Road, traffic let off obnoxious fumes that soured the air and dirtied the already grim-looking architecture.

But behind the main roads, in the back streets and back yards, there was excitement in the air. It was an excitement born of action: an excitement which had been building up and which was now reaching a peak.

Dalston had, for a long time, been an area where families, black and white, lived quietly side by side. But rising house prices, a corresponding influx of the young white middle classes into the family homes and a growth of militancy amongst the black community had changed the atmosphere. The events of the summer had only accelerated the trend.

Two years ago when I had walked down Amhurst Road what struck me most was the deteriorating housing stock and the dead feel of the area. Now, as I walked towards Kang's supermarket, what I couldn't avoid was the strong smell of marijuana.

I looked across to where a pool hall had been constructed in an abandoned building. Outside it, about twenty black men stood in bunches talking aimlessly. It was a casual crowd but as I watched it gained shape. The little groups formed into one mass as two policemen walked towards the entrance.

I wasn't the only person watching. By the time the first policeman had arrived, more men had appeared. From all directions they walked up, purposefully and confidently. The policeman was swallowed up in the growing crowd; loud voices could be heard coming from inside. The second policeman kept his distance; he began speaking into his pocket walkie-talkie.

He got his instructions just in time. The crowd was growing louder in its denunciation when he stepped into the group. He called out something to his colleague who pushed his way out with a look of relief on his panic-stricken face. The two men left, walking fast from the scorn that followed them.

From across the road, eyes looked at me. They looked like they wondered what I was doing there. I wondered myself: stuck on a divide between black and white, male and female, that I didn't know how to cross. I gave a brief smile. Then I went and did my shopping. By the time I came out the men had gone. Things were as relaxed as when I'd arrived.

The atmosphere in Amhurst Road had been tense: in the Limehouse Basin, it was surreal. I'd left my house early but only just arrived on time. I'd got lost, caught on the Commercial Road and going the wrong direction, before I'd managed to turn back. Then I tried a number of streets which led nowhere but couldn't be bothered to tell the passing vehicle that. Finally I gave up, parked and walked the rest of the way. I arrived, dead on five.

I was unprepared for the sight that greeted me. Open-mouthed, I stood at the barrier. The whole area was swarming with activity, none of it normal. Crowds of people in various stages of dress and undress, fork-lift trucks, cranes, musical instruments and strange constructions competed for space. All this was taking place within the confines of the square dock. Chairs had been stacked on a raised plinth so they looked forward on to a roughly constructed wooden stage and beyond it to the muddy Thames. A huge old schooner was moored by the side of the bank, slightly obscuring the rotting frames of abandoned warehouses.

I told the silent man at the gate that I had an appointment with James Stanford and he let me in with a curt nod. When I asked him what was going on he managed to say 'an event', before he became immobile. He looked like he was practising for catatonia.

'What's he doing?' I asked a woman who was standing aimlessly beside him.

'Practising catatonia,' she said. 'He represents alienation. I'm passivity.'

'A woman for passivity?' I asked.

'Oh it's okay. We rise up in the end,' she answered, before slumping back against the wall.

I wandered around the concreted ground that led up to the water and I stood still by the edge of the basin. Two groups of three people each, white-hooded and gowned, were rowing fragile rafts perilously close to each other. Another group was standing on a half-sunk hulk, setting up fireworks. I concentrated on them for a minute, admiring their exotic face paint, and so I missed the collision of the two rafts. When I next looked the six people had disappeared under the water. I scanned the surface anxiously but I needn't have worried. Within seconds they returned, dragging a monster inflatable that bore some similarity to a whale. I revised that opinion when red fire spurted from its huge mouth.

Things were no less exotic on the land. Large models of all types of jungle animals were being lifted and inflated. On the two stages, competing bands made music. Or I thought they were competing until I closed my eyes and realised that between the two of them the cacophony they were creating sounded very much like a distant sound of lions roaring and elephants stampeding.

I walked through the confusion, asking everybody I passed for James Stanford. I didn't have much luck. They'd either shrug or point in directions I tried, but failed, to follow. Occasionally people pointed in an upwards direction. I couldn't work out what they were getting at and they weren't interested in explaining.

I was on the verge of turning back towards the gate when it all became clear. I stepped forward, looking over my shoulder at another water collision, and bumped into a piece of wood. I tried to circumvent it, when a voice stopped me.

'Hold my legs a minute,' it said.

I looked up. I was standing under a thin giant. Nine foot up was a man. I followed his instructions and held on to his stilts. With complete assurance the man unhooked himself from his ballooning trousers, grasped the top of the two poles and somersaulted down. He ended up standing in front of me. He held out a yellow-gloved hand.

'Kate Baeier? I'm James.'

We shook hands while we sized each other up. He had an easier job than me. I saw he was tall, I knew he must be fit, but apart from the fact that his eyes were brown, I got no further. His face was painted a pale sort of yellow and he was wearing the red cheeks and big nose of a clown. The line of his mouth turned downwards under the weight of dark red lipstick.

The real James Stanford obviously wasn't so gloomy. As he led me out of the action he was continually stopped by the passing workers. He dispensed advice, sympathised with problems, gave instructions and pecked cheeks as he went.

'This is amazing,' I said, when we'd sat down on some white garden chairs which were placed around a white iron table.

'I like to think of it as a rebirth of the sixties,' he said.

'Not so easy these days,' I said.

'I wouldn't say that. I know I'm being heretical but I honestly don't think the sixties were what they're cracked up to be. Plenty of people got burned, you know,' James said.

'And they still do,' I answered.

'Yes, but that's out of their control,' he said. 'In the sixties we promised ourselves the world but we never stopped to think whether we were ruining it.'

'But what did we ruin?'

'Ourselves maybe,' he said. 'We had no roots, we had no responsibilities, and more than that, we had no discipline.'

'But we had vision. And political involvement. And fun.'

'Well, yes,' he said. 'Fun. If that's what you call it. I prefer real organisation myself. I've worked hard to create this group which has both purpose and structure. Not for me the collective fantasies of the past. You know, I think that too many people refuse to face the eighties. I know they're tough but let's acknowledge that they're also real.'

I opened my mouth to argue with him but I closed it almost immediately. I hadn't come to re-run the sixties and neither of us was going to change the other's mind.

'You know something about Paul Holland,' I said.

'I used to know him. He was my therapist.'

'His death must have been a terrible shock.'

'It was, even though I hardly ever saw him. I left therapy with him a while ago. I got to feel too introverted—bound up in myself.' He flashed me a smile and then turned to a rather taut-looking man who'd been waiting by his side. James reassured him about the explosive potential of fireworks. He did it smoothly, with only a touch of condescension.

'I've been at this for a long while,' he said when the man left. 'People rely on me. I encourage them to use their own knowledge but it's difficult breaking out of old forms.'

'I bet it is,' I said. 'Did you like Paul Holland?'

'I think I loved him,' James said. 'For a while he was my anchor in life. Then I realised that he had no solidity. He changed personality like he changed clothes. That's not what you want out of a therapist. So I left. We still kept in touch though. We became friends.'

'Did you meet often?'

'It was a casual thing. Paul made the running. He would come and visit me occasionally. We'd smoke a joint together and catch up on developments. I think talking to me made him feel involved.'

'When did you last see him?'

'Sometime in April. He dropped round. But he was killed near my house. He might have been coming for a visit. He never arrived.'

James finished talking and we sat in silence. I couldn't work out why he'd asked to see me and he seemed to be in doubt himself. He leaned back and crossed his arms, stretching his legs out in front of him. He stared at me as if asking a question. He didn't hide his scrutiny and I tried not to get flustered by it. At last he spoke.

'You investigated Tim Nicholson's death?'

'Yes.'

'Were you pleased he was killed by a man?'

'I wasn't pleased he was killed at all,' I said.

James nodded to himself. It looked like I'd passed whatever sort of test he'd set me.

'I have some friends—street kids—I occasionally hang out with. I got them involved with this organisation once.'

'Oh yes,' I said.

'They saw Paul run over.'

'But the police said there were no witnesses.'

'Yeah, well that's the thing. They wouldn't go to the police. But they saw it all right. And they say it looked deliberate. The street was empty and the car had plenty of room.'

‘Did they get the number plate?’ I asked.

‘I don’t know. I didn’t press them further. I know my limits—Paul taught me that. They said that if I thought you were okay they’d talk to you.’

‘And do I pass?’

‘You’ll do,’ he said. ‘With one proviso. The police are kept out of this.’

‘It’s a deal,’ I said.

James gave me an address. I wrote it down. For a while we sat in silence surveying the activity. Impossible as it seemed, the pace had speeded up. I watched as somebody got into a fork-lift truck and moved it forwards. They were having trouble keeping in a straight line and were edging ominously close to the water’s edge.

James was watching too. He got up.

‘Better see to that,’ he said. ‘Good luck.’

‘And to you. Thanks.’

He nodded absent-mindedly and was off, his mind bent on the scene removal.

There was a man standing on my front steps when I got back. All I could see of him as I came up behind him was a broad back encased in a tight-fitting grey suit. His back was slightly bent as if he was trying to do something to the door.

I coughed when I got behind him. He gave an almost imperceptible start and his right hand moved to his pocket. Then he turned round. His face was calm. He looked at me blankly, staring with blue eyes which were set deep in a squarish face. His short brown hair was neatly clipped with a hint of brylcreem for good measure.

‘There’s nobody in,’ he said. ‘I was just going to leave my card.’

I nodded and got out my key. He stepped aside to give me access to the lock. When I had the door open, he spoke again.

‘Do you live here?’ he asked.

He smiled in a self-deprecating way when I held up my key.

‘I’m not on the ball today. Of course you do,’ he said.

He threw me another smile, a more engaging one. He removed his brown plastic pocket case that he’d wedged under his left armpit and unzipped it. He took out a card which he showed to me.

‘The name’s Cross of the Ashley Agency. I’m terribly sorry to bother you but I have a proposal which might be of mutual benefit. Could I come in and put it to you?’

‘What’s the Ashley Agency?’ I asked.

'Estate agents. We handle many of the properties in this area. I believe we have one on our books in this street at present.'

He turned his back to me and searched the road. He pointed into the distance. Sure enough there was a 'for sale' sign printed in grey and pink and bearing the legend 'Ashley for A 1 service'.

'Your husband contacted us for a list and we do like to make personal calls. We pride ourselves on face-to-face interaction. That way we can be fully briefed on what the customer requires. He doesn't have to go to unsuitable properties, thus aggravating both himself and the owner.'

'Maybe you should talk to him then,' I said.

'Figure of speech,' he chuckled. 'Old habits die slowly. If I could come in?'

'It's not really the best time for me,' I said.

The man shifted uncomfortably. He must have developed a big repertory of smiles because this time he produced one of a different genre. It spoke of genteel embarrassment mixed with boyish charm.

'Penalty of the job,' he said. 'We are always on the move. I'm sorry to trouble you but could I use your bathroom?'

I sighed and nodded. I climbed the stairs and he followed. When we got upstairs I showed him the toilet and went into the kitchen.

He didn't take long. He came out looking relaxed, cheerful and grateful.

'Very kind of you.' He looked around the room with an eye practised in taking in his environment. 'Nice place you have here. I do hope you give it to us to handle. Your husband said you were only contemplating a move, but should the wish gell, we would be more than happy to help you out. I'll make a note of it in your file, Mrs Watkins.'

'Baeier,' I said.

The man looked up from the piece of paper he'd been scribbling on.

'I beg your pardon?'

'My name's Baeier.'

'I do beg your pardon,' he said. 'So Mr Watkins is not your . . .?'

He looked at me as I shook my head.

'It's not at all unusual,' he said quickly. 'We're getting an increasing number of mixed-sex sharers.'

He put his paper back into his bag and moved to the door. He already had his hand on the knob when something occurred to him. He turned round and looked startled to find me so close behind.

'Baeier,' he said. 'There can't be many of them around. You aren't by any chance the detective mentioned in *Street Times* are you?'

'One and the same,' I said.

'How utterly fascinating. It's a hobby of mine, collecting unusual professions. You meet so many in my line. How's it going?'

'Slowly,' I said.

'I assume these things take time. I do hope *Street Times* follows your progress. Now I've met you I'll be doubly interested in the outcome.'

I nodded and tried a smile. I wondered how long he was going to keep us at the door.

The man wasn't insensitive. He got the message in the nod and his face showed regret.

'I'll leave you to it,' he said. 'Do let us know if you want us to market your property.'

He went out and I followed him down. When he got to ground level he handed me one of his cards, muttered a pleasantry and was off.

The phone was ringing when I got back upstairs.

I picked up the receiver.

'Hello,' I said.

Nothing happened.

'Hello,' I tried again.

'I'm coming tomorrow,' the voice instructed.

'I know,' I answered.

'Tell him,' he said, before the dialling tone hit my ear.

I sighed. I thought about it and I looked through my filofax until I found his number. I dialled it. He answered on the second ring. I knew that he'd answered, not because he said anything, but because I could hear him breathing. He never had been a silent breather.

'Tell Sam what?' I asked.

'To pick me up from George's house. I am going there after school . . .'

In typical Matthew style, he hung up again. I took a piece of paper from the desk and wrote Sam a note telling him that his recalcitrant six-year-old wanted to be picked up later than usual from his friend George's house. Matthew was often like that with arrangements. He didn't mind taking two hours to describe the closing sequence of Star Wars, but he didn't like to waste his breath on personal information. I suppose it was because he so often moved home: at his mother's in the week and Sam's at the weekend.

As I finished writing the note, Sam turned up. I showed it to him and he nodded. I poured us both a Glenfiddich, gave him his, and he nodded. I switched on the news. Sam sat down in front of the TV, still without uttering a word. I went and sat next to him. He put his arm round my shoulders. I wondered why the boys in my life were both being so obtuse. I thought about asking Sam, but then I thought I'd just get another nod.

We watched in silence as pictures of burning cities and police in retreat came on to the screen. As a counterbalance, Michael Heseltine got on and off buses shaking hands with small businessmen. He tried to convince us that this was the way he'd solve mass unemployment in Liverpool. It wasn't impressive. He was followed by the mute faces of the seven dead hunger strikers. I switched the set off as Humphrey Atkins was mouthing words about Northern Ireland that had no meaning.

By this the time the Glenfiddich had done its work and Sam had found speech.

'Sometimes,' he said, 'I wish I'd become a lawyer.'

'Oh yeah,' I said. 'And I, that I was a housewife. What happened?'

Sam gave a long sigh. He put his face in his hands and groaned.

'Nothing happened. Absolutely nothing. Unless you count the fact that one of my students asked me a penetrating question about the foliation of space which took me all of thirteen minutes to answer, I got five circulars, two of them identical and I had an argument in the canteen with a Spartacist while eating a soya-bean casserole.'

'You're in a bad way,' I said. 'Arguing with a Spart.'

'Yeah, well he tried to tell me that soya was a sop thrown at the working class to divert it from the struggle.'

'So how was it?'

'The soya? Terrible. If that's a sop, then I think we're saved. Anyway, what time are we leaving?'

My mouth opened. I felt it happen but there was nothing I could do to stop it. I did manage to shut it pretty quick but Sam still caught me at it. 'To the Simpsons,' he said. 'You forgot. I've reminded you three times, and you forgot.'

I tried to think of an excuse but I couldn't. I had to admit it was odd. Sam had set up a date for us to go and eat with the Simpsons at least two months ago, and because he knew how resistant I was to it, he had been reminding me about it constantly. I'd still managed to forget.

It wasn't that I hated the Simpsons: it was that I found them hard work. She was as sweet as syrup and as glutinous. He was apparently charming, but he always succeeded in making me feel uncomfortable. He had a sort of brooding quality which made me think he was watching my every move and hating it.

They were both old friends of Sam. When the three of them got together they could reminisce about the past as if the present had brought no differences between them. I didn't mind that, as long as they kept me out of it. But the Simpsons had their own plans. Uneven numbers disturbed them and they demanded a foursome. Every three months or so they got one. I knew that I should have put my foot down about it, but somehow I never got round to it. So instead I tried to forget that we were due at their house. It didn't work. It never does.

That evening was different. We didn't get our foursome. We arrived to find Arthur Simpson entertaining a third couple. Norah Simpson said a brief hello as she rushed about busily seeing to the food and the kids. She managed both with admirable efficiency and the occasional dirty glance in Arthur's direction. He didn't seem to notice.

We sat for a while in their pastel living room, chatting desultorily. We couldn't find much common ground between the five of us and so the conversation was uneasy. Arthur tried hard, steering us through a whole series of topics, none of which was totally unsuccessful, but none of which took off. The calm of the room, with its low lighting and sqashy sofas, softened the discomfort, but even so everybody was relieved when Norah called us to the table.

Norah has a gift for presentation and as usual the table looked wonderful. It wasn't only the food—perfectly timed roast beef with three crisp vegetables to accompany it—but also the white tablecloth with its tiny yellow flowers that echoed the two glass vases filled with yellow freesias. We started on the food and the compliments. Norah looked pleased as we told her how good it all tasted. Arthur kept silent. She shot him a challenging glance.

'Pass the mustard,' she said to him, 'if that's not too much trouble.'

Slowly Arthur moved the mustard from in front of him. He

stopped before he reached Norah's outstretched hand. He put the mustard down in front of me. I picked it up and helped it to its destination.

'Thank you very much Kate,' Norah said, 'that is kind of you.'

'Had a spot of trouble at our ward meeting the other night,' Arthur said.

'And what are you up to now?' Norah asked.

There was silence. I looked up from my food to find that everybody was staring my way.

'Sorry,' I said. 'I didn't realise you were asking me. I'm doing some detective work.'

'You journalists,' Arthur said in a voice that didn't quite make it to the jovial. 'You're always delving in the mire.'

'You wouldn't say that if she was a man,' Norah said.

'Oh woman, don't be so ridiculous,' Arthur snapped. 'Not everything is directed against you.'

Norah ignored him. 'What are you investigating?' she asked.

'The death of a therapist.'

There was gasp from Arthur. We all looked at him. He was choking. His hand still on the thin-stemmed wine glass shook as he struggled for breath.

'So sorry folks,' he said. 'Swallowed it the wrong way.'

Norah got up and went into the kitchen. When she came back she was holding a cloth. She wiped furiously at the red stain that was spreading towards one of the intricate flowers. She only helped to diffuse the red.

'That was clumsy dear,' she said.

'You should be pleased you're not the only one that spills things around here,' he hissed.

'This food really is delicious,' the woman opposite me said quickly.

'She is a good cook,' Arthur conceded.

He ignored the flash of resentment that Norah shot across the table at him as he meticulously cut a slice of beef into four equal parts. He forked one of the pieces and was raising it to his mouth when he seemed to notice the silence. He placed the fork down on his plate so that it lined up with his knife.

'As I was saying, we had an interesting debate at the ward meeting last night.' He stopped, waiting for a challenge from Norah that never came. 'About Northern Ireland,' he said, 'and the tactics of the bullet.'

Nobody was willing to help him out but Arthur acted like he didn't care. 'It's a difficult situation,' he said. 'Very tricky indeed.'

It was then that I realised what Arthur was trying to do. He was throwing bait at Sam across the table. It was a well-worn routine between them. They'd met in the early seventies when they'd both served on a Vietnam solidarity committee. It had been a transition period for both of them. Arthur was moving from the freedom and uncertainty of the Young Liberals into the more bureaucratic area of moderate Labour politics; Sam was becoming increasingly disenchanted with the way the hard left paid lip service to personal politics at the same time as it did its utmost to discount them.

Because they both felt so uprooted, they had formed a tenuous alliance. It hadn't lasted long. Arthur was opposed to American policy in Vietnam but his lifelong belief in an abstract justice meant that he could never fully commit himself to a struggle. He admired the way the Vietnamese people would not let up but his distaste for violence meant he was always too ready to compromise. His attitude had led to intense clashes with Sam, the one arguing for petitions, the other for storming the US embassy. And, whenever they met subsequently, the arguments about strategy and tactics would continue, albeit over the dinner party table.

That evening was no exception. I always considered Arthur too set in his opinions to be worth challenging, but Sam seemed to like tangling with him. He sat up straight in his chair and he too deposited his cutlery on his plate. The lines of battle were joined.

'You can't help admiring the hunger strikers,' Sam said.

Arthur shook his head. 'They're on to a losing wicket. Thatcher won't budge.'

'Come on Arthur,' Sam said. 'That's always your mistake. You place Thatcher in the centre of the stage, just where she wants to be. The Irish people aren't so gullible.'

'It's not a question of gullibility,' Arthur said, 'but of reality. What good is such a waste of young men's lives?'

Sam was about to reply but Norah beat him to it. 'You don't care about people,' she said. 'You're just interested in being right.'

It went on like that the whole evening. Norah and Arthur fought on while the rest of us pretended it wasn't happening. At one point Sam tried to intervene. At that point the two of them united in failing to understand what Sam was getting at. He gave up.

By 10.30 we made our excuses and got ready to leave. Norah started to protest that it was too early but her half-heartedness showed and the other couple also got up.

'I'll show you to the door,' Norah said, taking me firmly by the arm.

She pulled me out of the room quickly. When we were away from the others she stopped.

'I think he's having an affair,' she said.

She was facing me. She flashed a brave smile that couldn't conceal the tears welling up in her eyes.

'Have you asked him?'

'I wouldn't demean myself,' she whispered and then turned to where the others had appeared.

'Everybody ready?' she said brightly. 'Nothing left behind?'

We exited in a flurry of polite thank-yous and barely concealed relief.

In the car, Sam and I tried to work out what was going on. We didn't get far. Arthur hadn't told Sam anything, which didn't surprise either of us.

'He never does talk about himself,' Sam said. 'I don't think he knows what to say.'

'I don't understand what you see in him,' I said.

Sam thought about it for a moment.

'Do you think he was seeing Paul Holland?' I asked.

Sam laughed. 'Arthur? Never. Not the type for introspection.'

'So why did he spill the wine?'

'Him and Norah I guess. He pretends to ignore her but if she pays attention to anybody else, he soon pulls her back. Only time they've ever been separated was when Arthur did his disappearing act.'

'Which act?'

'In the early seventies,' Sam said. 'Arthur vanished off the face of the earth. Norah was frantic. She thought he'd left her for another woman and was too much of a coward to tell her.'

'Had he?'

'Not Arthur. I reckon he was depressed and didn't want anybody to know. As I said, he's not one for introspection. When he came back he reverted to normal and proposed to Norah. They've been together for a long time: the most stable couple I know.'

'And not too happy with it,' I said.

Sam didn't comment and we lapsed into silence.

I wondered how the two of them could bear to live in that atmosphere. I wondered what it was doing to their kids. And then I got to thinking about friends and I wondered how Anna and Daniel were doing. I realised how much I was missing them and I wondered whether I would ever forgive them for leaving.

All that wondering didn't help me sleep. I didn't lie awake all night but I didn't get any rest from my sleep. Instead, I had dreams so intense and at the same time so frustrating that I kept wanting to pull myself out of them.

The dreams were crowded with people—people from my past held arguments in Portuguese with people I'd come to know in England. Nobody kept their shape: one minute I would be looking at Franca and the next she'd turn into Anna and walk away from me. No matter how hard I tried to intervene, nobody took any notice.

I forced myself to wake up by fighting my way out of the dreams. I was exhausted. I reached across the still sleeping Sam and looked at the clock. It was eight. I'd been asleep a long time and I was still exhausted. I took a shower to clear my head. It helped, but not enough, so I got out the percolator and made myself an espresso as strong as it was dark. That also helped.

I opened the front door and went downstairs to the hall. I came back with the paper. I sat on the balcony with it. There was nothing much to read. Too many things were happening and the newspaper reporters no longer had anything to say. They were biding their time, waiting to see which way things would settle.

By nine o'clock I was feeling better. I said goodbye to a barely awake Sam and walked to the tube. We'd settled on Sam's flat the night before and so when it began to drizzle I had no clothes suitable to keep the rain off. At least I could have an integral wardrobe, I thought, if we ever got to live together.

It didn't take me long to get to Laura Maxwell's restaurant. It was on the outskirts of Soho, near enough to Oxford Street to attract shoppers and tourists, but also deep enough in Soho to cater for office workers. Even at nine-thirty in the morning the place was full.

I went in and glanced around. 'Grains' was like a clone of so many of those health food outfits that had sprung up during the last five years. It had the standard shop attached that sold dried fruit and pulses at exorbitant prices.

The restaurant was beside the shop. It had a healthy look, thanks mainly to the liberal use of over-lacquered brown wood. The shiny tables were long and narrow, which was probably just as well because so were the benches. Behind the shiny counter people with rigid backs doled out large portions of fibre. I joined the queue.

I worked out the layout of the place while I waited to be served. It was of a utilitarian design. Behind the counter was a door which led into a spotless-looking kitchen. Every now and then the door would open for more fibre and I'd catch a glimpse of the five kitchen workers, chopping vegetables on butcher block tables.

The kitchen had a low ceiling, built to accommodate another room on top of it. This room was Laura Maxwell's office. I could see that because, instead of a wall, the room had glass windows, floor to ceiling. Laura Maxwell was looking out of it. As I was being served her eyes flicked on me. She gave no sign of recognition.

The woman behind the counter caught my upward glance. She smiled.

'Makes you feel like stealing from the till,' she said.

I returned her smile and waited while she put a fresh pressed orange juice and wholesome looking muffin on my tray. I paid, reflecting that if I spent much time here Laura would blanch at my expenses bill. Then I took the tray, squeezed myself into a side bench that gave me a view of the whole place, and got ready for a long watch.

Three fruit juices and one coffee later I hadn't learned much. The staff were too busy to notice me so I got a good view of their activities. The queues in the place were constant. Breakfast over, we got the morning tea brigade, mainly tired shoppers carrying too many parcels, and then lunch, which was a mixed affair. I didn't see anybody doing anything except ringing up the prices round the till. I did see a lot of Laura Maxwell. Every time I looked up she was there, watching. I got the impression she was more interested in me than in the operation of her restaurant.

By one o'clock I'd had about as much of health food as I could take. I pushed my tray to one side and prepared to squeeze my way out. At that point Laura appeared.

'Hold it a minute,' she said.

She wheeled round so I could admire her elegantly tailored fawn suit and went to the counter. When she came back she was carrying a Granny Smith on a shining pottery plate. She put it on the table. To its right she placed a lethal looking knife.

'Can't stand the skin,' she said.

She slid into the bench with ease. When she'd managed to block my exit, she came to a stop. She got the knife and went to work. She did it with deadly precision. In one motion she got the skin off and she got it off clean. I couldn't help feeling glad I wasn't the apple. She cut off a thin sliver and slipped it into her mouth. Then she turned her attention to me.

'Where were you going?' she asked.

'I've seen enough for today,' I said. 'I have other work to do.'

'What sort?' she said.

'All sorts.'

The knife was lifted again and a thicker sliver cut off. She lifted it up and held it between her thumb and forefinger. She gazed at it as if fascinated.

'Anything interesting?' she asked.

'Quite,' I said. 'Tell me, how much goes missing every day?'

'What?' Her eyes focused on the chunk of apple and she disposed of it almost without chewing. She put the knife down.

'I was wondering how much is stolen from your till?'

She got up. 'Oh that. Not much. A tenner a day. But it's the principle, isn't it? And now, I do have work to do . . .'

She got up and walked towards the kitchen. On her way she stepped in front of one of her healthy looking employees who was carrying a pile of dirty trays. Laura moved to brush her aside. Instead, she knocked the trays off balance.

The silence that followed the crash of descending wood meant that the whole restaurant could hear Laura's shouts.

'You creep! You absolute dunderhead! Can't you get out of my way? I'll have you for this.'

She was shaking with rage. She clenched a fist, almost as if she was going to hit the woman, and then she stopped herself. She came to, as if suddenly realising that the whole restaurant was watching her performance. She mumbled an apology, and then quickly she walked behind the counter and was gone.

It took a while for conversation to start again but as people got back to their food the hum reached its normal level. I watched as the assaulted woman pulled her brown hair forward over her face to hide her tears. She knelt down. Another woman came from behind the counter and knelt beside her. I got out of my seat and walked past them.

'I don't see why I should put up with it,' the first woman said.

'Don't take any notice. She's been in a terrible state all week. You wait, in half a hour she won't be able to do enough for you,' the second woman said.

I got to the exit. Before I went through it I glanced up. Laura Maxwell was at her station. She was standing motionless, staring into the space in front of her.

Kate was cursing the room. She hated it, she said. She hated the pictures on the wall, the Habitat of the polished floorboards and, more than anything, she hated the white, bright walls.

'It's so empty,' she said, shifting her eyes from left to right as she looked for another target to attack.

'You once commented that you liked the sparseness of the design,' Franca said softly.

Kate's eyes stopped moving, but the hunted look remained. She rounded on her companion. 'Taste changes,' she said. 'People change.'

'And is that frightening?'

Kate glared across the space.

'Don't change the subject,' she said.

This time the look that went across the two chairs was brittle with frozen anger. Franca faced the look without blanching. She sat, waiting.

After a while Kate spoke again. It was an effort for her to do so and the words came out slowly, separated by long pauses.

'I find it hard to disagree with you,' she said, and wished she could sound more adult. 'We have different ways of looking at the world. Why shouldn't we?'

'Why indeed?' Franca said.

'But it matters,' Kate insisted. 'It's vital. You're supposed to be helping me. How can you if we fight about the difference between the outside and the in?'

Franca looked puzzled. Kate waited for her to reply. When she didn't Kate spoke again, exasperation oozing.

'It's the ideology that I find so difficult. I was talking about the disintegration of the left in Portugal and you put it down to psyches. There are world forces out there, you know.'

'I don't think you were talking about them,' Franca said.

'I was trying to,' Kate said. 'It's not easy you know. And it doesn't help to hear that the people I trusted and worked with are, in your eyes, crazy.'

'I don't think I used that word,' Franca interjected.

'You never do,' Kate said. 'But it's the thought that counts.'

This time the silence between the two seemed almost final. Kate looked down at her shoes. Franca waited for the look to shift. After a while, she realised it wouldn't. She needed to speak, she felt.

'You lived through turbulent times,' Franca said to the bent head. 'I cannot deny that, nor would I want to. The world moved fast for you and your friends. But I think that a moment ago you were talking about a different aspect—about the pain you all carried with you, and how that interfered in your attempt to really change yourselves. You were, I think, talking about political growth and opportunity that ran ahead of personal awareness. And the problems that caused.'

Kate's head had lifted slowly while Franca spoke. She still looked down at her shoes but she no longer seemed to be trying to worm into them.

'And now,' she said, 'we have personal growth without political movement. I'm not sure that's any better.'

'Perhaps you're right,' Franca answered. 'We do not have the power to choose the world we live in.'

'I hate to believe that,' Kate said. 'We have the power to change it.' She grinned to herself, pleased by a joke only she had caught. Franca looked at her enquiringly.

'Mad logic,' Kate explained. 'I seem to be switching positions. Before I thought you were saying that the outside world was irrelevant, now I'm treating it as if it is.'

'It's not a simple matter,' Franca said.

'What is?' asked Kate. Her voice was a long, long way away.

Finsbury Park was a strange area. Like Dalston and many other Inner London boroughs it was going through an uneasy period of transition. While some parts were being renovated beyond recognition, others were falling into decay. The area still had a rough reputation despite concerted attacks by police and property speculators to purge the place of the dispossessed, but proximity to the tube meant that takeover by the white middle classes was becoming inevitable.

The day I went to seek out James Stanford's friend, Marcus Jones, Finsbury Park looked a mess.

The drizzle had stopped and the sun was making a bid for attention. It hadn't been trying long and so far it had produced more light than heat. The light shone on the drawn faces of the passers-by and on the soggy cardboard boxes that littered the pavement. Bits of glass from shattered windows had been kicked into the gutters to join the empty crisp and cigarette packets. Even the newly planted trees along the pavement looked like they were struggling for air.

It took me five minutes to walk to the house. It was one of those Victorian monsters that had seen better days. Paint peeled off the doors and the two lions that guarded the entrance looked sadly neglected. I rang the bell. Nothing happened. I rang again and again and waited, with no results. I turned to go but then I heard a window opening directly above me.

'You're early,' a man's voice called. 'Wait. Me come now.'

It was more than a minute before he opened the door. When I saw him I also saw why he'd taken so long. He was a big man and he should have been a tall one but he was bent sideways, leaning heavily on a cane. His brown skin was tinged with a grey pallor which was echoed in his hair. Black braces held up the trousers which stopped short of his highly polished but scuffed brown shoes.

'Come in,' he said. 'You catch me unawares; everybody usually come late.'

Limping, he showed me into a large front room.

'Sit down,' he said. 'I back soon.'

I sat on a large imitation leather settee and looked around. My eyes widened. It was the busiest room I'd ever seen. Not only was it crowded with furniture but on every piece lay more detail. The chairs and settees had arm covers and bright pieces of materials on their backs; the tables had large lace doilies to compete with the huge vases of garish plastic flowers; the walls were covered in pictures of weddings, christenings and graduations. In pride of place hung a 3-D picture of Jesus. Below him, on the mantelpiece, was a menagerie made of glass: tiny animals all shapes, sizes and colours. Beside them, in a small glass-enclosed bookshelf, were three volumes of Virtue's *Household Physician*.

When the man returned, he had put on a jacket to cover his braces. He stayed by the door.

'Where you want to start look?' he asked.

I stood up.

'I'm afraid there's been a misunderstanding,' I said. 'I'm looking for Marcus.'

'You not come to buy the house then?'

'No. I wanted to talk to Marcus. Does he live here?'

The man pushed his cane in front of him and limped to a seat. He lowered himself into it.

'Is my son,' he said. 'He in trouble?'

'Not at all. A friend, James Stanford, thought Marcus would help me with something.'

The man's brow cleared. He smiled and pointed with his cane to the settee. I went back to it.

'James he a good man. He spend he time with the youth. He keep my boy occupy and happy with his acting. It not easy for them round here, you know.'

'It isn't,' I agreed. 'Are you planning to move?'

'We going back home—St Lucia. This no place to grow old in and since I'm not working no more.' He gestured to his leg. 'People should die on them born spot.'

'Are you taking the whole family?'

He laughed. 'Not the kids. They have a different attitude. This they country but they so critical of it. I know this country harsh but they must learn toleration.'

He talked a bit more about his children and then he offered me some tea. I accepted. I followed him to the kitchen and he told me about his wife, who was sleeping after doing a day and night shift, and about what it felt like when he moved to England. While we were talking he told me I would be unlikely to find Marcus at home and suggested a few places where he might be. I got the impression he was scared for his son and for what the world would do to him. Behind the fear lay an anger. The man couldn't understand why his son was so quick to reject the values by which he'd tried to live. He had struggled to make a life in a country which had offered riches and delivered little. His son, born to the society, was ready to reject it.

Two cups of tea later, the real house buyers turned up. I left them looking, with their critical eyes, in search of a bargain.

One of the places Marcus's father had told me about was a café on the way to the tube, so I stopped at it. It was almost empty when I walked in. All the customers were white and silent. I bought a cup of tea and for a while I toyed with it. Then I asked the man behind the counter for Marcus. He shook his head, and he looked suspiciously at me. I told him that I was only after a conversation with Marcus, but he still looked suspicious. I didn't think I was going to get anywhere so I made my way back to Islington.

Sam and Matthew were in front of the television when I arrived. Sam managed a smile in my direction but Matthew, who was sitting on Sam's knee, didn't even register my presence. I shrugged and joined them.

Half a hour later when Charlie Chan had solved the mystery of the two hats, Matthew looked up. He got off Sam's lap and flicked his arm at me. He still didn't talk.

'How's school?' I asked.

'All right,' he said, in the bored monotone he had perfected.

'What did you do?'

'Nothing much,' he said.

He walked out of the room. Sam and I exchanged information about our day and then he went into the kitchen and started to cook. I switched off the television. That attracted Matthew back.

'I got my bronze,' he announced as he clicked the TV back on.

'Very good,' I said. 'You're not watching anything.'

'So what?' he said and walked to the door. 'Will you take me swimming tomorrow?'

'If it's not too early,' I said.

Having got what he wanted, Matthew decided to fill me in on his week's activities. I heard all about how red desk beat yellow desk for the smiley prize but how red desk had really cheated. Matthew was, of course, a member of yellow desk. I heard about how marbles, the new status symbol in Matthew's class, were banned after Miss nearly twisted her ankle when she walked in on a marble race. I could go on describing what I heard but the fascination was more in the telling than in the information. And anyway, it would take too long, since Matthew talked solid for four and a half hours. He even carried on talking to himself after he was put to bed.

Five

He was still talking when he woke up. All I could manage was a series of groans. Sam soon got the message and led Matthew out of the room. I tried to go back to sleep against the talking that penetrated through two closed doors.

I did manage to drift off for ten minutes but was woken when Matthew plonked a cup of coffee on the table beside me. I thanked him weakly and closed my eyes. The next thing I knew something soft descended on me, smothering me. I pulled at it and opened my eyes. I was looking at my swimming costume. Beside it stood a grinning Matthew. He was already dressed in his.

We got to the Caledonian Road baths at eleven o'clock and queued up along with half the families in Islington. I thought about giving it a miss but Matthew wouldn't hear of it. Then he refused to go into the women's changing room with me so I spent a few minutes trying to tell him to wait for me when he'd put his clothes away. He listened patiently but I could see that scepticism and contempt were about to surface. Matthew was growing up, faster than I realised.

When I was changed and out near the pool, I owned up to myself that the reason I'd wanted Matthew to wait was that I couldn't see. I'd taken off my contact lenses and the place was a huge blur on me—a huge screaming blur. I screwed up my eyes, looking for the small white body, but all I saw was what seemed like hundreds of small white look-alikes. Only when I walked to the side of the pool did I manage to identify Matthew, who was swimming furiously through the throng. He was spending more energy keeping afloat than in moving forward, but in a crowd like that it probably wasn't such a bad thing.

I got into the water to join him. It was its usual lukewarm bromidy substance. I gritted my teeth. I'd long ago discovered that crawl was one of the few ways to ensure that people got out of your way in overcrowded swimming pools, so I launched off.

As usual, it worked. I managed to force my way to Matthew to check on him and then I managed to do two lengths with only minimum interference. I was on my third when it happened. I was halfway down the pool and going strong. I took a breath to the side and out of the corner of my eye, noticed a blur that was a man planted dead ahead. I didn't take much notice. He was just standing there but I assumed that he, like all the rest, would get out of the way before I reached him.

I couldn't have been more wrong. On the next stroke I catapulted straight into him. I cursed and tried to get round. It didn't work. When I moved to the left, so did he. When I moved to the right, he followed. I stopped swimming and tried to get a proper look at him. Before I could get upright his hand reached out to my head, and then I was under water.

He held me under for a while, let me up for one breath, and then pushed me down again. This time he held me down for what seemed forever.

It seemed like forever, but when I think about what went through my mind, it wasn't much. Parts of me was convinced that I couldn't possibly drown in a pool the size of Caledonian Road, where nowhere is too deep to stand, and where at least fifty people were within shouting distance. The other part felt like I was fighting: fighting for my life. The man was at least twice my weight and strong with it. I began to feel I was losing the fight.

Somewhere in the distance, beneath the bubbles, I heard a whistle and a shout. It didn't mean anything to me until I realised that the pressure on my head had gone. I floated up, almost too weak to breathe. When I got to the surface the man was swimming furiously away from me. I hadn't the strength to follow him.

Matthew paddled up while I stayed in my place, gulping for air.

'You're not supposed to do that,' he said.

'Do what?'

'Play rough games. The guards are very cross with you.'

'Where did that man go?' I gasped.

'He left. They made him. You better watch out.' Matthew turned as if about to swim off. I held him by the leg.

'Did you see what he looked like?'

'A man,' he said.

I got out of the water and rushed into the changing rooms. My contact lenses were in within two seconds and I was dressed in ten. I stationed myself by the exit to watch the men coming out of their changing rooms. I was there for twenty minutes. Plenty of men passed by but none of them had the look of someone who'd tried to drown me. Several of them did throw me a glance that meant if I stared much longer they'd definitely be interested. I tried to show them how much they were kidding themselves.

By the time Matthew came out demanding crisps I was feeling a whole lot calmer. The swimming pool was on display through the glass doors giving the sight but not the sound of the frantic activity inside it. It made such an innocuous scene that for a moment I thought I might have imagined the entire experience. Only Matthew's insistent 'Did you know that man you were playing with?' stopped me from doubting myself. That, and the dirty look from the life guard.

We drove back via the Angel. When we passed it, Chapel Market was in full swing with stalls piled high with ordinary vegetables and guarded by stall-holders who looked like they'd hit you as soon as give you your change. I needed to buy some basics and an empty parking space just near the market was too much of a temptation. I stopped, accompanied by heavy heckling from Matthew in the back.

'I'll take you to an amusement arcade after,' I said.

'Why?'

I turned round to look at him. He was sitting with his feet up, his back hunched and his arms clasped in front of him. His lips were set firm against an adult trick. Suspicion glinted in his half-closed eyes.

'You never do anything like that,' he said. 'You don't like those places.'

'I'm looking for somebody,' I said. 'Name of Marcus. His father said he hangs out in one of those arcades called the "Glittering Prize". It's just round the corner.'

Matthew's eyes opened a fraction, but only a fraction.

'I knew you had another reason,' he said as he shrugged. 'But all right.'

We left the car. I managed some minor shopping before the weight of the crowds and Matthew's protests drove me out. We walked towards the 'Glittering Prize'. On the way we passed people selling left-wing papers. They were bunched together defensively trying to ignore the group of men who stood opposite, cracking jokes that had never been funny. On the outskirts two policemen kept jaded eyes on the length of pavement between the two groups.

The 'Glittering Prize' didn't live up to its name. Outside the air was dirty but the sun was shining. Inside was unmitigated gloom. So dark was it that both Matthew and I had to stand still to give our eyes time to acclimatise. We were hit by a barrage of sound as we stood there: booms, whirrs and whines punctuated by the swearing of the clientele.

It was a long room lined with machines and lit by fluorescent streaks which struggled vainly through the dirt that had accumulated on them. Down the middle of the room was another bank of machines. The atmosphere was sticky with smoke and a sort of frustrated anger that showed in the backs of the men, intent on scoring high. The room was almost exclusively male, filled with men of different ages and sizes but all with the common stance that came from concentrating on a game that ate their money and reflected their aggression.

There was only one other woman in the place and she was sitting in a kiosk with a sign underneath that read 'Change me here'. I went up to her and handed her a pound. Without looking up she thrust ten-pence pieces towards me. Only as I reached to scoop them up did she throw a glance my way. She looked puzzled.

'Don't get many women in here?' I asked.

She smiled and then shrugged as her eyes flickered over the room.

'Do you blame them?' she said.

Her skin seemed to have taken on the colouring of her environment: it was a pallid grey which her slapdash powder couldn't conceal. Her brown hair looked like it had given up on its hairdresser and was hanging around waiting for inspiration. Only her grey eyes showed a spark of life—a liveliness which boredom and Marlboros had done much to conceal.

'I'm looking for someone,' I said. 'Name of Marcus Jones. His father said he hangs out here.'

She looked at me and then her eyes passed me by. When her eyes caught mine again, they were a uninterested blank.

'Never heard of him luv,' she said. 'One's like any other in this place.'

She looked down, shutting me out. There was nothing I could do but walk away, towards an impatient Matthew.

On my way to him I glanced at the corner opposite her kiosk. A thickset man stood there, his back against the wall, his legs crossed, his arms folded in front of him. He had the air of a man who was not to be trifled with. His face was flat. His nose looked like it had gone through many breaks, which increased his appearance of brutality.

As I watched him, two seventeen-year-olds passed him by. They were talking animately and one of them tripped over the man's leg. He didn't move when it happened. He didn't have to. The teenager backed away nervously. Their apologies could be heard right down the noisy room. The man just stood there ignoring them.

It was another half an hour before I could persuade Matthew to leave. He, a squirt amongst the men, didn't care if he had no direct access to the machines. He was content to watch the others at their play, to drink in their atmosphere and to feel part of them. He would stand outside a group as they worked the machines. After a while a space would open up and he'd edge forward, negotiating their knees. Eventually he'd end up in front, beside the main operator and watching intently. Nobody ackowledged his presence, nor did they try and get rid of him.

I was left on the sidelines to wait for him. There was nowhere to sit so I propped up a corner and tried to bide time peaceably. The incident in the swimming pool had drained me and so I almost succeeded in falling asleep on my feet—which, in that environment, would have been some feat, even for me. But it was just too uncomfortable and too noisy.

And on top of that I couldn't shake off the feeling that the man in the corner was waiting me out. It wasn't that he looked at me or that he made any movement towards me but he had a stillness that was eerie and a stance that was ready for action. Only once, when I went to get more change for Matthew, did he make as if to move. When I didn't speak to the woman behind the counter, he leaned back once more.

Matthew finally got to play a fruit machine where the two-pences came tumbling out. We decided to leave on an up. I went up to the booth and asked the woman to change my money. Without looking at me she counted the coins and rang her cash register.

When she handed me the fifty-pence piece she was staring past me. Her lips hardly moved as she spoke and her voice sounded curiously disembodied. I had to concentrate hard to hear what she said.

'Marcus isn't welcome in here. They'll get him if he comes round. Try the "Green Horse" in Hackney. Tell him I said keep away if he knows what's good for him.'

That was all. She kept her face averted as I took hold of

Matthew's hand and pulled him out of the arcade. When we left the man was still there, propped up and motionless.

The rest of the afternoon passed uneventfully enough at Sam's. I hung around lethargically, picking at a variety of books. By eight o'clock I was beginning to feel restless. I looked towards my companions to see if they could offer anything in the way of entertainment. Nothing doing. Matthew was stretched out in front of the television and by the way that Sam's eyes were wandering, I guessed that he wouldn't have minded joining him.

'I'm going out,' I said.

They both nodded.

I left the flat, got into my car and, for the second time that day, drove to Caledonian Road.

The pool was just closing when I arrived. I stood on the pavement watching as the staff walked out, some talking animatedly, some showing their exhaustion by their bent backs and disinterested eyes.

The life guard was one of the last to leave. He came out with another man. He waited while his companion locked the glass doors. Then they both set off down the road swaggering as they went.

I ran up behind them and tapped the life guard on the arm. He tensed up and turned, his fists already formed into a tight ball. When he saw me he relaxed and smiled, a greasy confident smile. He glanced at his friend who shrugged.

'I told you you had a tasty job,' he said. 'See ya,' and he walked off.

The life guard was positively beaming.

'Remember me?' I asked.

'We get so many beautiful girls in the pool,' he smirked, 'come and let me buy you a drink. You can refresh my memory.'

He propelled me along to the pub on the corner and up to the bar. He looked slightly disappointed when I ordered a lime juice but he was man enough to shake it off.

With his arm around my back he guided me over to one of the plastic seats that lined the wall. He placed himself beside me, in close proximity, with one arm casually draped along the back of the bench so that it all but touched my hair. He twisted his body round so he faced me.

'What can I do for you?' he asked.

'I was in the pool today,' I started.

‘And you couldn’t help noticing the body beautiful,’ he said. He flexed his biceps before he caught the look on my face.

‘Only kidding,’ he said and thrust out a hand. ‘My name’s Gordon.’

I gave him my name and we shook on it. He held my hand that extra second longer than was necessary. When he let go, he dropped his arm so it hit my knee. I shifted position.

‘I was the person you blew your whistle at.’

‘We are fated to meet,’ he said. ‘I always pick the best.’

‘I was with a man,’ I said.

He shifted himself an inch. It was enough to move his arm back on to the bench curve and away from me. He frowned.

‘I don’t know who he was,’ I said.

The frown went, the hand returned.

‘Who’s an active one?’ he said. ‘And what can I do for you? As if I didn’t know.’

I moved away from him.

‘Does it ever happen?’ I asked.

‘What?’

‘Do you ever get picked up by strange women outside the swimming pool?’

He narrowed his eyes and looked at me.

‘There’s always a first time,’ he said. He sounded doubtful.

‘I only want to talk,’ I said.

‘The educated type,’ he replied and accompanied it with a sleazy smile, ‘I like a good chinwag myself.’

‘Come off it,’ I said. ‘Wrong fantasy. All I want to know is whether you recognised that man.’

‘Which man?’

‘The one who was trying to drown me.’

Again his eyes narrowed but this time they focused back into disapproval.

‘That was you, was it? You shouldn’t get up to those tricks. You might get into trouble.’

‘Do you know the man?’ I asked.

He removed his hand from the bench. He downed his pint in a virtuoso display of the open-throat technique before he spoke again. When he did, he was indignant.

‘Lady, I’m a life guard. It’s a responsible job. Thousands of people come and go in the swimming pool and some of them are not altogether right in the head. You get what I mean?’

'Not exactly,' I said.

'You get all types. So somebody tried it on with you. That's no reason for the Spanish Inquisition. The man was just making contact. They haven't made that a crime . . . yet.'

'Did you recognise him?'

'Never saw him in my life before,' he said. 'Forget him. He was looking for a bit of recreation and he picked the wrong girl. Happens all the time.'

With that he got up and walked to the bar. He didn't turn round when I left.

On the way back I thought about it. The encounter had left a sour taste in my mouth. It wasn't so much the man's attitude to me: it was the uncertainty I now felt about the incident in the swimming pool. Maybe it had been a casual encounter, an angry man who took it out on me because I happened to be passing.

All the way to Sam's flat I thought about it. By the time I arrived back I was still feeling unsettled. So instead of going upstairs. I decided to take a walk.

It was one of those rare evenings when a chill hadn't descended with the sun. I walked through the twilight enjoying the warmth and the company. The street was alive with groups of people, gathering on pavements, chatting together, walking with energy. They transformed the Essex Road from an ugly traffic-ridden waste to a place with a purpose. It was a transformation that had been building all summer and that had reached its peak. The street had been taken over by the young who had no money and no prospects but who carried with them a need for action and a willingness to go get it.

Because the daylight had gone, police foot patrols had ceased. Instead, down side streets and in garages sat whole carloads of men in blue waiting for the signal to move. The people in the street knew that, but the people didn't care.

I had started by walking aimlessly but in the end I followed the crowd towards Dalston. As I got nearer to the Kingsland Road, I was no longer walking alone. The groups of people had formed into one crowd, the pace had increased. So did the noise, but it wasn't only coming from us. For, as we rounded the corner towards Dalston Junction, we came upon an already established set-piece.

The street was flooded with police. They stood at every corner, they sat in vans no longer concealed, they had set up riot shields in doorways. They carried with them an air of business and efficiency that couldn't hide their feelings of confusion. They didn't understand what was happening but they knew they didn't like it. What they'd once considered their own, the right to control the streets, was being taken away.

As I stood watching, the scene took shape. From right to left came a group of black youths. They were running fast and they were doing it with ease and with glee. No one was organising them but they seemed to flow effortlessly past. When they saw their spectators, they lifted their hands in the air in a gesture of victory. The crowd cheered.

It must have been a disheartening sound for the group who were pursuing. They were the police, running in a three-column formation, and moving with discipline. They looked like they were hating it. Their feet hit the hard surface with a regularity and beat that spoke of their anger. They ran at a constant pace, intent on the group in front of them. But however fast they ran, they couldn't bridge the gap. They had the organisation: those they pursued had the inspiration. As they rounded the corner I could see that their shoulders spoke of their defeat.

Just then I was shoved forwards. I turned round to find a young policeman glaring at me.

'Move along,' he ordered, 'or I'll have you for obstruction.'

I shrugged and started walking. Around me other people were doing the same. We walked as a group until we noticed that the police seemed to be moving to surround us. At this, the crowd scattered. Noises rang out in the night as people made their escape through alleys and back gardens.

I knew the area well and I didn't have much trouble getting away. I soon found myself alone. It was then that I felt some of the tiredness the excitement had brought. I thought about making my way back to Sam's but then I remembered the Green Horse. It wasn't far from where I'd landed and it seemed worth a try.

The place was buzzing when I walked in. Disco music pounded from the juke box against a high level of conversation. In one corner the darts were flying. As I went to the bar one of the contestants scored a bullseye. The group around her cheered loudly.

I had to stand by the bar about ten minutes before I got served. I could have got my drink quicker but I spent the time trying to identify a possible Marcus rather than catching the barman's eye. It wasn't worth it. The pub was crowded with young men round about

Marcus's age. I would have had to go and try at least ten strangers and ask their names. I didn't think I would be kindly received if I did that.

Eventually I gave up and got my half of lager. As I handed my money over the bar I leaned across it.

'Is there a Marcus Jones here?' I asked the barman.

He nodded and took the moment of stillness to wipe the sweat from his brow. Without speaking he pointed to a table by the window where eight people were sitting talking animatedly.

I took my drink and walked towards the group. I leaned against the wall and prepared to listen to the action. A couple of the people arranged around the table sent a quizzical glance my way but they were too involved to take it further.

It was more an argument than a conversation. Two men, sitting opposite each other, were intent on getting their version across.

'. . . You go too far,' the older one was saying. 'This country have treat me bad but it have also treat me good. Youth, them have no respect and no patience. There has been racism, true, true, but times is changing.'

The younger man pursed his lips and then blew through them, making a dismissive sound. He was a good-looking man with strong clear features and long dreadlocks. I guessed he was the same age as Marcus Jones.

'We have won victories,' he said, 'but they hold on to their power. They don't give up easy.'

The man opposite him thumped his fist on the table. '*You* have won victories,' he shouted. 'It's easy for you. It your parent them who have smooth your path. Because of they hard work you accepted now.'

'It's like my father you speak,' his opponent said. 'You all think because you turn the other cheek things would get better for you. Check with the real situation. Let me tell you man, soon we have no cheek left.'

'Your father him a good man.'

'Good!' the young man said. 'How that help him? My father him a work as labourer for thirty years in Babylon. He never complained. And then one day while he was working, profiting the boss, a wall collapsed on him. His leg mash up. Nobody now will give him a job.'

'That bad luck,' the older man said.

'That firm specialise in a it.'

'He should prosecute them. The law there for use.'

'He try,' the young man shouted. 'Certain he try. You know what happen? Only one man witnessed the wall fall, a white man, one of the friend them, you talking about. He refused to give evidence. He say he scared for him job. So my father have no proof. He get nothing. An' you know, five years later, when my father cannot claim compensation by the law you have faith in, they sack the man. Five years to the day they tell him to go. They not even look after they own. What we expect?'

'Serve the man right,' somebody said.

While the general nods of agreement went round the table I stepped nearer to it. I looked at the younger of the men.

'Are you Marcus Jones?' I asked.

The atmosphere froze. Outside the group things went on as before, but inside a wall of silence and hostility built up to hit me. A woman got up from the table and stood in front of me.

She was a tall woman and she looked down on me. The tight clustered curls of her hair were cropped close to her head, allowing her features to stand out clear. Her dark brown skin was faintly tinged with red and it hung tautly, accentuating her high cheek bones. Her eyes were a deeper brown than her skin and they should have been warm. But they stared at me with rage.

'Who wants to know?' she asked. She had the easy stance of one accustomed to her strength and ready to use it. I moved to remonstrate and her hand knocked my glass. The beer spilt on to the ground.

'Who wants to know?' she repeated.

'My name's Kate Baeier,' I said. 'James Stanford put me on to Marcus.'

The young man grinned. The tension broke. The woman stepped out of my way and gestured to her chair. I sat down on it.

'We can't be too careful,' she said. 'You drinking lager?'

I nodded and looked at my glass. It was only a quarter full. The woman smiled and moved to the bar.

Marcus leaned across the table, holding out his hand. We shook.

'This is the detective I telling you about,' he said to the others.

I got a murmur of hellos and a few handshakes. I thought I also saw a few uneasy glances mingling in there but if they were caused by me they weren't meant to be intercepted.

'I looked for you at the arcade in the Angel,' I said. 'The woman behind the kiosk said to warn you not to come round.'

This time the glances were out in the open. Nobody spoke. The woman came back from the bar. She put a half pint of lager down in front of me. I thanked her and took a sip. The silence waited for me.

'Are you in trouble?' I asked.

'Black people live in a state of trouble in this society,' the woman said. It wasn't a hostile statement but it contained a warning. I don't think the warning was meant for me: I saw that Marcus, who looked like he'd been about to say something, shut his mouth.

'I'm investigating the death of Paul Holland,' I said. 'James must have told you.'

Marcus Jones nodded. He still wasn't going to speak.

'James said you saw the accident.'

'Wasn't no accident,' the man beside Marcus cut in. I looked at him. He was small and wiry with a body that needed more food and a face that needed more love. His white skin was pasty and blotched. Under my gaze, he blushed a faint pink.

'Were you there?' I asked.

'Terry and I were there together,' Marcus said.

'What happened?'

'A man run down by car,' Marcus replied.

'Maybe the driver was drunk,' I said.

'He wasn't drunk.'

'How do you know?'

'Because of what happened next,' Terry blurted out. His voice was excited and it came out too high and too loud. As if hearing the echo of it, he didn't continue. His look of embarrassment returned with a vengeance.

'What happened?' I asked.

The table was quiet as Marcus leaned forward. When he spoke, his voice was low.

'The man run over deliberate,' he said. 'We two saw it. The car started to drive off and Terry and I ran to help the man on the ground. Then the car reversed back down the road and stopped. We hid in a doorway. We see the driver get out. He walk up to the man on the floor and peer down into his face. Then he kick the man hard, hard, two or three times. When the man don't move, the driver get back into the car and drive off. Him know what he doing.'

'Did you get the car number?' I asked.

Terry made as if to answer but was cut off by a drawn-in breath from Marcus.

‘We minding our own business on our way home,’ Marcus said. ‘We never think to carry pencils and papers nor to look for numbers.’

‘What did he look like?’ I asked.

‘It was dark,’ Marcus said quickly before Terry could answer.

‘And you never told the police?’

As if on cue the door of the pub opened. Normally I wouldn’t have noticed, since the night was warm and my back was towards the door. But it was immediately apparent that something had happened. All conversation stopped as Grace Jones finished singing the final verse of ‘Everybody Hold Still’.

I turned to look. In the doorway stood two policemen with flat caps. They stood in silence, surveying the room. The room kept right on staring back. Finally the policemen broke the deadlock. They went back into the street, leaving the door swinging behind them. Gradually, conversation in the place started up again.

‘I guess you never did tell the police,’ I said.

I didn’t stay long after that. I’d already had my fill of lager and I had the feeling that my presence was inhibiting the conversation. So I said my thanks and my goodbyes. Then I walked back to Sam’s flat through streets that seemed strangely quiet.

Six

I woke up on Monday morning with Laura Maxwell on my brain. I knew it was time for me to go to 'Grains' again, but it was more than that. Something about her was bothering me.

Sam rolled over towards me and put his arms around me.

'You know what?' he said.

'What?' I answered, my mind with Laura.

'I've been thinking about us, Ms Baeier,' he said. 'And about our relationship. You know I really feel good about what's going . . .'

He never had a chance to finish. I jumped out of bed.

'Laura Maxwell!' I shouted. 'That's it!'

I ran into the living room and came back with my bag. I pulled out the piece of paper I'd taken from Paul Holland's floor.

'There, you see,' I said, pointing at where Paul had written the initials. 'I knew there was something odd about her.'

Sam turned over, his back to me.

'I'm sorry,' I said. 'Got carried away. What were you saying?'

'It doesn't matter,' he muttered.

I tried to get him to talk again but he wasn't having any of it. Eventually I gave up and went into the living room to get a better look at Paul's doodles.

The initials LM were somewhere in the middle of the paper. They were connected by an arrow to another set of initials: AA. I played with the idea that Laura was an alcoholic, but rejected it. I looked closely at the rest of the paper. There were a lot of other arrows on the page, but they led to scrawls that were all indecipherable. I could only make out one other set of initials and it was sitting in a red circle on its own. GP, it said.

I got dressed and made a pot of coffee. I took a cup into Sam, who was still lying with his back to the door. There was a small hump beside him. I pulled the duvet up and saw that it was Matthew, curled up in a ball and pretending to be asleep.

I had my coffee along with a piece of brown toast and marmalade.

After that it was time to go.
Just before I left I went into the bedroom.
'I'm going now,' I said.
'See ya,' said the lump that was Matthew.
Sam didn't speak.

It was filled with sadness, the room, that day. In the garden spring was coming and the colours held the bright promise of youth. But in the room, the reflected glitter only served as a contrast to the ache Kate was experiencing.

She didn't understand the sadness. Not that that made it any easier to bear. For the sadness pervaded her body and welled up in her throat. It was a sadness of the moment, but it meant more than that. It came from deep inside and it came from times past.

She crumpled the tissue in her hand and, not for the first time since she'd been in the room, wondered why the waste-paper basket was so far away. She put the tissue into her pocket and reached for another.

'It's not that he doesn't give to me,' she said. 'That's not it at all. It's that he doesn't give enough. Not entirely, absolutely as I want.'

'And you feel disappointed?'

'I feel more than that. I feel savagely let down. I feel like I opened myself up to receive and then I'm betrayed. It's so inappropriate. How can I expect Sam to understand that?'

'Perhaps he can. If you try to explain.'

Kate laughed. It was a laugh devoid of humour.

'Not so easy, when what you're after is care without explanation. It's so needy, so childish. And if Sam guesses wrong, I turn away. Pretend he's nothing to do with me. It's so self-destructive.'

Kate paused to wipe away the tears. She didn't do it very efficiently.

'I'm the same with you, aren't I?' she asked.

Franca kept silent. Kate didn't like that.

'Aren't I?' she insisted.

'You came to me for help,' Franca said. 'I try to. We both try together.'

Kate sat in silence, the tissue at her face. When she spoke again her voice was almost a whisper.

'What would I do if you weren't so trustworthy? If you used the situation against me?'

'Therapy can make you feel vulnerable,' Franca said.

'You're not kidding,' said Kate as she screwed up the second tissue.

By ten o'clock I'd been at 'Grains' for twenty minutes and was becoming impatient. When I arrived I'd bought myself a camomile tea and sat down to watch the till. The camomile was undrinkable, the bench uncomfortable and my mood deteriorated every time I looked up to find Laura Maxwell staring at me from behind her glass screen.

I had definitely had enough. I got up and went to the counter.

'I'd like to talk to your boss,' I said to the woman who was serving fruit juices with an air of complete boredom.

She was about to reply when a sharp tapping from above distracted us both. We looked up. Laura Maxwell was at her window, rapping with her knuckles. She gestured an impatient come-on to me and a dismissal to her employee.

'How much longer?' the woman muttered as she lifted up a hatch in the counter and let me through. 'Up the stairs, first right, first left,' she said in a louder voice.

The room was small but its glass front made it appear almost grandiose. A body of red four-drawer filing cabinets was placed by one of the walls, underneath a large chart. Opposite these a standard issue wall calendar was studded with stars, crosses and scrawled writing.

Laura was seated in her executive swivel chair behind her enormous desk. She was shuffling papers in an attempt to look busy. She wasn't doing very well. As I approached, one of the pieces of A4 refused to go into line so she picked it out and crumpled it up. She took aim and threw it across the floor. It landed amongst a pile of paper which had met the same fate and was lying around a red waste-paper bin.

'Well?' she demanded as I sat down.

'I'm ready to send you my bill.'

'Who is it?'

'Who knows? Could be anybody. I'd advise you to pay more attention to your staff.'

'Don't tell me how to run my business,' Laura snapped. 'You types don't like to get your hands dirty. I hired you to do a job and I want it finished.'

'It's the nature of the job that confuses me,' I said.

'Don't talk in riddles. Just because I make money doesn't mean I'm stupid.'

I pointed to the chart on the wall. It was a graph, traced by the month and headed upwards at a perilous rate.

'I'd guess those are your profit figures,' I said.

'And now you're going to tell me it's immoral to earn profit,' she said. 'I built this organisation from nothing. I pulled myself out of worse than nowhere and I have a right to what I earn.'

'That's not my concern' I said. 'What I do know is that you wouldn't need my help to catch a petty thief.'

'If that's how you feel, send your bill,' Laura said. She threw another piece of recalcitrant paper in the direction of the others. This time her aim was even worse. It landed by my feet. I picked it up and placed it back on the desk.

'How well did you know Paul Holland?' I asked.

'I don't know what you're talking about.'

'Yeah, and I bet you didn't read the *Street Times* article either. I'll send the bill.'

I got up and walked to the door. I put my hand on the knob and pulled. Nothing happened. I tried again but with the same result. I turned back to look at Laura. She was still seated at her desk. She lifted up her right hand to show the button she'd had built into the desk.

'Very security conscious,' I said.

'I've learned to be,' she said. 'He was my therapist.'

I turned away from the door and walked back to her.

'I wanted to know what you found out,' she said. 'I didn't know how to get the information out of you.'

'You could have asked.'

'You don't get anything in this world for free.'

'What exactly do you want to know?'

'Who killed Paul,' she said.

'You don't believe it was an accident?'

'Don't give me that,' she snarled. 'Accidents didn't happen to Paul. He was in control one hundred and fifty per cent of the time and I'm in a position to know that.'

'What do you want with his killer?'

'I want to congratulate him,' she said. 'What else?'

The last sentence was punctuated by a sharp giggle that seemed to come from nowhere. Laura Maxwell heard it and for a moment she looked puzzled. Then a laugh broke from deep inside her. It welled up and overcame her composure. It was a laugh devoid of all mirth and seemingly without end. It spilled into the room, that harsh sound. It bounded off the walls and came back to hang heavily around me. But the laugh was not for me: it was for a dead man and that's what it was—a dead laugh.

And then, abruptly, it stopped. There was a second's silence before Laura's hands went up to her face. She rocked her head in them and her body started to shake. When she next looked up her face was covered with tears that had made rivers through her powder. I reached into my bag and handed her a tissue. She took it and held it to her eyes, which stared into space. Then she got up, punched the button on her desk, and left the room.

When she returned the make-up was back in place. Only a slight redness around her eyes gave her away.

'I loved Paul,' she said in a dull tone. 'And now he's gone.'

'How often did you see him?' I asked.

'Once every two weeks in therapy. And at other times.'

'Paul didn't confine the relationship to the therapy room?' I asked. The surprise must have shown in my voice. Laura sneered.

'He didn't believe in the élitism of therapy. He considered us equals and if he liked us, he liked to spend time with us.'

'And if he didn't like you?'

'That wasn't my concern,' Laura said, a glint of pride in her voice. She smiled, a distant smile, as if she was remembering some special times. When the smile faded, it left a wistful look.

'We understood each other and were getting somewhere. I have this terrible guilt thing you see.'

'Guilt?' I asked.

'I used to be different,' she said. 'Not happier. But I did make different choices. Material reality meant little to me. I took risks, all sorts of risks. Paul helped me to see that I was just searching for security and that my rejection of social values was an escape from my own needs. He showed me that anything I wanted to do was permissible.'

'Including murder?'

Laura went red. Her lips sketched a thin line of disapproval and barely suppressed anger.

'You don't understand,' she hissed. 'You've obviously never tried self-exploration.'

'I've been to psychotherapy.'

'With some charlatan, I bet. Who was he?'

I told her.

She had a strange reaction to Franca's name. The red flush had been fading anyway but with the mention of the name it went double quick. It was replaced by an almost deadly white.

'You make me sick,' she said. 'Coming round uninvited, worming my feelings out of me.'

'You hired me,' I reminded her.

She opened her mouth to retort but couldn't think of anything to say. As if she could no longer bear the sight of me, she swivelled her chair round to face the restaurant. It looked like she was going to turn full circle, but suddenly she stopped.

I followed her gaze to where a woman was standing, looking around her as if trying to spot someone. From a distance she seemed small and timid, as if she didn't quite know what she was doing there. While I watched her, she looked upwards. She saw Laura and took a step towards us. Then she saw me. She put one hand to her breast, drew a deep breath and then turned on her heels.

'Who was that?' I asked.

Laura swivelled her chair back to face the room.

'Nobody,' she said. 'Why are you hanging around me?'

'Admiring the histrionics,' I said. I turned to leave but when I heard Laura move behind me I swung back again. My hand reached the desk first. I put it on top of the button and reached to the wires underneath. I gave one pull and the whole arrangement detached itself from the desk.

'How dare you!' Laura shouted.

'I don't like to be played with,' I said.

'Don't flatter yourself,' she said. 'You couldn't detect a pint of milk in a dairy.'

I walked to the door. When I reached the red bin I dropped the electrical affair into it. It clanged loudly.

The woman was standing just outside the exit. She was staring blankly at a window which had been decked out in grains and pulses. I looked at her reflection.

There was something waif-like about her, as if she was asking to be looked after. Her curly brown hair framed a face that was pale and flat. Over her shoulder a brown leather handbag hung down to her waist and she gripped it to her as though scared that somebody would make a grab for it.

When her eyes went into focus she saw me. She took a shrinking step to the right, ready to run away. I smiled at her and then I walked away down the street.

Once round the corner I waited until the count of ten. Then I walked back towards 'Grains'. The woman was no longer outside the restaurant. I gave another count of ten and after that I walked inside and looked up at Laura's office.

They were both there, Laura and the nervous woman. They were in the middle of an argument and oblivious to the possibility that anybody could be observing them. Laura, her back to the restaurant, was gesticulating at the woman, who had shrunk down into her seat. Every now and then she made a move to protest but she was no match for Laura Maxwell. As the argument continued she sank further and further back into her chair.

Then suddenly it ended. Laura stopped talking and went up to the woman. She knelt by her chair and hugged her. The woman returned the gesture. For a short time they stayed still, holding each other. Then Laura got up, touching the woman's hair gently as she did so. The woman gave a smile. She got out of her chair and the two of them walked towards the door, arm in arm.

The cheese and yoghurt section of the 'Grains' shop was set back in an alcove presumably to ensure privacy for customers who wanted to read the special methods that manufacturers used to guarantee pure products. I took refuge in it. With my back to the sheep and goats' shelf, I could just about see to the outside.

The woman came out slowly. She used her sleeve to wipe at her eyes and then, head down, she walked up the road. I followed. She walked as if the world had descended on her stooped shoulders. Each step looked like an effort which she overcame by sheer will power.

It was agonising following her. I am, at the best of times, a fast pacer and my interview with Laura had left me wanting to speed things up. Instead I found that to keep a distance between myself and her, I had to put one foot in front of the other as if in slow motion. I felt pretty silly and must have looked so too.

She walked like that for two blocks before turning the corner. It was as if she was dragging herself to a place she didn't want to reach. Once or twice the sleeve went up to her face again.

When she came to the shop, she stood outside, hesitating. She glanced at her watch and then, for confirmation, at the church clock. Then, slowly, she went inside.

By the time I reached the glass front, she had walked down one of the aisles. It was one of those shops that sells everything you might want and nothing you really need. I watched her as she went to the end of a row of garish paper flowers. They were overblown, brightly coloured models of flowers I found difficult to look at even when fresh. They took on a new dimension of ugliness in paper.

The woman walked with more purpose. At the end of the aisle she stopped. She'd reached her destination by a particularly large array of chrysanthemums. There was a man standing behind them. He had his back to the window and all I could see was his brown hair.

The woman went up to him. She moved round him to face the door, and started talking. Her story spilled out rapidly. At one point the man moved as if to slow her down. He placed one hand on her shoulder. A ring glinted on his third finger: a large gold ring.

The woman flinched away from his touch. It was then that she saw me. Her eyes widened. Without taking them off me, she said something to her companion. His back stiffened. He didn't turn round. Instead he moved forward, propelling the woman in front of him. They disappeared round the back of the aisle.

I went through the door, running. I found myself facing a high counter behind which a bored looking shop assistant slumped. There was nobody else in view.

'Where did they go?' I snapped.

'Can I help you?' she said brightly. She raised her eyebrows as if to prove that I hadn't caught her napping.

'The man and woman who were here. Where did they go?'

'I guess they left,' she said. Her eyes shifted towards the other side of the aisle which led to a second exit.

I ran to it. I flung the door open. It stuck where it hit a bulging card stand. Ignoring the protests of the shop assistant, I rushed outside.

I was just in time to see the woman getting into a taxi. The man had disappeared.

I had two choices. I could either try for a taxi to follow the woman or I could search the streets for the man. It took me a second to decide between them. I had two choices and in that second I lost both. The taxi drove round the corner and was gone. There was no other taxi in sight and, to make it worse, the man seemed to have vanished into thin air. No matter which direction I looked, I couldn't see any back remotely resembling his.

Without knowing that I was doing it, I hit my head with the open palm of my right hand. There was a giggle from behind me. I turned round to see two small people gazing up at me. A closer inspection showed that they were children dressed in scaled-down versions of adult clothes. Their white legs were scrawny, their faces dirty.

'Are you going to do that funny walk again?' one said, before giggling again.

I took no notice. I walked off. I had someone I wanted to see.

One hour later I was in Franca's room.

'Paul Holland was killed,' I said. 'I found an eye-witness.'

A look of pain flashed across Franca's face. Slowly she let out the breath she'd involuntarily held. I saw how tired she seemed, her face almost blank as if she'd been scrubbing at it to remove the distress. She hadn't been able to get rid of the tinges of red that lined her grey eyes.

'One of Paul's clients hired me. Name of Laura Maxwell.'

Franca nodded.

'Do you know her?' I asked.

'I know of her. As I told you, I was Paul's supervisor.'

'Laura seems angry with Paul,' I said.

'That would be a common reaction to his death. She probably feels enraged at the abandonment.'

'She only saw him once every two weeks,' I said. 'For therapy, that is.'

Again Franca nodded. I saw her throat tighten.

'I get the impression that Paul Holland didn't exactly restrict his clients to the therapy room,' I said.

'What do you mean?'

'At a guess, he was sleeping with Laura Maxwell.'

Franca didn't move but she looked like she wanted to. I glanced at her hands, resting uneasily on her lap. White showed around her knuckles.

'What happened to your wedding ring?' I asked.

'Do you really want to know?'

'Therapist's trick,' I said.

She smiled.

'I went to see Dr Edgar Greenleaf,' I said. 'He doesn't seem to like you.'

'Does that matter to you?'

'You're doing it again,' I said. 'Reversing the questions. What goes on between you and Greenleaf?'

Franca frowned as if trying to remember. Then she used her middle finger to smooth the lines that had gathered just above her nose.

'We have theoretical differences,' she said. 'And Dr Greenleaf is very keen on safeguarding his position in the profession. He sees all those not trained at his institute as interlopers who need to be pushed out. One of his clients left him and went to Paul Holland. Dr Greenleaf is very concerned about his own dignity.'

'Were you sleeping with Paul?' I said. 'I have to ask.'

'I should not have brought you into this,' she said.

'I gather that means yes.'

'It does.'

'What a mess!' I said.

She nodded.

'Did he mean a lot to you?'

'He was very charming,' she said. 'But I knew it would never last, especially when I began to examine his professional conduct.'

'Which wasn't great?'

'As you have already discovered, he was intimately involved with a woman client.'

'Not very therapeutic,' I said.

'That's one way of putting it.'

'Did your marriage break up over Paul?'

'It was over a long time before that. The fact that I no longer wear a ring is nothing to do with Paul. It's a pure coincidence. I felt the need to free myself from an identity of, if not a married woman, then at least a once-married one.'

'You taught me to doubt coincidence,' I said.

'You feel angry to find all this out?' she said. 'It's not easy.'

'I'll get over it. But I can't go on like this. I need more information. I have to know about other of his clients. Unless you give me more directions to investigate I will seriously consider stopping.'

She looked at me sympathetically. The look almost finished me off. It was so reminiscent of the times I had regularly received it. For a moment I was pulled back into the room, dissecting my own thoughts, my own life, my own inner fears. Sitting there opposite Franca, the expert of the unspoken word and the promise of fulfilment, the world started to recede. Paul Holland's death was fading into one of those incidents of the outer reality which could be forgotten in a search for the inner.

I made my voice deliberately cold to shake off the feeling. A flash of pain crossed Franca's face when I spoke.

'Let's try a question-and-answer session,' I said. 'Number one,

Laura Maxwell was a client of Paul who knew you were sleeping with him.'

She didn't answer that one. She didn't have to.

'How did she find out?'

'She made it her business,' Franca said. 'Laura has many resources and, when determined, nothing can stop her.'

'She could have killed him out of jealousy.'

Franca shook her head.

'Laura had known for some time. I suspect that was the motive for entangling herself with Paul.'

'You seem to know a lot about Laura,' I said.

'I supervised Paul. One learns much from such work.'

It was said non-committally, with a face devoid of expression. I examined her face. And a piece of the puzzle fell into place.,

'Laura used to come to you for therapy,' I stated.

Franca nodded.

'Why did she leave?'

'I recommended it. I did not feel that I was the right person to help her through her defences. I felt she needed a therapy less verbal, and that her own self-loathing stood in the way of her confiding fully in a woman.'

'So you sent her to a man,' I said, 'who slept with her.'

Franca flinched. 'I have made some bad mistakes,' she said. 'I am responsible for them.'

'Forget it,' I said. 'I guess I'm expressing my own jealousy. Not every day you find your ex-therapist involved in a triangle with one of her clients.'

Her lips twitched but she said nothing.

'How about Laura killed Paul Holland to get at you for rejecting her?'

'Psychologically that is possible,' she said musingly. 'But I doubt she would have acted it out. I think she received sufficient pleasure from joining with me through Paul.'

'You weren't married to Paul, were you?' I asked.

'No. It was a short episode. When I discovered his involvement with Laura, I knew matters were getting out of control. I ended our affair. In many ways Paul was unsuited for his profession. He was too interested in control.'

'Is that what killed him?'

'I think so,' she said. 'But I cannot be sure. He was mysterious.'

'Did you continue to supervise him?'

'Yes,' she said. 'I could not discard him and his clients at an important juncture. It would have been irresponsible.'

'But you couldn't stop his death.'

There was a bitterness in my voice and Franca heard it for what it was.

'Kate,' she said softly. 'I am not perfect.'

I smiled and blinked away the tears that had welled up in my eyes. I felt a terrible sadness for the destruction of an ideal. I had always known it would happen, that the special contact of therapy creates its own delusions, but it was still painful to take.

I hardened my voice again.

'What about a man called Arthur Simpson,' I said. 'Was he seeing Paul?'

'Yes.'

'Is he a possible suspect?'

'I cannot say.'

I gazed at her in exasperation. She smiled, a trifle sadly.

'Laura has an acquaintance.' I described the woman who had visited Laura at 'Grains'. 'Is she another of Paul's clients?' I asked.

'Sounds similar to one of them.'

'What's her name?'

Franca looked, for a second, as if she were going to refuse, but she changed her mind. She got up and walked to the small desk. Out of a top drawer she took a piece of paper and a small leather address book. She wrote on the paper and then she handed it to me.

There were two names on it. The first was a Stephen Braithwaite. I looked enquiringly at her.

'He was another of Paul's clients,' she said. 'We didn't talk about him much but it might be worth visiting him. I don't think he will suffer from such attention.'

I looked back at the paper. Abbey Ashurst was the second name. The AA of Paul's chart, I thought.

I folded the paper and put it away. I looked across at Franca who was still, quite still.

'I'm sorry this happened,' I said.

'I have to take responsibility for my mistakes,' she said.

I got up and walked to the door. Before I left the room I turned to face her.

'Who were you married to?' I asked.

'Edgar,' she said. 'Edgar Greenleaf.'

I walked out and shut the door softly behind me.

I wanted to go back and say something but didn't know what it was. Not everything can be parcelled and put away, I thought. Franca had taught me that. I stood there, listening at the thick oak for a while but no sounds penetrated.

The few days that had passed hadn't helped Regina Holland come to terms with her father's death. When she opened the door I got a flash of genuine *déjà vu*—she looked exactly the same from the unwashed hair to the jeans and pink sweater now a shade more crumpled. She even gave me the same kind of stare—a blank, uninterested and unfeeling stare. I wasn't sure she knew that she'd ever seen me before. I told her my name and she shrugged it off. But she widened the door and she showed me upstairs.

The living room was also unchanged, cushions on the floor, papers scattered and neglect all round. Regina left me standing by the door as she went to sit in the same place on the sofa as she'd picked on my last visit. She put her feet on the sofa, drew her knees up to her face, clasped her arms around them and hugged them close as she looked at me.

'I came before,' I said.

'I'm not stupid,' Regina answered in a voice which could not be bothered to change tone. 'I remember.'

I moved into the room and pulled up an easy chair so that I was facing her. it was covered with papers. I bunched some of them and put them on the floor to make room for myself. As I did so, I saw Regina's face move almost as if in protest, but she didn't speak.

'I'm investigating your father's death,' I said.

Regina nodded once and then she nodded again. She took her hands off her knees and used them to physically stop the nodding.

I didn't know what to say. Regina looked on the edge, but it was more than that: she looked as though with one tiny nudge from me she'd fall right over. There was silence between us. She read my mind across it.

'Don't spare my feelings,' she said. 'I look thin but I'm strong. Stronger than you could guess.'

I took a deep breath and I decided. It probably didn't take me long in real time but it felt like an age. I had to argue with myself, to persuade myself that my presence wasn't going to make the difference, that one sentence from me wasn't going to crumble Regina. I didn't quite believe it, but I did persuade myself to speak.

'I've found out,' I said carefully, wishing I could just get to the point, 'by talking to a number of people, that your father was murdered.'

'I know that,' Regina said.

I looked up in surprise. Her face was still as blank as ever. I realised she wasn't going to make it easy for me.

'He was murdered,' I repeated. 'Deliberately run over.'

'By whom?' Regina asked, as though asking the name of my dressmaker.

'I don't know. I'm still investigating. That's why I came . . .'

I hadn't been looking at her and so it was the noise that stopped me. It was a low, choking, eerie noise. When I raised my head to it I saw that Regina had folded herself into a tight ball. The noise came out in almost a hiccup—each time it came her body jerked.

I watched the dry heaving of Regina's sorrow and each time I felt an arrow of pain shoot through my body. After a while I could stand it no more. I went to the sofa and sat beside her. Nervous lest I scare all sign of emotion away, I gingerly put one arm around her.

It was my own fear, I realised, that had stopped me from approaching her. I realised that as soon as I moved. For in response to my arm, Regina unfolded. She cuddled up into me, and the dry agony turned into a flood of tears.

We sat there a long while, me still, Regina letting out a grief she'd stored too long. When she finished her face was a mess, tear-streaked and furrowed but it had life I hadn't seen before. She moved away from me, inch by inch, and I let her. I got up and walked back to my seat. She avoided my gaze. I sat there until I got edgy. I looked around the room and then at Regina who sat completely still on the sofa.

What the hell, I thought, I can try. I got up and began clearing the room. Regina didn't move. I got bolder in my movements until I was caught up in the activity: clearing, wiping, throwing out. I was so involved that it was some time before I realised that I wasn't alone. Regina was besides me, cleaning with me.

By unspoken consent we moved into the kitchen. We were working together like pros—not touching, or getting in each other's way, but cleaning to a rhythm, without interference from each other. By the time we stopped, both the living room and kitchen were sparkling.

I opened the fridge and looked inside. There was a piece of Camembert, dry on the outside but still moist in the middle, and a few tomatoes. I put them on a plate, found some bread in the freezer which I toasted and took it all into the living room.

Regina had the coffee ready. She poured herself a thick strong cup and looked at the food. I took my cup and also looked. There was a pause and then Regina reached forward and grabbed a tomato. She bit into it. She smiled as the juice spilled out. She followed it up with a couple of slices of toast and some cheese. When she had finished she smiled again.

'Thank you,' she said.

I nodded.

'What do you want to know?' she asked.

'Are you sure you're ready to talk about it?'

'It's better to talk,' she said and grimaced to hold back the tears. 'That was Paul's theory. Maybe he was right about that.'

'You didn't get on?' I asked.

'He had no time for me,' Regina said softly. 'Not since I was a baby. Paul was great at pretending the big emotions but not so good at the nitty gritty. I got in the way.'

'What of?'

Regina looked down at her fingernails. They were short, bitten almost down to the skin. She raised her hand as if to have a go at them again but she changed her mind. Instead, she took a gulp of coffee.

'I was in the way of his life. Of everything. His precious work, the manipulation of all he knew, his discoveries.'

'What discoveries?' I asked.

'He was excited about something. Kept talking about a coincidence and the connections.'

'Which were?'

Regina frowned. 'I don't know. He never really let me in. Just taunted me with the edges. Everything I know I got by picking up by mistake.'

'Did you ever have the temptation to listen in on his sessions?' I asked.

Regina blushed. The colour came quickly and was gone almost as soon, leaving two red spots on her cheeks.

'I did listen once,' she said, slowly, 'just before Paul . . . die . . . was killed.'

'To a session?' I asked.

'Not exactly. The room's semi-soundproofed. But for some reason Paul had left the door ajar. I'd never seen the man before. He was arguing with Paul. He was very angry.'

'What about?'

'Couldn't make it out,' she said. 'The man accused Paul of interfering in something and of being irresponsible. He said . . . he said . . . it was dangerous and somebody could get hurt.'

As she spoke the tears welled up again. I sat watching her do battle with them. She won. When she looked at me, her face was dry.

'It's enough for today,' she said. 'That's all I can say.'

'Could you just give me a description of the man?' I asked, hoping I hadn't now reached the line over which I shouldn't tread. I needn't have worried. Regina frowned, remembering.

'Slight build,' she said, 'mousy brown hair, brown eyes. Insignificant looking really.'

'Sounds like Arthur Simpson,' I said.

'Oh no, not that wimp,' Regina said quickly. She stumbled when she heard her own voice. 'That's what Paul called Arthur. He was a bastard, my father.'

'It doesn't make the loss easier,' I said.

Regina nodded. She moved restlessly. I got up. Relieved, she followed me to the door. Before I turned to go I squeezed her hand. She returned the pressure.

'Thanks again,' she said, before closing the door quietly behind me.

Arthur Simpson was sitting behind his desk when I arrived at his office. He looked like he'd been marooned. It was one of those square council offices in a square council building that spoke of bureaucracy. The fact that there was only one desk in the room and one and a half windows (the leftover from hasty partitioning) spoke of Arthur's seniority. He didn't look like he was enjoying it. He was picking gloomily at a thick brown bread sandwich that he'd placed on top of a chaotic pile of buff files. He looked up and frowned when he heard me close the door.

'They said you were having a working lunch at the desk,' I said. 'Hope you don't mind the interruption.'

'You found me out,' he muttered.

'Only that you were one of Paul Holland's clients. Is that so bad?'

Arthur let one corner of the bread fall back to cover the sweating cheese. He pushed the whole affair away from him.

'I never should have done it,' he said.

'Done what?'

'Expose myself like that. I knew it was a mistake. I should have carried on regardless. Plenty do and what harm does it do them? Nobody can help me anyway.'

'Why—what's wrong with you?'

Arthur's face formed into a pout. He bent his head so I could see the crown where the mouse-brown hair was shrinking. When he lifted his head again I saw that his blue eyes had filled with tears that wanted to get out but that would never make it.

'I'm mad,' he said. 'No two ways about it.'

'Oh come on, Arthur,' I said.

'I wake up sweating in the night. Sweating with fear. I pretend it hasn't happened. Then halfway to work I feel as if I'm not going to be able to go through with the day. I force myself to come in. I work for eight hours and then go home to look at the kids who are strangers to me—demanding, screaming strangers who want more than I can give—and a wife who is dissatisfied no matter what I do. I can't go on.'

'Maybe it's time to stop.'

'That's what Paul said,' Arthur whined. 'None of you understand, you do-gooders echoing your satisfaction with the world of emotions. You don't know what it's like to be the breadwinner, to do things you don't like, smile at the boss who you have no respect for. You think it's all easy, but I tell you I can't stand it much longer.'

'Why don't you leave?'

Arthur's voice had risen to a pitch in his preceding speech and now he looked all played out.

'What does it matter anyway?' he said. 'I've a lot of work to do. What do you want from me?'

'To see if you have any ideas about Paul Holland's death.'

'Couldn't take my moaning.'

He tried it as a joke but it didn't quite come out that way. I nodded sympathetically towards him. He flashed a look of hatred over his curling sandwich.

'Did Paul seem different the last time you saw him?'

'How could I tell?' Arthur muttered. 'He asked the usual questions.'

'Like what?'

'Early childhood shit. You know, the type of stuff they use to try and persuade you that you're all fucked up. All that garbage about being bottle-fed too early and my brother taking my place in the family and how my mother didn't love me properly. Sometimes he could even make me weep for pity of my poor neglected years.'

'Did they need weeping for?'

'Mine and the rest of the world,' Arthur said. 'But come to think of it, mine were probably less interesting than the rest of the world. Paul had obviously got bored with my adolescence in Ipswich and the conflicts with my insurance salesman father. He started trying to get me to go on about my student days. Of course he drew a dead end there too. I never took an active part in the sit-ins. Too busy struggling to make ends meet, what with Norah pregnant and all. Not that I hold much truck with the activists: those endless meetings and accusations. Still, if I had got into the action instead of settling down, maybe this would be different.'

He gestured with his right hand to the office where nothing but his own misery was out of place.

'It's never too late,' I said.

'And other slogans. You seem to forget we're not in the sixties now. The eighties are a harsher critic of foolish ideas.'

'And you forget those ideas gave life,' I said.

'Who cares?' Arthur muttered. 'Look how resentful those ideas made people. Norah does nothing but moan about my sexism. What am I supposed to do?'

'She thinks you're having an affair,' I said.

'Well, I couldn't tell her I was consulting a shrink, could I? I could never live it down. She's just waiting for some chink in my armour.'

'It might make her more understanding if she knew.'

'More understanding than what?' Arthur said. 'Norah's left me. She packed her bags and the kids and moved out at the weekend. Said she never wants to see me again.'

Abruptly he picked up the wilting sandwich. Leaning back in his chair, he unhooked the window catch and held the glass pane back a fraction.

'Environmental health department and the fucking windows won't stay open,' he said. He flipped the sandwich through the gap and then let the window bang shut. A shout of protest from outside which had begun to invade the room was abruptly cut.

'And I didn't ask for your help,' Arthur said. 'I just want all you women to let me get on with my own life.'

From the top of the pile he pulled a file towards him. He opened it and picked a pen from the plastic container on the right of his desk. Without looking up he started to write a note in the margin of what looked like a four-page memo on noise. He managed two words before the pen ran dry. Swearing, he shook it and tried again. When he didn't have any luck he flung the pen across the floor. He looked up at me.

'Don't know what you're still doing here,' he said.

'What were you doing the night Paul was run over?' I asked.

Arthur laughed. 'Why would I want to kill Paul?' he said. 'I wasn't worth a damn to him.'

'Maybe that's why,' I said. 'What were you doing?'

'Fighting with Norah. One of our marathons. We specialise in them. As dearly as Norah would like to get me into trouble, I think you'll find that she'll confirm it. I'm no murderer, not predictable Art.'

The last two words had a ring to them. For a short moment, I got a glimpse of the man who wanted so desperately to be what he wasn't that he turned his contempt on himself. That's right, I thought, he'd love to be called Art. It had a certain panache he would never quite achieve.

'You disappeared in the early seventies,' I said. 'That wasn't predictable. Where did you go?'

'None of your beeswax,' he said. He looked startled at the words he'd chosen but he also looked stubborn.

'Do you know an Abbey Ashurst?'

Arthur looked down at his desk. He started scrawling across an internal memo. I'd lost his interest.

'James Stanford? Stephen Braithwaite?'

He carried on doodling.

'Laura Maxwell?'

I'd got his attention. The doodle turned into a blob and his pen went through it, digging a hole. He looked at me defiantly.

'You know her?' I asked.

'I used to. What do you want to make of it?'

'Paul was sleeping with her,' I said.

The pen went deeper through the page and Arthur pushed it into the desk.

'I knew her once,' he said.

'Norah thought you were with a woman when you disappeared. Was it Laura?'

'We were going to run away together,' he said, 'to the Greek Islands.'

'Why didn't you?'

'It didn't work out,' he said blankly.

'She left you?'

'She said she was scared. That she had to go away, escape from everybody around her.'

'What scared her?'

'No idea. Probably just an excuse to get rid of me.'

'Was Paul interested in your affair?' I asked.

'More than in me,' Arthur muttered. 'Sometimes I think he only took me on because I knew Laura. If you ask me, Paul was the one with a problem.'

'What type of problem?'

'Leave me alone,' he said. 'You've got enough from me.'

His upper lip quivered. I got up.

'I hope things work out with you and Norah,' I said.

Arthur shrugged. He picked up the pen and worked on the hole in the paper. I left him to it.

There was one other man on Franca's list and I decided to see him on my way home. He lived in the back streets of Camden Town in one of those elegant Georgian houses that are crumbling from neglect and lack of money. They wouldn't be that way for long. The new bourgeoisification that had started in the late sixties had crept through Camden Town and was now only a few streets away.

Stephen Braithwaite answered the bell almost immediately. He smiled when I told him my name and ushered me in eagerly. He showed me through the back hallway with its crowd of cycles and peeling wallpaper and into a room that was covered in the untidy accoutrements of student living. Books lay on the floor and chairs and mingled with unwashed clothes. On a chipped white plate on the carpet a piece of cod and some baked beans were congealing.

Stephen brushed some clothes off the only chair in the room and gestured me to it. He took two long steps across the room and pulled the bed covers up to hide the disarray beneath them. Then he sat on the edge of the single bed and grinned across at me.

'Studying for my exams you know,' he said. 'A chap doesn't seem to find much time to keep things tidy.'

I looked at the desk, piled high with library books, their covers firmly closed. He followed my gaze.

'Well, actually I am having some trouble getting down to work,' he said. 'Just displacement activity and I'll soon work it through.'

He folded his lanky body into a U, his large hands clasped round his bony knees. I thought I heard a cracking sound as the two connected.

'I'm investigating the death of Paul Holland,' I said.

Stephen nodded and pushed back a lock of his thick black hair which had flipped on to his forehead and was threatening to impair his vision.

'Poor Paul,' he said. 'He had so much to offer.'

'Had you known him long?'

'A year or so. My course tutor sent me in Paul's direction after he realised that I was having trouble adjusting to the big city. Couldn't settle down to work, you understand. Now I know it was just a resistance to taking myself seriously. Scared that if I were to make it in the world I'd turn out like my father—externally ordered but in fragments inside.'

'When did you hear Paul was dead?'

'The day after. I had an appointment. I turned up to be met by some concerned friend who seemed to think I needed consoling. But I'm tougher than that.'

He paused for a while as if trying to get his words in order and then he let them spill out again.

'Of course I was shocked by Paul's death, upset and shocked, you understand. But I really do feel that I got the maximum from him. He taught me to face my defences and to deal with them, even to use them for my own good. It's ironic really. At the point where Paul brought me to the separation–individuation phase he disappeared out of my life. It's a challenge, I must admit, but I'll see myself through it.'

'How do you think he died?'

For the first time a look of uncertainty crossed Stephen's face.

'He was run over,' he said slowly before the doubt cleared. 'Oh, I see what you mean. You're talking symbolically of course. Death by hit and run could be seen as a sudden overwhelming of emotions from outside the ego. Could fit into Paul's psychic structure because he was externally in control all the time. That the sort of thing you're getting at?'

'Not exactly,' I said. 'Have you any reason to think Paul was murdered?'

'None whatsoever,' he said. 'In fact I don't believe in the concept. People select their own fates. You only have to analyse the minutiae of a person's actions to understand why he lands in certain situations. The individual is responsible for his own environment and his actions determine what happens.'

'You obviously don't believe in class politics.'

'Oh don't misunderstand me,' Stephen said. 'My theory isn't crude. Of course there are forces in the world that impose certain conditions. But in the end the state of mind is the ultimate determinant. To be working class is to be told that one cannot change one's circumstances. To be starving is to give up the will to make one's own food. What these people need to do is to take their fates into their hands and wrest control.'

He had stood up and was towering over me. As he spoke, small rivulets of spit came from his mouth and dripped on to my forehead. I got up and backed towards the door.

'Yes, well thanks,' I said. 'Must be off now.'

'Wait a minute,' Stephen said. He strode back to his bed and knelt down beside it. As I opened the door, he was pulling papers from underneath it. He held a bunch up into the air.

'I've worked it all out,' he called. 'And written it down. Paul was very impressed although he did tend to analyse my theory as an attempt to avoid dealing with the transference.'

I walked quickly down the hall, pursued by the sound of his voice. When I got outside I breathed a sigh of relief. I crossed the road and got the door of my car open before I looked back at Stephen's house. He was standing by the window, his face pressed against the glass. He was laughing. I couldn't help feeling he was laughing at me.

I drove to Crouch End, to where Abbey Ashurst lived. On the way I thought about Arthur Simpson and about the seemingly mad Stephen Braithwaite. They were men of apparently different types—Arthur outwardly confident and secure, and Stephen a jittering mess—but they had something important in common. Beneath their facades, the two of them were floating in a vacuum of uncertainty. The world they'd been brought up to expect, had changed without them. Neither of them had the inner resources to deal with the harsh realities of Britain in the eighties. The changes feminism had wrought had only further twisted their insecurities. Ten years ago they would have felt safe at least in their own homes. Now even their personal conduct was up for examination. Maybe they'd both gone to therapy to try and deal with the problems. I wondered how much help Paul Holland would have been able to give them.

Abbey Ashurst wasn't in when I arrived. Instead, the door of the double-fronted house was opened by a three-year-old with large brown eyes and no clothes on. He stared at me interestedly for about thirty seconds before a woman came running through one of the varnished wood doors that opened on to the entrance hall. Her hands were covered in wet blue paint.

'Get in here Alastair,' she said. 'I haven't finished with you.'

She saw me standing there and she smiled apologetically. I asked to speak to Abbey and she said she wasn't in. I asked when Abbey was expected back and she said she didn't know. Her voice implied that she couldn't care less. I asked her to tell Abbey I'd called round and she nodded absent-mindedly. She asked me to close the door behind me and gestured with her blue hands to back up the request. I closed the door. From behind it I could hear the woman shouting at the naked child who was chortling maniacally.

I got home an hour later after getting stuck in a traffic jam. A lorry had jack-knifed outside Jones Brothers and it lay there surrounded by gloating passers-by and angry motorists. Loud complaints competed with the noise of the lorries as they revved up, belching exhaust fumes into our faces. The fact that the sky was blue and the sun hot didn't help matters. It never does on the Holloway Road. But eventually the lorry was righted and I managed to get home.

I was starving. I climbed up the steps at breakneck speed and rushed into the kitchen. Out of the freezer I took a piece of pitta bread and put it into the toaster to unfreeze. Then I cut slices of Gruyère to go with some honey-roast ham and dug out the Dijon mustard from the back of the fridge. The pitta popped up but it still wasn't ready. I pushed it back into the toaster and went to the living room to listen to my answerphone.

There was only one message and it was from Tony at *Street Times*.

'How did you like your publicity?' Tony's voice was suave, as if to prove that he wasn't intimidated by recorded messages. 'It's just occurred to me what I'd forgotten about Paul Holland. Ring me before five, or in a couple of days' time. I'm off to Lothian to see if they can resist the cuts.'

It was a quarter to five but I was feeling too hungry to tangle with Tony. I reckoned I could get in a few mouthfuls to satisfy the most severe of the pangs and still reach him in time. Tony was notorious about organising everything to a punishing schedule to which he could never adhere.

I went back into the kitchen and took out the hot pitta. Then I cut it in half and separated the two folds. I was just in the process of slipping the ham, cheese and lettuce into the pockets when the doorbell rang. Cursing, I went up to the intercom and asked who was there. I got no reply and I ran out of patience. I hit the button to release the door lock and went back to the kitchen.

I had made one half of the sandwich and taken a bite when a knock at my flat door reminded me that I had a visitor. Pitta in hand, I opened the door.

The woman I'd last seen in the pub guarding Marcus was there, leaning against the hall wall for support.

'Can I come in?' she said. Her voice had lost all traces of the confidence it had carried on Saturday.

I stepped out of the way and gestured her in. I took her to the living room. I sat her down in a chair because it didn't look like she'd have made it on her own. I offered her tea, coffee or something to eat and she didn't respond. I went out of the room and got her a brandy. I put it in her hand and guided the glass to her mouth. She coughed when the liquid hit the back of her throat but she kept it down. I sat opposite her.

'What's the matter?'

For the first time she looked at me. Tears welled up in her eyes and ran down her face. She made no attempt to push them away.

'Marcus is dead,' she said.

I opened my mouth to say something but nothing came out.

'I just found out. I went to pick him up from his home and his father told me.'

'I'm so sorry,' I said.

'He was my friend,' she shouted.

I let the anger die out before I spoke again. 'How did it happen?'

'Nobody knows. The police say they found him late on Saturday night, lying in the gutter near home. They've done a post mortem and all. Said he died from a blow to the head. They're saying it's gang warfare, some revenge killing. They say a white youth had the same thing happen last week except he survived to say he'd been attacked by some black youths.'

'And what do you think?'

The woman snorted her derision. 'Marcus was no kid. He wasn't into gangs and he could defend himself against those punks. The police just want to file this away so they don't have to bother their heads no more about it. When I left Marcus on Saturday night he was going home to sleep. He wasn't out for a fight.'

'Was he in any trouble?'

'Black folks always have trouble,' she said. 'You not know that?'

'Why did that woman at the arcade warn him away?'

'He wouldn't say. I think it was something to do with the accident he saw but he didn't want to go into it and so I didn't press it.'

'What about his friend?'

'Who? Terry? That one wouldn't tell his name to his own mother. He disappeared since Saturday. He often does that, takes off and then comes back a couple of weeks later without saying where he's been.'

'It might be a good idea to find him,' I said.

She shrugged. 'I wouldn't know where to look,' she said. 'Never did have much time for him. Marcus was the one who believed in integration. I thought he was wasting his time with white kids like Terry.'

'Why did you come to me?' I asked.

'His father wanted me to. He asked if you could go visit them. And . . .' she paused while a fresh pool of tears coursed their way down, '. . . it was something to do.'

I looked down at my right hand and noticed the sandwich was still in it. I put it down on a side table and stared out of the window. The weather had changed. Blue skies had gone to be replaced by a spread of those light grey rain clouds which are a speciality of the English climate. The drizzle had already started up. I went to the cupboard and got out a jacket.

'I'll drive over there now,' I said. 'Can I give you a lift?'

We didn't speak at all on the way to Finsbury Park. When we arrived outside Marcus's house the woman made no move to open her door.

'I cannot face it,' she said. 'Not again. I'll sit here.'

I nodded and left her to it. When somebody opened the door of number 45 I turned to glance at the car. She was slumped in the front seat, her head in her arms, her body racked with sobs. There was nothing I could do. I went into the house.

The door had been opened by a large woman dressed in a brown A-line skirt and a voluminous yellow blouse. She took both my hands in hers and looked intently at my face.

'I'm Kate Baeier,' I said. 'Mr Jones asked for me.'

'Ah yes,' she said. 'You must make allowances. He is in terrible grief. Marcus, him favourite son. It like he never get over this.' She shook her head and introduced herself as a member of the church. She took my jacket and asked me if I wanted some tea. Then she ushered me into the sitting room.

It was crowded with people but it was almost totally quiet. Every now and then somebody would say something, but they did it in hushed tones which hardly penetrated the concentrated silence. On the sofa sat Marcus's father. He was hugging a small woman, who looked just like Marcus. She was dressed in a nurse's uniform. A minute after I arrived Mr Jones lifted his head.

'My son,' he said. 'Him a good boy.'

From round him there were murmurs of agreement.

'He right,' Mr Jones continued. 'This a vicious country.'

The woman who'd let me in was standing just in the door, holding a cup. She gave it to me.

'Hush up now,' she said. 'This is a sorry time for you but the Lord is righteous. He lead us to this country and this country been good to us.'

Mr Jones leaned forward and pointed a finger at himself.

'That's what I been saying for twenty years. I deceive myself like you. We recruit to come here, we work hard and we never gain no place here. Our pickney no get work, they have abuse in the street and now they killed. Marcus right. This country rotten, rotten to the bone.'

'Hush now,' the woman said. 'You upsetting you wife.'

Beside Mr Jones the woman in nurse's uniform looked up. Her face was crumpled with grief but her voice was calm and clear.

'He's right. This is one bad country. Marcus and the youth speak the truth. For too long we have been keeping silence.'

Her husband moved closer to her and hugged her to him. When he next spoke he looked straight at me. 'You a detective. Find out who did this to our son.'

'I'm not sure I can,' I said.

'We have money,' he said. 'We pay you what you want.'

'It's not the money. I'm not sure that I'll be able to find out.'

His gaze held an entreaty that I couldn't avoid.

'Find out,' he said. 'Do that for we.'

'I'll try.'

He nodded, satisfied, and sank back into the sofa.

I didn't stay long after that. There didn't seem any point. The woman who'd let me in showed me out.

'He will recover himself in the Lord,' she said. 'And with it, forgiveness. Him not a man to look seek revenge.'

I nodded and went to my car. It was empty. I made the slow drive home with the grief of Marcus's parents weighing heavy on me.

Sam was sitting in the kitchen when I arrived. Pointedly he looked at his watch.

'A terrible thing has happened.' I said. 'I . . .'

Sam got up and slammed two pieces of paper on the table.

'What are those?'

'Two tickets,' he shouted, 'for a film you wanted to see. Remember? We were going to the early show and for a romantic meal afterwards. I was to buy the tickets. You were to turn up on time, that's all.'

'I'm sorry,' I said. 'I forgot. Let's try and cash these in.'

I reached for the tickets but Sam's hands got there first. He grabbed them and tore them into little pieces that he scattered in the air.

'Forgot!' he shouted. 'You just about forget everything these days. You forgot you were going out to the Simpsons, you forgot we're trying to find somewhere to live and you forget I'm waiting in the rain. Well baby, maybe we just better forget it full stop.'

He pushed me from the doorway and rushed through it. The sound of the front door when it slammed against its hinges echoed over the house.

Two hours later he phoned up. I had spent the intervening time making myself something tasteless to eat and forcing myself to swallow it down. I didn't feel like talking and my voice showed it when I answered the phone.

'I'm sorry,' Sam said. 'It's just that I don't feel loved by you.'

I didn't know what to say so I didn't try. Sam's voice sounded harder when he next spoke.

'Let's go away,' he said. 'Just the two of us. I could get a few days off and we could find somewhere in the country. Without Matthew and work to get in the way.'

'I can't now,' I said.

'You mean you don't want to.'

'No, I mean I can't,' I said. 'I'm in the middle of this investigation and something happened today, something terrible.'

'Now you choose to tell me,' he shouted. 'You dole out

information when it suits you. Ever since you started playing detective you've had no time for me.'

'You're no angel yourself,' I said. 'Sending estate agents round as a way of getting me to find a house with you. Where's the consultation in that?'

'I don't know what you're talking about,' he shouted.

'Cross,' I said. 'The Ashley Agency. Ring a bell?'

'Leave me alone. You and your cryptic comments.' He slammed the phone down.

I was asleep when the phone rang again. I floundered about trying to find it and when I managed to, I picked it up and shouted hello into the wrong end. I reversed the handpiece.

'There have been major new improvements on the transatlantic lines,' Anna said. 'Called satellites. You don't have to shout.'

'Oh, hello,' I said.

'Good welcome,' Anna said. 'What's up?'

'Sam,' I answered. 'And please don't say you told me so.'

There was a pause and, although I couldn't be sure I thought I heard a gulp coming from so far away. Against the static Anna's voice sounded subdued when she spoke again.

'I'm your friend. I want to help. Not rub things in.'

This time it was my turn to wait before I spoke. When I found the words, my voice came out shaky.

'I'm sorry. Everything's weird here. I know I'm antagonising Sam without reason but I can't stop myself.'

'Maybe you should talk to him about it,' Anna said.

'That's the trouble,' I said. 'I don't seem able to intervene in my own life. It's this investigation. It's taken over.'

'Is it Franca?' Anna asked.

With the mention of that name I froze. In that instant I realised that it *was* to do with Franca: that somehow I'd slipped back into an old way of relating, an old way of coping with difficulties. And at the same time as I realised this, I continued to do it.

'Why should it be?' I heard myself saying. My voice was still, unfriendly and ungiving and I hated myself for it.

Anna got the message. While I wished she would intervene, do something to break into my solitude, I heard her muttering pleasantries on her way to goodbye. My voice was cold despite my need to unfreeze it: hers was careless and not a little hurt.

By the time she hung up I was fully awake and doubly miserable.

I lay motionless in bed willing myself back to sleep. But it was a good few hours before I managed to recapture my dreams.

Outside, dusk had come and gone. It left the already bare garden looking even more destitute. Cold is what came to mind when you looked on the thin branches, the frosty soil and the icy path.

Inside, though, it was different. True, the room was still empty of embellishments, but today it was warm and even cosy.

Kate smiled, an open even smile. She had been talking for some time and she was getting ready to finish up.

'So I managed perfectly,' she said. 'It wasn't easy but I really feel that I came through for myself. You would have been proud of me.'

Franca returned her smile. For a moment the two of them sat there in silence. It was not the silence of previous years. Instead the quiet embraced them: joining rather than separating.

Kate reflected on how far she'd got in the time she'd sat in the room. A feeling of almost contentment enfolded her.

But the silence went on too long and it still had a power. As Kate sat there, her smile faded. Something seemed to be nestling on her shoulder, something cloying and familiar, but something she did not want to know. She shook herself roughly. Franca looked startled.

When Kate spoke again, her voice had changed. Gone was the lightness. Instead it was replaced by a bitterness—a kind of recrimination.

'Small victories,' she said. 'That's what I've learned here. I used to think we could change the world. Now I'm just proud if I survive a hostile encounter with myself intact.'

Franca nodded. She was not ready to speak.

'And what's the use?' Kate continued. 'Don't you sometimes think you're spending a lot of energy to teach us to conform?'

'Us?' asked Franca.

'Your clients,' said Kate, 'or patients. Whatever you call them.'

She waited for a reply to the challenge. When it didn't come she got up abruptly. Or found herself getting up—it was as though she had become separated from her actions. While a small frightened part of herself still lurked in the chair, she found herself striding across the room. She pulled a straight-backed chair away from the small wooden desk. She turned the chair round and sat on it, facing Franca, her arms crossed. From this viewpoint, her old familiar chair seemed very distant.

'You look small,' she said. 'Has my anger shrunk you?'

'It's probably because you've changed position,' Franca answered. 'You've never done that before.'

To Kate, the sentence seemed to crash through the air. She looked embarrassed, fearful, as if she'd been caught out doing something forbidden. She got up from the chair. Her body was rigid as she pushed the chair back under the desk and walked towards her familiar setting. When she sat down again, she seemed defeated. Franca frowned to herself.

'I think it is an achievement,' Franca said, picking her words carefully across what now seemed like a dangerous crevass, 'that you felt free to move in this room.'

Kate did not reply, but the words had their impact. It showed in the way she began to relax.

When she spoke again, her voice was small, almost childish.

'I was happy,' she said. 'And I ruined it.'

Kate frowned when her statement was met with silence. Some of her irritation returned. 'You're too rigid,' she said. 'Break out of the mould. Say something daring once in your careful career.' Her face twitched when she heard what she had said.

'Funny,' she mused, 'I get to unfreeze and move in the room and I accuse you of being too rigid.'

She looked across to see if Franca would return the grin. She seemed oddly reassured when no answer came back.

'But I mean it,' she continued. 'I do need more help. Tell me, for a change, instead of leading me painstakingly to the right place. Make it easy.'

'Nobody said it would be easy,' Franca said.

'Oh don't be so prim,' Kate snapped. 'Tell me. Why did I just flick from confidence to gloom?'

'I think you got scared,' Franca said. Kate couldn't be sure but she thought she detected a look of, could it be, fear crossing her companion's face. But when Franca spoke again, her voice was as modulated as ever.

'I think perhaps that it is difficult for you to express happiness because it brings with it a feeling that you will be abandoned . . . in this case by me. Feelings of insecurity and depression may come easier because they are known and because they appeal for help. Perhaps you feel that the strength that comes with being whole will mean a removal of support, a denial of any misery you might still feel.'

'Does that mean I'm not ready to leave therapy?' Kate asked.

'Come off it, Kate,' Franca snapped before catching herself.

This time the silence between them was one of surprise. Kate looked straight at her companion, as if trying to reach a decision. The older woman met her gaze evenly but there was a discomfort in the meeting. An unspoken taboo had been broken.

Kate smiled and as she did so, Franca's shoulders seemed to relax.

'I am being annoying,' Kate said, 'restless I suppose.'

The eyes of the two women met and locked together for a second in a look that could not be expressed in words.

'And it isn't so terrible if you broke the rules,' Kate finished, 'is it?'

Franca dipped her head. When she looked up her gaze was clear.

'Let's take it up next time,' Kate said.

Seven

My dreams weren't really worth recapturing. All night I had arguments with people who turned out to be variations of myself. Sam wandered in and out of them, ignoring me but muttering curses to himself. When he walked towards me I got scared: when I tried to catch up with him, he disappeared.

All predictable stuff, which didn't help my mood when I woke. I made myself a cup of coffee and dialled Sam's number. It was engaged. I read the paper and then dialled the number again. It was still engaged. I gave up.

I phones the Joneses and asked Marcus's father to look for Terry's phone number. Within five minutes he rang back with an address. He sounded as low as a man could sink.

I stretched for the phone book and found the number of the Ashley Agency.

It was engaged on my first, second and third tries. On the fourth, it rang for an age. Finally a woman answered. She sounded flustered and I thought I knew why when I heard the sound of telephones ringing in the background.

'Ashley's,' she said. 'Hold the line.'

I held the line until I thought it would melt in my hands. I put the phone down and dialled again.

'Ashley's,' the woman answered. 'Hold the . . .'

'I have been,' I shouted.

'Can I help you?' she said wearily.

'Mr Cross.'

'I'm afraid he's in a meeting,' she said. 'Can I get him to ring you back?'

'It's okay,' I said. 'I'll come in.'

She'd hung up before I finished my sentence.

Their office was just off Stoke Newington Church Street, in a bijou little cul-de-sac. They'd done their bit to blend by going in for colour toning. The outside of the building was painted a subtle pink, the window frames a mellow grey and the lettering above the door a colour in between the two.

A bell rang when I entered the charcoal-carpeted office. It added to the sound of a lone telephone. A woman was seated behind a grey desk. She looked as though she might have started the day neatly dressed but the pressure was taking its toll. Her black hair was mussed up and desperate and it echoed the creases in her beige silk shirt. She was talking simultaneously into two receivers, one held to each ear. A third phone was struggling for attention.

The woman smiled when she saw me. The change in her facial muscles meant that one of the receivers clattered to the desk. She picked it up, put it to her ear and then, frowning, slammed it down.

'No way to treat the customer, Gladys dear,' said a man who was sitting behind a bigger, and almost empty, desk.

The woman pouted and she frowned at the man. She looked like she was going to follow that up by sticking out her tongue. The man pretended not to notice. He turned back to contemplation of the empty space in front of him.

He was dressed like a shark. Greasy hair slicked down close to his face and swept behind his flat ears. His suit was white cotton, imitation gangster and immaculate. His tie was white silk and broad.

'Can I help you?' the woman said.

'I'm looking for Mr Cross.'

The man got up from behind his desk and walked towards me, hands outstretched. 'At your service,' he said.

I looked at him more closely. 'You're not Cross,' I said.

'Cross by name but not by nature,' he joked. The woman let out an audible sigh.

'I'm looking for another Mr Cross. The one who visited me.'

The man laughed jocularly. 'I'm an original,' he snickered. 'Couldn't stand the competition from another.'

'But he visited me,' I said. 'He had one of your cards.'

The man frowned.

'He got my name from Sam Watkins,' I continued. 'Who asked for your house lists.'

The man walked up to a pink three-drawer filing cabinet and opened the top compartment.

'Watkins,' he said. He leafed through a list of names. 'Wassen, Watson, Wilkinson.'

He looked up at me.

'We have no Watkins on our list,' he said. 'Unless Gladys left it off.'

The woman glared at him from behind her desk. She didn't speak. She didn't need to. The man flinched.

'Easily remedied,' he said, slicking the shoulder of his suit in a much-practised gesture. 'What sort of property are you interested in?'

'I'm not buying,' I said.

'Selling?'

'Investigating,' I said. 'A murder.'

The man froze. His hand stopped in the air, six inches from his shoulder.

'You're from the police?'

'No, private,' I said.

'Leave me alone then,' he hissed. He reached over his desk, grabbed a dirty white briefcase and was out of the door in a flash.

From behind her three telephones, now all ringing, the woman smiled brightly at me.

'He's nervous, your boss,' I said.

'Had a bit of trouble recently,' she said. 'The police were all over the place.'

'What about?'

The woman shrugged. The telephones carried on.

'Irregular dealings,' she said. 'Sold a house for more than the asking price and pocketed the difference. Must have made a packet. I didn't see any of it. He's a mean bastard that one.'

She smiled again. The phones rang. The sound was beginning to get on my nerves. I wasn't the only one. Abruptly the woman picked up two receivers.

'Ashley's,' she said into each and then she put the receivers down so their wires crossed and each phone got a different top. The third phone she left ringing.

I went through the door. The bell jangled behind me.

Terry lived on a council estate at the back of the Hornsey Road. It was one of those developments that had gone lengthways rather than upwards as a protest against high-rise architecture. I parked and walked into the estate. To all sides were what seemed like miles of sprawling three-storey buildings, all surrounded by walkways and corridors. At every turn, and there were many of them, stood signposts pointing to different block names and different block numbers, but they were the sort of signposts that pointed straight ahead and petered out when you followed them. Eventually after I'd had to ask directions from three separate groups of children I found the right block, the right walkway and the right number. I rang the bell.

The man who answered the door wasn't taking any risks. He only opened it a fraction and when he saw me he resisted opening any further.

'Yes?'

'I'm looking for Terry.'

'What's he done?'

'Nothing. I just want to talk to him.'

'Tell me another,' he said. 'He's out there somewhere.' And he closed the door firmly in my face.

I found my way down the gangway again and wandered around the estate. One part looked much like another and after about ten minutes I was well and truly disoriented. I carried on walking anyway. Finally I got to an open space. Straight ahead was one of those squat round windowless buildings that pass for community meeting places, plus a more angular construction: the cross over its doorway gave away the fact that it was masquerading as a church. To the right of them stood a playground: concreted over, with a couple of swings, a roundabout and a slide with two missing rungs on its ladders. Terry was sitting on one of the swings, his feet on the ground. He was rocking himself listlessly backwards and forwards.

When he saw me a look of panic swept his face. He gripped the chains of the swing as if to lift himself off but there was only one exit to the place and I was standing by it. He changed his mind and sat still while he tried to replace the fear with nonchalance. I walked up to him.

'Did you hear about Marcus?' I asked.

He nodded and rocked some more.

'I need some information from you,' I said.

'Don't know nothing,' he muttered.

'You left something out when you told me about the man you saw run over,' I said. 'What was it?'

Terry put his index finger of his right hand into his right nostril. He twisted it there while he looked at me. He took it out when I didn't faint with horror. 'Nothing,' he said. 'We told you everything.'

'Who was the man at the amusement arcade?'
'What man?'
'Come on Terry,' I said. 'Marcus was warned not to go near the place. There was a man waiting for him.'
Terry threw back his head and tried to dismiss me with a laugh. He was too young and too scared to do it with conviction. While he was trying it, two nineteen-year-olds passed by the playground fence. They stopped when they saw us and nudged each other.
'You're all right there Terry,' one of them called, and accompanied the words with a heavy wink to his companion. Terry blushed, which brought on another bout of jostling and winking. They soon got bored, though, and strolled off in search of other diversions.
'I don't want to talk to you,' Terry said when they'd gone.
'Just tell me who the man was and I'll go away.'
He looked down at his fingernails and then quickly up at me.
'You don't want to take no notice of him,' he said. 'He likes to play the big man. Nobody will talk to him because he's a nark.'
'What did he have against Marcus?'
'Nothing,' Terry said. 'That's how he is. He takes it on himself to terrorise street kids. He thinks it keeps them in line. The week before he picked on someone else.'
'And did they end up dead too?'
Terry's eyes widened. 'He didn't kill Marcus, did he?'
'Somebody did.'
'But they said it was a gang. Another kid got done in there the week before.'
'Marcus didn't belong to a gang,' I said. 'Who wanted him killed?'
Terry got off the swing in such a hurry he almost landed on his face. He brushed past me.
'I have to go,' he said.
His shoulders slouched as he walked quickly out of the playground. I followed after him. Just before he rounded the corner the two youths reappeared. Terry muttered something to them before disappearing from sight. When I tried to go after him the path was blocked. The two boys stood in front of me, not touching, but threatening to.
'Where's she going?' one asked the other.
'Search me. Following our Terry,' the other replied.
'We can't have that can we?'
'We don't like birds that don't know their own place.'

'Stupid cunt.'

It was all said in a half jocular manner but there was menace in their voices and rage on their faces. They were moving closer as they spoke as if they were building up the courage to push at me.

I turned away and started walking in the opposite direction. They followed. I tried not to run but couldn't stop myself from speeding up. So did they. It was broad daylight. There was nobody around. The only sound was my heart thumping and the distant shouts of kids playing somewhere else in the maze.

By the time I got to the road I was running. I burst out, leaping over the fire barrier, and almost catapulted into an elderly woman who was dragging her shopping trolley behind her. I managed to stop just in time. Breathing heavily I turned to look at the estate. There was nobody behind me, nobody in pursuit.

'I'm sorry,' I said to the woman as I walked away.

'Young people,' she called after me. 'No manners.'

I sat in my car to give myself time to find my breath and my courage. Then I drove up Hornsey Road and into Crouch End. I parked near Abbey Ashurst's house and rang the bell.

I recognised the woman who opened the door. She was the woman who'd visited Laura Maxwell. She'd had a change of image but it was definitely the same person. She was dressed in jeans and a V-necked pink T-shirt. On top of them she wore a long black apron made of thick plastic. Her hands were also gloved in plastic and she was holding some wet pieces of paper. She gave off a curiously strong chemical smell.

She looked at me blankly for a second and then she remembered. She pushed with her shoulder at the heavy oak door. I stuck my foot in the gap. For a moment we stayed in combat, her pushing, me resisting and then she gave up. Silently she opened the door. I went in and closed it behind me.

She nodded and made her way down the hallway and into a room on the right. I limped after her.

It was a living room in which the polished floorboards shone and were echoed in the stripped pine shutters that lined the bay windows. The walls were painted an almost white colour and decked with various sizes of black and white photographs. Double doors led into a kitchen whose theme was also wood, arranged country style. The floor was of heavy red tiles and the french windows opened up into a carefully landscaped garden. It was all in perfect order except for the traces of blue handprints climbing up one wall.

'Alastair been expressing himself?' I asked.

'The girl can't control him,' Abbey said as she removed her apron and gloves and threw them in the kitchen sink. The chemical smell stayed there with them. She dropped the paper she'd been carrying into the bin and washed her hands. Then she moved back into the living room and sat down on a chrome and corduroy chair.

'What do you want with me?' she asked.

'I'm investigating the death of Paul Holland,' I said.

'I gathered that,' she said. Her expression stayed still but I thought I detected a faint quivering of her thin mouth.

'You were a client of his.'

'That's confidential,' she said.

'Did all Paul's clients hang out together?'

'I don't know what you mean,' she said.

'I saw you talking to Laura Maxwell yesterday. At "Grains".'

'That's different. I've known Laura for many years.'

'What were you arguing about?'

'You're imagining things,' she said. 'We've been through a lot together and we have no reason to argue.'

While she talked the brass doorknob of the hall door had turned slowly. As I watched, the door opened. Alastair Ashurst crept in, his hand on his lips. He moved round the walls, stalking. When he got up to Abbey's chair he jumped out at her.

He'd meant to give her a fright but he hadn't reckoned on the extremity of her reaction. Turning a shade paler than white, she screamed. She gripped the chair as if it might collapse beneath her.

Alastair looked at her and then his face screwed up. He began to sob. His mother hugged him.

'I'm sorry,' she said.

The consolation made him sob louder. Abbey threw me a look-what-you've-done-now look and picked him up. 'Come on, love,' she said. 'Let's get your train set out.'

She left the room carrying the kid. When she'd gone I got up. I went to the sink and sniffed at the apron. Then I picked up the lid of the swing bin and poked around inside it. The crumpled paper was there. I fished it out and smoothed it down. It was a half-developed photo, running at the edges. It was beyond salvage and all I could make out was that it was a group composition—several people ranged round some sort of van.

I heard the sound of Abbey's footsteps and I threw the paper back into the bin. When Abbey came back in I was only halfway back to my chair.

'What are you doing?'

'Why are you so nervous?'

'I don't know what you're talking about,' she said. 'My child is upset. I'd appreciate it if you would leave me to calm him.'

I stayed where I was and I looked at her. She tried to outstare me but her heart wasn't in it: her eyes dropped.

'What were you talking to Laura about?' I asked.

Abbey picked up a paper napkin that was lying on a sideboard. She worked at it, folding it into smaller and smaller shapes.

'We were discussing you,' she said. 'If you really want to know.'

'What about me?'

'You're interfering. You're not wanted. As far as I'm concerned, Paul Holland's better off dead.'

'But he was your therapist,' I said. 'Doesn't that mean anything?'

'He never liked me,' she said. 'Thought I was too scared of life. Maybe he's right.'

The paper was as small as she could get it. She unfolded it and examined the marks she'd made.

'Paul used his charm on people,' she said. 'He had his favourites . . . and his neglected. I could never get into the first category. All that talk about equals and honesty: he was on one big power trip.'

'Why did you go to see Laura?' I asked.

'I've told you,' she said impatiently, 'to discuss you.'

'And how did you know about me?'

She started tearing at the paper, insistently and viciously. When it was almost totally destroyed she looked up defiantly.

'Laura told me. Said you came nosing around.'

'She hired me,' I said, 'to nose.'

Abbey looked at the shreds in her hands as if she didn't know what to do with them. Her face had gone hard and stubborn.

'Who was that man?' I asked. 'The one you met?'

'My husband,' she said.

I looked at the wall where a framed photograph of a grey-haired man looked back at me.

'Your husband taken to dyeing his hair?' I asked.

Abbey took a step towards me. There was hatred in her face.

'Get out of here,' she said. 'You're not wanted.'

She muscled me out of the room and pushed me down the hall.

When I was through the front door she slammed it behind me.

Outside, I looked around. Abbey lived in one of those detached double-fronted houses surrounded by garden. To one side was an alley-way leading to a tall garden gate. I tried the gate. It was locked.

I went back into the street and checked it out. There was nobody in sight. I hoisted myself up on to the wall that divided Abbey's garden from her neighbour's and I balanced myself along it until I reached the gate. The wall was stepped gradually and by the time I got to the gate I was considerably higher than when I'd started but I still wasn't high enough. I grabbed hold of the top of the gate with both hands and pulled myself up. Then laboriously I put first one leg and then the other over the gate. After that there was nothing I could do but jump for it. I landed—clumsily—but safely enough.

Shaking myself off I walked down the path and into the garden. The double doors leading to the kitchen were still open. There was nobody inside. I crept through the room, into the living room and then out into the hall. Sounds of playing drifted down the stairs. In a distant room a woman was talking.

Quietly I crept down the corridor, opening doors as I passed them. I got to see a second sitting room and what looked like two studies. There were all furnished, like the living room, in seventies Habitat, full of the trappings of respectability.

I found the room I was looking for at the end of the corridor under the stairs. I opened the door to what had once been a large cupboard. It was pitch black inside. I felt around the walls until I found a light switch which I clicked on. The cupboard had been converted into a small darkroom, the walls painted black, two tray-size sinks installed in a corner and a series of hooks holding negatives above them.

To one side of the sinks a white sheet of perspex had been laid. I went up to it and searched around underneath. My hand felt a switch and I pressed it. The perspex lit up, flooded with light from below.

One by one, I took the string of negatives and placed them on the plastic surface. The first three were a series of family snaps made up of combinations of people who looked like Abbey, Alastair and a man whose name probably also began with A. The last strip was even less interesting to me. It had picture after picture of a cherry tree I'd seen in the garden. It had been snapped through the seasons until it was in full flower.

That was all. Carefully I put the negatives back on their holders. I searched the bin underneath the sinks but found nothing interesting. Then I rifled through the shelves but all I learned was that Abbey prided herself on her still lifes.

It was on the way out that I got lucky. I noticed an in-tray filled with blank shiny paper. I picked up the wad of paper and flicked through it. A negative fluttered to the floor. I put it on the perspex. It was of a group of people ranged around a van. I put it in my pocket.

I switched off the light and stepped out into the deserted hall. The woman's voice was still talking. I walked down the hall to a side table that held a black telephone. Quietly I picked up the receiver.

'. . . And what happens if she looks further back?' Abbey's voice was saying. Abruptly she stopped talking.

'Who's there?' she called.

I replaced the receiver and left quietly.

It didn't take me long to get back home. On the way I stopped off at a photographic shop. The assistant looked at me peculiarly when I asked him to develop one lone negative fast but he didn't say anything. I left him behind the counter. He had the negative in one hand and was holding it up to the light, a bemused expression on his face.

Lowri was on my doorstep when I arrived home. She greeted me with a weary smile and followed me upstairs. When she got into the kitchen she fell into a chair, dumped her canvas bag overflowing with files on to the floor, and put her feet on the table. That accomplished, she gave me another smile.

'Yes please,' she said. 'Coffee would be great.'

I flicked the switch for the kettle and measured some Java into a filter paper.

'What brings you here?' I asked.

'Railings,' she said. 'What I haven't learned about cast iron railings this morning, you wouldn't want to know.'

'Aha,' I said.

Lowri was at it again. A freelance journalist, she was constantly on the trail of obscure details. She was one of the most original researchers I'd ever come across, and her persistence tended to pay off. She would ask why a different councillor had signed a routine memo and she would uncover a major palace coup; she would investigate why her neighbour's son fell off his new bike, and discover a scandal to severely embarrass the bicycle manufacturers. If Lowri was into railings, then cast iron manufacturers should watch out.

'Your tenants' association is being taken down the garden path,' she said. 'If you'll forgive the metaphor. They're spending far too much on their front fences and the graft is spreading far.'

'Shocking,' I said. I poured the coffee into two mugs and handed her one along with a jug of cream.

'I can see militant consumerism is far from your mind,' she said. 'What's happening between Sam and you?'

'What do you mean?'

I turned away from her. Suddenly I felt hungry. I cut two slices of egg rye and buttered them. I remembered Lowri as I was finishing. I looked back at her, tilting my head at the bread. She nodded so I cut another two. I put a couple of layers of toscano salami on all four. I gave Lowri hers on a plate: mine I started immediately. I concentrated on the chewing and while I did so I kept my eyes fixed firmly on the table.

'I saw him this morning,' Lowri said as soon as I'd wolfed down the sandwiches.

'Who?' I asked. I knew I sounded ridiculous but I didn't care.

'Sam,' she said. 'He wasn't talking either.'

'We had a rift,' I said.

'Mendable?'

'I don't know.'

'Need a go-between?'

'Not at the moment,' I said. 'Let me pick your brains.'

Lowri pulled the glass coffee pot towards her and poured herself another cup.

'Fire away,' she said. 'Although don't say I didn't try to get personal.'

I ignored the crack. I asked her if she'd ever heard of an Abbey Ashurst and she shook her head. Laura Maxwell got a similar response, although Lowri seemed less sure on that one. When I pushed her further she remembered doing a write-up on 'Grains' at the time it celebrated its millionth customer. Marcus Jones drew another blank.

It was when I mentioned James Stanford that Lowri got interested. She knew who he was and she knew all about his theatre group, but it was more than that.

'Our paths crossed a long while ago,' she said.
'In what way?'
Instead of answering, Lowri looked at me. Her eyes glazed over. She carried on staring in my direction but she wasn't seeing me.
'Don't mind me,' I said.
Lowri shook her head as if to recall it into the present. She laughed.
'I'm sorry Kate. My scurrilous past came flooding back.'
'I never knew it was scurrilous,' I said.
'It was before you came to England. I was a different person then.'
'Apart from the fact that you pretended to be heterosexual?'
'That was part of it,' she said. 'But there was more.'
'Like?'
'It's funny—it probably wouldn't matter at all now, but I can't bring myself to talk about it. The taboo's too strong.'
'Give us a hint.'
'I was into some heavy stuff in the early seventies,' she said. 'So was James Stanford.'
'Like Angry Brigade stuff?' I asked.
'Something like,' she said. 'Not quite. If you're going to dig into it, be careful.'
'Why? Where's the danger?'
Lowri threw the remains of her coffee down her throat and smiled.
'Yeah, I am probably being overdramatic. But people are sensitive about those times. They might not like you digging into their pasts.'
She reached for the coffee pot and poured herself another cup.
'You'll get caffeine poisoning,' I said.
'I should care,' she answered. 'You should see what goes into the paint they daub those iron railings with.'
We sat together a while longer, catching up on news. Lowri tried to mention Sam again and I prevented her. After an hour, the coffee pot was empty. Lowri said she'd have to be going anyway and so I walked her down the stairs. Her bicycle was outside, chained to one of the new railings. It had only one wheel. Lowri gave a groan of despair.
'There's been a rash of that around London,' I said. It wasn't much of a consolation.
I said I'd drive her to the nearest tube. Before we got into the car

Lowri picked up the snapped bicycle chain and threw it into her bag.

'It's advertised as unbreakable,' she said. 'I'll get the manufacturers for this.'

The photographer's shop was on our way so I stopped opposite it. Lowri came in with me. The bemused man was still there and he still looked bemused. When he saw us he went into the back room before returning with a white envelope.

'We don't normally do this,' he said, 'develop odd negatives. I'll have to find out how much it costs.'

He disappeared again. While he was gone I opened the envelope. I took out the black and white print and looked at it. Some familiar faces stared back at me.

It was a blurred picture of six people lounging on an old post office van. The three men and three women stared straight at the camera with tight lips and stern eyes. Laura Maxwell was in the middle of the group wearing a loose and long dress which, embroidered on the top half, managed to effectively conceal her whole body. Abbey Ashurst was standing beside her, separated by a small space. She was wearing flared jeans topped by what looked like a cheese-cloth rag. James Stanford, who was on the outside of the group looking like he wanted to get in, also sported denims. His chest was bare and his bones showed through his scrawny skin.

There were three other people in the photo: one woman and two men, none of whom I recognised. I handed it to Lowri. When she looked at it, she nodded as if confirming something to herself. Silently she pointed to James Stanford. Then her finger touched the third woman who was standing on the left-hand side of the picture flanked by the two other men.

'That's Jane Grappling,' she said. 'The whole photo's blurred but I'm sure it's her. She works in a women's refuge in Holloway.'

She held the picture up to the light for a moment. Then she got out the negative and examined it closely.

'Abbey must have lost the negative,' she said.

'What do you mean?'

'This has been taken off a positive. That's why the definition's gone.'

'Maybe it wasn't her picture.'

The man came back behind the counter.

'That'll be twenty-eight pence,' he said. 'Plus VAT.'

I paid him. We left the shop. I dropped Lowri off at Archway tube, took directions to Jane Grappling's place of work and drove back down the Holloway Road.

It was a monster house beside a church near the Caledonian Road. I walked through the immaculately kept front garden and went up to the brightly painted yellow door. There were four bells to choose from. They all bore the same name so I picked the middle one.

The loud ring sounded through the house. It was followed by the sound of a woman's shouts and then some scuffling. Eventually the door opened a fraction. A pair of eyes peered out from between the crack made by the door and the chain which restrained it.

'Yes?'

'My name's Kate Baeier,' I said. 'I'm looking for Jane Grappling.'

The door slammed shut and the footsteps retreated. It was another two minutes before the door was opened again, this time fully.

Jane Grappling was just about recognisable from the photograph. She looked a lot healthier. She was wearing a pair of stylishly cut brown shorts and a white shirt, both of which gave her smooth tan maximum value. Her fair hair was cut short and fluffily and allowed her pretty face to speak for itself.

'Kate,' she said. 'Sorry about the welcome. One of the men tried to make a voluble complaint last night and everybody's on edge.'

'I didn't realise you had men here,' I said.

'That's exactly what he was complaining about.'

She held the door wide and ushered me into the hallway. It was of a size that well matched the dimensions of the house. Light flooded in from tall windows which lined the side wall and reflected off the polished banisters. Two corridors led off in opposite directions. They were lined with closed doors, newly painted in a shiny blue gloss. The whole place smelt of paint and cleaning fluid.

As Jane Grappling led me through the maze, a small tousled girl came out of one of the doors. It swung shut silently behind her. When she saw me, she planted her feet firmly on the ground, stuck a thumb into her mouth and stared. I tried to smile at her. She stared back. I tried another and suddenly her face beamed. Then, as quietly as she had arrived, she disappeared back behind the door.

'In here,' Jane said.

We walked into what was an enormous kitchen, glassed in on all sides. Stairs led down one end into an open-plan living room. It in turn led to a garden. Shouts of children playing floated through the windows.

'Tea?' Jane asked.

I shook my head and sat down on one of the many chairs that surrounded the long wooden table. Jane sat opposite me.

'Lowri gave me your address,' I said.

Jane nodded. I took out the photograph and gave it to her. She looked at it and then smiled before placing it on the table.

'That's times past,' she said. 'Me surrounded by two men.'

'I'd like to know about them,' I said. 'The times, I mean, as well as the men. It's in connection with a case I'm investigating.'

'Yes, Laura told me,' she said.

'Laura Maxwell? What else did she say?'

'That you're an interfering busybody who wrecked her security system.'

'Does that put you off?'

'Laura can be a bit abrasive,' Jane said. 'Making up for lost time. What do you want to know?'

'For a start who these people are. I've met Laura, Abbey and James. What about the other two?'

Jane picked up the photograph again and stared at it. It was a while before she spoke.

'The one in the middle is Mich Dwight. Calls himself Michael S. Dwight now and earns a living publishing learned papers. The one on the edge is Bob Francis. I'm not sure what's happened to him. I don't spend much time with any of them. We grew apart.'

'But you saw Laura recently?'

'She and Abbey made a special trip from the past. To warn me to keep silent,' Jane said. 'Laura's paranoid. She wants to disown those years. I think she'd like to wish them away. Money is all she's after now.'

'What about Abbey?'

'Look at her,' Jane said, pointing at the picture. 'Trying so hard to fit in. In those days it was okay to side with rebellion. The late eighties changed all that. She's made a home for herself and her own and doesn't want anybody messing about with it.'

'And you?' I asked.

Jane smiled. She sat back in her chair, her legs stretched out in front of her, her hands pushed deep into her pockets.

'I work here,' she said. 'In those days we would have sneered at it, called it working for the state, doing social work. Maybe it is, but

I enjoy it, living with women and kids, sharing each other's experiences.'

'Is it really enough,' I asked, 'restricted to your own small niche?'

'It's what I've got,' she said. 'Sometimes the world gets too large. Even to be contented is an achievement.'

Jane got up as the small child from the hall wandered in, looking disoriented. Jane went up to her and picked her up.

'My, don't I sound smug?' she said.

'What's smug?' the girl asked.

'Pleased with myself,' Jane said. 'I suppose I am. We're not going to regret our pasts, or our presents, are we?' She held the girl high in the air and looked intently at her.

'I want to get down,' the girl said.

Jane laughed and put her gently on her feet. The girl threw me an uncertain look and climbed down the stairs, holding tight to the wooden banisters. She walked through the sitting room, and into the garden.

'What did you get up to in those days?' I asked.

Jane went to the fridge and opened it. She pulled out a bowl filled to the brim with courgettes, aubergines and red peppers. She selected a knife from the rack high on the wall and began to work, slicing the peppers into thin strips.

'We were going to change the world,' she said. 'We did partially succeed. The women's movement is the proof of that. But we were too ambitious. And foolhardy. It got us into some heavy action.'

'Like what?'

She finished with the peppers and began on the aubergines, slicing them thin and laying them out, flower-like, on a large china plate.

'It doesn't do to get too specific,' she said. 'Even after all this time. We thought the world was ours to change and we acted on the assumption. We played with fire.'

'Did anybody get burned?'

Jane poured sea salt over the first layer of aubergines before returning to her cutting.

'Bob Francis was picked up,' she said. 'I don't know why. Maybe the police wanted a scapegoat and he was the most vulnerable without a middle-class family to back him up.'

'What happened to him?'

'They mauled him about a bit,' she said. 'And then let him go. He got very bitter. The whole incident meant the end of our unit. I suppose we were breaking up anyway. Times had changed.'

The aubergines lay in their plate. Little drops of liquid slowly appeared on their surfaces. Jane reached for the courgettes and diced a few of them.

'Mich kept in touch with Bob,' she said. 'Why not talk to him?'

She reached under the sink and pulled out a heavy skillet. She poured some corn oil into it. She followed it with a couple of cloves of garlic. The aroma soon filled the room. As if on cue, three children appeared from the garden.

'Is tea ready?' the eldest shouted.

'Of course not—it's too early,' Jane said. She smiled at me. 'I'll walk you to the door. I'll dig out Mich's address on the way.'

Michael S. Dwight made sure that everybody knew about the S. It was engraved in copperplate and stuck beneath a lighted bell on the outside of his Georgian house which was situated at the back of the Angel.

Michael S. was a tubby man who had some difficulty getting his yellow cotton shirt to connect to his grey flannel trousers. His hair was having the same kind of trouble. Brushed forward to conceal a growing bald patch, it didn't quite make it.

Michael was a busy man. I knew that because he managed to tell me so at least three times in between the time he opened the door and the time he showed me into his sophisticated living room.

It was sparsely, if expensively, furnished. Two light blue sofas stuck at right angles to each other and centred by a huge perspex table provided the seating. A thick pile fawn carpet and a few nicely chosen modern sculptures provided the ambience, and Michael himself came up with the conversation.

It was more in the way of a long complaint than anything else. He was, he informed me, a busy man. He had two books on the go, an insatiable editor who didn't know his syntax from a hole in the wall and a PhD student who not only wanted to base his entire thesis on Michael's work, but also insisted on talking to Michael daily.

'I gave all this up once,' Michael said. 'And I've a good mind to do it again.'

'You gave it up in the sixties?' I asked.

Michael S. looked me over. He made no bones about it. His watery brown eyes started at my feet, slowly went to the top of my head and down again. When he'd finished he smoothed some strands of hair across his bald spot.

'I know about you,' he said. 'Kate Baeier. You're the person Laura Maxwell told me about.'

'She has been doing the rounds,' I said.

'Laura regards herself as somewhat of an organiser,' Michael sniffed. 'And I suspect she sees herself as my soul mate. Ridiculous. Just because she's gone straight she thinks we move in the same circles. But I have not, for a minute, surrendered my integrity. Pure financial considerations would play havoc with my life.'

I looked around the room, giving it the head-to-toe treatment.

'You don't seem to be doing badly,' I said.

'Nonsense,' Michael scoffed. 'I am in no way what one would call well off. I watch the pennies. I suppose you want some coffee.'

He disappeared for a short while and came back bearing two white mugs of coffee. The mugs were cracked. The coffee was instant.

'I gave up a lot in the sixties,' Michael said. 'I wasn't playing at it. I put my whole career on the line. The rest of them hadn't even started theirs. What do they know about suffering?'

'I hear Bob Francis got into trouble,' I said.

'What did he expect? The man had no discipline. I'll tell you now what I told him then. I would have backed the group with my life, I repeat—with my life—if I had agreed with and been consulted about their actions. But Bob was an individualist, pure and simple.'

'What did he do?'

'How would I know?' Michael asked. 'He didn't deign to consult me. All I know is that he was taken away in the middle of the night. When he got out, he acted even odder than usual. Wouldn't speak to any of us. As a matter of fact the other day I tried to contact him about a piece I was writing on working-class culture and he slammed the phone down on me.'

'Have you got his address?' I asked.

'I thought you were investigating Paul Holland's death,' Michael said. 'The faker.'

'Did you know him?'

'I consulted him once. Or attempted to. I was writing a paper on psychopathology and socialisation. Paul dabbled in the field and so I went to see him. Pure waste of time. The man was not only anti-theory, he was downright rude about it. I cannot tolerate those who use their own ignorance as an excuse for rampant anti-intellectualism. I know it's fashionable to criticise structuralism but surely one should do so from a standpoint of knowledge. Paul

Holland hadn't even read Foucault, never mind understood him.'

'And you know nothing about his death?'

'Only that it happened,' Michael said. He picked up his cup and rose from his end of the sofa. He stood in front of me. 'I think you've used enough of my valuable time,' he said.

I gave him my cup and followed him out of the room. On the way to the door he dropped off in the kitchen and riffled through some papers which were piled by the phone.

'Must have thrown Bob's number out,' he said. 'Sorry. You know the way out.'

I left him there. As I went he poured the two full cups of coffee down the sink. Then he took out a cup and saucer and turned to one of the gleaming tile surfaces where a full coffee pot was percolating.

Nothing seemed to have changed at *Street Times*. Tony was in the same position I'd last seen him in, except he looked twice as gloomy.

'How was Lothian?' I asked.

'Council politics,' he muttered. 'Don't they understand where the real power is? They'll never get anywhere. And you didn't return my call.'

'Something came up,' I said.

'Lucky you,' Tony grumbled. 'All I come up with is help for other people.'

He reached across his desk and began fumbling in the middle level of his in-tray. Sheaves of paper came tumbling out. Tony cursed and used both hands to sort through them. Eventually he found a scrap of paper which he handed to me. It bore a man's name and a telephone number.

'Take this,' Tony said. 'He knows something about Paul Holland.'

'Graham,' I said. 'Has he got a surname?'

'Let your fingers do the dialling,' Tony said. 'That way you'll find out.'

I removed some cuttings from the chair opposite Tony and sat down. 'What's the matter?'

Instead of answering Tony pulled a pack of Woodbines across his desk and stuck one of them into his mouth. He lit it, took a drag and then coughed. He couldn't stop coughing. I got up and walked to his side of the desk and slapped him on the back. After a while the coughing subsided.

'I'd start on Silk Cut if I were you,' I said.

Tony stubbed the Woodbine in an ashtray already brimming over with barely smoked cigarettes.

'Look at me,' he said. 'Not even grown up enough to smoke. I'm not ready. How can I have a baby?'

'Caroline's pregnant?'

'So she told me this morning.'

'And you're terrified?'

Tony reached for the packet and pulled out another Woodbine. He looked at it, then threw it away in disgust.

'Not only,' he said. 'Maybe it'll be good. But I'll be a terrible father. What should I do?'

'Stop smoking,' I said.

'Actually I want a baby. It's my article that's giving me the trouble.'

I nodded.

'I mean it's about time, isn't it?' he said.

Again I nodded.

'How's your investigation going?' Tony asked.

'I'm not sure,' I said. 'Ever heard of a Bob Francis?'

This time it was Tony's turn to nod.

'A while back,' he said. 'He was picked up on a so-called anti-terrorist raid by the men in blue. They wrecked his house and then never charged him.'

'What was their excuse?'

'They said he was implicated in a bombing of a police computer centre. Those were heavy days. Everybody was free. And single.'

A faraway look crept into Tony's eyes. He picked up a pencil and began scrawling on some paper in front of him.

'Maybe I could write a piece on it,' he said. 'The sixties recaptured. Could make a splash.'

'Everybody's doing it,' I said.

'Can't be wrong then,' Tony said. He smiled. His eyes still hadn't come back. I left him sitting there.

There was a familiar figure waiting on the pavement when I got out of the *Street Times* office. It was Sam.

'Saw you going in,' he said. 'Thought I'd say hello.'

I felt confused. I couldn't think what to say. 'Caroline's pregnant,' I ventured.

'So there is some commitment in the world,' Sam said.

'What do you mean?'

Sam kicked his shoe against a lamppost. He looked down.

'Forget it,' he said. 'Just a cheap point.'

There was a silence between us. After a while I tried for a smile and he tried to imitate it. Neither of us was successful.

'How are thing . . .' I started.

'I thought you'd phone,' Sam said simultaneously.

Our words sprang from our mouths and clashed in the space between us.

'I tried,' I said. 'You were engaged.'

'Some try,' Sam said. 'A friend of Marcus Jones did manage to get me, difficult as it obviously is. Here's her address. See you.'

He thrust a note into my hand and walked away from me, his head bent. I stood there and watched his misery retreating. I thought about calling after him but I couldn't find the words.

I walked to the nearest telephone box and waited outside while a man used the telephone to lean on as he thumbed through a crumpled *Evening Standard*. He looked like he was waiting for a call that was never going to come. Eventually he got bored, folded his paper carefully into three segments and opened the door. He threw me a long cold stare before he walked off. I think it had something to do with tears that were congealing on my face. I wiped them away, went inside and dialled the number Tony had given me. A man answered on the second ring.

'Graham?' I said. 'Tony gave me your name.'

'Can't talk,' the man said. 'Do you want to meet?'

I told him I did and then I stood around while he made up his mind about something. It took an age and another ten-pence piece before he gave me an address and a time. He told me to wait by the third lamppost in a street in Kentish Town. He also said that if he didn't turn up within five minutes I should walk away. While he was issuing the instructions his voice got lower and lower. By the end it was all I could do to catch his muttered goodbye before he hung up abruptly.

The address Sam had given me wasn't far from where Marcus's parents lived. The woman who answered the door was Marcus's friend.

'Thanks for coming,' she said. 'Let's go upstairs.'

I followed her up the uncarpeted stairs and into a small flat. It was barely furnished but spotless and cared for with love. By the wall a gas fire burned slowly, adding heat to the English summer. Above it on the mantelpiece stood a framed picture of the woman holding a baby.

A small vase of tulips stood on a low side table. The girl from the picture, now grown to five years old, was crouching by the table, drawing. She gave me a radiant smile when I went to look at her picture.

'That's my mum,' she said, pointing to a stick figure that towered above a narrow house. A bright yellow sun looked like it was about to fall into the figure's shock of hair. The figure reflected the sun's warmth in her mouth, which was drawn so its upwards curves covered a full half of her moon face.

The girl got bored with me and returned to her drawing. She picked up a blue pencil and began to fill the sky with birds whose huge claws bore no relation to the size of their feet. I looked at the woman. She seemed far from happy.

'I never got your name,' I said.

'Carmen,' she said. 'My parents were Harry Belafonte fans. Thanks for coming.'

She heard the repetition as soon as it came out of her mouth. She gave a self-deprecating grimace and pointed to a chair. I sat down and looked about the room some more while she fixed me a drink. It came in a tall decorated glass and on its surface floated pieces of lime. I took a sip.

'Delicious,' I said.

'My mum's the best cook in the world,' the girl said. She got up from the table and gave Carmen a long, sloppy hug. Then she picked up her drawing and left the room.

'Marcus's parents asked me to speak to you,' Carmen said. 'They want you to stop investigating his death.'

'Oh?' I said.

'It's Mr Jones. He was in a rage the day Marcus was killed and he wanted to take action. But doing that doesn't come easy to a man who's always put up with his life. Now his anger has given way to grief he feels that it's the police's job and he shouldn't be interfering. Marcus's mother tried to argue with him but he's so fearful and so upset, she gave in. They want you to stop.'

'I see,' I said.

'But I don't,' Carmen continued. 'I want to know who killed Marcus. I want my revenge.'

'I might never find out.'

'You can try. We can try.' A look of fierce determination crossed her face but it was replaced by something less certain. There was a pause before she spoke again.

'I can't pay you,' she said.

'That wouldn't matter. But I still might not succeed. Marcus's death is connected with Paul Holland's. Which leads back to a group of people. I can't make any sense of it yet.'

I told her what I'd learned about Paul Holland and the group of six. She listened intently, only stopping me when she needed clarification. None of the people's names meant anything to her. None except Terry's, and when I told her about my encounter with him and his friends she frowned. When I finished, she spoke.

'Terry's disappeared,' she said.

'But I saw him today.'

'He took off afterwards. I tried to look him up this afternoon. Nobody knows where he is. And it being Terry, nobody cares.'

'Do you think something's happened to him?' I asked.

'I think he's scared. Courage was never one of Terry's major attributes. He knows something and he doesn't want to tell. I'll find him.'

I looked at her face as she spoke. I didn't have any doubt that, if Terry was alive to be found, she would do it.

'I'll look tomorrow,' she said. 'After I've taken the kid to school.'

As she'd been talking a smell had wafted from on top of the stove. Carmen noticed how my nose kept catching it.

'Would you like something to eat?' she asked.

She got out a plate and spooned some lamb curry and a portion of rice and beans on to it. She sat me down at the table and watched while I ate with appreciation. Her daughter was right: Carmen was a pretty good cook and I told her so.

She smiled while I finished the food. Not many words passed between us, but I felt a peace I hadn't experienced in days. Carmen laughed when I told her so.

'Sounds like man trouble,' she said. 'He does have a brisk phone manner.'

It was time for me to be going. We agreed to keep in touch. On the way out her daughter accosted me in the hall.

'Come and see what I done,' she said.

I went into her bedroom and followed her pointing finger. The picture she'd been drawing was stuck up crooked on the wall with blobs of Blue-tack showing through it. It had been placed next to a whole series of pictures of the same stick figure standing by narrow houses.

'That's lovely!' I said.

'It's not straight,' she said. 'Bye.'

Dusk was falling when I reached the right lamppost in the right street. There was nobody beside it. I checked my watch and found I was ten minutes early. Lolling around a lamppost earned me some odd looks, so I took a walk around the block.

The inmates of the small terraced houses were enjoying the evening's warmth. They sat about on their doorsteps exchanging gossip on the latest street disturbance. Everywhere there was a feeling of togetherness. A feeling from which I was completely excluded.

I went back to the lamppost and waited. Five minutes past the deadline nobody had appeared. I walked away from it.

I'd walked about fifty yards when I heard the sound of footsteps behind me. I didn't take much notice. Instead I turned right down a long narrow road. The footsteps followed. I walked faster. So did the person behind me.

The area that had seemed so full of life was now devoid of it. Doors were closed while families stayed inside to eat together. Occasionally the sound of what the TV moguls call light entertainment drifted into the street. That, the footsteps behind me and the sound of my own breath, were the only company I had.

I turned round to take a quick look. I was being followed by a man I'd never seen before. I quickened my pace again, trying hard not to panic. It wasn't easy. The road stretched in front of me; the footsteps behind echoed in the empty space. I decided the time had come to run. On an optimistic reckoning, I might just make it to the tube.

At that point a hand gripped my shoulder. I turned round with as much bravado as I could muster and made my hands into fists. I found myself facing a man, height about five foot nine, short brown hair and a scar above his left eyebrow. A frown wrinkled his forehead and made the scar an ugly red.

'What do you want?' I asked.

'Making sure you weren't followed,' he said. 'I'm Graham. Follow me.'

He turned on his heels and walked back the way we'd come. He didn't bother to check on me, he just walked, intent on his destination.

It took about eight minutes, and three crooked turns down side streets before he was satisfied. He reached into his pocket and took out a key which he used to unlock a gate, embedded in a tall wooden fence. He stood aside to let me pass.

I was facing a narrow passageway that led to a courtyard and then to the back door of what looked like a long-abandoned house. Ivy clung to its walls and pushed its way through the windows.

Everywhere the plant life was dominant. On one side of the passage a climbing rose was protesting its neglect by spreading. Its dark red pulpy flowers drooped against each other, defeated by a white powder that crept on them. Willowherb competed with the rose for the light. They stood tall, in their prime, their purple flowers jutting out.

'Hurry up,' the man said. 'We can't be seen.'

'What's the security for?' I asked.

'Paul Holland got killed, didn't he?' the man said, shutting the gate firmly behind him. It made a loud noise as its catch fell into place.

The man took a step towards me but when he noticed me shrink backwards, he held up his hands, palms open.

'I'm a friend,' he said. 'I have some information for you.'

He walked up the path, kicked some bottles lying by the broken door, and went into the house. I followed him. When I got there the man was sitting on a broken-down chair he'd arranged so its three legs were supported by the wall. The room was worse than the garden. On one wall water dripped from a tap through a hole in a mouldy sink and on to the floor. The moss underneath the sink looked like it was enjoying the gift. Scattered about the floor, competing with the moss, were newspapers, old tins and empty cider and sherry bottles.

'One of my students showed me this place,' the man said. 'Winos use it when it rains. Take a seat.'

He pointed across from him to an orange crate. I sat on it.

'Name's Graham Parsons,' he said. 'I'm a teacher.'

'GP' I said, almost to myself. 'What do you teach?' I asked in a louder voice.

'Policemen,' he said. 'I teach at the college. Social studies.'

I looked at him.

'I needed a job,' he said. 'Just out of teachers' training school and they invented falling rolls. I looked everywhere and then these hours came up—teaching liberal studies to trainee policemen. It wasn't what I wanted but I kidded myself that I could, if not enlighten, then at least influence in a small way. I thought I could produce a true breed of community policemen.'

'You chose the wrong decade,' I said.

'If not century,' he replied. 'It's proved impossible. Education doesn't work in a vacuum.'

'So you left?'

'No,' he said. 'I persevered. I brought in outside teachers thinking it would help. That's how I met Paul Holland.'

'He taught at the college?'

'He gave a few lectures. The authorities were keen to have him. I thought it was my influence, getting some progressive ideas across to the boys. I soon learned that the powers that be in the police force need to move with the times. Psychological assessments they call it. Cultural differences and all that. It's another way of learning about force.'

He got a faraway look in his face. He touched the scar above his eye with his right hand and worried at it.

'So Paul Holland taught there,' I prompted.

'Only a couple of times. The first time he gave a general introduction to therapy and its techniques. He went through gestalt, bio-energetics, psychotherapy, the lot.'

'Was it popular?'

'Hardly,' he said. 'It was part of an optional course. Only two students turned up. But the second time was different.'

'How?'

'He said he'd thought of a method of getting their attention. He made me advertise in advance. He chose as his topic the psychology of the terrorist. It couldn't have been better. The room was packed. And Paul seemed to know his stuff. He talked about the people as if he'd met them. He had it all, their family backgrounds, their fears, their hates, their motives.'

'And then what happened?'

'Nothing,' he said. 'Paul was applauded, congratulated and paid. The next thing I heard about him was that he was dead.'

'Why are you telling me this?' I asked.

The man looked down at his fingernails. They didn't pass muster. He lifted his left hand to his lips and began to chew on one of his fingers. 'My old friends won't talk to me,' he said. 'They think I've sold out.'

He changed fingers and looked straight at me. 'I'm only doing a job,' he pleaded. 'They're my students. How can I refuse to socialise with them?'

'It's your choice,' I said.

'Who has free choice with all this unemployment? It's only a job but I'm called a collaborator. I walk into the pub and people back away. Specially black people.'

'Tough,' I said.

'It's a terrible strain and I tell you I'm not the only one that suffers from it. We have young lads, working-class boys, whose whole self-image deteriorates.'

'What happens to them?'

'They're sent to analysis.'

'To anybody in particular?' I asked. I got off the orange box and stood by the door. Graham Parsons carried on biting at his nails.

'A Dr Greenleaf,' he said. 'Nice man. You better go first. I'll follow in a while.'

I left him there amongst the wreckage of what was once a home.

The phone was ringing when I put the key in the door. I opened it, threw my bag on the floor and made a grab for the phone. By the time I reached it the ringing had stopped and all I heard was the dialling tone.

I went into the kitchen and fixed myself a vodka and tonic. I was just about ready to drink it when the phone rang again. It was Tony.

'Sorry about today,' he said. His voice had come out of the gloom and into the light. I could hear smoochy music playing in the background.

'You had your troubles,' I said.

'Caroline's got her period,' Tony said.

'And you're celebrating.'

'We both are. We've decided to have a baby. Today persuaded me that it won't be so bad.'

'Congratulations.' I tried to make my voice match his joy but I didn't succeed.

'I heard about you and Sam,' Tony said. 'Are you sure you're doing the right thing? You always seemed so happy together. And that's a precious gift.'

'Watch it Tony,' I said. 'You're getting downright sentimental and the child's not even conceived yet.'

'Easy remedy for that,' Tony said. A sound of scuffling came down the phone followed by Caroline's giggles.

'I'd better leave you to it,' I said.

'Hold on,' Tony said. 'I phoned to find out what you thought of Graham.'

'Couldn't work him out. What motivates him?'

'It's a unique case,' Tony said. 'Not so much liberal guilt as reactionary *angst*. I think he's been passed up for a permanent job and is taking his revenge by telling all. He doesn't seem to know much.'

'He helped,' I said.

'I did some research for you this afternoon. I looked into the Bob Francis case. He was picked up after the police computer in Henley was bombed. Not much damage but the break-in was what really worried them. They never found out who did it but Bob must have had a great alibi because they weren't too coy about framing people to clear their books. Practising for the IRA.'

'Do you know how I could get hold of Bob Francis?' I asked.

'He's disappeared from circulation,' Tony said. 'Rumours are that he's gone completely straight. Nobody seems to know anything about him. And now, I better go back to my Caroline.'

The 'my' was said with a pride and possession that echoed down the phone. We said goodbye and I hung up. I looked at my empty kitchen. I took the vodka and went into my living room. I put an Al Green album on the stereo but when 'I didn't know' came on I had to turn it off. I sat for a while in the silence. It had been a long day. I was exhausted. I left the drink where it stood and went to bed.

The room no longer seemed important. It was both so familiar and so irrelevant to the interaction inside it, that the two women could have been stranded anywhere. And yet stranded was not the right way to describe it. For there was movement in the room, a movement which, even though it did little to disrupt the stillness, was fundamental.

'I've learned a lot,' Kate said.

'And I too,' Franca answered.

Kate looked surprised. She opened her mouth to interject but instead she looked across to the other chair. She took in the seriousness of the face and the gentleness within. And she believed the statement.

One solitary tear journeyed down her face, softening the skin as it passed.

'It's a sick world,' she said. 'I finally learn to love and accept you and the answer is to leave.'

'You can always come back,' Franca answered.

'That's not the point. Why give up what I've gained?'

'Because you're not giving it up. You hold it inside you. You can carry me and our relationship with you.'

'Sounds like another form of loneliness,' Kate said.

'In many ways we are all alone.'

'As long as I don't cut off from it, like I used to. Pretend not to need,' Kate said.

'Don't make life too difficult for yourself. Nobody is perfect. You may find that these feelings come and go. You may find yourself doing things you thought you'd left behind. But remember what you've learned, and, more important, feel it. And you can always come back.'

'Same time next week then?' Kate asked.

Franca smiled: a long slow smile that filled her face and the room with it.

They both rose together.

They walked towards the door.

And then they both stopped. They turned to each other and in silence they hugged each other, long and hard. When they parted there were tears in their eyes.

Kate squeezed Franca's hand and then quickly left the room.

Eight

I was fast asleep when the doorbell rang. I opened one eye. A soft light was coming through a crack in the curtain. I reached for my watch. It felt like dawn: in fact it was seven-thirty a.m.

The bell rang again.

'Go away,' I muttered to myself and turned in my bed.

The bell carried on, hard and insistent.

Cursing, I got out of bed. I pulled on my dressing-gown and stumbled to the door. I picked up the doorphone and muttered into it.

A woman's voice, bright and cheery, responded. The voice sounded familiar but it was distorted by the cables. I couldn't be bothered to ask again so instead I pushed the entry buzzer.

She didn't take long to reach my door. She had a strong, sprightly step, which like the voice seemed curiously familiar. Fully awake now I stood by the door and watched.

I wasn't prepared for the surprise. When she rounded the corner and came towards me I felt my jaw drop. She smiled, a wide, friendly, familiar smile.

'Anna,' was all I could manage.

She bounded up the last stairs and hugged me.

'Anna,' I said again.

'Right first time,' she said. 'Let's have coffee. I've been on a plane all night.'

She propelled me into the flat and towards the kitchen. She sat me down and I watched while she moved surely round the room, getting out cups, putting the milk into a jug and scooping the coffee into the filter.

Her energy took over as I watched. Within minutes she'd laid the table with an assortment of cheeses, and some black rye bread. She put a plate and knife down in front of me.

'I'm starving,' she said. 'God knows why. It's two in the morning for me.'

'What are you doing here?' I asked.

Anna smiled and sat down opposite me. She buttered a slice of bread and spread some ripe Camembert on it.

'Thought you'd never ask,' she said, and took a large healthy bite.

'Anna.' I heard the anger in my own voice and I stopped myself.

Anna put the bread down. She looked at me. The smile was still there but it was mixed with something else—a sense of friendship and some pity. I didn't think I could stand it. I felt the tears well in my eyes. She reached across the table and grasped my hand.

'I told you,' she said. 'If you need me, just call.'

'But I didn't,' I said.

'Come on, Kate. I'm your friend. I heard the call despite the words—or lack of them.'

It was like a weight was suddenly lifted. I was no longer alone. But more important, for the first time in a long while, I realised how alone I'd been feeling.

'You did this for me?' I asked. 'You, the plane hater of all time?'

'You're more important than that,' Anna said. 'Anyway it's probably good therapy for me. I spent all the time worrying that I should have come earlier and didn't get a chance to think we were going to plummet from the skies.'

'What did you think I would do?'

'Self-destruct,' Anna said. 'Was there a chance?'

I nodded and then the tears came. They came strong and fast and they came as more of a relief than I would ever have expected. Anna waited them out and when they were finished we talked about what had happened. We talked about Sam and about Franca and about Anna leaving town. We talked about my past and my future. In between that we talked about nothing—a healing, glorious nothing.

I was human again, when the phone rang. I picked it up gaily.

'I found Terry,' Carmen said.

'Alive?'

'Just about. He's scared to death. He was hiding out with a friend.'

'Can I see him?'

'He says he has to sign on and take care of some other business. After that he'll come and see you.'

'We won't lose him again?'

'We sure won't,' said Carmen, 'because he's not going out of my sight. See you at six-thirty.'

I said goodbye and I hung up.

When Anna came back into the room, she was wearing the cotton jacket she'd arrived in.

'Where are you going?' I asked.

'Home,' she said. 'I need some sleep. And you have work to do.'

I stared at her incredulously.

'You've come all this way, and you're going home now?' I asked.

Anna nodded. She held up a couple of film cans that were lying beside her.

'Got to get these to Pinewood,' she said. 'That's where the fare came from. I sneaked in on a courier run.'

'You're going?' I asked again, incredulous.

'It's not the time, it's the quality,' she said. 'It worked didn't it?'

It was my turn to nod.

Anna gave me a last smile. She hugged me quickly. Then she was gone.

It didn't take me long to get dressed. For once in my life I went to the cupboard and reached for the right clothes first time. They turned out to be light, bright and carefree—a perfect match to my mood.

Then I went back to the kitchen. I threw the old vodka and tonic down the sink, put a leaf of jasmine into a mug and poured some hot water over it. By the time I'd got halfway through it I was ready to tackle the feast Anna had left.

I was just finishing off the marmande tomato I'd had to accompany my cheese when the doorbell rang.

Laura Maxwell and Michael Dwight slipped into my flat looking like they wanted me to know that they had better things to do with their lives.

'We have to talk to you,' Laura said.

'I was just about to make some coffee,' I said. 'Come into the kitchen.'

While I poured water into the filter, Michael and Laura sat down and followed my every move. They both wore the same expression on their faces: boredom combined with disgust. In the time it took the water to drip through the filter Laura looked at her watch three times while Michael showed his impatience by tapping his foot arhythmically on the floor. When I gave them their coffee they each took one sip and then they looked at each other.

'I think you should tell her,' Michael said.

'If you're sure,' Laura answered.

'It's for the best,' Michael said.

'She's all ears,' I contributed.

Laura put her cup down in front of her. She glared at me.

'You've caused us immense problems,' she said.

'Oh,' I said.

'And as a result I am going to have to tell you about matters best left unsaid. Michael and I were once part of a group, a secret group.'

'Oh,' I said again.

She ignored me. She was in stride now.

'There is no need to go into details. Suffice it to say that we were involved in actions that could have been interpreted as being somewhat outside of a legal framework.'

'And were they?' I asked.

'Were they what?' Laura snapped.

'Illegal.'

'We planned certain actions,' Michael said. 'That's all you need to know.'

'We have nothing to be ashamed of,' Laura said. 'Speaking, that is, for the two of us. We always saw eye to eye, didn't we?'

Michael returned the self-satisfied glance that Laura offered. For a moment the two of them stayed locked together in their common memories. By the look of it, the memories included more than a remote sexual attachment and they were wondering whether to go for a revival.

I cleared my throat.

'What about Bob Francis?' I asked. The question broke the romance.

'I'd appreciate it if you would allow me to tell you the story in my own time,' Laura said. 'We have come to tell you about Bob Francis.'

'He was an extremist,' Michael said.

'And an individualist,' Laura said.

'And a spy,' Michael added.

'Now Michael, you can't know that.'

'He was always disappearing. Specially at night. What else explains it?'

'Excuse me,' I said. 'Remember me?'

Laura opened her mouth to say something but Michael beat her to it.

'Bob Francis was involved in actions that we were never informed of. In particular he was involved in the bombing of a police computer.'

'How do you know,' I asked, 'if he never told you?'

'He was picked up for it,' Michael said.

'The police have been known to pick on the innocent,' I said.

'Why did they let him go then?'

'Because he was innocent?' I said.

'Now you're being naïve,' Michael said. 'After Bob was arrested all types of strange things happened. My mail was opened. They didn't even bother to conceal the fact: it arrived half stuck together. My telephone was tapped. And I wasn't the only person in the group to suffer that way.'

'Surely the police might have known about you without help from Bob,' I said.

'Yes,' Michael answered, 'but why then did Bob refuse to see us? Why did he refuse to say anything?'

'You have a point,' Laura said.

'And then,' Michael continued, 'two weeks ago, out of the blue, Bob contacted me.'

'You said you phoned him.'

'Let's not split hairs,' Michael said. 'As a matter of fact I was the one that dialled the number. But Bob said he'd like to talk to me. He said something was going on.'

'And?'

'And then Paul Holland was killed,' Laura said. 'My therapist.'

'What's the connection?'

'You must draw your own conclusions,' Michael said. 'All I can say is that Bob never bothered to get in touch with me to tell me what had been so important.'

'Why did he hang up on you?'

'How should I know?' Michael said. 'He always was unbalanced.'

They got up together.

'Wait a minute,' I said.

'We are busy people.' This from Laura.

'I need Bob Francis's address,' I said.

They walked together towards the door. I skirted the table and got there before them. We three stood by it, glaring at each other.

'Oh, give it to her,' Laura said. 'I have an appointment.'

Michael reached into his bulging pocket and took out a small black book. He opened it and read out an address. I stood aside and then they went out without another word.

I didn't have to go far to find Bob Francis. He was an almost neighbour of mine. He lived in a small cul-de-sac just near Dalston Junction, in one of a row of small two-up. two-down houses. I recognised him when he opened the door.

'Bob?' I said. 'I'm Kate Baeier.'

'Yeah,' he said. 'Saw you at the last cinema meeting. Come in.'

He showed me into a small living room which was packed with furniture. It was all frills with little bits of bright material decorating almost every flat surface. Ornate lace blinds shrouded the window.

'My mum goes for covering things,' Bob said when he saw me look around. 'As if her life isn't crowded enough.'

'You live with her?' I asked.

'Had to,' he said, 'when I lost the last job.'

'I heard you were active in an engineering firm. What happened?'

'Got the sack. Modern style. They call it redundancy. Funny how all the most active in the union were the first to go.'

'And you weren't defended?'

'People were scared for their jobs. Can't blame them, I suppose.' He said it in a tone of voice that belied the charity of the words.

'What can I do for you?' he asked.

I thought about everything I'd heard about Bob, and I decided I'd have to play it straight. I took a deep breath.

'You've been pointed out to me as Bob Graves,' I said. 'Your surname's Francis, isn't it?'

Bob got to his feet and stood above me. He was a short man but an obviously strong one. Years of working on the line had tightened his arm muscles and given confidence to his stance.

'I'm not interested,' he said, 'whatever you're after.'

I sat where I was and looked up at him.

'I've just seen Laura Maxwell and Mich Dwight,' I said.

'I'm even less interested.'

'A man's been killed.'

'Yeah, Paul Holland. Don't go on. I'm positively bored now.'

'He's not the only one,' I said. 'A young black man, aged nineteen, name of Marcus Jones, was also found dead the other day. The police are not doing their best to discover how.'

Bob backed off from where he'd been standing and went to lean against the wall. The look of threat on his face had abated slightly, or so I thought. I wondered whether it was wishful thinking.

'What's he got to do with this?' he asked.

'That's what I'm investigating,' I said. 'I thought you might be able to help.'

He went to sit down on one of the imitation leather chairs. He took off his watch and placed it on the lace-covered table in front of him.

'You have five minutes,' he said.

'Paul Holland was murdered in Finsbury Park,' I said. 'Marcus Jones saw it happen.'

Bob nodded.

'Paul Holland was a therapist. He'd once been James Stanford's therapist. Laura Maxwell and Abbey Ashurst were also seeing him.'

'They never could separate,' he said. 'You have four minutes and twenty-five seconds.'

'You knew Paul Holland,' I said.

'That's a lie,' Bob cut in quickly.

'I have a witness,' I replied. 'His daughter. She saw you arguing with Paul.'

'So?' Bob said. 'It was my first and only encounter with the creep. Michael gave me his name. I went to check him out.'

He glared at his watch again.

'Time's marching,' he said.

'What were you arguing about?' I asked.

'I heard Paul was asking questions about things that didn't concern him—or anybody any more. I wanted him to stop. I thought he was stirring a pile of shit, old hard shit. But when I got there I realised he knew nothing—or next to nothing. Just a few names.'

'So why was he killed?'

'How should I know?' Bob asked.

'What was your group up to, so long ago?' I said.

'Action,' Bob answered, 'militant action. We thought we were changing the world. We had nowhere else to go and nothing to lose. We were, for the first time in our lives, part of something.'

His face glowed with the memory of it. Then it cooled again as he pulled himself reluctantly back to the harsh realities of the eighties.

'It's gone now,' he said. 'And so has your five minutes.'

'Paul Holland used to lecture at the police college,' I said. 'On the subject of terrorism. I think he was collecting his background information through Laura and Abbey. I found some scribblings of his that identify both of them. He was drawing up the connections.'

Bob nodded again, and the absent disinterest was gone from his face. He picked up his watch and strapped it back on his wrist.

'I think Paul Holland found something out that none of you knew. I think he pieced it together from his clients' stories. He wanted to find out more. Somebody stopped him finding out and then they killed Marcus because he knew too much.'

'Like what?'

'The person who killed Paul,' I said. 'I think Marcus and his friend Terry who was with him at the time, knew more than they told me.'

'What happened to Terry?' Bob asked.

'A friend's watching him.'

'He better be good.'

'It's a she,' I said. 'And she can look after herself. I'm seeing Terry later.'

'I'd like to talk to him.'

'Maybe you can. But first I need some answers.'

'Try me,' Bob said.

'What happened when you were picked up—what did they want?'

'You're asking me,' Bob said. 'I don't know. I didn't know then and I haven't been able to work it out since. They said it was something to do with a bombing of a police computer but that was nonsense to me. There's only one thing I can think about it.'

'Which is?'

'We were infiltrated,' he said. 'And I was picked up just to check us out. Somebody fingered me.'

'Do you know who?'

'That would be telling,' Bob said. 'I have my suspicions but don't believe in throwing accusations about with no proof. I was very angry when I was released. Refused to see any of them. But now, ten years later, it doesn't seem so heavy. We were part of a much larger movement that was threatening the state. An arrest was small beer.'

'Why did you say you wanted to talk to Michael after all this time?' I asked.

'Something happened recently. Something suspicious.'

'That connected back to those years?'

'Not really,' Bob said. 'But in a way. I have a friend who works for an engineering firm. Not the one I got the push from. He walked into the boss's office one day and saw a confidential memo. He just happened to pick it up.'

'And I assume he happened to read it?'

'As a matter of fact he did,' Bob said. 'And photocopy it. I'll show you.'

He went out of the room and came back carrying two sheets of paper. He handed them to me. The top sheet was written in normal type as a letter. 'Dear Employer,' it read,

> We at the League are delighted that you are interested in availing yourself of our services. We, like you, believe that in times like these employers have a duty to help each other to keep British industry going. We are under severe financial strain. The government is willing to help alleviate it but we must guard against another enemy: the enemy within. For this purpose we have drawn up a list of employees who, from our experience, are less than willing to pull their weight in a proper manner in a factory environment. Our current list, updated six monthly, is attached. We strongly recommend that should one of these persons apply for a job in your factory, you check carefully with their previous employers.

The letter was signed by someone with indecipherable writing. Underneath the scrawl was written one word, 'Director'. The paper was unheaded.

'A blacklisting service,' I said. 'A shoddy one.'

'Yeah,' Bob said. 'It's not new, specially in engineering. Look at the list.'

I turned to the second page. It was an A4 page, unheaded, but containing a long list of names. So many were there that the type was small—the page had obviously been reduced.

'Look under Graves,' Bob said.

I did. There it was: the name Bob Graves.

'No unusual,' Bob said. 'I've always been active in the union and we don't keep involvement like that quiet. Now look under Francis.'

There it was: the name Bob Francis. It had a number beside it. I looked to the bottom of the page. There was nothing there. I shot a silent question at Bob.

'There were three pages,' Bob said. 'My friend never got time to copy the third. But he looked to see what it said.'

'I can guess,' I said.

'Alias Bob Graves.'

'How did they know?'

'That's what I wondered. I changed my name a while ago. It wasn't difficult. I couldn't get a job and so I tried the names switch and nobody ever checked on it. When I saw this I got paranoid. Thought it might be somebody from my past following me up. That's why I contacted Michael. But after I'd been to see Paul Holland and decided he was playing spy games, I thought I was also being stupid. It would only take a person in records to look at my NI number and they'd cotton on to the switch. The only thing that must have protected me up to now is the sheer inefficiency of British management. I decided I was panicking over nothing.'

'And now?' I said.

'Yes,' he said. 'Paul and Marcus. That changes things. I'll have to get involved.'

'Before we go any further, I've got a question,' I said. 'Why did the police let you go?'

'I had an alibi,' Bob anwered.

'Which was?'

'I had a part-time job as a night watchman. I never told the others, they would have laughed. I happened to be talking to the local policeman about a break-in down the road from the factory when the bombing was done.'

'I think we'd all better get together,' I said.

'I think you're right,' Bob answered.

We discussed what was the best way of doing that. In the end we agreed that Bob would ring the other five and ask them to come to my house at six. He said he'd put the pressure on. He also said they'd all be there.

That left me with seven hours to kill. I went back to my flat and looked at Paul Holland's flow chart. It didn't tell me anything I didn't already know. I ran a bath and got into it. I held my head under the water for a while listening to the amplified sounds of the pipes knocking against each other. I got out and picked a book at random from my shelves. It turned out to be a science fiction saga collected in the days when I read science fiction. I read through it, cover to cover. I didn't remember ever reading it before. When I finished it, I put it down. Five minutes later I couldn't remember what it was about. I made myself something to eat and then ate it without tasting. I picked up the phone a couple of times and dialled Sam's number. I never got to find out if he was there since each time I put the phone down before it began to ring. I tried to get myself to work out why I couldn't drop my pride and get in touch with him. No luck. I put the television on and watched the second half of an Australian soap opera. Somebody called Pamela was playing havoc with somebody else's marriage while her daughter lay dying of peritonitis. A sticky situation. It looked like whoever made the programme was going to ensure that it got stickier before it was resolved.

I learned how to balance a coin on a glass and how to toss a pancake by watching children's television. I thought I'd take the advice of the presenter and never toss a pancake without my mother being present. I also realised I didn't much care for pancakes. I switched the TV off after seeing the latest unemployment figures on the news.

By five to six I was ready for action.

Bob was the first to arrive.

'They're all coming,' he said. 'Some under protest.'

We sat opposite each other waiting for the bell to ring. Neither of us could think of anything to say.

At 6.10 Jane arrived. She and Bob greeted each other like old friends and set to talking about old times. I listened with half an ear. At 6.15 Laura Maxwell arrived. She was closely followed by Michael. I got the impression they'd come together but didn't want anybody to know.

Their presence somewhat inhibited the conversation. Soon we all lapsed into silence.

At 6.22 James Stanford turned up. He walked into the room full of confidence but three minutes in the room seemed to stunt that. I wondered whether everybody was reverting to how they'd been when they were together. All James's assurance at work seemed to crumble in the face of the past.

'What the hell's holding her up?' James said in an over-loud voice. 'She always did like to keep people waiting. Only way she could assert herself.'

'She has a child,' Jane said.

James's retort died on his lips as the bell sounded. I pressed the buzzer, went to the door and opened it. Standing on the doorstep was Carmen. She was clutching on to a terrified Terry. I put Terry in the kitchen and explained what was going on. Carmen agreed to sit and wait with him.

'He'd go out of the window as soon as my back's turned,' she said.

At that point Abbey arrived. White-faced and drawn, she sidled into the flat and into the living room. She mumbled a greeting to the others and then sat on a chair as far away from the action as she possibly could. I closed the door.

'Thank you all for coming,' I said, as soon as I sat down.

'Well, show your appreciation by making it snappy,' Michael said. 'I have another appointment.'

'Can it, Michael,' Bob said to him. 'We all know you're important.'

I interrupted before Michael could reply.

'The six of you hold the key to Paul Holland's death,' I said. 'And to Marcus Jones's. You're all here so we can work out what it is. To do that we have to go back ten years. To the time when Bob was picked up. For bombing a police computer.'

'He never told me nothing,' Michael said. It came out of the side of his mouth as if he was cracking a joke. But Bob didn't think it was funny. He slapped his fist on to the side of his chair.

'I had nothing to do with it,' he said.

'So why didn't you come back and tell us?'

'Because,' said Bob and his fist again hit at the wood, 'somebody shopped me. I have my suspicions.'

Michael went red in the face. He held his breath. He held it for a long while as if deciding on the best course of action. Then he slowly let it out and stood up.

'I will not tolerate the accusation,' he said. 'I'm leaving.'

He got two paces towards the door before Jane interrupted.

'Don't be childish,' she said. 'You can't bring your past grudges into this. You always were competing with Bob for the power. You boys at play.'

Michael wheeled around towards her.

'Don't give me any of that feminist garbage,' he said. 'Bob has as good as accused me of being a spy. My reputation is not to be sullied.'

'My, you are showing your class background,' Jane taunted. 'And I never heard you be sparing with your accusations of treason in the group.'

Michael puffed himself. He seemed to lengthen by at least six inches and his stomach slowly disappeared into his diaphragm. Who knows what further transformation would have occurred if it hadn't been for the disruption next door. There was a loud scuffling from the kitchen. I got to the hallway just in time to see the front door slam. Carmen came slowly out of the kitchen. She was using her left hand to clasp her right wrist. When she took it away I saw scratch marks which went up her arm. A trickle of blood flowed from them.

'Terry made his escape,' she said.

I rushed towards the door.

'It's okay,' she said. 'I got the information out of him. Tell you later.'

'Are you hurt?' I asked.

'Not as badly as Terry is,' she said.

We walked back into the living room, where a heavy silence had descended. Michael was back in his chair looking more like his normal shape. I introduced Carmen and she took a seat. Laura made as if to protest at her presence but gave up when the others didn't join in.

'Let's start again,' I said. 'Was any of the group planning to blow up a police computer?'

Nobody said anything.

'I take that as no,' I said. 'Was any of the group involved with anybody else who might have been planning to blow up a police computer?'

This time I got a few nos.

'Okay,' I said. 'Let's take that on trust for a minute. And let's consider the following. Police computers are valuable objects. The police know this. The police probably go as far as to make sure there is some security around their computer. I assume none of the group would have access to any such security plans.'

Carmen had leaned forward while I was saying this, and when I looked at her she shook her head. Everybody else in the room stayed still, dead still. I turned my chair so that I could get a better view of where Abbey was hiding.

'Where did you get this picture?' I said. I held up the group photo.

'I should be asking you that,' she hissed. 'Except I know—you stole it. You broke into my house and stole it. I could report you for this.'

'You could,' I said. 'Where did you get the photo?'

'What do you mean?'

'The one I stole was a negative taken off a positive,' I said. 'Where is the original?'

'You don't know what you're talking about,' she said. 'I've been taking photographs for years. That one was part of a roll of film. I never had another positive. I just developed it to see how my technique had improved.'

'Let's put it another way,' I said. 'Who took the photograph?'

'I . . .' Abbey started before she realised how ridiculous it sounded. She opened her mouth to say something else but was interrupted by one word from Jane.

'Howard,' she said.

'Howard who?'

'That's right,' Bob said. 'We never really counted him in.'

'Howard who?' I asked again.

'Just Howard,' said Jane. 'Creep who used to hang out with us. I forgot about him. Preaching schoolboy revolution and action. We couldn't get rid of him, however much we tried.'

I turned back to Abbey. Her face had blanched a whiter shade than the wall.

'Okay, Abbey,' I said. 'When did you get the photo from Howard who has no surname?'

'I don't have to tell you,' Abbey said.

'Tell her,' Jane said.

Abbey turned a mute appeal Laura's way. Laura looked the other way.

'I don't know why you're picking on me,' Abbey said.

'Because you were having an affair with him,' I answered.

Nobody spoke. Nobody moved. Abbey kept her eyes fixed on a spot in the carpet. Her voice, when it came out, sounded defeated.

'I met him,' she said. 'Some months ago. In the street. Outside my house. It was a coincidence. He happened to be passing by.'

'Some coincidence,' James Stanford mocked. They were the first words he'd uttered in a long time and even he seemed surprised to hear them.

Abbey didn't lift her face.

'Everything's so dull,' she said, 'since the group broke up. I thought I wanted to settle down. I thought having a family would help me to feel part of the world. I was wrong.'

'So when Howard turned up you looked for excitement,' I said.

'It was a way of joining the past to the present. I couldn't talk to the rest of you.' Her eyes glanced over the other occupants of the room but they didn't register anything. 'But Howard loved going over old ground. He felt like me: that we all really had something when we were together.'

'Did you tell Paul about Howard?'

Abbey's eyes misted over. 'It was the first time Paul showed any real interest in me. He couldn't get enough of asking about Howard. He said it all made sense—he kept on talking about the missing link.'

'Was Howard interested in Paul as well?' I asked.

'We never discussed him. We talked about the old days. That's why I was copying the picture Howard had although he'd lost the negative. He said it was his only memento.'

'What else did he say?'

'That the group had never taken him seriously. That he did something which proved his capabilities but then everything went wrong.'

'Something like bombing a police computer,' Bob said. 'Everything like my arrest.'

'But how would he have got in?' Michael said. 'Given all the security shit Kate's been educating us in. He was an ineffectual guy.'

It was at this point that Carmen chose to speak.

'I think it's time to tell you what Terry is afraid of,' she said. 'Paul Holland was killed by a policeman. Marcus had been harrassed by him the week before and recognised him. A plain-clothes cop.'

'Howard?' Laura asked. It was a question spoken to the air.

'Terry doesn't know his name,' Carmen said. 'It's not the sort of thing you ask cops. And if I know Terry he won't be seen for dust from now on. We have no way of finding out.'

'I have a way,' I said. 'I'd better go and see somebody. Let yourselves out.'

Edgar Greenleaf opened his door within seconds of my ringing at it. He showed his surprise by a slight twitch of his lips.

'Ms Baeier,' he said. 'I'm afraid I do not consult after hours.'

'I do,' I said. 'And I'd advise you to see me.'

I pushed past him and into the hallway. He didn't move from the door.

'I can see you're in a state of some considerable distress,' he said. 'I can put you in contact with our emergency service.'

'I'll put you in contact with somebody else,' I said. 'Like your professional body. You can explain to them about Howard.'

His face registered nothing, but he did close the door.

'Could we please conduct this conversation in a civilised manner,' he said, 'not in the hall. I try to spare my family the rigours of my work.'

He led me into the room I'd visited before. I thought about making a break for the comfortable chair but decided it would only drown me. I sat on the rickety one instead.

'You see policemen,' I said.

'I treat them,' he said.

'Howard is one of them.'

'You must know that in my profession one cannot break a confidence of the patient,' he said.

'Howard's a killer,' I said.

Greenleaf laughed. The sound filled the room. He laughed for a long time, holding his sides. When he finished I looked at him. His face was an unamused blank.

'Give me some credit for years of experience,' he said. 'Howard couldn't hurt a fly.'

'He killed Paul Holland,' I said. 'Somebody saw him.'

For the first time a real expression registered on Edgar Greenleaf's face. It was an expression of panic, sheer unadulterated panic.

'It was fantasy,' he blustered, 'pure fantasy.'

'The person who saw him is dead,' I said.

I could have sworn that this time Greenleaf was feeling relief. He made as if to get up.

'There was another witness,' I said. 'And he is well and truly alive. And planning to stay that way.'

Greenleaf sank back in his chair. 'What do you want from me?' he asked.

'Howard's address.'

'I cannot release that,' he said.

'But can you stop him killing?'

'My reputation,' he said. 'It was fantasy. I know it was.'

'So give me his address and pretend that's fantasy too,' I said.

Greenleaf got up and went to his antique desk. He looked through a large embossed diary. Then he tore a sheet off a prescription pad and wrote on it. He handed me the paper.

'I'll show myself out,' I said. Greenleaf nodded as if he hadn't heard me. He looked as though it would be a while before he heard anybody else.

I recognised Howard as soon as he opened the door. His hair was as short as the day he'd come to my flat posing as the estate agent. On the third finger of his right hand a large gold ring sat.

'You found out,' he sneered. 'Come in.'

He waited until I'd got inside and then he closed the door behind him. It banged with finality. It was only then that I came to my senses. I'd walked into the house of someone I knew was a killer, who'd gone so far as to kick the man he'd just run over. Who'd broken into Paul Holland's house and ripped a cushion to shreds. Who'd killed Marcus Jones because of a casual sighting.

Howard stood behind me breathing heavily. He knew what I was thinking and he was enjoying it.

'Straight ahead,' he said. 'First door on the right. Let's do this in comfort.'

My feet stepped one in front of the other while I willed them to stop. Howard prodded me in the back to make sure that I kept moving. We went into a room remarkable only for its bareness. It was furnished, but with the most inconspicuous of cheap items. Not a picture on the wall, not a book on the shelves. It was a room devoid of personality.

'Take a seat,' the man said and pushed me down.

He sat opposite me and laughed when I looked at the barred windows.

'I knew we'd meet again,' he said. He crossed his arms and leaned back in his chair, watching me. I said nothing. Nothing seemed appropriate.

'You recognised me from my visit to your house,' he said. 'I wanted to reassure myself that you were no danger. One look was enough.'

'But I found you,' I said.

'Alone,' he said.

He paused to allow the words to sink in. He smiled to himself in satisfaction. My face felt like it was on fire; my fingers were icy cold.

'You should have listened to the first wet warning,' he gloated.

'It was you in the Caledonian Road pool,' I said dully.

'The penny's dropped,' he said.

'Why?'

'Don't you listen?' he said. He showed his impatience by tapping his forefinger on his neat grey trousers. Each word he spoke was emphasised by a tap, and each time he tapped, his finger descended from a higher point. He didn't seem to know that he was doing it.

'Why did you kill Paul?' I asked.

'I didn't like him,' he said, his finger now going furiously. 'I didn't like him at all.'

'Is that a reason to kill?'

'He was in my way. He knew too much. He had to die. Like you. And your friends.'

'They used to be your friends,' I said.

The finger came down with ferocity. It stopped on his knee. He looked as if he didn't know what it was.

'They never meant anything to me,' he said. 'I didn't want them as my friends even if . . . even if . . .'

The childish sentence ended on a high note. The finger took over again.

'You were always a policeman. Even when you were with them,' I said.

'You finally got there.' He smiled. 'I was on special duties. Infiltrating the loonies.'

'And bombing computers,' I said. 'I hear your superiors weren't too happy about that.'

'The force isn't naïve,' he said. 'They knew we'd have to prove ourselves to the groups. Bombing the computer was my way of doing that.'

'I don't believe you,' I said.

Howard jumped out of his chair and stood in front of me, towering above. His face which started off as bright red, lost its blood. His words were filled with the same white anger as his eyes.

'How dare you,' he shouted. 'What do you know?'

'I know you killed Paul because he worked out that you bombed the computer. He wasn't going to do anything about it, but he wove it into his case studies. His understanding was a threat to you. So you killed him, just like you killed Marcus Jones because he recognised you. And because you killed Paul, I know that you bombed the computer without permission—either from your so-called friends or from your boss. So I asked myself, why would you go so far?'

'And what did you come up with?' His voice came from far away. He seemed mesmerised.

'That you wanted to prove yourself to the group. You wanted to belong, really belong, not just as an interloper but as a full-time member who could take risks. But it didn't work out like that, did it?'

'The group disintegrated,' Howard said. 'They just dispersed. It was okay for them, but what about me? They left me with nothing. I couldn't tell anybody what I'd done. I would have been damned by both sides. What could I have done?'

'It was a tricky situation,' I said. I tried to make my voice as soothing as possible. That was a mistake. Howard heard the honey, and it brought him back to the present.

'Who's a clever girl,' he said. 'But not quite clever enough.'

He moved nearer to me. I edged away but there was nowhere to go. The side of the sofa was pressing against me and the door was a million miles away.

'It'll be easy to kill you,' he said.

'You'll never get away with it,' he said. 'People know where I am.'

'I understand those people,' he said. 'I spent days with them. They can't do anything.'

His hands reached up to my neck. I opened my mouth. Nothing happened. I opened it again and forced myself to scream. The noise that came out was eerie. It was me but I was completely dislocated from it. It filled the room, a loud ugly panicking noise.

But not for long. One of the man's hands clamped firmly against my mouth. He hit me in the stomach with the other and the wind left my body. Then I felt his hands around my neck again.

A calm descended on me. A glorious, inexplicable calm.

'I'm dying,' I thought, as the world turned wavy in front of me. I could hear sounds of battering from outside the room.

'Funny what you imagine when you're dying,' I thought.

The next thing I knew was silence. A long calm silence. I lay there revelling in it. Then a hand reached to touch me.

I screamed and tried to get away. The sound this time was strangled. Just like me, I thought.

The hand retreated and somewhere from a long way away I heard a voice.

'It's okay, Kate,' it said. 'You're safe.'

I opened my eyes. To see Jane sitting next to me. She took my hand.

'What happened?'

'We followed you,' she said. 'Carmen, Bob and I. We thought you might be in danger.'

'Good thinking,' I said. I began to laugh. The laugh turned into a cry and the tears flooded down my face. Jane sat there, holding my hand, saying nothing. Just when the crying was ready to stop Bob Francis burst into the room.

'We've got to get out of here,' he said.

'What happened?'

'Get out of here,' he said. 'The police will be coming soon.'

Between the two of them they supported me out of the door. I noticed, in a detached kind of way, it'd been broken in.

'Not very good burglar-proofing for a policeman,' I said.

Neither of them replied. They almost carried me to my car. Carmen was sitting in it. Jane got into the driver's seat and Bob closed the door on me.

'I'll take your car back,' he said to Jane. 'I think we should separate.'

He walked towards an old VW which was crookedly parked outside Howard's house. He got into it and drove off, brakes squealing.

'Where's Howard?' I asked.

From the back Carmen spoke. 'He's dead.'

Jane drew in a breath as she pulled out.

'What happened?' I asked.

'Bob and I chased him over that wall,' Carmen said, pointing behind her, 'on to the railway line. A train was coming. We shouted at him but he didn't listen. He kept on running, right into that train.'

'He killed Marcus,' I said. 'You got your revenge.'

'Yes,' she said. 'I got my revenge.'

There were no words left.

I spent the next day in Carmen's flat admiring the pictures her child produced by the minute. I had to do it in a muted voice. My throat was bruised. I was in agony. Carmen made me soup and kept me drinking.

'Chicken soup from a Trinidadian,' she said, shaking her head. 'What next?'

'What is next?' I asked.

She sat on the bed.

'His death was reported as an accident,' she said. 'The police are saying that he was chasing the people who broke into his flat. We're all right I think.'

'You're all right,' I said.

'Your boyfriend phoned,' she said. 'He'd like to see you.'

I turned over to face the wall.

The next day I made the trip to Franca's therapy room. She was waiting by the door when I arrived. She saw the scarf around my neck and reached out and touched me lightly on the arm.

'It's all right,' I said.

'Are you sure?' she asked.

I left the question unanswered and went to the window. With my back to her I told her everything I'd learned. When I finished I turned round to face her. There were tears in her eyes.

'You did good work,' she said. 'It was too much to ask.'

'I'll recover,' I said. 'Can't go for a scarf job for the rest of my lfe. It ruins my style.'

'Sit down a minute, Kate,' she said. 'I've been thinking about you. There is something I want to say to you.'

I nodded and sat down.

'It's about what has happened to you.'

'Thought it might be,' I quipped.

'I feel responsible,' she said.

'I'm a free agent.'

'Don't push me off so quickly.'

I looked at her. I tried to smile, to reassure her. But my mouth was frozen. Like my heart.

'I mean it,' I said. 'I take responsibility for myself now. I'm no longer in therapy with you. I chose to do the job.'

'I do not deny that,' Franca said. 'But does that mean you can no longer accept help from me—even as a friend?'

The last word dropped into the space between us and I hung on to it. I breathed it in, trying it out. It felt good.

This time I managed the smile. 'Pax,' I said.

Franca smiled back. 'And more than that,' she said. 'I hope.'

All of a sudden the investigation seemed to be slipping away from me. I felt tiredness wash over me. For the first time since I'd seen her in Hyde Park I relaxed.

'I've been dumb,' I said. 'Caught on a roundabout of confusion about you and not acknowledging it.'

Franca leaned forward. She clasped her hands together. Her

voice was filled with an urgency.

'Don't be too hard on yourself.'

'What do you mean?' I asked.

I think I really knew what the answer would be but I wanted to hear it from her: wanted perhaps to hear the therapist talking before I could allow the friend to take over.

'You have been pushed to extremes. Forced to define yourself almost in opposition to me. I can imagine that the emotional toll was large. But remember, that is not failure. You survived. You haven't lost anything you didn't want to lose.'

'Sam?' I asked.

'That is for you to decide,' she said. 'I think we both know the answer. But what I am trying to say is that you are strong. Showing weakness, seeming to go backwards, doubting yourself, all these things can often be a sign of your strength. Be generous to yourself. You're doing fine.'

'I don't feel fine,' I said. 'I feel alone.'

'You're not alone,' she said.

Sam was sitting on my doorstep when I arrived home. He looked at me, a question in his eyes. Franca was right about that too, I thought—I know what I will do.

'I'm sorry,' I said.

Sam looked uncertain, unable to interpret the words. I smiled at him. He got up.

'I'm sorry too,' he said. 'I pushed too hard. You had a lot on your plate.'

I walked towards him but stopped halfway, hoping he'd take the final steps.

Ess

KU-432-174

Normandy

by

ROBERT KANE

Robert Kane is an art historian specialising in Renaissance poetry, art and architecture. He has written several guides to Italy and holidays regularly in Normandy

AA

Produced by AA Publishing

Introduction and Background

INTRODUCTION

Normandy is one of the largest regions of France and full of variety. Towards its eastern end it borders on the suburbs of Paris, and its capital, Rouen, straddles Paris's river, the Seine. Much of the Normandy coast is Paris's playground: the rich go to Deauville, with its race-course and its long, straight beach of perfect white sand, while other Parisians go year after year to their houses, favourite family hotels, chalets or caravans scattered along the

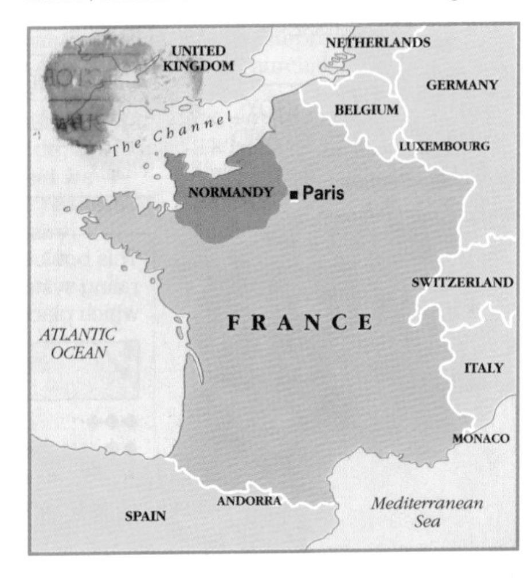

The Porte des Cordeliers in the town walls at Falaise, birthplace of William the Conqueror

almost endless coast. Here, in summer, they will mingle with visitors of every nationality, the British above all but also many Germans, Dutch, Belgians and Italians.

This is the Normandy of the old-fashioned family holiday, with all the joy of a northern temperate zone summer. Normandy caters for it brilliantly. The coast has the beaches, cliffs and harbours, the isolated, forgotten spots, the old-fashioned resorts. Even if it has no mountains, Normandy has vales and rivers, orchards and pastures, hundreds of old farmsteads, many abbeys, and more castles, *châteaux*, churches, museums and gardens than you can possibly visit.

Many of these places recall Normandy's history. For the French, this was once a wild region, outside the pale of the Ile-de-France, a land occupied by the Norsemen and not finally conquered until the second half of the 15th century. For the British it is a land of origins – birthplace of William the Conqueror, site of the Bayeux tapestry, source of the Caen stone with which many English churches were built,

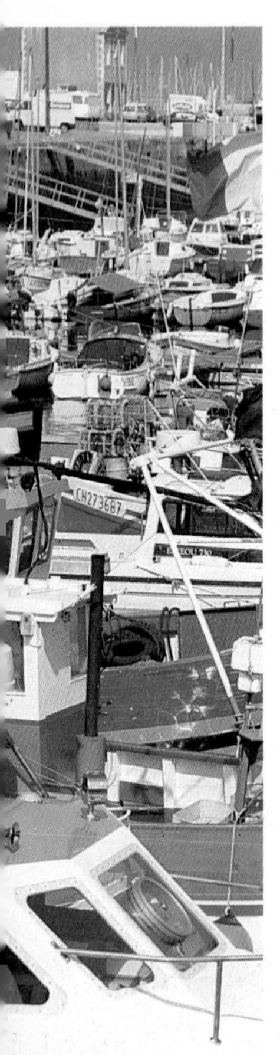

Boats at Cherbourg

and the perfect setting for towering medieval walls of the kind associated with Shakespeare's Henry V.

For other people Normandy will be associated particularly with the Impressionist painters, who came on their own family holidays to a coast made newly accessible by the railway. Many of the resorts and landmarks they painted have changed little. Despite the oil refinery at Le Havre and the industry straddling the Seine up to Rouen, despite the destruction wrought during the 1944 Allied invasion, Normandy is an unspoilt land. It has not budged from its traditions, and is more homely and hospitable than many other parts of France. Less severe and bleak than Brittany neighbouring to the west, it has much more character and variety than the dreary flats of Picardy to the east.

Normandy (Normandie) can be divided into east and west, conventionally known as Upper (Haute) and Lower (Basse). In fact, apart from the sea, it has only one strong natural boundary – the River Seine, which cleaves Upper Normandy in two and has been bridged below Rouen only in the last 20 years. Northern Upper Normandy, the administrative *département* of Seine Maritime, includes the coastal ports and resorts of Dieppe, Fécamp, Etretat and Le Havre, and has its capital at Rouen, with its historic centre on the north bank of the Seine. Known as the Pays de Caux, this is a region to itself, while the rest of Normandy – comprising the four *départements* of Eure, Orne, Calvados and Manche – extends over forest and farmland, between a dense pattern of small towns (and a few large ones), without any obvious break. Only a shallow chain of hills separates it from the Loire Valley region to the south. However, the countryside tends to become rather less lush as you go further westwards, into the *département* of Manche. The Cotentin (Cherbourg) Peninsula is wild and rugged at its northern tip, but the southern extremity of Manche is low-lying and marshy, except for the isolated rock of Mont-St-Michel. Historically, Normandy has only two capital towns, Caen (in Calvados) in Lower Normandy and Rouen (in Seine Maritime) in Upper

Normandy. Heavy industry is essentially limited to the valley of the Seine, though Caen is a steel town and a number of nuclear power-stations have been built along the coasts. There is only one motorway, the A13, which comes down the Seine from Paris, passes to the south of Rouen, and dies out at Caen, though there is dual carriageway extending to Bayeux and in patches beyond that up to the important port of Cherbourg. The rest of Normandy is not on the way to anywhere, but abounds in country roads and local traffic, shuttling between the various villages and small towns about its own business.

Normandy is almost always reached by land or sea (through the ports of Cherbourg, Caen, Le Havre and Dieppe). This has helped the region to keep its character and its own tastes, for instance in its architecture or in its food. It still serves, for instance, the kind of cream-sauce dishes that the new cuisine has driven out elsewhere, not to mention its fish and shellfish still caught, sold and eaten the same day. It has a largely land-bound or peasant population unswayed by changing fashions or the big city, though opportunistic enough to prosper.

Bathing at Trouville, 1884. Family holidays are a long-established tradition on the Normandy coast

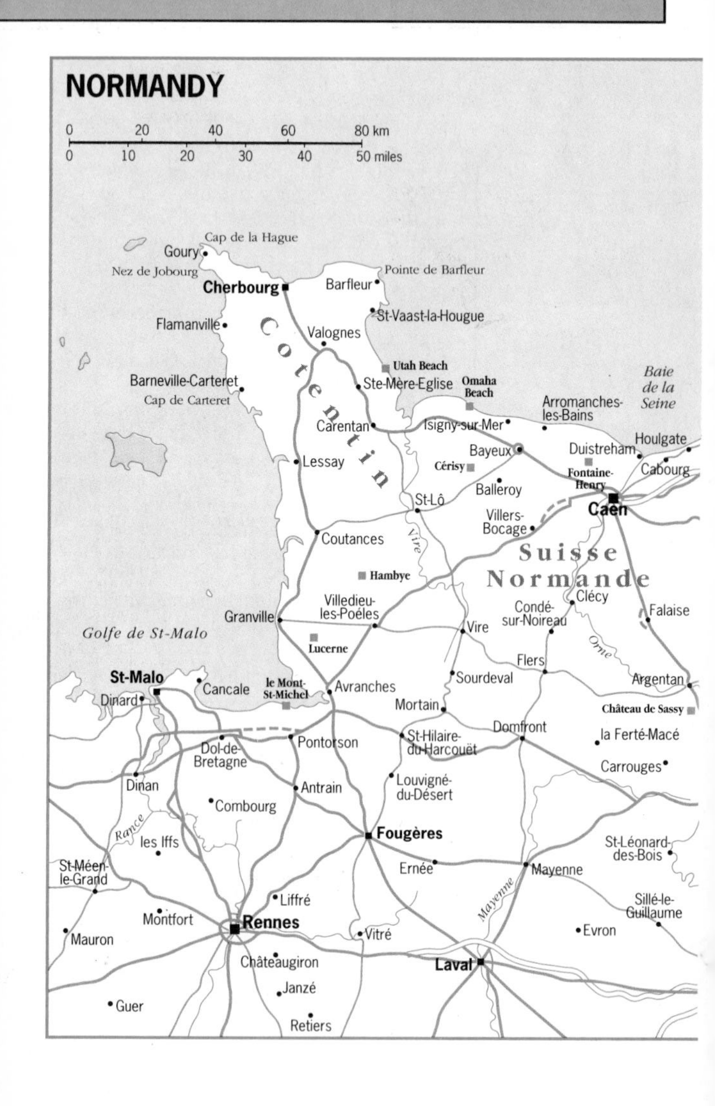
NORMANDY
0 20 40 60 80 km
0 10 20 30 40 50 miles
Cap de la Hague
Goury
Nez de Jobourg
Cherbourg
Pointe de Barfleur
Barfleur
St-Vaast-la-Hougue
Flamanville
Valognes
Cotentin
Utah Beach
Barneville-Carteret
Cap de Carteret
Ste-Mère-Eglise
Omaha Beach
Baie de la Seine
Arromanches-les-Bains
Carentan
Isigny-sur-Mer
Houlgate
Bayeux
Duistreham
Cabourg
Lessay
Cérisy
Fontaine-Henry
Balleroy
St-Lô
Caen
Villers-Bocage
Coutances
Vire
Suisse Normande
Hambye
Clécy
Villedieu-les-Poéles
Condé-sur-Noireau
Falaise
Granville
Vire
Golfe de St-Malo
Lucerne
Orne
Flers
St-Malo
Cancale
le Mont-St-Michel
Avranches
Sourdeval
Argentan
Dinard
Mortain
Château de Sassy
Domfront
Pontorson
St-Hilaire-du-Harcouët
la Ferté-Macé
Dol-de-Bretagne
Carrouges
Dinan
Antrain
Louvigné-du-Désert
Combourg
Rance
Fougères
les Iffs
St-Léonard-des-Bois
St-Méen-le-Grand
Ernée
Mayenne
Mayenne
Liffré
Sillé-le-Guillaume
Montfort
Rennes
Vitré
Evron
Mauron
Châteaugiron
Laval
Janzé
Guer
Retiers

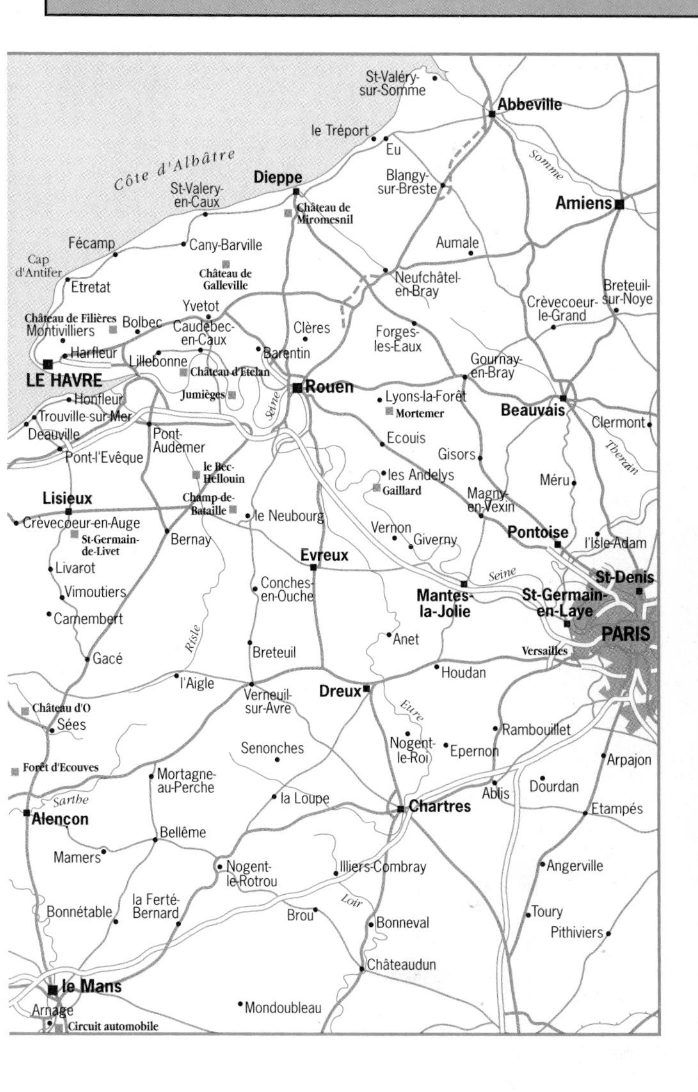
St-Valéry-sur-Somme
Abbeville
le Tréport
Eu
Somme
Côte d'Albâtre
Dieppe
Blangy-sur-Breste
Amiens
St-Valery-en-Caux
Château de Miromesnil
Fécamp
Cany-Barville
Aumale
Cap d'Antifer
Château de Galleville
Neufchâtel-en-Bray
Breteuil-sur-Noye
Etretat
Crèvecoeur-le-Grand
Yvetot
Château de Filières
Bolbec
Caudebec-en-Caux
Clères
Forges-les-Eaux
Montivilliers
Harfleur
Barentin
Lillebonne
Gournay-en-Bray
LE HAVRE
Château d'Etelan
Rouen
Jumièges
Lyons-la-Forêt
Beauvais
Honfleur
Seine
Mortemer
Clermont
Trouville-sur-Mer
Deauville
Pont-Audemer
Ecouis
Therain
Pont-l'Evêque
Gisors
le Bec-Hellouin
les Andelys
Méru
Gaillard
Lisieux
Magny-en-Vexin
Champ-de-Bataille
le Neubourg
Crèvecoeur-en-Auge
Vernon
Pontoise
St-Germain-de-Livet
Giverny
l'Isle-Adam
Bernay
Evreux
Livarot
St-Denis
Seine
Vimoutiers
Conches-en-Ouche
Mantes-la-Jolie
St-Germain-en-Laye
Camembert
PARIS
Risle
Anet
Breteuil
Versailles
Gacé
Houdan
l'Aigle
Dreux
Verneuil-sur-Avre
Château d'O
Eure
Sées
Rambouillet
Senonches
Nogent-le-Roi
Epernon
Forêt d'Ecouves
Arpajon
Mortagne-au-Perche
Ablis
Dourdan
Sarthe
la Loupe
Chartres
Alençon
Etampés
Bellême
Mamers
Nogent-le-Rotrou
Illiers-Combray
Angerville
Loir
la Ferté-Bernard
Bonnétable
Toury
Brou
Bonneval
Pithiviers
Châteaudun
le Mans
Arnage
Mondoubleau
Circuit automobile

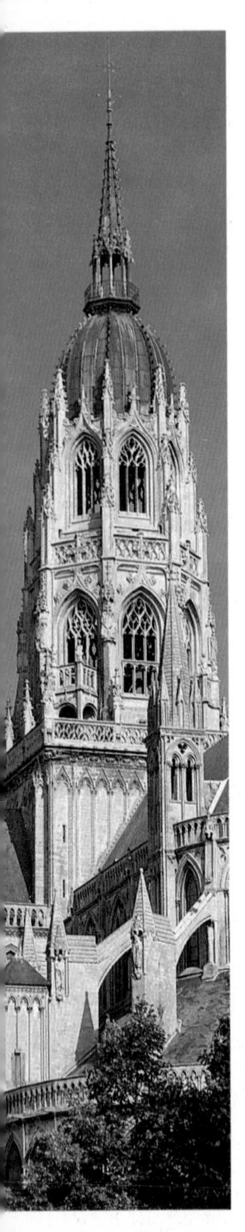

Bayeux Cathedral

BACKGROUND

Early history

Before it was Norman, Normandy was part of the vast Celtic commonwealth of 'tribes' (as the Romans called them) with close relations not only to the rest of Gaul but also across the water to England. During the Bronze Age tin from Cornwall was imported up the River Seine, but otherwise few traces remain of settlement in 'Armorica' (Upper Normandy and Brittany) before the Roman conquest. Nor is there any trace of the little Gaulish village in which the comic-strip character Astérix once lived, though it is meant to be somewhere on this coast!

Once Gaul had been conquered by Julius Caesar in the mid-1st century BC, towns were founded at nodal sites, some of which survived the Dark Ages and remain Normandy's capitals today. Rotomagus became Rouen, Caracotinum became Harfleur (now engulfed in Le Havre), Mediolanum became Evreux, Cosedia/Constantia became Coutances. Others had little posterity, for instance Juliobona (modern Lillebonne) or Noviodunum (Jublains, near Mayenne, just to the south of modern Normandy), and at these, accordingly, there is still something Roman to see. The archaeological sections of the museums at Rouen and Evreux display fragments, artefacts and models.

Normandy's Dark Ages were very dark. Scarcely a name or a legend has survived from that time between the 4th and the 9th centuries when invaders and raiders, first Saxons then Norsemen, had their will of the country, both along the coast and inland as they made their way up the many navigable rivers. Most of Normandy, of course, remained impenetrable forest. Frankish rule under Clovis at the beginning of the 6th century extended down the Seine, but reached no further westwards – however, there had been a glimmer of life at Sées (north of Alençon) under Bishop St Latuin in the early 5th century, and in the early 8th century, in the extreme west, St Aubert was induced to get up from Avranches and found Mont-St-Michel.

The Norman Achievement

The establishment of medieval Normandy was the work of Rollo, Normandy's first duke or *dux* – the Byzantine term for an autonomous military governor. In 911 he agreed with Charles the Simple of France to cease raiding beyond the Seine tributaries Epte (to the north) and Avre (to the south), which have remained the borders of Normandy ever since. Rollo, too, was the first of the Norsemen or Vikings to settle, making Rouen his capital. The early development of the dukedom of the Norsemen or *Normands* as the French called them was centred, not surprisingly, around the timeless highway of the Seine.

The 10th century, if only more were known about it, was a vital period of transformation in Normandy. More swiftly and effectively than the old Carolingian centres, the dukedom developed as an organised state and as a focus of that main vehicle of civilisation for the high Middle Ages, monasticism. While outstanding intellects of the day, such as Lanfranc from northern Italy, came here to join the flourishing abbeys, the Normans themselves set off in numbers to conquer the world. The Normans of this period demonstrated a genius for the two great requirements of the age, worship and warfare. The latter involved not just berserk Viking bravery, but strategic and technological innovations, while the former was not merely about singing and copying ancient manuscripts, but included composing and building. Above all the Normans were builders, of the new-fangled motte-and-bailey castles and of churches in a new style and technique called Romanesque.

As in the case of Bayeux Cathedral, mostly rebuilt in the 13th century, few Norman churches of the early, formative period have survived, but, as well as Lessay in the Cotentin, two great exceptions are the Abbaye aux Hommes, founded at Caen by William in the year of the Conquest, and the still earlier abbey at Jumièges on the Seine. Jumièges is itself said to be dependent on the Norman-style cathedral built at Westminster in London about 1050 by Edward the Confessor, now lost. But at Jumièges there are both signs of throwbacks to

Carolingian architecture, the Normans' starting point, and some novelties, developed more strongly at Caen.

Essentially, the Normans inherited churches conceived loosely as long halls with pierced walls, and developed instead the idea of a rigid, almost mathematical structure composed of identical repeating units. Hence early Norman Romanesque, even though massive and primitive, also has a marvellous regularity and purity.

It was the cultural and technical as much as the military prowess of the Normans that enabled Duke William (1028–1087) to conquer and to hold England. He arrived not as an adventurist but as a legitimate claimant whom the previous king, Edward the Confessor, had honoured and to whom, according to the Bayeux tapestry, he had wished to leave the throne. The Bayeux tapestry, reflecting largely Anglo-Saxon skills in depiction and narration, is itself a sign of the Norman capacity to assimilate as well as to dominate. (An account of the early Norman achievement is set out in the new museum in Bayeux where the tapestry is exhibited.) William removed most, but not all, Saxons from secular and ecclesiastical power. Despite their support for Harold, the pretender he defeated, William was able to integrate the country swiftly, as well as satisfying the hunger of his own barons.

Undoubtedly an atavistic Viking desire for plunder and glory animated the men who set sail from Dives-sur-Mer with William – a desire so strong that the conquest of England only partially fulfilled it. Since the very first years of the 11th century Normans had also been

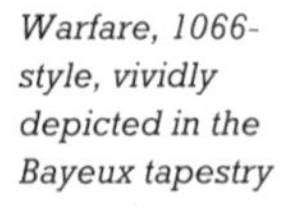

Warfare, 1066-style, vividly depicted in the Bayeux tapestry

slipping southwards, and only five years after William had won one new kingdom the landless sons of Tancred of Hauteville near Coutances had united their compatriots in south Italy and won another, with the capture of Bari and Palermo in 1071. When he died in Corfu, the great Robert Guiscard was bound for Constantinople, and his son Bohemund, architect of the First Crusade ('the little god of the Christians', as the Muslims called him), was the hero of Europe on his return from Antioch in 1104. However, there was comparatively little in common between the two kingdoms, despite the marriage of Joanna, the daughter of Henry II of England and Normandy, to William II of Sicily in 1176. The couple remained childless, and the inheritance of the Normans' 'kingdom in the sun' went to the German emperor with William II's sister Constance.

Normandy Torn Between Two Crowns

The cohesion of the two lands of England and Normandy was always difficult to sustain – William Rufus, William's successor in England, had had to reconquer Normandy from his brother Robert Curthose. Despite the efforts of kings Henry II, Richard I and John, Normandy was eventually taken from the English crown – partly with the help of its own subjects – by Philip II Augustus of France. The surviving castles in Normandy mostly date from this time of conflict, the 12th century. Many were rebuilt in stone by Henry I, then strengthened during the wars of Henry II with his own sons and with Philip Augustus, or by Richard I – who founded from new the magnificent Château Gaillard on the Seine at Les Andelys – or by Philip Augustus once he had conquered Normandy from John in 1204.

Established securely as part of France by the Treaty of Paris in 1259, Normandy joined in the general peace and prosperity under St Louis IX. From this time date its wonderful cathedrals such as those of Rouen, Bayeux, Coutances, Evreux, Lisieux – rebuildings of existing churches but in the new Ile-de-France style of Gothic. Fine though they are, however, they did not make an original contribution to the development of the Gothic style.

In the mid-14th century peace was shattered by the outbreak of the Hundred Years War, as Edward III of England claimed the French crown in 1337, and by the onset of the Black Death in 1348. For Normandy, one of the main theatres of war, this was a period of decline. Still worse was to come after the spectacular successes of Henry V, landing at Harfleur and fighting his way to a brilliant victory at Agincourt in Picardy in 1415. The two crowns were jointly settled on the infant Henry VI, and the English held Normandy, with their capital at Rouen, for the next 35 years, despite the preference of most of its people for France. Joan of Arc, the Maid of Orléans, appeared on the scene in 1428. Having persuaded the French pretender, Charles, to trust in her, she rallied the French troops and drove off the English from besieged Orléans in 1429. Further victories in the Loire Valley followed, and under their impetus Charles was crowned Charles VII at Reims. In the following year Joan was captured; she was brought to Rouen and there tried as a witch, on the two main charges of having incorrect visions and wearing male clothes. She was burnt at the stake in the Vieux Marché in Rouen in May 1431. But it did the English little good. After desultory war, the French quite suddenly rolled up the English possessions in mainland France in the years 1448 to 1450, while Henry VI's madness in 1453 and the outbreak of the Wars of the Roses in 1455 prevented any English retaliation.

The Maid of Orléans – an Italian representation

The Age of the *Armateurs*

The departure of the English heralded a new era of enterprise and prosperity for Normandy, especially for its seafaring ports. Mariners from Dieppe had already reached Africa, in the wake of the Portuguese, in the late 14th century, and in the early 16th century, led by the *armateur* Jehan d'Ango, French privateers waged successful war against these rivals. Another such *armateur*, or builder and owner of privateering ships, was Jean Le Pelletier of Rouen. Like the English, these French dogs of the sea also preyed on Spanish ships, laden with the treasures of the New World, but at the same time explored in their own right: the

Florentine Verrazzano, for example, sailed from Dieppe to discover modern Manhattan (New York) in 1524. Such enterprise was actively encouraged by King François I, who founded Le Havre in 1517, and several Normandy men had an important part to play in affairs of state at this time, notably Georges d'Amboise, cardinal archbishop of Rouen. The seafaring tradition continued well into the next century, and Honfleur had a conspicuous role in the colonisation of French Canada, Samuel de Champlain having sailed from its harbour to found Québec in 1608.

Signs of Normandy's late 15th- and early 16th-century wealth and success are abundant in its churches and in many secular buildings as well. Jehan d'Ango's country residence survives at Varengeville, near Dieppe, also Jean Le Pelletier's outside Rouen; unfortunately Georges d'Amboise's *château* at Gaillon has not fared so well. Numerous churches or chapels in the late Gothic style called Flamboyant are to be found especially in Upper (eastern) Normandy, and number some of the finest examples in all France. St-Maclou in Rouen is an exceptionally large church wholly in the Flamboyant style.

The Hundred Years War had caused an almost total disruption in architecture, and the Flamboyant style developed directly out of 13th-century Gothic. Already in the 13th century the ribs of the vault and the tracery of the windows had begun to merge to produce an overall, harmonious effect, rendered dazzling by colourful painting and stained glass. But although Flamboyant was an independent French development, it had been anticipated by the overall 'Perpendicular' style – its equivalent in England.

In earlier Gothic, ornament and structure are one; in late Gothic the decoration takes over. Although Flamboyant often seems an extreme of the Gothic style, its decorative nature actually made the penetration of Italian Renaissance forms much easier. These start appearing at the very end of the 15th century, in the wake of the French invasions of Italy. They were assimilated easily also because the Italian influence came not from the heart of the

Château d'Anet

classical Renaissance, in Florence and central Italy, but from the north, around Milan, which the French ruled from 1500 to 1521. Where a quite different, highly ornate, crowded style was favoured, you could say that the French simply exchanged one form of incrustation for another. Fine examples of Early Renaissance architecture are to be seen especially in the old government buildings and *hôtels* at the centre of large towns in Normandy.

However, by the middle of the 16th century a more profound change had taken place, represented by the *château* at Anet on the very eastern edge of Normandy, by Philibert de l'Orme. Indeed Anet is almost a suburb of Paris, and from this period Normandy reverted to a reflection of the styles decided by an increasingly centralised government. Not that the royal government remained indifferent to Normandy. Two initiatives by Louis XIV's minister Colbert are worth noting: the building of the Vieux Bassin harbour at Honfleur, and the establishment of a lace-working industry at Alençon. Also, Rouen and Le Havre continued to exploit their excellent trading positions, and in Rouen significant industries in both textiles and in faïence were established during the Ancien Régime.

The vernacular tradition of building in timber was not affected, even though Normandy is not short of fine *châteaux* in stone built or rebuilt over the 17th and 18th centuries.

Extraordinarily enough, half-timbering has remained common up to the present day. To some this may seem artificial and false, but there is no doubt it helps to keep alive the Normandy sense of tradition – one of its strongest points.

Beaches, Railways and Aesthetes

The Revolution was not well received in conservative Normandy, where the so-called Chouan resistance continued throughout the 1790s. 'Chouan' derives from the Norman French for owl: supposedly a call imitating an owl was used as a signal by the royalist peasants. But with the 19th century there came increasingly rapid changes. The growth of Paris brought new prosperity to the farming regions of Normandy, and the development of deep-sea fishing imparted new life to its ports, notably Fécamp. At the same time certain towns and ports became favourite residences of eminent persons, for instance Louis-Philippe, who spent much time at Eu in the northeastern Bray region, and was visited there by Queen Victoria. Dieppe became a favourite haunt of English high society, despite the presence for a year or so of Oscar Wilde, who died there a social leper in 1900.

However, resort Normandy was really a product of the railways, which after the mid century rendered holiday breaks to the seaside feasible and fashionable for a much larger number of people. With its spacious beaches, pleasant breezes and atmospheric fishing ports, the Normandy coast was an ideal refuge during the hot summer months for those condemned to wear Victorian clothes. The paintings of the Honfleur artist Eugène Boudin document life and times on the promenades that began to be built, particularly along the Côte Fleurie, at that time – Cabourg is the most remarkable example of a complete Edwardian resort complex, but many other Normandy resorts still have glittering Second Empire casinos.

Above all, Normandy in this period will be known through the paintings of the Impressionists, either because, like Manet and Monet, they belonged to the class that took their family summer holidays in Normandy anyway, or because their chosen subject matter was now, with the revolution that was overtaking art, typical scenes of contemporary life – in which going to the seaside ranked high. Their own seaside still ranks high with the French, whose schools have long summer holidays that render package holidays in more exotic places impracticable. Many Parisians own houses in Normandy to which they have been coming now for generations. Modern resort Normandy has also been well documented in French films from Truffaut to Blier, and, above all, Louis Malle.

Not only the visual artists but also writers recorded the recreations of 19th-century Normandy. That does not include the sardonic

Gustave Flaubert, a native of Rouen, who instead wrote of bourgeois life inland (*Madame Bovary*), but Victor Hugo wrote a famous lament over a boating accident at Villequier on the lower Seine. At the end of the century Marcel Proust often camped in the Grand Hôtel at Cabourg, where he wrote some of *A la Récherche du Temps Perdu* (*Remembrance of Things Past*). He also created a synthetic picture of an Impressionist painter in the figure of Elstir, and depicted the new spell that Norman Romanesque architecture had begun to exert in his descriptions of 'Balbec' church.

Gustave Flaubert (1821–80)

The Battle of Normandy

During the summer of 1942, Allied military planners began to envisage the re-invasion of Europe, following the disastrous 1940 British retreat from Dunkirk. An important preliminary to the D-Day invasion on 6 June 1944 was an unsuccessful commando raid on Dieppe and nearby points in August 1942. This convinced the masterminds of 'Operation Overlord' that it would be costly, if not futile, to attempt to capture any existing port.

It was decided to opt for a beach landing, which would be supported by artificial harbours (the so-called Mulberry harbours), towed out and anchored behind the invasion force. Normandy's flat, sandy beaches were ideal for the purpose. Much of the purpose-built new technology worked well, though subsequent fighting was hard. Of course, there were mistakes and tragedies, as the numerous cemeteries reveal, but the Allies managed in many cases to land without heavy loss.

Damage to the towns and villages of Normandy was substantial, however, and the ravages of the Invasion are still evident in the many places that were gutted of their historic buildings. Reparation was not always attempted, and resulted in some eyesores.

Also much in evidence, and highly evocative, are the many museums of the Invasion – to be found in Caen, Bayeux and at many sites along the coast. Their dioramas, films, photographs and military memorabilia tell a story that, for many people, remains a vivid chapter in Normandy's history.

What to See

The Essential rating system:

 'top ten' sights

◆◆◆ do not miss
◆◆ see if you can
◆ worth seeing if you have time

NORTHEAST NORMANDY: THE PAYS DE CAUX

Strange though it may seem, the Pays de Caux was historically a rather isolated region. This northeastern area of Normandy – now corresponding broadly with the *département* of Seine-Maritime – is cut off from the rest of Normandy by the lower Seine, which used to be unbridgeable beyond Rouen.

The fertile Pays de Caux was first developed during the 19th century, when its agriculture geared up to feed Paris's expanding population, and when Le Havre, at the mouth of the Seine, grew into a major transatlantic port. Apart from Rouen, which links the two halves of Upper (eastern) Normandy, it has only one historic centre of any importance – the port of Dieppe. With its castle, old streets and unchanged ways, Dieppe is easily the most attractive of Normandy's Channel ports.

Most of the character of the Caux region is round its edges. Especially around Fécamp and Etretat, with its famous chalk cliffs (*caux* means chalk), it has a beautiful coastline. Between the resorts you will find some charming unspoilt nooks and coves directly adjoining open or wooded countryside. Its beaches are piled with great round pebbles, but there is sand below the high-water mark. To the south, the Pays de Caux is bounded by the lower valley of the Seine. Despite the heavy presence of industry here, there are woods and forests and inspiring ruins such as Jumièges, one of many important abbeys that flourished in Normandy from the 11th century. Several of them are linked together by the *Route des Abbayes* – one of.20 or so *routes touristiques* in various parts of Normandy. You will see signposts for these special-interest routes, such as the *Route des Marais* (marshes) and the *Route du Cidre*, as you travel around the region. Others to follow in Seine-Maritime include the *Route des Ivoires et des Epices* (ivory and spices) around Dieppe, the *Route des Colombiers* (dovecotes) and a *Route des*

Fromages, which explores the cheese country around Neufchâtel-en-Bray.

On its eastern side, the Caux region has a number of old forests that follow the line of river valleys, providing views and variety for walkers, cyclists and picnickers. Examples are the Forêt d'Eu along the River Bresle (which separates Normandy from Picardy), and the Forêt d'Eawy (pronounced 'ee-a-vi') along the River Varenne south of Dieppe. The Eawy forest adjoins the northern point of the charming Bray region, famous for its cheese and apples. Here there are many timber-framed houses and barns (known as *chaumières*) set among orchards – a similar landscape to that of the flat parts of the lower Seine Valley. Some of the farms where cheese is made are open for visits or tasting – definitely a bonus as you tour this attractive region. Classic local cheeses include Neufchâtel, Gournay and Petit-Suisse.

In the centre of the Caux plateau, towns like Yvetot and Tôtes are scarcely more than built-up crossroads. There is little to see out of the window as you travel, only open and flat arable countryside. Perhaps for this reason, many British visitors arriving at Le Havre miss this part of Normandy by using the great toll-bridge – the Pont de Tancarville – near the mouth of the Seine. However, it can be just as convenient to stay north of the Seine and cross by the Pont de Brotonne or, further east, at Rouen.

WHAT TO SEE

ARQUES-LA-BATAILLE

southwest of Dieppe

The **castle** at Arques was one of the great early castles of Normandy, on a classic hilltop site overlooking the confluence of the rivers Béthune and Varenne. Abandoned in the 17th century, it is now all ruins. The typically Anglo-Norman square keep and the bailey are due to Henry I, who took it over in 1123. The entrance was refortified in the 16th century, and its four larger towers were built to house cannon.

Open: at all times.

The village takes the 'Bataille' (battle) part of its name from the victory won here in 1589 by Henry of Navarre. As a result he became Henri IV of France and settled the Huguenot Wars which had divided the kingdom. A monument marks the site.

◆◆

CANY, CHATEAU DE

east of Fécamp

This fine *château,* built between 1640 and 1646 and attributed to the royal architect François Mansart, is wonderfully enhanced by its superb setting. A stately approach between service blocks is set off by a series of moats and canals fed from the nearby River Derdent. The *château* is surrounded by a park that was landscaped *à l'anglaise* in the early 19th century. The main house, reached by an elegantly curved double staircase, preserves much of its original 17th-century furniture, woodwork and decoration.

Open: Saturday to Thursday, July and August.

Closed: 4th Sunday in July.

◆

CAUDEBEC-EN-CAUX

on the Seine, south of Yvetot

A small town with views out from its cliff over the Seine on to the **Forêt de Brotonne**, Caudebec sits beside the newly built **Pont de Brotonne** (toll). Most traffic whistles past Caudebec up to Yvetot or down to the Seine valley floor without stopping, but Caudebec was once a more important place and is well worth a visit.

Its church of **Notre-Dame**, dominating the market square, is a fine example of the Flamboyant Gothic style, in which the region of Normandy is so rich. Look closely at the stained glass, as well as the tracery. There are also statues taken from the nearby great abbey of Jumièges (see page 28).

The so-called **Maison des Templars** near the church dates from the 13th century. Another beautiful Flamboyant church, dated 1519, lies just north of Caudebec at **Ste-Gertrude**, on the D40.

Castle ruins, Arques-la-Bataille

Accommodation and Restaurants
Caudebec is also worth visiting for a meal. Try the highly acclaimed new restaurant in the **Manoir de Rétival** hotel, rue St Clair (tel: 35 96 11 22) or the established **Normandie**, 19 quai Guilbaud (tel: 35 96 25 11).

Tourist Office
Hôtel de Ville, place Charles de Gaulle (tel: 35 96 20 65).

◆
CLERES
north of Rouen
The park of the *château* at Clères was landscaped in the 19th century, and since 1920 has been a **parc zoologique**. Here you can see exotic birds (such as flamingos, cranes and ornamental ducks), antelopes, kangaroos, emus and monkeys. Clères offers not theme-park thrills, but an old-fashioned 'paradise' in a woodland setting. The *château* is a pretty 19th-century Gothic revival building on an ancient site. *Open*: daily Easter to August; weekends in spring and autumn.
Also at Clères is the **Musée d'automobiles de Normandie** (Normandy Car Museum). The collection includes several very early cars, as well as military vehicles of World War II and a diorama of the 1944 invasion. *Open*: daily all year.

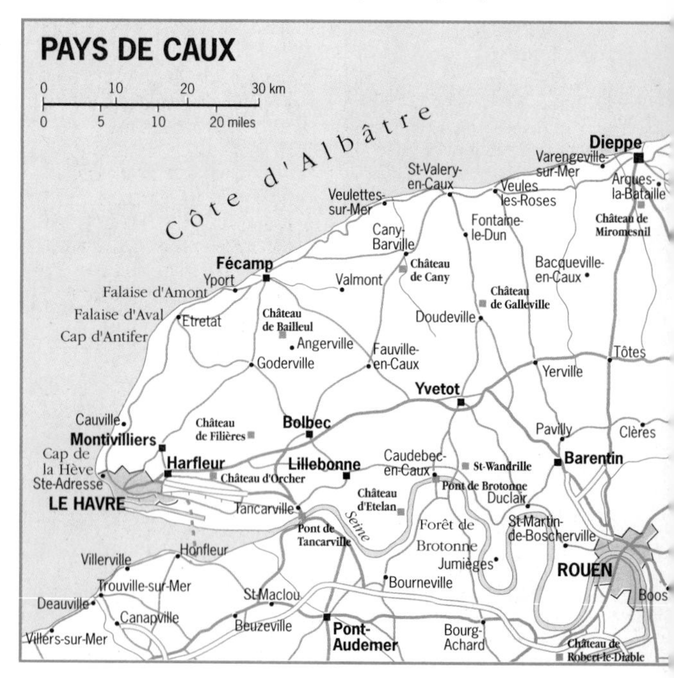

◆◆◆
DIEPPE

Dieppe still uses its typically Norman river-mouth **harbour**, a long thin slit between the cliffs which penetrates right into the town, and along which the ferry from Newhaven in England slowly threads its gigantic way, dwarfing the rooftops. It only just has room to turn round, and the route is only just economic. In general, Dieppe is said to be in decline, although this tends only to increase its charm for the visitor. Besides its harbour, also used by a fishing fleet, Dieppe has a long, flat pebble **beach** on an esplanade currently occupied for much of August by an enormous funfair. The town itself is mostly a warren of small streets, with the fresh, pleasant atmosphere of a historic seafaring place. It is justly famous for its **fish markets**. Its streets rise steeply to the **castle**, which belongs not to the Anglo-Norman period, but to the 15th and 16th centuries. The castle houses a **museum**, which includes a collection of ivories – reflecting Dieppe's former links with Africa – and paintings by Courbet, Boudin, Sisley, Braque and others; also memorabilia of the composer Saint-Saëns. *Open*: Wednesday to Monday, June to September.

The port and waterfront at Dieppe

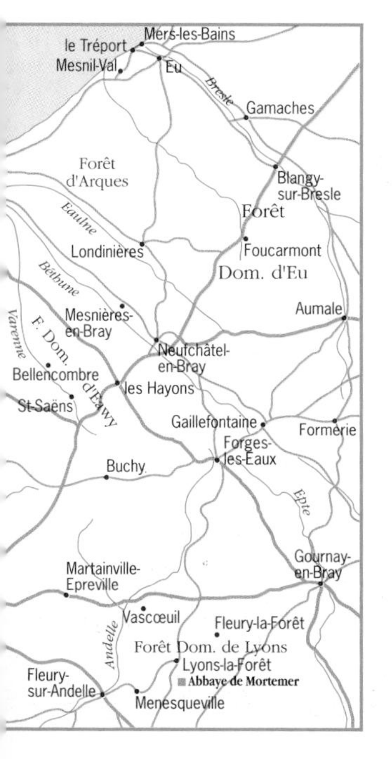

Dieppe was a flourishing port by late medieval times. As it grew, mariners from here in their tiny ships regularly crossed the Atlantic and the equator. Famous names of the early days are Jean Parmentier,

who reached China as well as America, Jean Denis, who got to Brazil, the Florentine Verrazzano who sailed from here to land for the first time on the future site of New York, and also Jean Fleury who captured the Spanish bullion fleet returning from Mexico in 1521. A famous Dieppe citizen was the *armateur* or privateer magnate Jehan (Jean or John) Ango who, in the early 16th century, built and equipped a series of squadrons which successfully attacked the Portuguese and Spanish in the seas around Africa and America. Ango became rich enough to ransom his king, François I, after his capture by Charles V in 1525. He is buried in **St-Jacques**, the main church of Dieppe, which also contains other mementoes of the town's seafaring heyday. During World War II, Dieppe was the object of what Churchill called a 'reconnaissance in depth' in August 1942, when several thousand Allied troops, including many Canadians, landed and suffered heavy losses. This 'Operation Jubilee' demonstrated how well defended the Channel ports were, and the Allies made no further attempts to recapture existing harbours. The lessons learnt were important for D-Day strategy two years later.
The best **beaches** are to the west of Dieppe. Inland, off the Paris road, is the **Forêt d'Eawy**, along the valley of the Varenne; the D154 to Bellencombre and St-Saëns is a pretty drive, and the forest tracks are good for walking and cycling. A fire-break, the Allée des Limousins, cleaves the length of the forest. Originally the Eawy joined up with the similar Forêt de Lyons further south.

Accommodation
The main hotels are along the boulevard Verdun, facing the beach: the moderately expensive **La Présidence**, 1 boulevard Verdun (tel: 35 84 31 31) with an upstairs seaview restaurant; the more modest **L'Univers**, 10 boulevard Verdun (tel: 35 84 12 55); or **Epsom**, 11 boulevard Verdun (tel: 35 84 10 18). There are cheaper ones in the back streets.

Restaurants
Dieppe boasts some superb fish restaurants, for example **La Mélie**, 2 Grande rue du Pollet (in the fishermen's quarter, tel: 35 84 21 19), or the **Marmite Dieppoise**, 8 rue St-Jean (just by the church of St-Jacques, tel: 35 84 24 26). Others are on the quai Henri IV, the street beside the ferry dock.

Tourist Office
1 boulevard du Général de Gaulle (tel: 35 84 11 77).

◆

ETELAN, CHATEAU D'

near Norville, southeast of Lillebonne
To match its Flamboyant Gothic churches, Normandy has some excellent surviving secular buildings of the same period. This historic *château* is a beautiful example, with its bands of red brick and white stone, and its exquisite weathered pinnacles, some of which adorn a grand external

staircase on three storeys. *Open*: Wednesday to Monday afternoons, mid-July to August.

◆◆

ETRETAT

Etretat is a classic family-holiday place in the delightful Norman tradition. Dead in winter, it is packed with visitors of every nationality in summer, when parking is an achievement. You may have to go at least as far out as the church of **Notre-Dame,** east of the town centre. This sizeable Romanesque building was rendered even more Romanesque in the 19th century.

The town itself is small, full of timber-framed buildings creaking with not terribly old antiquity. Etretat's happy atmosphere is its best quality. There is a typical beach promenade and pebble beach, set off by two great cliffs at each end, one of which has split away spectacularly to form one detached 'needle' (*L'Aiguille*) with another still clinging. There are walks from the town up both cliffs, but the path becomes a human ant-stream in August. There is a famous painting of one of the cliffs by Seurat, and several other Impressionists also painted here.

Etretat is the prettiest resort of the so-called **Côte d'Albâtre** (Alabaster Coast). But the coves and beaches between Etretat and Fécamp – some accessible only on foot – are also charming, and quieter. The town has a few central hotels, such as the **Falaises**, boulevard Coty (tel: 35 27 02 77). There

The Falaise d'Aval, near Etretat

are also a couple of reasonably good restaurants on the promenade, including **Roches Blanches**, terrasse Eugène Boudin (tel: 35 27 07 34). But there is not a wide choice.

Tourist Office

Hôtel de Ville (tel: 35 27 05 21).

EU

Eu is an historic town (only just in Normandy), much dwindled from its former importance, when William the (future) Conqueror was married here in 1050. Its centrepiece is the church of **Notre-Dame et St-Laurent**, a High Gothic building with some fine 15th-century fitments and tombs, including one of the St Lawrence to whom it is dedicated – actually an Irish saint, St Lawrence O'Toole, who died at Eu in the 12th century.

The *château* has a late 16th-century Renaissance core, but was entirely refitted when it became one of the French royal pretender Louis-Philippe's favourite residences. He received Queen Victoria here in 1843 and 1845. Unfortunately fire later gutted the interior, and though the building houses the **Musée Louis-Philippe,** it has virtually no decoration dating from his time.
Open: Wednesday to Monday, Easter to October.
Inland the **Forêt d'Eu**, following the line of the River Bresle, is broken up by several large open clearings. There are paths for walking and cycling.

Tourist Office
41 rue Bignon (tel: 35 86 04 68).

FECAMP

Until recently Fécamp was a leading fishing port, specialising in deep-sea cod-fishing; its harbour has now become more of a yacht marina. The **beach** here is typical of the Caux coast, wide, bare and pebbly. The town lacks the character and atmosphere of nearby Etretat, but it is larger and not so exclusively a resort.
Fécamp was the home of one of the greatest of Normandy's famous Benedictine monasteries. Its origins go back to the 7th century, and its early 11th-century abbot, William of Volpiano, was one of the leading churchmen of his age. The enormous abbey church of **La Trinité** has traces of Romanesque here and there. Mostly, however, it is a High Gothic building, much altered, especially in the 18th century. Politely you might call it dignified and majestic; impolitely, vast and dull.
The **Musée de la Bénédictine** is best known as a museum of the well-known Bénédictine liqueur, but has other memorabilia of the monastery where the liqueur was first made in the 16th century.
Open: daily all year.
Fécamp's **Musée Centre-des-Arts** has a small collection of 19th-century paintings and obsolete items of local craft and industry. Facing the sea, the **Musée des Terre-Nuevas et de la Pêche** revives Fécamp's prestigious maritime past through boats, models, tools and paintings.
Open: both museums Wednesday to Monday.
Closed: major public holidays.

Accommodation and Restaurants
A pleasant small hotel, also a restaurant, is the **Auberge de la Rouge**, just inland at St-Léonard on the D925 to Le Havre (tel: 35 28 07 59). There are good fish restaurants by the harbour, for example the unpretentious **L'Escalier**, 101 quai Bérigny (tel: 35 28 26 79).

Tourist Office
113 rue Alexandre le Grand (tel: 35 28 51 01).

FILIERES, CHATEAU DE

off the N15 from Le Havre, near Gommerville
This splendid, if understated Neoclassical *château* of the late 18th century is attributed to the

Fécamp's Musée de la Benedictine

architect Victor Louis. It was an incomplete rebuilding of a 16th-century *château*, of which one wing remains. Its park setting and precious but severe interiors are its main features. *Open*: afternoons daily, July and August; Wednesday, weekends and holidays, Easter to June and September to October.

◆
HAVRE, LE

Said to be Europe's third largest port, Le Havre is chiefly about oil: a bank of shiny refineries stretches from its harbour for several miles up the north bank of the Seine. It is also a ferry port, with links to Portsmouth as well as to Rosslare and Cork in Ireland. This is what brings most visitors to Le Havre today. The town was once a popular centre for sailing and family holidays (a big regatta is still held in July), but it was bombed flat in the War. Though rebuilt according to modern principles under the aegis of the distinguished architect Auguste Perret, Le Havre is now a soulless place, lacking the charm that might tempt visitors to linger. Numerous main roads lead here, nonetheless. Le Havre has a special link to the Paris-Caen motorway by the arching **Pont de Tancarville** (toll) and by another bridge due for completion in 1994 which will come out close to Honfleur. Reminders of old Le Havre can be seen in two museums. One – the **Musée de l'Ancien Havre** – recreates the town from its foundation in 1517. The other – the **Musée des Beaux-Arts André Malraux** – is one of the best museums in Normandy. It is devoted chiefly to the paintings of Raoul Dufy and Eugène Boudin , whose strong, delicate pictures are on show here in their full variety (see also page 54).
Open: both museums Wednesday to Monday.
Closed: major holidays.
Just west of Le Havre, **Ste-Adresse** – once a fashionable

summer residence – is a name that features in Impressionist painting. Today it has little atmosphere even as a village. There is, however, a beach (with even more pebbles than most on the Caux coast), used mostly by locals. Further north, the coast is inaccessible (partly because of a second port for tankers at Le Havre–Antifer) until you come to Etretat.
To the east, **Harfleur** is an older port than Le Havre: it features in Shakespeare's *Henry V*. Though engulfed by its neighbour, it has just kept its identity. Further east still is the **Château d'Orcher**, which Henry V gave to Sir John Falstolf, the formidable soldier on whom Shakespeare's Falstaff was based.
Open: afternoons daily, July to mid-August.

Accommodation

The two major hotels are the **Bordeaux,** 147 rue Brindeau (tel: 35 22 69 44), and the **Mercure** (one of the chain), chaussée d'Angoulême (tel: 35 21 23 45). There are several more in the Quartier Moderne, south of avenue Foch.

Restaurants

The classy restaurants are at **Ste-Adresse**, for instance **Beau Séjour, Nice-Havrais, Yves Page** – it is not easy to choose between them. Good food is available in Le Havre itself at **Le Montagné**, 50 quai Féré (tel: 35 42 77 44), and **La Bonne Hôtesse**, 98 rue Président Wilson (tel: 35 21 31 73).

Tourist Office

1 place de l'Hôtel de Ville (tel: 35 21 22 88).

JUMIEGES

on the north bank of the Seine, west of Rouen; also accessible by ferry from Port-Jumièges on the south bank
On a flat peninsula jutting into the winding Seine, Jumièges is one of the most beautiful empty choirs in a land rich in ruined abbeys. The west end of the church (**Notre-Dame**) still rises to its full height, but the nave is roofless and the east end razed (it was used as a quarry after the Revolution). There are also substantial remains of the monastic buildings.
The church is early Romanesque in style: it was consecrated in 1067, well before the great Abbaye aux Hommes at Caen (see page 57). The west end has an upstairs chapel over the porch, between flanking towers, and the nave, once roofed in timber, was braced by stone arches across every other bay. The nave opened into a crossing over which there rose a tower, and a chancel with an ambulatory. This, however, was enlarged in the Gothic period. From the choir there is a passage into a second, older church, **St-Pierre**, which had been outgrown by the abbey; there are 10th-century parts at the west end. The **chapter house** is of the early 12th century – its later date shows in its slightly pointed arches. A gnarled yew stands in the former cloister, and pleasant grounds surround the ruins.
Open: Wednesday to Monday.
Closed: major holidays.

The abbey at Jumièges

LE HAVRE see HAVRE, LE

LE TREPORT see TREPORT, LE

◆

LILLEBONNE

Today a satellite of Le Havre to the west, in Roman times Lillebonne was the major port at the mouth of the Seine. The considerable **amphitheatre** of the former Juliobona, dating from the 1st and 2nd centuries AD, has been excavated.
Open: Friday to Wednesday. Key available at café near Hôtel de Ville.

Tourist Office
4 rue Pasteur (tel: 35 38 08 45).

MARTAINVILLE

east of Rouen
Privateer or *armateur* Jacques Le Pelletier of Rouen built the *château* here about 1481. It was originally a square, moated castle with four round towers. Some 30 years later, the castle was remodelled by Le Pelletier's nephew, who dismantled the battlements, built the present steep roofs and replaced the tiny windows by large ones. He also filled in the moat, ripping out the drawbridge and introducing the present portal and beautiful Flamboyant Gothic bay window above it. Not neglecting defence altogether, he protected the house with a wall with four towers (three survive). This was not to guard against siege from an army, but to prevent robbery by marauding bands – a serious problem in the late Middle Ages.
This castle, almost untouched, was bought by the state in 1960. It now houses a collection of Normandy furniture and utensils.
Open: Wednesday to Monday.
Closed: major holidays.

MESNIERES EN BRAY

northwest of Neufchâtel-en-Bray
The *château* here is one of the few in Normandy to rival those of the Loire – at least, those of

the same date. Situated on the River Béthune, it was started about 1500 and finished about 1546 by the powerful Boissay family. It consists of a square block with four massive round towers at the corners. The central courtyard was opened up on the river side in the early 18th century, and a previously hidden Italianate loggia now forms the central feature of the garden front. The interior is known for unusual 17th-century wooden statues of stags.
Open: guided visits only, Saturday and Sunday afternoons, April to October.

◆

MIROMESNIL, CHATEAU DE

south of Dieppe

Built in a superb baroque style of the mid-17th century, the *château* is famous as the birthplace of the brilliant writer of short stories Guy de Maupassant – friend of Zola and Proust – and has memorabilia of him. A 16th-century chapel survives from the *château*'s predecessor on the site.
Open: Wednesday to Monday afternoons, May to mid-October.

◆

ST-MARTIN-DE-BOSCHERVILLE

beside the Seine west of Rouen

The former 11th-century abbey here became a parish church – **St-Georges** – at the time of the Revolution, and so avoided destruction. It is a solid example of mature Norman Romanesque, datable between 1080 and 1125, except for the 13th-century vaults. It has some figurative capitals, though many have been mutilated.

◆

ST-VALERY-EN-CAUX

With its two flanking cliffs, St-Valéry is sometimes regarded as a smaller version of Etretat. However, it has more of a harbour – now full of yachts rather than fishing smacks – and less of a beach.

The harbour, St-Valéry-en-Caux

Accommodation
The hotel **Les Terrasses**, 22 rue Le Perrey (tel: 35 97 11 22), is right on the beach.

Restaurants
Two good restaurants for fish are the **Port**, on the harbour (tel: 35 97 08 93), and the **Pigeon-Blanc**, by the old church (tel: 35 97 03 55).

Tourist Office
place Hôtel de Ville (tel: 35 97 00 63).

◆

ST-WANDRILLE

east of Caudebec-en-Caux

The **abbey** of St-Wandrille is an historic and holy site. Its monastic origins lie in the 7th century, and though the ancient buildings have long been in ruins, the abbey has been refounded. Today, the monks' services are held in a vast but starkly beautiful medieval barn, painstakingly transported here piece by piece from its original site and rebuilt.
The old church at St-Wandrille consists only of stumps, but the **cloister**, dating from the 14th and 15th centuries, has survived better. Not far away, the chapel of **St-Saturnin** is heavily restored, but its trefoil plan probably goes back at least to the 8th century.
Open: guided visits only, Monday to Saturday afternoons, Sunday and feast-day mornings.

Restaurant
The **Auberge Deux Couronnes** is a good restaurant opposite the abbey (tel: 35 96 11 44).

TREPORT, LE

This most easterly of Normandy's resorts is much frequented by Parisians in summer. Today much less chic than Deauville, it was an extremely fashionable resort more than 100 years ago, when Louis-Philippe used to reside at nearby Eu (see page 25). Like Deauville, Le Tréport has a quieter sister the other side of the river-mouth harbour – **Mers-les-Bains**. There are reasonable fish restaurants along the harbour quay.

Tourist Office
Esplanade de la Plage (tel: 35 86 05 69).

VALMONT

east of Fécamp

The castle, church and town here were once the property of the d'Estouteville family, first recorded in the 9th century, who later followed William across the Channel and did well from the Conquest. Of the **abbey** only the Chapelle de la Vierge (Lady Chapel) and some other parts of the east end remain standing, though they are flanked by remaining buildings dating from the monastery's revival in the 17th century. The chapel still has some fine 16th-century fittings and sculpture inside.
Open: Wednesday to Monday, April to September.
Closed: 15 August.
The **castle** has a great Norman keep with an incongruous steep tiled roof, added to match the rest of the *château* that was

built on to it, one part in the 15th century and the rest in the mid-16th century. Unfortunately this Renaissance wing was spoilt by a 19th-century restoration, though the arcades of the loggia survive.
Open: afternoons daily in July and August; Saturdays and Sundays only April to June and September to October.

◆

VARENGEVILLE-SUR-MER

west of Dieppe

The **Manoir d'Ango**, near this small seaside village, was built by the famous 16th-century Dieppe *armateur* Jehan Ango (see page 24) as a country house where he could retire in style and enjoy his wealth. Unfortunately the house was later badly damaged and was unfaithfully restored, but the outlines remain, as do some outstanding original features, such as the large round dovecote richly decorated in terracotta and flint. Dating from 1532–44, the house is an example of the French Early Renaissance, much influenced by the Po-valley styles the French had seen on King François's campaigns in North Italy – hence the Manoir's loggia and the broad frieze running above it.
Open: daily Easter to October; weekends and holidays in winter.

A window in Varengeville church

Also at Varengeville is a slice of Edwardian England, the **Parc des Moustiers**. The house was designed in 1898 by the young Edwin Lutyens (much influenced by Norman Shaw and the Arts and Crafts movement). An exquisite garden was laid out by Gertrude Jekyll. In this period Dieppe was a favourite resort for the English aristocracy.
Open: house by special arrangement only; gardens daily Easter to October.

◆

VEULETTES-SUR-MER

between St-Valéry-en-Caux and Fécamp

This coastal resort is no more than a village on a beach that hums into life in the season, despite the new nuclear power-station round the headland. It is a pleasant place, with a good small hotel and restaurant overlooking the sea: **Les Frégates,** rue de la Plage (tel: 35 97 51 22).

Tourist Office
esplanade du Casino (tel: 35 97 51 33).

ROUEN

Rouen is where it is because it was until recently the lowest point on the Seine that could be bridged. A Roman settlement here was revived by Rollo, the Viking ruler of Normandy, in the early 9th century.

Of Rouen's early prosperity its great 13th-century cathedral is the most obvious sign, a High Gothic heaven-scraper to rival those of nearby Amiens, Beauvais or Chartres. From the 14th century it preserves among other things the belfry of the Gros Horloge (Great Clock), its most famous monument, arching over the oldest street in the city. But the later 14th century and early 15th century saw the troubles of the Hundred Years War with England. Rouen was a crucial city in Henry V's campaign to re-conquer Normandy, and once he had taken it in 1418 it remained in English hands till 1449.

It was during this low period for France that Joan of Arc entered on the scene, reviving French fortunes until she was captured and taken to Rouen, where she was condemned on false charges for witchcraft and burnt at the stake in 1431. The Place du Vieux-Marché, where the deed was done, is in the very centre of the old city, but is now dominated by an incongruous modern church dedicated to her (she was made a saint in 1920).

The end of the 15th century and the beginning of the 16th were Rouen's greatest period. It was the capital of a rich region, while its merchants and fleet-owners carried their trade to the Old and New Indies (or stole the cargoes of the Spanish and Portuguese who had been there). From this period date the church of St-Maclou and

The Gros Horloge

some of Rouen's famous half-timbered houses – more than 700 in all. The grander examples include the **Palais de Justice** (see below) and the **Hôtel de Bourgtheroulde** (off the Vieux-Marché), with its fine early 16th-century courtyard. Even after this heyday Rouen remained prominent. It was the birthplace of the classical playwright Corneille and of the severe novelist Flaubert. It became industrialised rapidly, capitalising on its colonial trading links to become a textile centre in the 18th century. As a port and centre of industry it inevitably became a target during World War II, but the ravages to its architecture have been repaired and its heavy industry once again lines the Seine. Its suburbs have spread to the river's south side and up into the heights overlooking the city from the north. The pedestrianised old city nestles among them like a pearl.

Rouen has museums enough for a week of rainy days. Those worth visiting even in the sunshine are described under **What to See**, below. Others cover various aspects of Rouen's history, from Joan of Arc (**Musée Jeanne d'Arc**) to ironwork, tools and locks (**Musée le Secq des Tournelles**) and from famous local writers (**Musée Corneille** and **Musée Flaubert**)to the

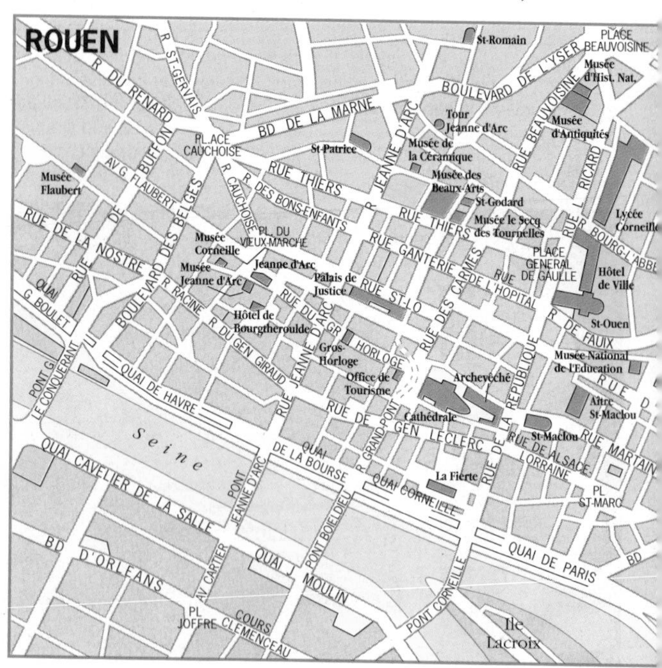

faïence industry in Rouen (**Musée de la Céramique**)
One way to see the sights of Rouen is to take the 'tourist train', which leaves the place de la Cathédrale on regular narrated tours in summer.

WHAT TO SEE

◆◆
CATHEDRAL

Rouen Cathedral was begun in 1145, just after Notre-Dame in Paris and Chartres, just before Amiens, Beauvais and Reims. However, it is not so well known as those because it represents no particular advance in the steady development of Gothic architecture during those years.

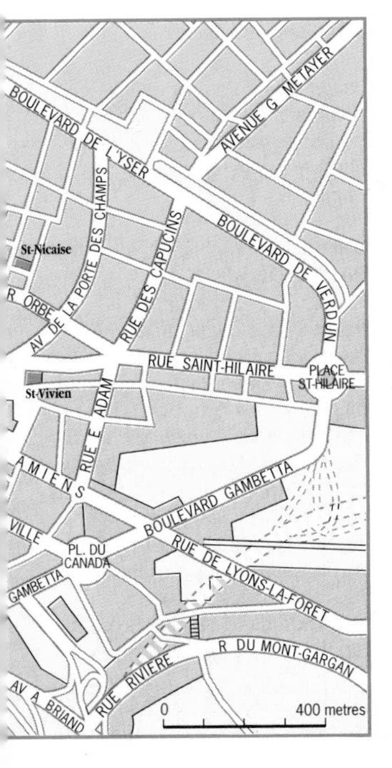

Its four levels or storeys are rather clumsy compared to the normal three, breaking up the vertical lines, and it lacks the breathtaking simplicity of Chartres or Amiens. That does not mean it is not impressive. It has the tallest medieval crossing tower in France. It has a rich heritage of sculpture and stone-carving, inside and out, of the 14th, 15th and 16th centuries. This includes especially its northern portal (Portail des Libraires) and the tombs in the chancel, one of them holding the heart of King Richard the Lionheart. Those in the Lady Chapel are some of the most ornate and splendid tombs of the French Renaissance. There is also good stained glass, mostly of the 13th to 16th centuries. Clodion's Christ, on the main altar, is a fine 18th-century work.
Circulation is restricted during services

◆◆
MUSEE DES BEAUX-ARTS

rue Thiers, beside place Vendreul, on the north side of the old city
Here you will find a small international collection of Old Masters and a larger one of French paintings (including works by Poussin, Champaigne and Géricault). Naturally there are also works by Impressionists, but only one of Monet's famous series of pictures of the façade of Rouen Cathedral.
Open: Wednesday afternoon to Monday.
Closed: some holidays.

The remarkable Aître St-Maclou, a 16th-century cemetery

◆

MUSEE DES ANTIQUITES DE LA SEINE MARITIME

198 Rue Beauvoisine, at the bottom of the hill where the N1 heads north to Dieppe

A comprehensive array of objects on display here documents the area's rich Roman and medieval history. *Open*: Wednesday to Monday. *Closed*: holidays.

OLD CITY

centres on rue du Gros-Horloge

The old city is just about a walkable proposition: go down from the Vieux Marché along the rue du Gros-Horloge to the Cathedral and behind it St-Maclou (see below). Then walk up to the outstanding 14th- and 15th-century church of **St-Ouen** and back again along the Ganterie or rue Thiers (with the Musée des Beaux-Arts). In this square there are numerous streets with old timber-framed houses, as well as the major churches, and also smart shopping streets such as the Ganterie.

PALAIS DE JUSTICE

rue du Gros-Horloge

Apart from houses, Rouen has several timber-framed buildings described as palaces or *hôtels*. The grandest – also incorporating stonework – is the Palais de Justice (Law Courts), a government building of the 16th century. The old belfry adjoining the Gros Horloge can be entered by a staircase of 1457, and houses a small museum of old clocks. From the top there is a view of the city. *Open*: Wednesday afternoon to Monday, Easter to early October.

◆◆◆
ST-MACLOU ✓

behind cathedral
In all France there is no finer piece of late Gothic Flamboyant architecture than this. Large churches wholly in this style are rare; Flamboyant appears mostly in chapels and by way of addition and repair to existing churches. In St-Maclou, despite a long building period (1437–1517), the slender, gently twining tracery ('flame-like' – hence the name) lends great homogeneity to the church. The organ dates from the same period as the building (1521), as does the Aître St-Maclou (St-Maclou Cemetery) close by. This is another rarity: virtually all such cemeteries were built over after the Revolution. A few figures of a Dance of Death survive on the columns supporting the 16th-century houses.

Accommodation
Rouen's grand old hotel is the **Dieppe** with its **Quatre Saisons** restaurant, place Tissot (tel: 35 71 96 00), but there are some other comfortable hotels both in the centre (**Colin**'s, 15 rue Pie, tel: 35 71 00 88) and south of the river by the Parc des Expositions. Otherwise there are several small, reasonably priced hotels in the old city. Two with parking are the **Québec**, 18 – 24 rue Québec (tel: 35 70 09 38) and the **Viking**, 21 quai du Havre (tel: 35 70 34 95).

Restaurants
Rouen has its fair share of smart, expensive restaurants,

Flamboyant Gothic – a Style for France
The ornate late Gothic style of architecture known as 'Flamboyant' is particularly associated with Normandy. Flamboyant derives from the flame-like tracery of the windows – though it tends to invade portals, porches and ceilings too. The decoration is almost an end in itself, taking over and masking the structure. Many churches and chapels in Normandy show, in part at least, the exuberance and richness of Gothic Flamboyant. However, St-Maclou is one of few large churches entirely in this style. This is partly for historical reasons. Flamboyant developed, as an independent French style, after the end of the Hundred Years War.
The century of intermittent conflict had halted architectural development, but the late 15th century was a period of relative peace and prosperity. The great cathedrals were already built, so the new style was used for personal projects such as tombs, chantry chapels, and other additions or embellishments to existing buildings. Rouen Cathedral has a splendid array of tombs, and a chapel in the Flamboyant style was added to Lisieux Cathedral by the 15th-century bishop Pierre Cauchon. Churches in the Flamboyant style can be seen at Caudebec-en-Caux, Alençon and Verneuil-sur-Avre.

Rouen has plenty of restaurants

offering both old-time Normandy favourites in cream sauces and modern cuisine. **Gill** (in the second category) is the top, 9 quai Bourse (tel: 35 71 16 14). Less pretentious and expensive but also outstanding is the **Beffroy**, 15 rue Beffroy (tel: 35 71 55 27). Both these are closed for part of the high season. A close third is the **Auberge du Vieux Carré**, 34 rue Ganterie (tel: 35 71 67 70). Besides these, in the old city you will find both tourist-traps – for example, the most famous restaurant in Rouen, **La Couronne**, 31 place du Vieux-Marché (tel: 35 71 40 90) – and excellent, reasonable places, for example, **Les Maraîchers**, 37 place du Vieux-Marché (tel: 35 71 57 73), or **Les Halles du Vieux-Marché**, 41 place du Vieux-Marché (tel: 35 71 03 58).

Tourist Office

25 place de la Cathédrale (tel: 35 71 41 77).

THE SEINE VALLEY

The region of Normandy between Rouen and Paris, along and around the valley of the Seine, seems to belong to a different category from the rest, being a long way from the sea and adjacent to Paris's suburbs. One of this region's most famous sights – Monet's garden at Giverny – is just the outermost of several places down the Seine from Paris where the Impressionists used to paint. The great ducal forest at Lyons-la-Forêt is comparable to that at Fontainebleau, south of Paris (though, as it happens, the French king never built a palace here). The *châteaux* at Anet and Bizy were not so much country houses as refuges from the capital a little beyond Versailles.

In the Middle Ages this was border country. The splendid Château Gaillard, on the Seine above Les Andelys, was built by Richard the Lionheart to hold the border between Normandy and the Ile de France. The modern boundary is nearer to Paris at Vernon.

Today, much of the Seine Valley is heavily built up, and its sights and amenities are well known and well used by the residents

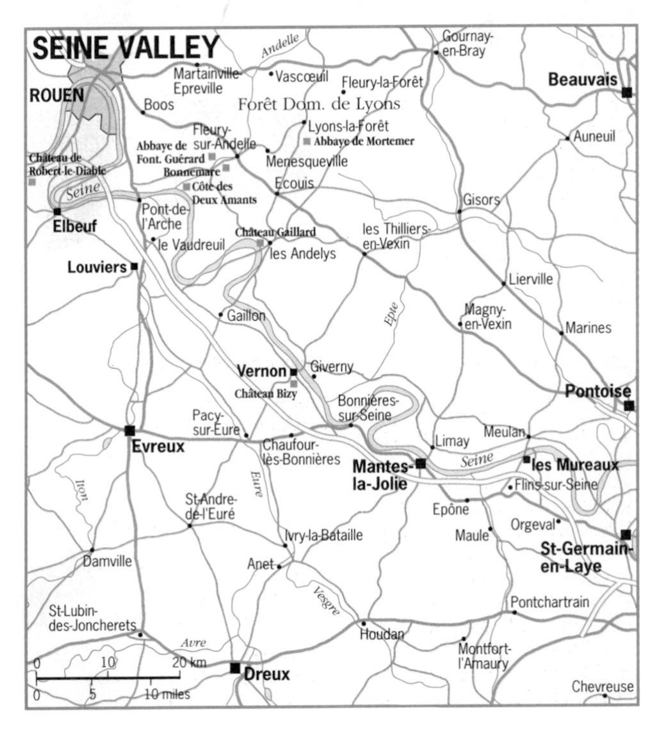

of nearby Paris. But although the proximity of Paris makes itself felt here, there are still patches of authentic Normandy. You will still find towns and villages with half-timbered houses and a rural atmosphere. Tracts of forest, a scattering of small *châteaux* and traditional farmsteads make it hard to forget that, despite the commuter age, this is still Normandy.

WHAT TO SEE

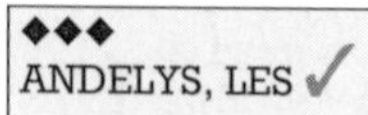

◆◆◆ ANDELYS, LES ✓

Beneath Richard the Lionheart's superbly sited Château Gaillard high above the winding Seine lie the merged twin villages of Petit Andely and Grand Andely. The old buildings of Petit Andely nestle below the castle on the banks of the Seine, where a riverside walk offers stunning views. Nearby, a

Château Gaillard and the Seine

typically French tree-lined square is overlooked by the simple 12th-century church of **St-Sauveur**.

Grand Andely has an altogether different feel, busier and more modern. Its square has a good **market**, and its church – **Notre-Dame** – is large and impressive. Visit Grand Andely for shopping and banks, but stay in Petit Andely – and visit the castle even if you don't like castles, for you are unlikely to find a better view of the Seine Valley.

Château Gaillard itself remains one of the best preserved and most interesting castles of its period. '*Qu' elle est belle, ma fille d'un an!*' (My lovely year-old daughter!), Richard the Lionheart is said to have exclaimed in 1197 as he saw the newly founded castle rise on its rock. Unfortunately Château Gaillard was taken by Philip Augustus in a night assault only seven years later. Philip's troops, entering through the conduits for the latrines in the towers, caught the defenders before they had time to scramble back into the keep.

Both Richard and Philip were professional soldier kings whose new castles were the technological masterpieces of their era. This one has been maintained but not modernised, so although some of the outer defences are gone, it is easy to see the original plan. Château Gaillard had four layers of defence: first the triangular *châtelet* protects the approach to the bailey walls; then within the bailey walls a *chemise* swelling with closely set towers rings the last refuge, the keep. *Open*: keep, Wednesday afternoon to Monday, mid-March to mid-November. Free access to the bailey.

Accommodation and Restaurants

The hotel-restaurant **Chaine d'Or**, 27 rue Grande (tel: 32 54 00 31), is a popular and attractively sited old inn. A runner-up, less expensive, is the nearby **Normandie**, 1 rue Grande (tel: 32 54 10 52.)

Tourist Office

24 rue Philippe-Auguste (tel: 32 54 41 93).

ANET, CHATEAU D'

on the River Eure, southeast of Evreux

The *château* at Anet, built for Diane de Poitiers, mistress of Henri II, during the 1540s and 1550s, is the most important surviving work by the hugely influential Philibert de l'Orme, the founding father of French classicism.

Though much of the *château* is no longer, his remarkable entrance gateway and chapel survive. The entrance is bold, massive and monumental, and represents the earliest attempt in France to reproduce fortress-like grandeur in the language of classical architecture. The chapel was the first French church with a centralised (rather than longitudinal) plan – inspired by Italian Renaissance architecture. Philibert evolved a complex scheme involving advanced geometry, producing a dizzying effect when you

The west front of Evreux Cathedral

enter beneath the dome.
Open: afternoons Wednesday to Monday, April to October; also Sunday and holiday mornings; Saturday, Sunday and holiday afternoons all year.

◆

BIZY, CHATEAU DE

on the southwestern edge of Vernon

Much of this once outstanding 18th-century *château* was destroyed after the Revolution, but it was rebuilt and refurbished in the 19th century. The outbuildings, including magnificent stables (now housing a collection of vintage cars) go back to the days of the *château's* original glory, when it was the scene of lavish fêtes put on by the fabulously wealthy duc de Belle-Isle. The grand avenues of lime trees are 18th-century, but the rest of the park was redesigned *à l'anglaise* in the 19th.
Open: Saturday to Thursday, April to October.

◆

ECOUIS

north of Les Andelys

The village of Ecouis marks the centre of the so-called **Vexin normand,** a region of fields and forests on the north bank of the Seine southeast of Rouen. Ecouis is known for its twin-towered 14th-century **church**, endowed by the local Marigny family. Inside is a remarkable collection of painted wooden sculptures of the same period.

◆◆

EVREUX

Evreux might be thought of as a smaller version of Rouen. This pleasant and historic country town is set on the little River Iton – the walk along the old ramparts by the river is one of the town's best features.
The **cathedral**, smaller than Rouen's though ambitious, has had its 12th-century core patched, rebuilt or improved many times as a result of repeated war damage all through Evreux's strife-torn history. The museum in the nearby **Ancien Evéché**

(Bishop's Palace) has a limited collection, though its archaeology section is extensive.
Open: Tuesday to Sunday.
Closed: Sunday mornings and holidays.
Like Rouen, Evreux has an historic clock, but for dedicated medievalists the town's outstanding treasure is the precious 13th-century reliquary of Louis XI in the pretty church of **St-Taurin,** a local bishop saint.

Accommodation and Restaurants
There is quite a wide choice of hotel-restaurants, from the modernised and rather expensive **France**, a restaurant-with-rooms overlooking the river at 29 rue St-Thomas (tel: 32 39 09 25), to the old-world **Normandy**, 37 rue Feray (tel: 32 33 14 40).

Tourist Office
1 place Général de Gaulle (tel: 32 24 04 43).

◆
FONTAINE-GUERARD
east of Rouen
The ruins of this 12th- to 13th-century abbey lie just outside the Forêt de Lyons in beautiful countryside beside the River Andelle.
Open: (guided tours only) Tuesday to Sunday afternoons, April to October.
A popular beauty spot to the southwest near Amfreville is the **Côte des Deux Amants**, a hilltop overlooking the Seine and surrounding countryside.

GAILLARD, CHATEAU see ANDELYS, LES

◆
GAILLON
northeast of Evreux
On the south bank of the Seine between Louviers and Vernon, the **castle** here was one of the earliest in France (1502) to show the influence of the Italian Renaissance. Once very grand, and historically important, it now has only an entrance pavilion and one small wing left, though excavations going on may make more of the site eventually.

◆◆
GISORS
southeast of Rouen
Chiefly notable in this market town on the very eastern edge of Normandy is the **castle**, a key point fortified by both English and French kings during their struggle for Normandy. The first keep was built in the 11th century, and the first curtain walls round the bailey followed under Henry I, around 1125. The present keep was rebuilt by Henry II at the end of the 12th century, and Philip Augustus, having won the castle from King John, built the much higher Tour du Prisonnier (Prisoner's Tower) overlooking the still untrustworthy town. This tower became a prison in the 16th century, when its incarcerated wretches began the drawings and inscriptions still visible inside.
Open: February to November.
Also worth visiting in Gisors is the 13th-century Gothic church of **St-Gervais et St-Protais**.

Tourist Office
3 rue Baléchoux
(tel: 32 27 30 14).

◆◆◆
GIVERNY: MUSEE CLAUDE MONET ✓

across the Seine from Vernon
Claude Monet lived at Giverny from 1883, when he had just begun to find a market for his paintings, until his death in 1926, when he had become a grand old man of art. Here he laid out the gardens made famous, above all, by the *Water Lilies* series he painted in the first decade of the new century, incorporating the distinctive motif of the arched wooden bridge that visitors can now cross during their tour. The gardens went to ruin, but were left to the country in 1966 and have recently been scrupulously restored. Though well worth a visit, Giverny is now very popular, and you will be lucky to miss the crowds.
Perhaps Monet's major inspiration was the English garden in Gertrude Jekyll's style. His borders build up from small plants at the front to larger ones at the back, with the very tallest plants at the centre. One of his favourite high plants was lemon yellow mullein, together with lilies and hollyhocks.
The garden also has a shady section at the back, by the river that feeds the lake, with a bamboo grove and a copse underplanted with several old English favourites, such as Solomon's seal. Some of the most beautiful planting is alongside the water, where some flamboyant autumn golds and oranges are dramatically

The bridge and water lilies at Giverny – Monet's inspiration

Claude Monet
Born in Paris, in 1840, Claude Monet moved to Le Havre as a child, and it was there that his lifelong connection with Normandy began.
Now familiar to everyone, the term 'Impressionist' was coined by Monet quite by accident. An early exhibition of work by Monet and like-minded artists caused uproar among traditionalist critics, who seized on the title of one of Monet's paintings – *Impression: Sunrise* – as a focus for their mockery of what were seen as slapdash painting techniques.
Monet's revolutionary method as a young man involved painting direct from nature, capturing fleeting effects of light and mood to give the feeling of a particular scene, rather than painstakingly portraying every detail. He had a small boat converted into a studio to enable him to work out of doors on the river; a famous painting by his fellow Impressionist Manet shows him at work in his boat.
In later life Monet worked from his studio at Giverny. Colour, light and mood remained his passionate concerns. He painted several series of pictures of the same subject, for example *Rouen Cathedral* (1892–5), which capture the swim of colour, light and shadow over the stonework. Most famous of his later works – verging on the abstract – is the *Water Lilies* sequence, inspired by his garden.

reflected. In Monet's old studio, now a bookshop, there is every opportunity to study the painter's career – especially in splendid old photographs of the bearded gentleman. In his extreme old age he never left Giverny, but drew all the inspiration for his famous late paintings from the colourful blur in which he now – because of his cataracts – saw his garden.
In Monet's lifetime, many young American artists came to study at Giverny. Their works – now famous in their own right – are the basis of the new **Musée Americain Giverny**, close to Monet's house.
Open: both museums Tuesday to Sunday, April to October.

LES ANDELYS see ANDELYS, LES

◆

LOUVIERS
in the Eure Valley, south of Rouen
A rather uneasy combination of half-timbered old town and 20th-century industrial estate, Louviers preserves at its centre a notable Flamboyant Gothic church, **Notre-Dame**. Its wealth of rich decoration was funded by the wool trade – the traditional business of Louviers, now replaced by modern industries. There are several places to stay and to eat in the town, and particularly in the countryside around. Three miles (5km) southeast on the N155 at Vironvay is **Les Saisons** (tel: 32 40 02 56); five miles (8km) north on the N15 at St-Pierre-du-Vauvray is **Hostellerie St-Pierre** (tel: 32 59 93 29).

Tourist Office
10 rue Maréchal Foch (tel: 32 40 04 41).

LYONS-LA-FORET
east of Rouen
The beech and oak forest in which the picture-postcard village of Lyons-la-Forêt nestles is one of the finest in Normandy. Wonderful not only for walking and cycling, it has more than its share of tourist sights: apart from **Fontaine-Guérard** (see page 43), the forest includes another abbey ruin, now with a museum of monastic life, at **Mortemer** to the south, where Henry I of England died. You could visit a Romanesque church at **Menesqueville** to the southwest, or a 17th-century *château* at **Fleury-la-Forêt** to the northeast. The old kitchens here house an exhibition of dolls and toys.
Conveniently situated within reach of all these attractions, and itself offering old buildings to see and antique shops to visit, it is not surprising that the village of Lyons-la-Forêt attracts the crowds in summer.

Accommodation and Restaurants
The old established hostelries of **La Licorne**, place Bensérade (tel: 32 49 62 02) and the **Grand Cerf**, place de la Halle (tel: 32 49 60 44) have no need to cut their prices in order to attract customers. They are restaurants with simple rooms offering good food in typical Normandy surroundings - if you can get in.

Tourist Office
Mairie (tel: 32 49 31 65).

PONT-DE-L'ARCHE
south of Rouen
If you pass this pleasant little village wedged between the Seine and the Forêt de Bord, it is worth stopping to look at its highly ornate Flamboyant Gothic **church**.

ROBERT-LE-DIABLE, CHATEAU DE
just southwest of Rouen
This 'castle' is something of a fake: 'Robert the Devil' never was a real person, and the real castle that was once here was largely demolished in the 15th century. Nonetheless, this is a popular place with the residents of nearby Rouen. Visitor attractions among the ruins include displays about the Vikings, William the Conqueror and the former castle. The towers have fine views over the Seine valley, and there is a children's play area.
Open: daily, March to November.

VASCOEUIL, CHATEAU DE
east of Rouen
This *château* on the edge of the Forêt de Lyons is an older red-brick structure modernised in the late 18th century. It became a fashionable country-house *salon* in the mid-19th century and is now a cultural centre holding modern art exhibitions. It also contains a museum concerning the 19th-century French historian Jules Michelet, who did much of his writing here.
Open: daily, afternoons only, March to November.

THE CENTRAL NORTH COAST: COTE FLEURIE AND COTE DE NACRE

Normandy's best known resorts are those on the so-called **Côte Fleurie** (Flower Coast), between the mouths of the Seine and the Orne. Honfleur, Deauville, Trouville, Cabourg and Houlgate were fashionable when St-Tropez was a fishing village, and are still flourishing. These resorts have a long history and are steeped in nostalgia. Whole families come here, grandparents and grandchildren returning summer after summer to the same chalet or villa or flat. It was on these beaches that the monumental French novelist Marcel Proust remembered watching his beloved Albertine play ball. But the resorts are still going. Their charm is not faded, their paint is not peeling and their appeal to Paris society, as well as to visitors from other places far and near, is undimmed.

The **Côte de Nacre** (Pearl Coast), further west between the rivers Orne and Vire, is a different story, because it was never developed in the same way. It has the same kind of beaches – superb white strands, with dunes rather than the mounds of pebbles of the Pays de Caux – but it has never had the same crowds. Its fame lies rather as the site of the 1944 D-Day landings. These beaches are now commonly known as *Les Plages du Débarquement* (the Landing Beaches), and individually by their wartime code-names – Utah, Omaha, Gold, Juno and Sword. Rusting hulks have been preserved, and museums up and down the coast tell the story again and again in vivid detail. (For the overall story see page 18.)

Trouville – less chic than Deauville, but smart enough for most

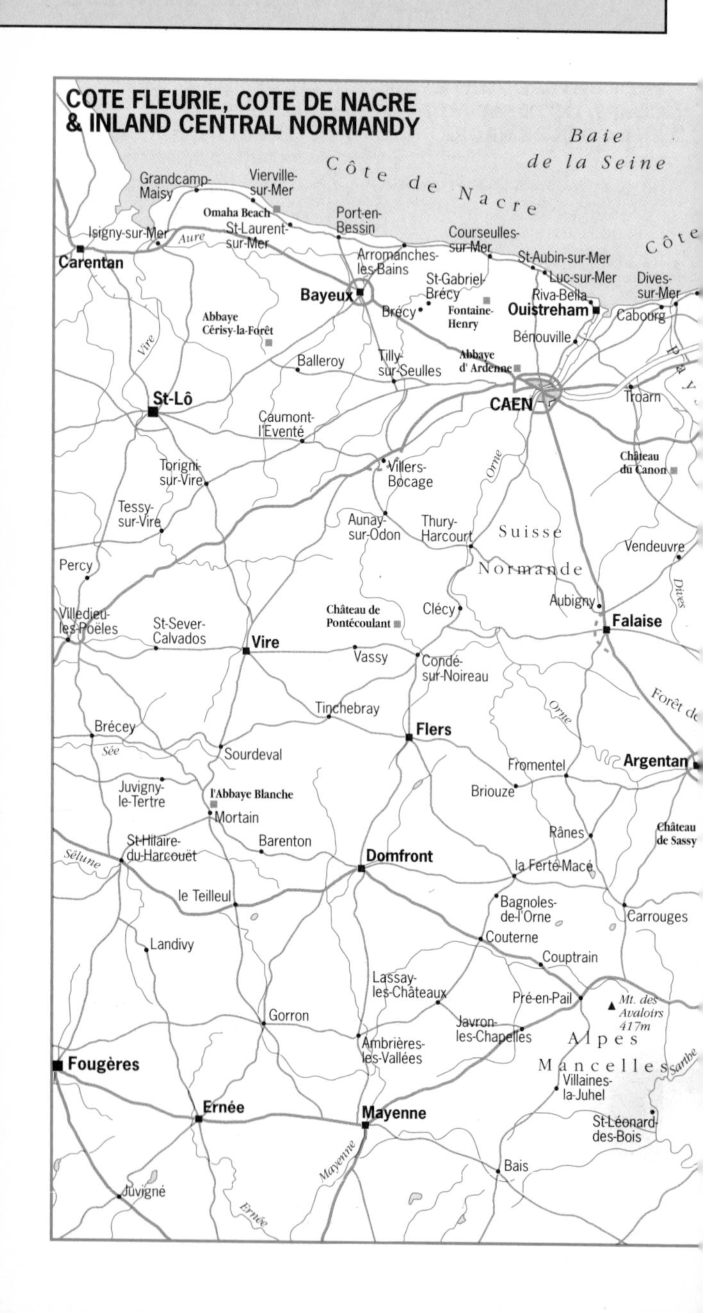

COTE FLEURIE, COTE DE NACRE
& INLAND CENTRAL NORMANDY
Baie de la Seine
Côte de Nacre
Grandcamp-Maisy
Vierville-sur-Mer
Omaha Beach
Port-en-Bessin
Isigny-sur-Mer
St-Laurent-sur-Mer
Aure
Carentan
Courseulles-sur-Mer
Arromanches-les-Bains
St-Aubin-sur-Mer
Luc-sur-Mer
Dives-sur-Mer
St-Gabriel-Brécy
Bayeux
Brécy
Fontaine-Henry
Riva-Bella
Ouistreham
Cabourg
Abbaye Cérisy-la-Forêt
Vire
Bénouville
Balleroy
Tilly-sur-Seulles
Abbaye d'Ardenne
St-Lô
CAEN
Troarn
Caumont-l'Eventé
Château du Canon
Torigni-sur-Vire
Villers-Bocage
Orne
Tessy-sur-Vire
Aunay-sur-Odon
Thury-Harcourt
Suisse Normande
Vendeuvre
Percy
Aubigny
Dives
Château de Pontécoulant
Clécy
Falaise
Villedieu-les-Poëles
St-Sever-Calvados
Vire
Vassy
Condé-sur-Noireau
Tinchebray
Forêt d
Brécey
Flers
Sée
Sourdeval
Fromentel
Argentan
Juvigny-le-Tertre
Briouze
l'Abbaye Blanche
Mortain
Rânes
Château de Sassy
St-Hilaire-du-Harcouët
Barenton
Sélune
Domfront
la Ferté-Macé
le Teilleul
Bagnoles-de-l'Orne
Carrouges
Couterne
Landivy
Couptrain
Lassay-les-Châteaux
Pré-en-Pail
Mt. des Avaloirs 417m
Gorron
Javron-les-Chapelles
Alpes Mancelles
Ambrières-les-Vallées
Fougères
Sarthe
Villaines-la-Juhel
Ernée
Mayenne
St-Léonard-des-Bois
Bais
Juvigné
Ernée

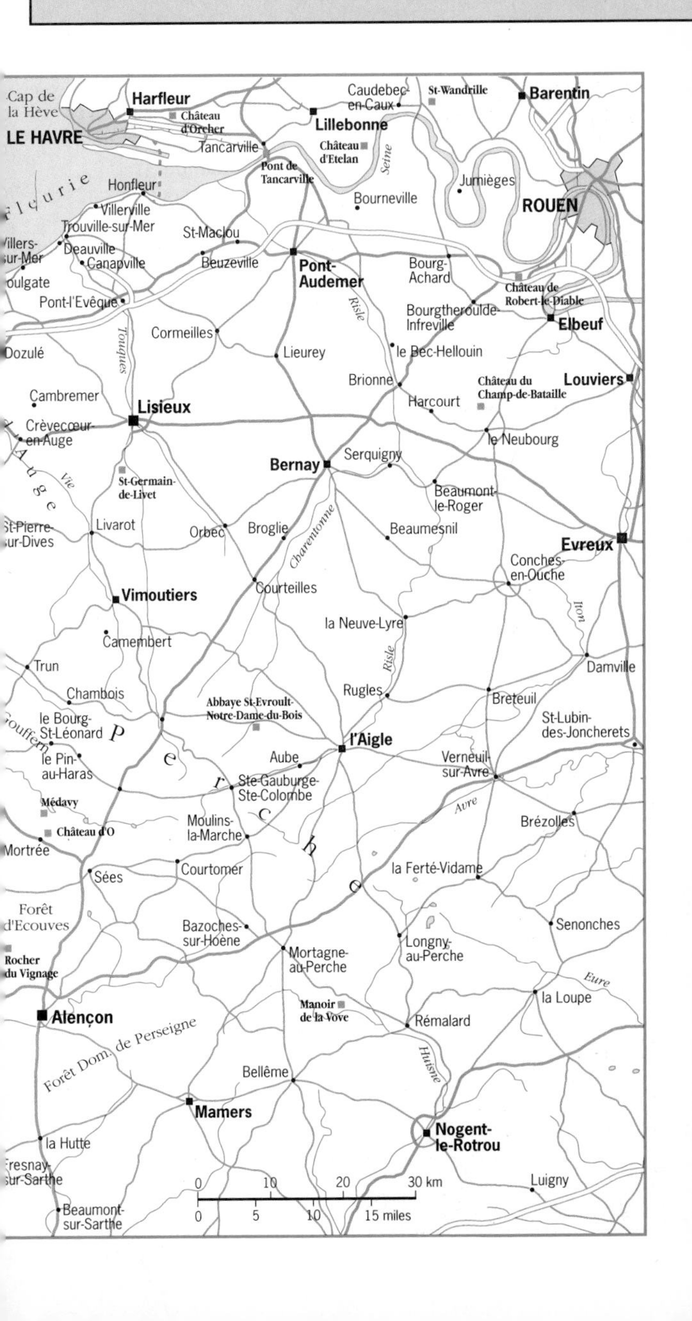

Cap de la Hève
LE HAVRE
Harfleur
Château d'Orcher
Tancarville
Pont de Tancarville
Caudebec-en-Caux
Lillebonne
Château d'Etelan
Seine
St-Wandrille
Barentin
Jumièges
ROUEN
Bourneville
Honfleur
Villerville
Trouville-sur-Mer
Deauville
Canapville
St-Maclou
Beuzeville
Pont-Audemer
Bourg-Achard
Château de Robert-le-Diable
Bourgtheroulde-Infreville
Elbeuf
Pont-l'Evêque
Cormeilles
Lieurey
Risle
le Bec-Hellouin
Touques
Dozulé
Brionne
Château du Champ-de-Bataille
Louviers
Cambremer
Harcourt
Lisieux
Crèvecœur-en-Auge
le Neubourg
Bernay
Serquigny
St-Germain-de-Livet
Beaumont-le-Roger
Vie
Livarot
Orbec
Broglie
Beaumesnil
Evreux
Charentonne
Conches-en-Ouche
Courteilles
Vimoutiers
Iton
la Neuve-Lyre
Camembert
Trun
Damville
Chambois
Abbaye St-Evroult-Notre-Dame-du-Bois
Rugles
Breteuil
le Bourg-St-Léonard
St-Lubin-des-Joncherets
l'Aigle
le Pin-au-Haras
Aube
Verneuil-sur-Avre
Ste-Gauburge-Ste-Colombe
Médavy
Avre
Château d'O
Moulins-la-Marche
Brézolles
Mortrée
Sées
Courtomer
la Ferté-Vidame
Forêt d'Ecouves
Bazoches-sur-Hoène
Senonches
Rocher du Vignage
Mortagne-au-Perche
Longny-au-Perche
Eure
la Loupe
Manoir de la Vove
Alençon
Rémalard
Forêt Dom. de Perseigne
Huisne
Bellême
Mamers
Nogent-le-Rotrou
la Hutte
Luigny
0 10 20 30 km
0 5 10 15 miles
Beaumont-sur-Sarthe

WHAT TO SEE

◆◆◆
ARROMANCHES-LES-BAINS ✓

northeast of Bayeux
This is an unpretentious family holiday resort – with a difference. Visitors flock here because of the extraordinary role Arromanches played in the liberation of France in 1944. Just off the beach can still be seen the remains of one of the two huge artificial ports or 'Mulberry Harbours' which were towed piece by piece from England to help land troops and supplies after the D-Day invasion.The scale of the operation is hard to comprehend: the ports involved half a million tons of concrete and several miles of floating roads. Amazingly, they were a success.
The large and popular **Musée du Débarquement** (Invasion Museum), on the sea-front, chronicles this remarkable invasion in its collection of photographs, maps, dioramas and military memorabilia.
Open: daily.
Closed: January.

Accommodation
The **Marine**, quai Canada (tel: 31 22 34 19) is a traditional, unspoilt hotel with a good restaurant.

Tourist Office
4 rue Maréchal Joffre (tel: 31 21 47 56).

◆
CABOURG

Cabourg is perhaps the exception to the rule that the Normandy resorts have changed little since their heyday. True, the Grand Hotel – centrepiece of the Edwardian town-plan – still gleams and remains true to the memory of Marcel Proust, who used to stay there. But the main street is gaudy and overpopularised, and you might say Cabourg's finest feature is now the extravagant fake architecture of the mini-golf on the promenade. In summer there are many foreigners, especially British, and few French. Cabourg merges into the former inland port of **Dives-sur-Mer**, now a yacht marina. From here Duke William set out to conquer England in ships hardly much bigger than today's yachts. The **Village Guillaume-le-Conquérant** (William the Conqueror's village) is a complex of ancient buildings so much refurbished as to look completely false. Better sights are the church of **Notre-Dame** – particularly the

Oyster beds, Courseulles-sur-Mer

east end, which survives from a fine Romanesque church here – and the 15th-century wooden **market-hall**.

Accommodation and Restaurants

One can eat amid the grand *salons* of the **Pullman Grand Hotel**, promenade Marcel Proust (tel: 31 91 01 79), at reasonable expense considering the hotel's excellent position, right on the beach. It also has some very large bedrooms. There are numerous alternatives in the town, or at the Village Guillaume-le-Conquérant.

Tourist Office

Jardins du Casino (tel: 31 91 01 09).

◆

COURSEULLES-SUR-MER

north of Caen

This is a more of a harbour and marina than a beach place, though it has one. Facing the beach, the **Maison de la Mer** features a 'tunnel' aquarium of local marine life and an extensive sea-shell collection. *Open*: Tuesday to Sunday, April to October.

Accommodation and Restaurants

The **Crémaillère/Le Gytan**, (boulevard de la Plage, tel: 31 37 46 73), is a good hotel. Courseulles is known for its oysters. One can eat them on the quay at the popular **La Pêcherie**, place du 6 Juin (tel: 31 97 45 84).

Tourist Office

54 rue de la Mer (tel: 31 37 46 80).

DEAUVILLE

Deauville is for the rich – and those who like to watch them. Private planes flock to its airport; racehorses are bought and sold here; exclusive shops sell designer labels hardly seen outside Paris and the world's major capitals. In Ciro's café bejewelled, deep-tanned Parisians pay a king's ransom to eat like sparrows. A week's hire of a beach-cabin here would probably buy you one elsewhere.

Not surprisingly, there are fewer foreigners in this resort than in any other along the coast. Deauville is for the Parisian jet-set. They take a large flat for the summer in one of the many 'prestige' mansion blocks, or a villa on Mont Canisy behind. In between commuting along the motorway to Paris, they spend their leisure hours yachting, horse-racing, at the casino or at one of the establishments lining the beach offering *thalassothérapie*. Probably only granny or nanny go to the beach itself with the children.

While in Deauville do not miss the ambience of **Les Planches**, a broad avenue of yacht's-deck hardwood extending alongside the beach, till it peters out in down-market neighbouring Bénerville-sur-Mer. Having strolled along Les Planches, looking out over a perfect white, flat, sandy beach, colourfully tented and meticulously clean, you should then go out to lunch at **Ciro's** café-restaurant to complete the Deauville experience.

Accommodation
Naturally Deauville boasts deluxe hotels such as the **Normandy**, 38 rue Mermoz (tel: 31 98 66 22) or the **Royal**, boulevard E Cornuché (tel: 31 98 66 33). More modest ones exist, but Deauville is not a cheap place to stay. Try the **Pavillion de la Poste**, 25 rue Fossorier (tel: 31 88 38 29). It has no restaurant, but there are plenty within walking distance and the bedrooms, though small, are attractive.

Restaurants
Except for **Le Spinnaker**, 52 rue Mirabeau (tel: 31 88 24 40), which is very good and not extravagantly expensive, and **Ciro's**, promenade des Planches (tel: 31 88 18 10) for lunch, it is difficult to find anything beyond the level of an overpriced *croque monsieur* in Deauville. Try Trouville.

Tourist Office
place de la Mairie (tel: 31 88 21 43).

DIVES-SUR-MER see CABOURG

GRANDCAMP-MAISY

northeast of Carentan
Grandcamp is a fishing port and marina frequented mainly by seafarers and those addicted to the shellfish abundant on its rocks. The atmosphere is different from the usual run of holiday places, and there are good fish restaurants. Two modest places you could try are **La Marée**, quai Cheron (tel: 31 22 60 55), or the hotel **Duguesclin**, 4 quai Crampon (tel: 31 22 64 22).

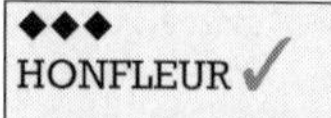

HONFLEUR

Stone and timber-framed houses, winding streets and open quays, ships and easels, an old-world ambience and a thriving, humming atmosphere – Honfleur is picturesque in the good old sense, a postcard of a town but a living one. Even though it gets very full in summer, it never loses its spirit or its character.

A series of galleries and artists' shops line the **Vieux Bassin** (Old Harbour), which was the new harbour when it was dug out in the 17th century, but was itself replaced by the other harbour basins in the 19th.

Honfleur's artistic tradition goes back to the generation before the Impressionists – to Gustave Courbet and Eugène Boudin, who was born here. The **Musée Boudin** houses a representative selection of his and other 19th-century painting, mostly of local scenes.

Open: Wednesday to Monday. *Closed*: weekday mornings in winter, and the first half of February.

Other museums are the **Musée du Vieux Honfleur**, full of bygone bourgeois and folk artefacts, and the **Musée de la Marine** (Maritime Museum).

Open: both museums daily in summer; Saturday afternoon and Sunday, February to mid-June.

Just back from the port, the remarkable 15th-century wooden church of **Ste-Catherine**, overlooking the market place, was built by Honfleur's skilled shipwrights in thanksgiving that the English had finally departed. During the following years Honfleur rivalled Rouen and Dieppe in its seafaring enterprise, and Samuel de Champlain founded Québec after sailing from Honfleur in 1608.

The sights are there to see, and the history is there to learn. But the greatest pleasure of Honfleur is to wander its streets, quays and squares, threading your way through alleys made narrow by tall, overhanging timber-framed houses. Take time to potter or to buy, to eat heartily or drink coffee, and above all to soak up the atmosphere.

Accommodation

Honfleur's most famous hotel is **La Ferme St-Siméon**, rue Marais (outside town towards Trouville, tel: 31 89 23 61). Once a fuelling stop for poor Impressionists, it is still thoroughly Norman, and beautifully run, with a fine restaurant – though prices have kept up with the times.

Generally, Honfleur's hotels are noticeably expensive, but several are well recommended. These include the **Hostellerie du Belvédère** (a good restaurant-with-rooms), 36 rue Emile-Rénouf (tel: 31 89 08 13); **Le Castel Albertine**, 19 cours Manuel (tel: 31 98 85 56); and **Le Cheval Blanc**, 2 quai des Passagers (tel: 31 89 13 49).

Restaurants

There is no shortage. **Au P'tit Marayeur**, 4 rue Haute (tel: 31 98 84 23), is in one of Honfleur's many pretty streets. It and the **Belvédère** (see under **Accommodation**, above) are perhaps best for value. **L'Assiette Gourmande**, 8 place Ste-Cathérine (tel: 31 89 24 88), is another in the tourist area, but still excellent. Other reliable ones include the nearby **La Lieutenance**, 12 place Ste-Catherine (tel: 31 89 07 52), and

Honfleur harbour – one of the classic sights of Normandy

L'Ancrage, 12 rue Montpensier (tel: 31 89 00 70). The decor is sometimes in modern style, but most of the houses are timbered inside as well as out. In spite of the many restaurants, few are empty during the season, and the place fairly pulsates with family *bonhomie* at the cheek-by-jowl tables. So start looking early if you haven't booked. Some restaurants may seem a little expensive for what they are, but the food is more than adequate – especially fish, of course, but succulent steaks as well.

Tourist Office
place Boudin (tel: 31 89 23 30).

Eugene Boudin
A generation ahead of the Impressionists, Boudin was a native of Honfleur and many of his works are local scenes. Art historians have tended to pigeon-hole Boudin as the precursor of Impressionism and move on, paying little attention to his pictures themselves – a pity, because the paintings repay closer study. Boudin specialised in small, horizontal pictures of beach parties, often seen from a distance with wide skies behind, and with light and shade featuring prominently. He befriended the young Monet – 16 years his junior – who did not, at that time, like Boudin's work. Nevertheless, Boudin was one of the exhibitors at what later became known as the First Impressionist Exhibition, in 1874.

HOULGATE

Situated between Deauville and Cabourg, Houlgate is a good choice, avoiding the excesses of either. This old-fashioned family resort, with turn-of-the-century villas and few modern buildings, has fine, long, flat sandy beaches but also rocks suitable for curious children. High cliffs to the east include the **Falaise des Vaches Noires** (Black Cow Cliff). The name was coined to describe the broken rocks covered by seaweed at its base.

Hotel and Restaurant
Le 1900, 17 rue Bains (tel: 31 91 07 77) is a central, simple restaurant-with-rooms.

Tourist Office
boulevard des Belges (tel: 31 24 34 79).

LUC-SUR-MER

north of Caen
A continuation of the resorts of Lion-sur-Mer and Riva-Bella, Luc-sur-Mer has an excellent **beach** and **gardens**, and deserves a mention, as does a local hotel called **Beau Rivage**, 1 rue Charcot (tel: 31 96 49 51)

Tourist Office
rue Charcot (tel: 31 97 33 25).

OUISTREHAM

north of Caen
This port and marina at the mouth of the River Orne is the dock for ferries from Portsmouth (Brittany Ferries). Places of interest here include a **lighthouse**, a small **Musée du Débarquement** (Invasion

Museum) and a Romanesque **church**. Ouistreham is full of small villas – a suburb of a resort. It runs into **Riva-Bella**, wtih its long, sandy **beach**.

Hotel and Restaurant
A recommended hotel and restaurant is the **Broche d'Argent**, place Général de Gaulle (tel: 31 97 12 16).

Tourist Office
place Thomas (tel: 31 97 18 63).

PORT-EN-BESSIN
northwest of Bayeux
This small working fishing port is claustrophobically flanked by cliffs and has no beach – rather unexpected on this coast. There is a museum of shipwrecks from the D-Day landings.
Open: daily June to September, also Easter and Pentecost.

Restaurant
One good fish restaurant is **La Foncée**, 12 rue Letourneur (tel: 31 21 71 66).

TROUVILLE
Trouville is a less expensive, smaller version of Deauville, on the other side of the River Touques. It has a similar but shorter **boardwalk** and a similar but less smart **children's train** regularly touring the streets. Trouville is more of a family place than Deauville, and more genteel. It also has better architecture, better restaurants, and (on the port) a **fish market** that is unbeatable.

Accommodation
There are several very pleasant small family hotels in Trouville, and choosing between them is difficult. Near the beach and in the heart of the town are the quiet **Carmen**, 24 rue Carnot (tel: 31 88 35 43); or the small but luxurious **St James**, 16 rue de la Plage (tel: 31 88 05 23). More anonymous modern ones are the **Beach**, 1 quai Albert (tel: 31 98 12 00), and the **Mercure**, place Maréchal Foch (tel: 31 87 38 38).

Shellfish at Trouville's fish market comes in all shapes – and sizes

Restaurants
The famous restaurant is **Les Vapeurs**, 160 boulevard Moureaux (tel: 31 88 15 24), but **Le Central** next door (tel: 31 88 13 68) is less brassy and perhaps even better. Boulevard Fernand Moureaux is packed with restaurants, and there are quite a number of adequate, reasonable places to eat.

Tourist Office
32–36 boulevard Moureaux (tel: 31 88 36 19).

CAEN

Like Rouen, like Le Havre, Caen suffered terribly in World War II. Unlike Le Havre, and still more than Rouen, it has nevertheless kept its old-world charm. That is due to its site, which has both level areas and hills, and to the easy pace of its streets and squares – it is more open than Rouen – and to the beauty of its stone, the yellow-grey, fine-grained Caen stone which was also shipped by the Normans to England for use in building. In this century its ore deposits made Caen a steel town, and it is surrounded by industry, but its population is only a third of Rouen's. It is a port, at **Ouistreham** (see page 54).

Caen was the creation of William the Conqueror, and its centre is bounded by his three great works, the Abbaye aux Hommes to the west, the Abbaye aux Dames to the east, and the castle overlooking the city in between. 'Guillaume le Conquérant' is a recurrent theme in Caen.

Open spaces in the town include the former **Cimetière St-Nicolas** (cemetery of St Nicholas), which has a Romanesque gate, and the **Jardin des Plantes** (Botanical Gardens).

Just outside the town to the west, off the D9 to St-Lô, the **Abbaye d'Ardenne** is a fine ruined 13th-century abbey.

There is access from the expressway round Caen to the **Mémoriale pour la Paix** on its northwestern side. Opened in 1988, the centrepiece of the memorial is a museum of World War ll, presented as a monument to future peace. Audio-visual presentations trace the events that led up to the war and portray life in occupied France, ending with a message of peace and hope for the future. The memorial centre is a convenient stopping-place, with a restaurant and bank.

Open: daily except Christmas Day and first half of January.

WHAT TO SEE

ABBAYE AUX DAMES

William the Conqueror is said to have founded Caen's two abbeys, one for men and one for women, in return for papal dispensation to marry his cousin Matilda. However, such dispensations were never a problem and the real point was to create burial churches or

mausoleums, one for himself and one for Matilda.

Matilda's foundation – the Abbaye aux Dames – is not so large, glorious or well furnished (or as well visited) as the Abbaye aux Hommes. The nave of its church – La Trinité – belongs to a slightly later, more ornate style of Romanesque, though it was actually founded earlier – in 1062. Matilda's plain tomb is in the chancel, which has been altered, though it still has its massive 11th-century barrel-vault. There are several figurative capitals in the church and in the crypt, including one with an elephant.

Open: daily; guided tours at 14.30 and 16.00hrs.

♦♦♦ ABBAYE AUX HOMMES ✓

Begun in 1066, the Abbaye aux Hommes has one of the grandest of all Norman Romanesque churches, St-Etienne. It is of enormous length and height for its day. It has wide, spacious galleries and a tall central crossing-tower (rebuilt) of the kind English cathedrals copied – for example, Ely and Norwich. Originally the nave had a wooden roof, but this was replaced in the early 12th century by a stone vault which was an important precursor of Gothic style. The east end, not completed until the 13th century, has a normal early Gothic vault. The outside view of the west end of the church is unique: a fortress of a church,

The Abbaye aux Hommes. The church of St-Etienne is flanked by 18th-century monastic buildings

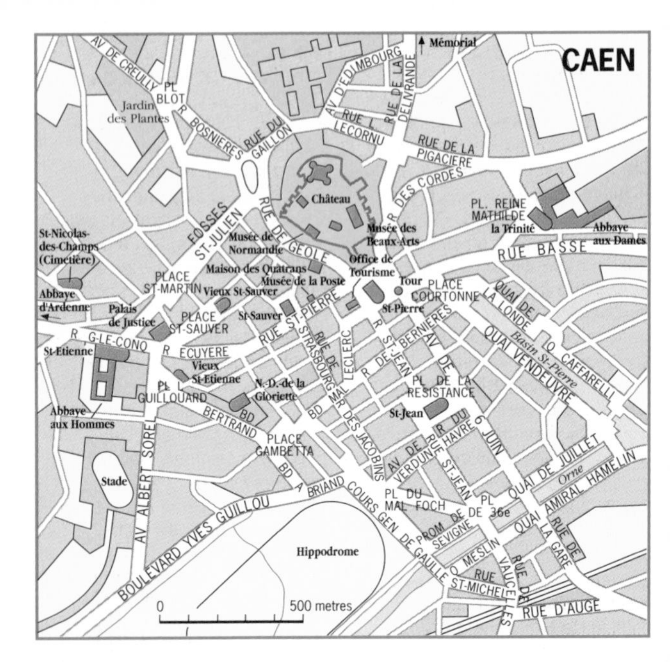

built like a Norman keep. Usually Gothic rose windows were inserted later, but this front has kept its primitive aspect.

The obvious thing missing from William's last resting place is his tomb – unfortunately destroyed in the 16th century. Some handsome church furniture of later date and the 18th-century monastic buildings (now the *Mairie* or town hall) are also worth seeing.

Open: guided tours daily.

◆◆

CASTLE

William's castle at Caen does not seem to have been very imposing. But later both English and French kings strengthened and refortified the site in their struggle for Normandy. By the 17th century, it had become obsolete both militarily and strategically, so was left derelict. Buildings grew up in its extensive bailey. The destruction wrought in World War II reduced it to a pristine archaeological site, in which the ruins are laid bare and two modern museums now stand. You enter the castle through one of two barbicans added in the 13th century and improved in the 14th and 15th. They once guarded drawbridges over a moat. Inside you can see the remains of the original keep, built in stone in the early 12th century by Henry I of England, and the so-called *Echiquier* (Exchequer), a palace of the same date, also the Chapelle St-

Georges (St George's Chapel). The curtain walls are due mostly to the French king, Philip Augustus.

The larger of the two museums in the bailey, the **Musée des Beaux-Arts**, has paintings from the Renaissance period, a substantial collection of baroque pictures by leading French and Dutch names, some good 18th-century French work and a collection featuring virtually all the best known French artists of the 19th century, from Romantics to Impressionists. The smaller **Musée de Normandie** is a historical museum concentrating on Norman rural life, with some excellent models and artefacts. There is also a good archaeological section.

Open: castle, free access; Musée de Normandie, Wednesday to Monday.

Closed: some holidays.

Note: Musée des Beaux-Arts *closed* at time of going to press, but due to re-open late 1993.

◆◆

MUSEE DE LA POSTE ET DES TECHNIQUES DE COMMUNICATION

rue St-Pierre

This museum of post and telecommunications is something out of the ordinary, and will particularly interest children. French telecommunications are some of the most advanced in Europe, so adults can catch up too. Besides the sophisticated systems of today, the museum also displays old equipment.

Open: Tuesday to Saturday, April to December.

Closed: mornings, except in summer.

Accommodation

There is no very special hotel in Caen, but two with good food, both near the castle, are **Le Dauphin,** 29 rue Gémare (tel: 31 86 22 26) and the **Relais des Gourmets**, 15 rue de Geôle (tel: 31 86 06 01).

Restaurants

The outstanding restaurant is **La Bourride**, 15 rue Vaugueux (tel: 31 93 50 76) – unassailably the best in town, some say in Normandy. It has a very Norman setting and equally Norman specialities, in both fish and meat. Nor is it the only one: **L'Ecaille**, 13 rue de Geôle (tel: 31 86 49 10), has outstanding fish and shellfish, or try the usually crowded **Le Boeuf Ferré**, 10 rue Froide (off rue Croisiers, tel: 31 85 36 40), or **Alcide**, 1 place Courtonne (tel: 31 44 18 06).

Tourist Office

1 place St-Pierre (tel: 31 86 27 65)

◆

ST-PIERRE

below the castle, in the centre of town (on rue St-Pierre)

This mostly 14th-century church has some splendid carving and an extraordinarily ornate early 16th-century east end, neither quite late Gothic nor early Renaissance. Opposite is the **Hôtel d'Escoville**, a merchant's mansion of the 1530s. Nearby streets feature half-timbered houses of equal antiquity. Few such buildings have survived in Caen, and almost all suffered heavy damage by bombs and fire in 1944.

BAYEUX

For visitors (and there are many of them, especially in summer), Bayeux is centred on the museum housing the famous Bayeux tapestry. There is more to the well-preserved medieval town than this, however. Unlike many towns and villages in Normandy, Bayeux escaped damage in World War II, and it has kept its historic feel. Do not miss its fine cathedral, its compact web of interesting old streets, such as the rue St-Malo and the rue St-Jean, and the fine half-timbered post inn, the **Lion d'Or**, which still serves excellent food.

WHAT TO SEE

BAYEUX TAPESTRY see CENTRE GUILLAUME LE CONQUERANT

♦♦
CATHEDRAL

The west end and the crypt date from the time of Odo, Bishop of Bayeux, one of William the Conqueror's close followers. His cathedral was completed in 1077, but much of this original church was subsequently rebuilt. The massive cross-ribs in the left tower are very early work, but most of the rest of the cathedral is 12th- and 13th-century.
Its splendid nave and choir, lit by a full set of enormous stained-glass windows, are beautiful High Gothic work. The nave is rather narrow because, despite the new Gothic elevations, the church was built on an original Romanesque plan.

♦♦♦
CENTRE GUILLAUME LE CONQUERANT ✓

rue de Nesmond
This is the new museum housing the **Bayeux tapestry** (*Tapisserie de la Reine Mathilde*). In the old days you might have taken your time to look at this extraordinary 11th-century embroidery with the story of the Conquest of England – but not any more. Before reaching the tapestry, visitors are led through a series of displays explaining the background to the events it depicts. Much of this is useful, but if the museum is crowded (as it usually is in summer), you have shuffled in a queue for too long by the time you reach the tapestry. This means you can expect to spend an hour or more in the museum, with perhaps only a few minutes looking at the tapestry itself.
The 230-foot (70m) embroidery is a crucial document, not just for the historical events of the Conquest, but for many different dimensions of Norman life – what the castles looked like before stone replaced the original wood; how oaths were sworn and treaties made; how people saddled and rode their horses. It is well known that the 'tapestry' is really an embroidery, but not that the end of it has been lost, so it breaks off well before William's coronation. It used to hang in the cathedral, and was probably made for Odo, Bishop of Bayeux, in an English workshop, perhaps in

Canterbury. The tale of the dispute for the crown of England is told from the Norman angle, putting the Saxon Harold in the wrong, but it is worth remembering that William had had the support of the previous Saxon king, Edward the Confessor, who admired Norman culture and had introduced it to England well before the Conquest.
Open: daily all year.

◆
MUSEE BARON-GERARD

north of the cathedral
A small permanent collection of paintings is displayed here in an old house of some charm. Some of Baron Gérard's own pictures are included: he was a rather theatrical follower of the great Neoclassicist J-L David in the early 19th century. The museum also represents the decorative arts with its displays of porcelain, ceramics and lace.
Open: daily all year.

◆
MUSEE MEMORIAL DE LA BATAILLE DE NORMANDIE

boulevard F. Ware
The Battle of Normandy Museum is in Bayeux because Bayeux was the first city liberated by the advancing Allied forces in 1944. It is an audio-visual paradise of models and dioramas, together with original military equipment, sound effects, and film footage from the campaign.
Open: daily all year.

Accommodation

The **Lion d'Or**, 71 rue St-Jean (tel: 31 92 06 90) is a traditional inn with a popular restaurant. There are other good hotels in the city, but none delivers quite the same experience. At the other end of the scale, **Family Home**, 39 rue Général de Dais (tel: 31 92 15 22), is a kind of boarding house, but good value and with generous portions of home cooking.

The cathedral, seen from the east

Restaurants

Apart from the restaurants of the two hotels above, there is no obvious choice, but try also **La Rapière**, 53 rue St-Jean (tel: 31 92 94 79).

Tourist Office

1 rue des Cuisiniers (tel: 31 92 16 26).

INLAND CENTRAL NORMANDY: AUGE, PERCHE AND SUISSE NORMANDE

If Normandy has a centre it is the **Pays d'Auge**, the region centred on Lisieux, traversed by the rivers Dives, Touques and Risle and spread across the *départements* of Calvados, Eure and Orne. This is archetypal Normandy, a green land of orchards and meadows grazed by spotted cows, and peppered with traditional *chaumières* – thatched and timber-framed houses or barns. From the orchards come the apples to make cider and Calvados, and from the cows the milk to make Camembert, invented near Vimoutiers in the Auge. The countryside is lush and varied, undulating and well covered with trees.

South of the Auge, in the region called the **Perche**, the houses revert to stone. There is a good scattering of turrets – perhaps the influence of the neighbouring Loire. The country is similar to the Auge, but the Perche has been known more for its horses than for its cows (there is a Percheron breed), and more for its *boudin* (black pudding) than for its cheese. There are some dense forests, too, and it is excellent territory for ramblers (*randonneurs*).

Due south of Caen, the **Suisse Normande** ('Norman Switzerland') is so called not because it has any real mountains but because it is the kind of place to go camping, walking or canoeing. Through the middle of this country of wooded hills, the River Orne

Normandy's countryside at its peaceful best – a farm in the Perche

courses through a series of rocky gorges.
One more region that could be mentioned is the **Ouche**, between the River Eure to the east and the Auge and Perche to the west. But with all these regions, borders are vague and still leave great tracts of land without a convenient label.
There is no dramatic change in the countryside as you travel through central Normandy, although it becomes a little drier towards the west. It is all quite lush enough, however, to make a superb touring or rambling holiday, or a delightful backdrop to a more indulgent eating-and-drinking stopover, staying either in one of the many delightful half-timbered inns or in one of the superb *châteaux*-hotels.
Dedicated sightseers will find plenty of notable *châteaux*, churches and abbeys in central Normandy, many of which are mentioned in **What to See**, below. However, a whistle-stop tour of the 'sights' would miss the point. Essentially this is a region for leisurely, and perhaps unplanned, touring. Almost wherever you go, you will be sure to discover unpretentious, timeless villages, bustling old country towns full of atmosphere, rural lanes and by-ways well off the beaten track, and a countryside that has for the most part escaped the ravages of late 20th-century agriculture and development. Abandon your schedules, arm yourself with a good map and – most of all – take your time!

WHAT TO SEE

(See map on pages 48-9)

ALENCON

This delightful old Norman town lies close to the centre of a huge conservation area – the **Parc Naturel Régional Normandie-Maine**. Alençon has its own forests – **Perseigne** to the east, **Ecouves** to the north – and, to the west, the hills called the **Alpes Mancelles**. Both Perseigne and Ecouves are mixed forests; in the Forêt d'Ecouves boar are reputed still to roam.
Alençon itself – famed in the past for its lace-making – has a church and a museum worth visiting. **Notre-Dame** is a Flamboyant Gothic church with fine stonework and stained glass; it also has a chapel commemorating Ste Thérèse of

Alençon's lace museum

Lisieux, who was baptised here. The **Musée des Beaux-Arts et de la Dentelle** (Museum of Fine Art and Lace) contains two disparate collections, one of paintings and one of lace. Its lace industry was implanted in Alençon by Louis XIV's minister Colbert – a kind of parallel to the royal workshops that made Gobelins famous for tapestries, or Sèvres for porcelain. Certainly the finest lacework in France was made here. The museum also has a collection of lace made by its European rivals, especially Venice.
Open: Tuesday to Sunday.

Lace-making in Normandy
Lace as we know it was probably first produced in Flanders, but by the 17th century the lace of Venice was considered the finest. By then, lace was an essential part of fashionable costume. Schools of lace-making sprang up elsewhere in Europe, including those at Alençon, Bayeux and Argentan in Normandy. Each lace-making centre developed its own stitches and techniques, and both needlepoint and bobbin lace were found. Many hours of painstaking, detailed work went into this hand-made lace, and patterns were a jealously guarded 'trade secret'.
The 19th century saw the burgeoning of the machine lace industry, notably at Nottingham in England. Passable lace could be made in a fraction of the time taken to produce the hand-made article, and commercial lace-making by hand began to die out.
Normandy produces little hand-made lace today, but examples of the exquisite workmanship of the past can be seen in the museums at Alençon and Bayeux.

Accommodation and Restaurants
The best hotel (and quite reasonable) must be the **Chapeau Rouge**, 1 boulevard Duchamp (tel: 33 26 20 23). It has no restaurant, so you will have to go out – perhaps to the edge of town, to **Au Petit Vatel**, 72 place Desmeulles (tel: 33 26 23 78).

Tourist Office
Maison d'Ozé, 1 place Lamagdelaine (tel: 33 26 11 36).

ARGENTAN
A historic small town with two Flamboyant Gothic churches, several hotels and restaurants and a good market, Argentan is bordered by the Suisse Normande to the west and the Forêt de Gouffern to the east. This makes it a good touring centre, with plenty of places of interest within easy reach. Famous for its lace – '*le point d'Argentan*' – the town was also a key position in the fighting that followed D-Day in 1944. Like so many other Norman towns, it suffered heavy damage.

Tourist Office
1 place du Marché (tel: 33 67 12 48).

AUBIGNY see FALAISE

The lake and casino at Bagnoles

◆
BAGNOLES-DE-L'ORNE

Bagnoles is a spa town, and though it is unique in Normandy it has the neat and tidy air of spas everywhere. The municipal gardens and casino by the lake are classic spa-town architecture. However, Bagnoles today is also a centre for rambling or cycling in the nearby **Forêt d'Ecouves** (see page 63).

Accommodation and Restaurants

Bagnoles has several well-run hotels; one especially worth noting for its food is the **Manoir du Lys**, out on the D235 towards Juvigny (tel: 33 37 80 69). This comfortable hotel is a converted 19th-century hunting lodge in spacious grounds.

Tourist Office

place de la République (tel: 33 37 85 66).

◆◆
BALLEROY, CHATEAU DE

southwest of Bayeux

Here is a remarkable and well-preserved house in the French classical style. Under the royal architect François Mansart, it rose in one build from 1626 to 1636, and has kept its interior decoration, by Charles de la Fosse, largely unaltered. Externally, though severe, the house is a fitting and rather splendid climax to a sequence of gatehouse, drive, service quarters and formal gardens designed by the famous French landscaper Le Nôtre. A **balloon museum** has been set up in recent years.

Open: Thursday to Tuesday, mid-April to October.

BEAUMESNIL, CHATEAU DE

between Bernay and Conches

This *château* is almost exactly contemporary (1633–40) with Balleroy (see p. 65) and very similar in design, though the façade is considerably more enriched. It, too, has beautiful gardens, including a lake, and an additional museum, this one of book-binding.

Open: Friday to Monday afternoons, mid-May to mid-September.

BEC-HELLOUIN, LE

southeast of Pont-Audemer

The fame of the historic **abbey** here on the River Risle goes back to the 11th century. In 1034 Herluin renounced the world and founded his own small hermitage here. It grew, beyond his original intentions, into a leading religious and intellectual centre. From it sprang the first two Norman archbishops of Canterbury, Lanfranc and St Anselm – the most distinguished theologian of his time.

The monastery remained in being until the Revolution, when, like many others in Normandy, it was pulled apart for the stone; monks returned in 1948 and built a new church beside the ruins. Today there is a rather incongruous **car museum** nearby.

Open: Wednesday to Monday.

Accommodation

The **Auberge de l'Abbaye** (tel: 32 44 86 02) offers simple bedrooms and good Norman cooking in a delightful village house.

BELLEME

Overlooking a superb oak forest in the Perche region, Bellême is an attractive, well-preserved little town on a hill. Little remains of its 15th-century ramparts, but there are some interesting old houses and a couple of hotels and restaurants. A pleasant short walk in the nearby **Forêt de Bellême** is round the lake known as **l'Etang de la Herse**.

Tourist Office

Hôtel de Ville (tel: 33 73 09 69).

BERNAY

This historic Norman town grew up around the now ruined abbey church in its centre. Founded in 1013 by William the Conqueror's grandmother, this was later rebuilt, but some very early parts remain. Close by is a small **museum** of local crafts.

Open: Wednesday to Monday.

The church of **Ste-Croix** dates from the 14th and 15th centuries. Among Bernay's half-timbered houses are some typically Norman hotels and restaurants. There is also a pleasant walk along the **Promenade des Monts**.

Tourist Office

29 rue Thiers (tel: 32 43 32 08).

BOURG-ST-LEONARD, LE

The late 18th-century **château** here has fine contemporary interiors including tapestries and Louis XV furniture.

Open: Thursday to Tuesday, mid-June to mid-September.

Closed: mornings except first half of August.

◆

BRECY

east of Bayeux

Brécy has a 13th-century parish church and, round the small 17th-century **château**, some very pretty formal gardens.
Open: daily, April to October.

◆

BRIONNE

northeast of Bernay

Another charming Norman market town, on the River Risle, Brionne has an 11th-century *donjon* (keep), a 15th-century church with a fine wooden roof, and a craft museum, the **Maison de Normandie**.
Open: all year. *Closed*: Wednesday, October to May.
There are two excellent hotel-restaurants, **Auberge Vieux Donjon**, 19 rue Soie (tel: 32 44 80 62), and **Logis de Brionne**, 1 place St-Denis (tel: 32 44 81 73).

Tourist Office
place de l'Eglise (tel: 32 45 70 51).

◆

CANAPVILLE

southeast of Deauville

The 15th-century timbered manor here is worth visiting as a fine example of traditional Norman building style.
Open: Wednesday to Monday afternoons, mid-June to August; weekends and holidays only out of season.

CANON, CHATEAU DE

southeast of Caen

This minor *château* is important for its 18th-century gardens. Embellished by statues and follies, the gardens are formal but influenced by contemporary English landscaping.
Open: Wednesday to Monday afternoons, July to September; weekend and holiday afternoons, Easter to June.

Le Bec-Hellouin village

The Pont du Vey at Clécy

◆

CARROUGES

east of Bagnoles-de-l'Orne

Domain for centuries of the prominent Le Veneur de Thillières family, the fine **château** just outside this hilltop village is a rambling but impressive mixture of ages and styles with a splendid early Renaissance gatehouse and surrounded by a moat. Its interiors also date from several periods.

Open: Wednesday to Monday.
Closed: some holidays.

◆

CERISY-LA-FORET

between St-Lô and Bayeux

The shorn abbey here is a Romanesque gem in a now greatly reduced beech forest. The church has lost four of its former seven bays, but remains worth seeing.

◆

CHAMBOIS

northeast of Argentan

The ruined keep at Chambois, built under Henry II of England though since modified, was long a key strongpoint of the region. The village's later fame is remembered in a monument in the square which commemorates its key role at the end of the Battle of Normandy in 1944.

◆

CHAMP-DE-BATAILLE

southwest of Rouen

Champ-de-Bataille is one of Normandy's grandest *châteaux*. The late 17th-century building has predominantly 18th-century Neoclassical interiors. It is now also a country club with a golf-course.

Open: afternoons, April to October.

◆◆

CLECY

A good centre for exploring the Suisse Normande, Clécy is an attractive village on the River Orne. Several walks are signposted; one goes to the **Musée du Chemin de Fer Miniature** (model railway museum).

Open: daily; mornings only October to Easter.

There is also a craft museum at the **Manoir de Placy.**

Open: guided tours daily afternoons only, July and August.

Cafés and restaurants cluster round the **Pont du Vey**, and landmarks and viewpoints further afield within walking distance include the **Viaduc de la Lande** and the **Pain de Sucre**. Paintings of the Suisse Normande by the artist André Hardy can be seen in the **Musée Hardy**.

Open: daily, Easter to September.

Accommodation and Restaurants
Several good hotel-restaurants include **Le Moulin du Vey**, by the Vey bridge (tel: 31 69 71 08).

Tourist Office
Mairie, place de l'Eglise (tel: 31 69 79 95).

◆
CONCHES-EN-OUCHE
Conches is another small Norman town with all the traditional ingredients: a large forest nearby; a ruined castle; a charming 16th-century church with notable stained glass; good restaurants including **La Toque Blanche**, 18 place Carnot (tel: 32 30 01 54).

Tourist Office
Maison des Arts, place Aristide-Briand (tel: 32 30 91 82).

◆
CREVECOEUR-EN-AUGE
west of Lisieux
The village called 'Heartbreak in the Auge' has a charming ruined **castle** with 500-year-old farm buildings in the bailey, restored and converted into a small museum of oil prospecting. Art exhibitions are also held here.
Open: afternoons, mid-February to mid-November.

◆
DOMFRONT
The castle here was once very grand and as late as 1578 withstood siege when held by the extraordinary character Gabriel de Montgomery, who killed the French king Henri II in a tournament, and was later beheaded. Beside the castle ruins and a Romanesque church there is a rather self-conscious old town, empty of hotels and restaurants, which are to be found in the new town at the bottom of the hill.
Two modest hotels, both with restaurants, are the **Poste**, rue Maréchal Foch (tel: 33 38 51 00), and the **France**, rue Mont-St-Michel (tel: 33 38 51 44).

Tourist Office
rue Dr Barrabé (tel: 33 38 53 97).

FALAISE
The birthplace of William the Conqueror in 1027, Falaise has a fine **castle** – much bigger than the one he occupied, but on the same site. The town's name (French for 'cliff') comes from the castle's site – a great bluff rearing over the valley. The keep, with outjutting chapel, is 12th-century, built by Henry I; the cylindrical Tour de Talbot was added in the early 13th century, and the curtain walls slightly later.
Open: daily except Monday and Tuesday in winter.
The rest of the town, which suffered badly in World War II, is somewhat characterless, but has adequate hotels and good-value restaurants. There is not a wide choice: for hotels try the **Normandie**, 4 rue Amiral Courbet (tel: 31 90 18 26) or the **Poste**, 38 rue Clémenceau (tel: 31 90 13 14). A nearby restaurant is **La Fine Fourchette**, 52 rue Clémenceau (tel: 31 90 08 59).
The tiny village of **Aubigny**, just north of Falaise, is worth visiting

for the outstanding tombs in its church. They show six former lords of the manor, all dressed up in a row ready for the Almighty.

Tourist Office
32 rue Clemenceau (tel: 31 90 17 26).

FONTAINE-HENRY

northwest of Caen
The grand **château** here was constructed slowly from the end of the 15th century through the 16th, and fascinatingly evolves – from south to north – from Gothic into classical. Inside there is a notable collection mostly of French paintings.
Open: Wednesday to Monday, mid-June to mid-September; weekend and holiday afternoons Easter to mid-June and mid-September to October.

HARAS DU PIN see PIN, LE

HARCOURT

southeast of Brionne
The **château** at Harcourt fronts a lovely ruined bailey in the unusual and tranquil setting of a mature arboretum. This is the ancestral home of the Harcourt family, whose name crops up again and again in French history. Members of the family have been involved in military and political affairs from the 11th century to the present day. Their castle here has suffered various damage, by warfare and by fire, over the centuries, but remains surprisingly well preserved.
Open: afternoons, mid-March to mid-November.

LE PIN see PIN, LE

LISIEUX

Lisieux is an historic bishopric and is today the leading town of the Auge region. It is also the home town of Ste Thérèse of Lisieux, which has transformed it into a lesser Lourdes. The pilgrim traffic to her house (**'Les Buissonets'**) and to the **Basilique Ste-Thérèse** – an enormous sugar-cake of a church, consecrated in the 1950s – is considerable.
Lisieux has a charming 13th-century **cathedral**, with a renowned Flamboyant Gothic chapel built by one of its bishops in the mid-15th century. While in Lisieux, take a few minutes to wander among the timbered-framed buildings of its old streets, and to visit the market – good for all sorts of traditional Normandy fare.

Tourist Office
11 rue d'Alençon (tel: 31 62 08 41).

LONGNY-AU-PERCHE

east of Mortagne-au-Perche
Though it is a pleasant little town well situated for exploring the wooded countryside of the eastern Perche, Longny has only a few hotels and restaurants. The chapel of Notre-Dame-de-Pitié dates from the 16th century.

Tourist Office
Hôtel de Ville (tel: 33 73 65 42).

MORTAGNE-AU-PERCHE

This attractive and unspoilt hill town is a good base for a stay in the Perche countryside. The

The Percheron – Normandy's Own Horse

The Perche region of Normandy, with Mortagne as its traditional capital, has long been famous for breeding horses. The best known, taking its name from the district, is the Percheron, a heavily built grey or black breed which was first reared by a small group of farmers in the Perche in the early 19th century – though the horse's ancestry is said to be traceable back to the Crusades. Energetic yet sure-footed, tremendously strong yet docile and easily broken, Percherons were highly prized for farm work in the days before tractors. Today, they may be less sought after for this purpose in many countries, but Percherons have been bred all over the world and their fine qualities are still much valued in cross-breeding.

church of **Notre-Dame** is a blend of Flamboyant Gothic and Renaissance styles, with some fine 18th-century carvings.

Restaurants

Two excellent, traditional restaurants are the **Genty-Home**, 4 rue Notre-Dame (tel: 33 25 11 53), and the **Tribunal**, 4 place du Palais (tel: 33 25 04 77). Both of these have rooms available.

Tourist Office

place Général de Gaulle (tel: 33 25 19 21).

MORTAIN

The historic town of Mortain has an attractive setting by river and forest. The 13th-century church of **St-Evroult** survived substantial war damage to Mortain in 1944. Nearby is the **Abbaye Blanche**, a 12th-century Cistercian church whose plainness reflects the early asceticism of the order. *Open*: Wednesday to Monday. *Closed*: Sunday morning.

There is good rambling countryside to the north of Mortain, around the valley of the River Sée. Nearer at hand, a steep track just off the Avenue de l'Abbaye-Blanche leads to the **Grande Cascade**, an 80-foot (25m) waterfall.

Reasonable accommodation and meals are available in the town. Two modest hotels serving local fare are the **Poste**, 1 place des Arcades (tel: 33 59 00 05), and the **Cascades**, 16 rue Bassin (tel: 33 59 00 03).

Tourist Office

place Hôtel de Ville (tel: 33 59 19 74).

A Percheron at the Haras du Pin

◆◆◆

O, CHATEAU D' ✓

southeast of Argentan

A kind of French Elsinore, with its tall gatehouse and witch's hat roofs, the strangely named Château d'O stands beside a dreamy lake.

The building has much of the Renaissance about it, but the oldest part dates from the 15th century. To this, two newer wings were subsequently added round a courtyard. The effect is a harmonious and enchanting whole, and the interiors are well worth seeing too. Several members of the O family, the one-time owners, were prominent government figures of their day.

Open: daily, July to September. *Closed*: February, and mornings from October to June. You can picnic in the park or dine in the restaurant (tel: 33 35 35 27) in the stable block.

◆

ORBEC

An attractive small town at the southern end of the Auge, Orbec has an assortment of appealing old houses in its busy main street, where a good range of everyday shops and a small country market can also be found. There are a couple of good hotel-restaurants: the **France**, 152 rue Grande (tel: 31 32 74 02), and **Au Caneton**, 32 rue Grande (tel: 31 32 73 32).

Tourist Office

rue Guillonière (tel: 31 32 87 15).

◆

PIN, LE

east of Argentan

Haras du Pin – the French National Stud – has been situated here since the time of Louis XIV. The *château* is not open, but the stables and carriage collection are.

Open: daily (guided tours only). On Thursdays at 15.00 hrs from mid-May to mid-September there is a parade of stallions.

The stuff of fairy-tales – Château d'O, mirrored in its lake

◆◆

PONT-AUDEMER

Though close to the Paris–Caen motorway and the industry of the lower Seine, Pont-Audemer is a quiet town full of charming back streets with half-timbered riverside houses and an 11th-century church, **St-Ouen**. The *pont* was for centuries the lowest bridge on the River Risle, and Pont-Audemer has long been a useful halting point for travellers.

Between Pont-Audemer and the Pont de Tancarville is the low-lying country of the **Marais Vernier**. Especially attractive in spring, this little-known, rural corner of the Seine Valley is surrounded by some fine viewpoints – ideal for a last 'breath of French air' before travelling on to Le Havre.

Accommodation and Restaurants

Pont-Audemer's **Auberge du Vieux Puits**, 6 rue Notre-Dame-du-Pré (tel: 32 41 01 48) is a fine '*maison ancienne normande*' and a former tannery. Traditional dishes are served in welcoming surroundings, and guests have a choice of smaller, simpler bedrooms in the main building or more modern ones in the new wing. An alternative is **La Frégate**, 4 rue La Seüle (tel: 32 41 12 03).

Tourist Office

place Maubert (tel: 32 41 08 21).

PONTECOULANT

southwest of Clécy

This serene, mostly 18th-century *château* stands in an English-style park in the Suisse Normande – one of the few *châteaux* in the region.

Open: Wednesday to Monday. *Closed*: October; mornings in winter.

ST-GABRIEL-BRECY

east of Bayeux

Only the east end remains of the ornate, late Romanesque priory church here, but the 13th-century gatehouse and the 14th-century prior's lodgings are intact. The priory is now a horticultural school whose gardens can also be visited.

Open: daily all year (guided tours July to September).

ST-GERMAIN-DE-LIVET

south of Lisieux

This splendid Renaissance *château* – one of the best in Normandy – evokes all the pageantry of a tournament, with its chequered walls and conical turrets. Surviving frescoes of the late 16th century show battle scenes.

Open: Wednesday to Monday. *Closed*: first half of October; mid-December to January.

ST-PIERRE-SUR-DIVES

southwest of Lisieux

The extraordinary market hall makes this ordinary, out-of-the-way little town worth visiting for its market alone. The great barn of a building, which now shelters chickens and rabbits on market days, was destroyed in 1944, but was later rebuilt. This was done using replicas of the medieval timbers and dowels (of which there are said

to be nearly 300,000) and no nails. A **museum of cheese-making** can be found in the former abbey.
Open: Wednesday to Monday.
Closed: mornings in winter.

Tourist Office
12 rue St Benoît (tel: 31 20 81 68).

◆

SASSY, CHATEAU DE

south of Argentan
This imposing 18th-century *château* with seigneurial views is still owned by the dukes of Audriffet-Pasquier, who were influential statesmen in the days of Louis-Philippe.
Open: gardens at all times; *château* Easter to October.

◆

SEES

This small town was an important place in late Gallo-Roman antiquity, when it became a bishopric. It still has a bishop, and a medium-sized cathedral rebuilt during the 13th and 14th centuries. Some of the fine stained glass dates from the same period. There are pleasant hotels and restaurants for countryside tourers or ramblers in the nearby Forêt d'Ecouves.

Accommodation
An old favourite is the **Cheval Blanc**, a timber-and-plaster inn, 1 place St-Pierre (tel: 33 27 80 48); also recommended is the **Normandy**, 12 rue Ardrillers (tel:33 27 98 27), with an inexpensive restaurant.
A good country hotel is the **Ile de Sées**, three miles (5km) away at Macé on the D303 (tel: 33 27 98 65).

Tourist Office
Hôtel de Ville, place Général de Gaulle (tel: 33 28 74 79).

◆

THURY-HARCOURT

One of several centres for visiting the Suisse Normande, Thury-Harcourt is on the northern edge of the area beside the River Orne. The *château* was one of many buildings destroyed in 1944, though its chapel and park – now fully restored to include a series of gardens – survive.
Open: afternoons daily June to September; Sundays and holidays May, June and October.

VENDEUVRE, CHATEAU DE

southwest of St-Pierre-sur-Dives
The *château* was the work of the distinguished architect Jacques-François Blondel, but is a conservative and unexceptional

Vimoutiers – Marie Harel's statue

design. Besides the intact interiors and fine gardens, there is a museum of miniature furniture, featuring apprentices' 'masterpieces' or exercises to demonstrate their cabinet-working skills.
Open: afternoons daily June to mid-September, weekend and holiday afternoons Easter to May and mid-September to October.

◆
VERNEUIL-SUR-AVRE

This one-time English stronghold in the southern Ouche region has little sign of its early history. The Flamboyant Gothic church of **La Madeleine** was rebuilt after Verneuil's final recapture by the French in 1449. The second church, **Notre-Dame**, has a notable series of 16th-century statues by local craftsmen. Verneuil is a good centre for touring or rambling.

Accommodation and Restaurants

There are a couple of good-value restaurant-hotels – the rather expensive **Hostellerie du Clos**, 98 rue Ferté-Vidame (tel: 32 32 21 81), and the simpler **Saumon**, 89 place Madeleine (tel: 32 32 02 36).

Tourist Office

129 place Madeleine (tel: 32 32 17 17).

◆
VIMOUTIERS

This is famous as the place where Camembert was first sold. Marie Harel, who brought it to the market here, made it in the neighbouring village of Camembert. There is a Camembert museum just by the tourist office.
Open: Monday afternoon to Sunday. *Closed*: Saturday afternoon and Sunday, November to April.
Vimoutiers is almost equally well known for its Calvados. Both are liberally offered for tasting in the town and on some of the nearby farms.

Tourist Office

10 avenue Général de Gaulle (tel: 33 39 30 29).

Exploring Camembert Country

Visitors to the Vimoutiers area of the Pays d'Auge will not escape reminders that this was the birthplace of this classic soft cheese.
Having visited the **Musée du Camembert** in Vimoutiers itself, you could seek out Marie Harel's home village (its name now a household word) just southwest of the town. Then why not drive along all or part of the **Route du Camembert**. Like the *Route des Fromages*, a little further north (taking in Livarot and Pont l'Evêque), the *Route du Camembert* is not only for cheese freaks. It should appeal to anyone who enjoys exploring the quintessential Normandy countryside of green pastures and orchards, tucked-away farmsteads and rural lanes. Tasting farm-produced cheeses, and perhaps buying some for a picnic lunch or to take home with you, is a bonus along the way.

NORTHWEST NORMANDY: COTENTIN, *BOCAGE* AND MONT-ST-MICHEL

The northern half of the *département* of Manche forms the Cotentin Peninsula (also known in English as the Cherbourg Peninsula). Inland, much of the country here and further south is all of a piece with the neighbouring parts of middle Normandy known as the *Bocage*. It is a pleasant, varied countryside of meadows, hedgerows, orchards and woods, rich in wild flowers and with a scattering of peaceful small market towns and historic abbeys.

The western coast of Manche, facing the Channel Islands, has many excellent beaches and unfashionable, uncrowded resorts that often have a refreshingly dated feel. This part of Normandy is a little too far from Paris for a comfortable day trip; other visitors also tend either to stop earlier or to travel further on to Brittany. However, it is quite easily accessible to the British, crossing the Channel to Cherbourg.

The southernmost stretch of this coast faces into the bay of Mont-St-Michel. Neighbouring Brittany forms most of the bay's southern and western edges, but tucked into its southeastern corner is a bit of Normandy that must not be missed – Mont-St-Michel itself. Visit early or late in the day: with up to three-quarters of a million visitors annually, this spectacular site is not a place to get away from the crowds.

By contrast, much of the northern Cotentin has a rather remote feel, and at the tip the character of its coastline changes. It is often compared to Brittany or Cornwall. Instead of flat strands, the coast rears up into storm-beaten cliffs, and it is a land of points and lighthouses, with a history of wrecks. Nevertheless the northeastern inland region known as the Val de Saire is pretty and friendly country. Here you are never far from the coast, which is punctuated by pleasant, quiet fishing villages. Further south, the flatter and rather featureless eastern seaboard has attracted much attention for its role – as Utah Beach – in the D-Day landings of 1944.

The upper Cotentin is sparsely populated except for the major industrial port of Cherbourg, which feels anything but remote. Next in size among the towns of Manche comes the historic but badly bombed St-Lô. These two modern towns have eclipsed the old capital, Coutances – which remains, however, one of the most agreeable towns in all Normandy.

WHAT TO SEE

AVRANCHES

This has been a kind of landing-stage for Mont-St-Michel (see pp. 85-86) ever since Aubert, Bishop of Avranches, was nudged rather violently by the angel Michael into founding the monastery there in the 8th century. You can look out to the Mount from the town and today, in summer, you can even go for a flight over it from Avranches'

Not a plant out of place – the public gardens in Avranches

little airfield. The **Musée de l'Avranchin** in the former bishop's palace has manuscripts from Mont-St-Michel, and an archaeological and popular art section.
Open: Wednesday to Monday, Easter to mid-October.
In its own right Avranches can now boast perhaps only its **Jardins des Plantes** (municipal gardens), in which it outdoes most other towns in the area, though they compete. On the site of the destroyed cathedral, the spot is marked where Henry II knelt to do penance for the murder at Canterbury in 1170 of Thomas Becket. On another preserved site the American General Patton stayed in 1944, at the time of the so-called Avranches offensive against the main German Panzer division. There is a war museum, **Musée de la Seconde Guerre Mondiale**, at **Le Val St-Père**, to the south.
Open: daily in summer; weekends and holidays in winter.

Accommodation
A number of small, reasonable hotels make Avranches an excellent stop for a tour including Mont-St-Michel. **La Croix d'Or**, 83 rue Constitution (tel: 33 58 04 88) is open only during the season. A modern contrast is **Les Abricantes**, 37 boulevard Luxembourg (tel: 33 58 66 64), or try the **Jardin des Plantes**, 10 place Carnot (tel: 33 58 03 68), with good-value home cooking.

Tourist Office
2 rue Général de Gaulle (tel: 33 58 00 22).

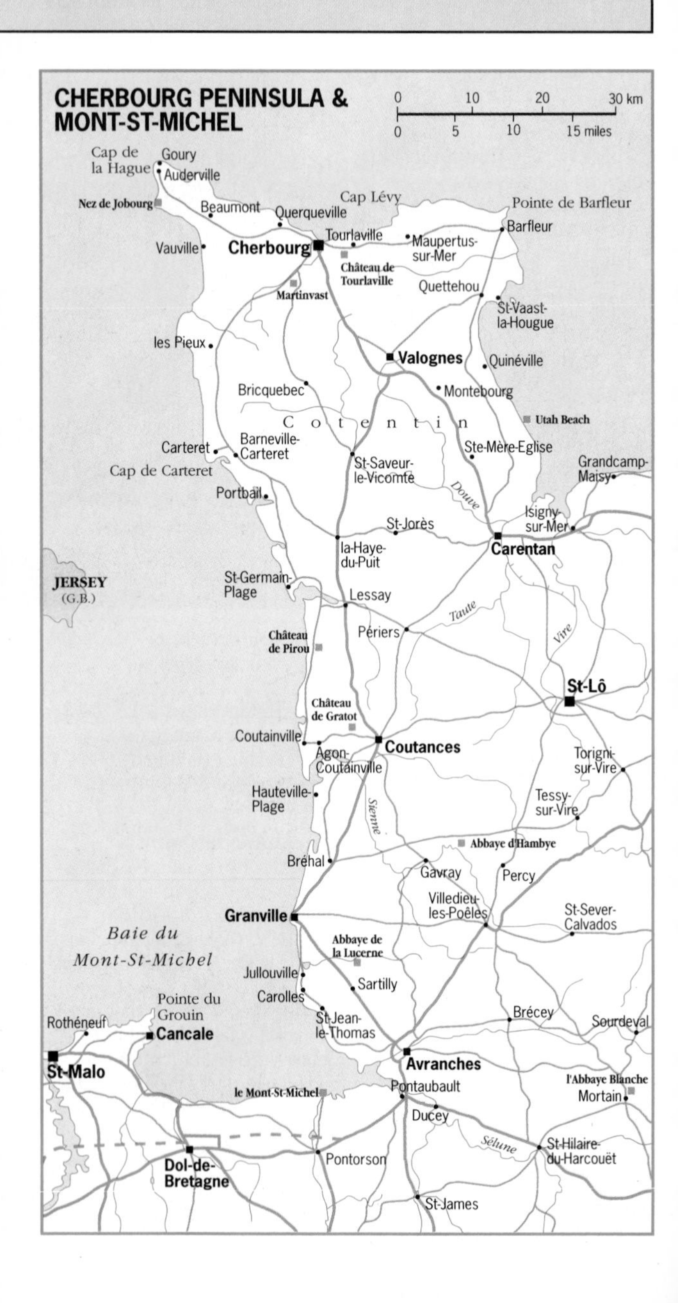
CHERBOURG PENINSULA & MONT-ST-MICHEL
0 10 20 30 km
0 5 10 15 miles
Cap de la Hague
Goury
Auderville
Nez de Jobourg
Beaumont
Querqueville
Cap Lévy
Pointe de Barfleur
Barfleur
Tourlaville
Maupertus-sur-Mer
Vauville
Cherbourg
Château de Tourlaville
Martinvast
Quettehou
St-Vaast-la-Hougue
les Pieux
Valognes
Quinéville
Bricquebec
Montebourg
Cotentin
Utah Beach
Carteret
Barneville-Carteret
Ste-Mère-Eglise
Cap de Carteret
St-Saveur-le-Vicomte
Grandcamp-Maisy
Portbail
Douve
Isigny-sur-Mer
St-Jorès
la-Haye-du-Puit
Carentan
JERSEY (G.B.)
St-Germain-Plage
Lessay
Taute
Périers
Vire
Château de Pirou
St-Lô
Château de Gratot
Coutainville
Coutances
Agon-Coutainville
Torigni-sur-Vire
Hauteville-Plage
Sienne
Tessy-sur-Vire
Abbaye d'Hambye
Bréhal
Gavray
Percy
Villedieu-les-Poêles
Granville
St-Sever-Calvados
Baie du Mont-St-Michel
Abbaye de la Lucerne
Jullouville
Sartilly
Carolles
Pointe du Grouin
Rothéneuf
Cancale
St-Jean-le-Thomas
Brécey
Sourdeval
St-Malo
Avranches
l'Abbaye Blanche
le Mont-St-Michel
Pontaubault
Mortain
Ducey
Sélune
St-Hilaire-du-Harcouët
Dol-de-Bretagne
Pontorson
St-James

BARFLEUR

east of Cherbourg

Barfleur is a romantic fishing-port and now a yachting marina. A stroll in its attractive and quiet streets offers a good first taste of France to visitors arriving at Cherbourg.

Barfleur was frequently used as a Channel port in Norman times and the White Ship, in which William Atheling (heir to Henry I) and his retinue drowned in 1120, foundered close by. The tragedy upset Henry's careful dynastic plans and gave rise, after his death, to the civil wars of Stephen and Matilda.

Today Barfleur has the tallest **lighthouse** in Normandy, for its waters are still dangerous, being shallow and with strong currents. The fit can climb its 365 steps for the view.

Open: daily April to September; winter, Sundays only.

Accommodation

The best hotel is the simple **Conquérant**, 16–18 rue St-Thomas-Becket (tel: 33 54 00 82). Duke William is said to have set off from here for Dives on his way to conquer England.

Tourist Office

rue St-Thomas-Becket (tel : 33 54 02 48).

BARNEVILLE-CARTERET

Barneville and Carteret lie on opposite sides of a sheltered harbour behind the point of Cap de Carteret. The amenities of these merged resorts include a port (departure point for the Channel Islands) and marina, cliffs with a walk, and two **beaches**. There is also an excellent **market**, for both sea and land produce.

In summer Barneville and Carteret swell with seasonal visitors, mostly French, staying close by on a traditional family holiday. The place is crowded enough for atmosphere, but not swamped, not pressured, and not smart.

Barneville's church is mostly Romanesque, with some notable carving on the arches and capitals.

Accommodation and Restaurants

There are quite a number of decent and reasonable places

Barfleur's historic fishing port

to stay and to eat. **Les Isles**, 9 boulevard Maritime, Barneville-Plage (tel: 33 04 90 76) is more of a family hotel, with straightforward cooking. The **Marine**, 11 rue de Paris, Carteret (tel: 33 53 83 31), is the grandest, with a starred restaurant.

Tourist Offices
Barneville – rue des Ecoles (tel: 33 04 90 58); Carteret – place Flandres-Dunkerque (tel: 33 04 94 54).

◆

BRICQUEBEC

inland, between Cherbourg and Barneville-Carteret
A remarkable 11-sided 14th-century *donjon* (keep) on a motte or mound dominates Bricquebec's ruined castle, which still also has its curtain wall and gatehouse.
Open: ruins at all times.
The big market place near by hums into life on Monday mornings.

CARENTAN

Set at the foot of the Cotentin Peninsula, on the main route to Cherbourg, Carentan would benefit from a by-pass. People come here for the market, which specialises in cattle and for the yacht marina, a successful new attraction. The church of **Notre-Dame** has perhaps the most easterly piece of Flamboyant Gothic architecture in Normandy.

Accommodation
A good hotel and restaurant is the **Hotel du Commerce et de la Gare**, 34 rue de la Gare (tel: 33 42 02 00).

Tourist Office
Hôtel de Ville (tel: 33 42 05 87).

CAROLLES

south of Granville
Slightly inland, Carolles village is situated in pleasant walking country (for instance, the so-called **Vallée des Peintres** – Artists' Vale – or the **Vallée du Lude**). **Carolles-Plage** is an equally pleasant beach resort.

CARTERET SEE BARNEVILLE-CARTERET

CHERBOURG

There is something gloomy about most of the Channel ports – perhaps because nobody looks at them, or stays in them unless they are stuck there. Cherbourg is no exception. It is a big town, but deserves only a short description – even for restaurants it is not exceptional. Its streets look like Normandy, it has a market, it has bars and restaurants and hotels, but none of them seem to match what one finds inland.
Cherbourg had some importance between the Wars – when transatlantic liners regularly docked here – and during World War II, once the Battle of Normandy was over and it became the main port for Allied supplies. The **Musée de la Guerre et de la Libération** documents this role. Pictures in the modern **Musée des Beaux-Arts Thomas-Henry** include local landscapes (notably by the 19th-century painter of peasantry J-F Millet) and a small international collection.

Open: both museums Wednesday to Monday.
Outside Cherbourg there is much to see. Westwards lies the rugged **La Hague** peninsula, eastwards the **Val de Saire**, pretty country giving on to some charming harbours. Out at **Querqueville** (off the D901 up the Hague peninsula), the little pre-Norman church of **St-Germain** is something of a curiosity. The trefoil plan and patterned stonework recall Early Christian or Byzantine building.

Accommodation and Restaurants

There are chain hotels in Cherbourg, and smaller, ordinary ones. Reasonable restaurants include **Le Grandgousier**, 21 rue Abbaye (tel: 33 53 19 43) and **Chez Pain**, 59 rue au Blé (tel: 33 53 67 64).

Tourist Office

2 quai Alexandre-III (tel: 33 93 52 02).

◆
COUTAINVILLE

This is the *plage* (beach) for Coutances inland, and more than enough of it – miles of sand and dunes on the exposed west coast. Though it has some modern facilities such as windsurfing, Coutainville is still not smart, but much more a family holiday place. There are several adequate places to stay and to eat along the front.

Tourist Office

place 28 Juillet 1944 (tel: 33 47 01 46).

◆◆◆
COUTANCES

The **cathedral**, still the centrepiece of Coutances, is one of the finest in Normandy, and definitely the finest for a long way around. Though retaining its 11th-century plan, foundations and piers, and even the older western towers, it was rebuilt in an Early Gothic style after a fire in 1208. Despite the constraints – which, for instance, produced a narrow chancel – the adaptation was skilful, and was completed within the 13th century (including the windows) without change of style . Only the spires over the front and the crossing towers are later, but equally harmonious.
Open: daily in summer; by appointment in winter.
The town is little more than one main street, giving on to quiet,

The clock tower at Carolles

bourgeois back streets. There is quite an elaborate municipal garden and a small museum (**Musée Quesnel-Morinière**). *Open*: Wednesday to Monday. *Closed:* Wednesday, Sunday morning and holidays in winter. Coutances has few hotels or restaurants.

Tourist Office
place Georges-Leclerc (tel: 33 45 17 79).

GRANVILLE
A lively place with several points of interest, Granville is primarily a summer resort, but is also known for its carnival or *mardi gras*. It takes on character not only from its fishing port and marina, but also from the cliffs of the **Pointe du Roc** and the surviving ramparts of the upper town, built by the English in the 15th century to threaten Mont-St-Michel.
The 'sights' range from the severe church of **Notre-Dame** to a peaceful public garden that once belonged to the family of Christian Dior, a waxworks museum (**Historial Granvillais**), a '**Palais Minéral**', a **'Féerie de Coquillage'** (shellwork extravaganza) and an aquarium . Such attractions have a Victorian, trip-to-the-pier ring, which is right for this old-fashioned but still thriving family resort.
Open: daily, summer only; Sundays and holidays in winter. You can see local artefacts and historical displays in the **Musée du Vieux Granville**.
Open: Wednesday to Monday April to September; winter weekends.

Boat trips are available out to the nearby **Iles Chausey** (Chausey Islands), with their 19th-century forts, and to the **Channel Islands**.

Accommodation
A really good, simple hotel is the **Michelet**, 5 rue Michelet (tel: 33 50 06 55); but there are others.

Restaurants
Several good eating places are another point in Granville's favour. **Le Phare**, 11 rue Port (tel: 33 50 12 94), is a packed favourite; also **Normandy-Chaumière**, 20 rue Poirier (tel: 33 50 01 71) and **La Gentilhommière**, 152 rue Couraye (tel: 33 50 17 99).

Tourist Office
4 cours Jonville (tel: 33 50 02 67).

The Abbaye de Hambye is off the beaten track, but worth findng

◆

GRATOT, CHATEAU DE

northwest of Coutances

This ruined *château* with its moat and its crumbling towers is delightfully picturesque. Only the offset square tower goes back to the 14th century, when the castle is first recorded; the other buildings date from the 15th or 18th centuries.

Open: daily all year.

HAGUE PENINSULA

northwest of Cherbourg

Reaching out towards the Channel Islands, with views over to them in fine weather, the peninsula of La Hague is a land of dry-stone walls, empty heaths, wind, gulls and dour granite rock. Between the **Cap de la Hague** and the island of Alderney, the Alderney Race is rendered deadly by its very swift currents; there is a heroic lifeboat station at the tiny port of **Goury**. Just south of the Cap, the **Nez de Jobourg** presents a memorable spectacle of raw rock and foaming sea. There is a walk along the western cliff, from Goury south to **Vauville**. Here a long, unspoilt beach stretches away southwards, backed by wild dunes. The stone buildings of Vauville itself, clustered round its stream, include a 16th-century *château* (not open).

◆◆

HAMBYE, ABBAYE DE

east of Granville

Hambye is one of the finest of Normandy's many ruined abbeys, partly because it is set in beautiful countryside. Most of the nave and chancel – dating from the 13th and 14th centuries – survive, though roofless. The later outbuildings, some of which are intact, house furnishings and tapestries.

Open: Wednesday to Monday.

Closed: mid-December to January.

Accommodation

The nearby **Auberge de l'Abbaye** (tel: 33 61 42 19) is an excellent country hotel.

JULLOUVILLE

south of Granville

This is another of those Normandy resorts where time seems to have stood still. The resort itself is small, with an extensive suburb of pre-War villas. It is a good place for young children.

Tourist Office

avenue Maréchal Leclerc (tel: 33 61 82 48).

LESSAY

north of Coutances

The little town is dominated by its ex-abbey **church**, founded in 1056. The style is Romanesque but with rib vaults anticipating Gothic structures. The church is an exceptionally beautiful and rare example of a fairly large Romanesque church completed in one building programme. Not on the scale of St-Etienne in Caen, but larger than a normal parish church, it has three storeys inside but only two outside. Masked on the outside by the aisle roof, the intermediate storey is a 'false gallery'. Unroofed in 1944, the church has been meticulously restored and any later additions have been removed.

The nearby beaches to the west – long, broad and sandy – are undeveloped and almost deserted. They are wonderful for children – and molluscs.

◆

LUCERNE, ABBAYE DE LA

southeast of Granville

The church of this ruined abbey, set in pleasant countryside, dates from the 12th century, and is transitional between Romanesque – a rather heavily decorated late Romanesque portal survives – and Gothic, for instance the tower over the transept. Not all the ruins are so old: the cloister is, but the ruined aqueduct was built in 1803 for a mill installed in the grounds.

Open: daily mid-March to mid-November; weekends and school holidays rest of year.

Closed: January.

The Normans and Romanesque Architecure

Although the Normans did not exactly invent Romanesque – a term usually used to describe a manner of building prevalent all over Europe in the 11th and 12th centuries – they certainly evolved a new variation, important not only in itself but also because it led directly to the development of the Gothic style. The most important forebear of the new vaulting system essential to Gothic architecture is the late 11th-century Norman Cathedral at Durham in England, but there are also contemporary signs in mainland Normandy of the new use of rib vaulting, for instance here at Lessay or in the lowest chambers of the twin towers of Bayeux Cathedral. Here we find cemented rubble vaults sustained not only by arches round the sides of the square, but also by great ribs crossing its diagonals. With the arrival of the Gothic style, ribs such as these became the basis of the whole vaulting system.

MARTINVAST

southwest of Cherbourg

The *château* here is a rambling, cobbled medieval castle updated in the Renaissance and then again in the 19th century. It is a fine backdrop for an extensive arboretum.

Open: afternoons at weekends and public holidays. Special events include a *son et lumière* in summer.

◆◆◆
MONT-ST-MICHEL ✓

Mont-St-Michel is a unique and memorable experience, a 'must'. No photograph can capture the drama that unfolds when you see it for the first time. As you approach it, the landscape changes completely. Empty, marshy flats give way to the bare strand itself and the sea. Several hundred yards (metres) from the shore, the extraordinary granite island rises from the watery levels, its steepness accentuated by the spire of the abbey church at the top.

The rock is not large, but can seem extraordinarily isolated, despite the modern causeway that links it to the mainland. Around it the tide comes in very fast – and deep – so an awareness of the tide table is an elementary caution (especially if you park in the lower car park).

Mont-St-Michel has a long history. The 'Michel' is Michael the Archangel, an important saint of the Carolingian era. Mont-St-Michel is one of several European shrines to him that date back to the Middle Ages. All of them are built on rocks where the angel was said to have appeared.

Architecturally, Mont-St-Michel is a hotch-potch of dates, styles and uses, from the 9th to the 19th centuries, and from place of pilgrimage to prison. Religious, domestic and military buildings sit cheek by jowl, and a tour involves a bewildering sequence of steps, passages, open spaces and rooms.

Unmissable Mont-St-Michel

High above the ramparts, the abbey buildings are well worth the strenuous climb. The earliest church on the site was converted into a crypt when the larger Romanesque church was built in the 11th and 12th centuries. Of this church the nave remains; the chancel was replaced in the 15th and 16th centuries in the Flamboyant style. Sadly, the old Romanesque façade and the last three bays of the nave were destroyed in the 19th century.

The finest architecture of the abbey is the part known as La Merveille, built by King Philip Augustus between 1211 and 1228, and opening off the north side of the church. On its topmost level the Merveille consists of a very beautiful cloister (often only to be peeped at, not entered) and a refectory; beneath there are a couple of large halls, and cellars. This was the guest wing, which had to be worthy of visiting kings, and the overall

effect of Philip Augustus's Gothic is indeed dazzling. On the south side of the church are the buildings for the monks themselves, later in date and not so ornate. Beneath are several crypts. The superstructure of the church, including the spire, is late 19th-century. Ramparts and gardens surround the immediate precinct of the abbey.
Open: abbey church, cloister and refectory daily except some public holidays, by guided tour only.
It is not surprising that, as Normandy's most famous sight, Mont-St-Michel becomes very crowded in summer (especially during the several festivals). Cars and coaches pack the car parks at the end of the causeway, their occupants choosing either just to stop and stare, or to follow the crowds toiling up through the ramparts on foot. Restaurants, souvenir shops and other tourist attractions line the Grande Rue – the steep main thoroughfare leading up to the abbey.
There are three museums – designed more for entertainment than for instruction. The **Archéoscope** is full of high-tech devices explaining the history of Mont-St-Michel. The **Musée Grévin** offers a series of tableaux with waxwork figures of people associated with the Mount through the ages. The **Musée de la Mer** contains local marine curiosities and gives film presentations on the tidal peculiarities of the bay.
Open: all three museums daily, February to mid-November.
The abbey is illuminated every evening at nightfall. During the summer season it is the setting for *son et lumière* shows, every evening except Sunday.
There are those who claim that Mont-St-Michel is best visited out of season. Certainly it is more atmospheric when free of the summer hubbub. However, it can be bleak in winter, and some of the hotels, restaurants and shops may be closed.

Accommodation and Restaurants

As in most tourist traps, the hotels, restaurants and shops on Mont-St-Michel do not offer very good value. However, there are a dozen or so hotel-restaurants to choose from, and staying the night offers the advantage of being here in the evening and early morning when day-trippers are few. The disadvantage is that you must carry your luggage up from the car park at the bottom.
The famous restaurant **Mère Poulard**, Grande Rue (tel: 33 60 14 01), has declined from its former glory, although it is still good, if expensive. (Mère Poulard was famous at the beginning of the century for her omelettes, and the restaurant still is.) A large place with a large turnover, the **Terrasses Poulard**, Grande Rue (tel: 33 60 14 09), offers perhaps the best available. Both are hotels as well as restaurants. The **Saint Pierre**, Grande Rue (tel: 33 60 14 03), has attractive bedrooms and a busy, informal restaurant.

Tourist Office

Corps du Gard de Bourgeois (entrance) (tel: 33 60 14 30).

Milestone on 'Liberty Way' at Utah Beach, near Ste-Mère-Eglise

PIROU, CHATEAU DU

southwest of Lessay

This rather shambling but charming castle dates from the 12th century with considerable internal modifications. It still has its moat, its curtain wall and a number of gatehouses, but has lost its keep. A modern 'imitation' of the Bayeux tapestry displayed in one of the rooms tells the story of the local Hauteville family, who conquered Sicily and South Italy in 1071.

Open: afternoons daily; also mornings in July and August.
Closed: Tuesday out of season.

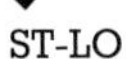

ST-LO

St-Lô's history goes back to Roman times, but the town suffered heavily when it was bombed in 1944 as a key strongpoint. It also suffered when it was rebuilt. The ruins of the church of **Notre-Dame**, which was not reconstructed, are a telling illustration of the damage.

A set of 16th-century tapestries is the highlight of the small collection in the **Musée Municipal des Beaux-Arts**.
Open: Wednesday to Monday.
South of St-Lô, in the valley of the Vire, there are beauty spots such as the **Roches de Ham**, a cliff above the winding river.

Accommodation
The town has perfectly good places to stay and to eat, all with a modern ambience. Among the several modest hotels is the **Terminus**, 3 avenue Briovère (tel: 33 05 08 60). The **Marignan** restaurant in place Gare (tel: 33 05 15 15) also has rooms.

Tourist Office
2 rue Havin (tel: 33 05 02 09).

STE-MERE-EGLISE

between Valognes and Carentan

The simple farming village of Ste-Mère-Eglise is the largest settlement in the rather featureless rural area north of Carentan. It has an early Gothic church and a farm museum, the **Ferme-Musée du Cotentin**.
Open: Wednesday to Monday, Easter to September (daily, July and August); also open weekend afternoons in October.
Ste-Mère-Eglise will be remembered by many as the scene of fierce fighting in 1944, when airborne troops were dropped to supplement the efforts of the US Army landing on the long expanse of '**Utah Beach**' to the east. The events of this period are commemorated in the **Musée des Troupes Aéroportées** (Airborne Troops

Museum). There is another war museum (**Musée du Débarquement à Utah-Beach**) at **Ste-Marie-du-Mont**, to the southeast.
Open: both museums daily in summer. *Closed*: mid-November to January.

◆

ST-SAUVEUR-LE-VICOMTE

southwest of Valognes

The remains of a powerful castle here include a 14th-century keep declared at the time to be 'impregnable to both machine and assault'. An older round keep also survives, and the remnants of the bailey's outbuildings.
Open: at all times.

◆

ST-VAAST-LA-HOUGUE

northeast of Valognes

Though it has not quite the appeal of Barfleur, to the north (see p. 79), St-Vaast-la-Hougue is an attractive fishing-port and resort with the remains of 17th-century fortifications – notably the **Fort de la Hougue** (not open), at the end of the long promontory known as the Grande-Plage.

Accommodation and Restaurants

A pleasant, well-run simple hotel and restaurant is the **France et Fuchsias**, 18 rue Maréchal Foch (tel: 33 54 42 26). There are some newly converted bedrooms in the annexe at the bottom of the pretty garden. Another is the **Granitière**, 64 rue Maréchal Foch (tel: 33 54 58 99). There are several good fish restaurants by the harbour.

Tourist Office

Quai Vauban (tel: 33 54 41 37).

TOURLAVILLE, CHATEAU DE

east of Cherbourg

Conveniently close to Cherbourg, this late 16th-century *château* may be worth visiting to pass the time while waiting for a ferry, rather than for its architectural merit. It was left to ruin and then so restored in the 19th century that nothing authentic remains. However, swans swim in its lily-covered lake, and it has an arboretum.
Open: daily.

VALOGNES

A straightforward market town, Valognes suffered terrible war damage in 1944. Its **Hôtel de Beaumont**, however, is an 18th-century building with a fine staircase and some good surviving furnishings.
Open: afternoons daily Easter weekend and July to mid-September.
The history of cider-making in Normandy is explored in the **Musée régional du cidre**.
Open: Thursday to Tuesday, Easter holiday and June to September.
Closed: Sunday mornings.

Accommodation and Restaurants

Valognes offers a choice of good hotel-restaurants. The best known is the **Louvre**, 28 rue Réligieuses (tel: 33 40 00 07); or try **Hôtel de l'Agriculture**, 16 rue Léopold-Delisle (tel: 33 95 02 02). Both offer good meals.

Tourist Office

place Château (tel: 33 40 11 55).

Peace and Quiet

Countryside and Wildlife in Normandy by Paul Sterry

Above all, Normandy is green. Its setting in the cool, moist northwest of France is clearly of paramount influence here, but the greenness is, if anything, intensified by traditional agricultural practices, which encourage pastures and orchards.

So the predominant 'feel' of Normandy as you travel through it is of a gentle place with venerable half-timbered farmsteads tucked away along tracks lined by equally venerable apple and pear trees. It all seems very slow and unhurried, but looks can be deceptive. This quiet landscape is actually very carefully tended, as you will realise if you look in the farmyards, nearly all of which have huge, neat stacks of firewood gathered from the hedgerow trees. (The reason that some of those trees look odd is that all of their lower branches are stripped off regularly as part of the wood-gathering process.)

For many people, the best time to visit Normandy is in the spring, when the blossom is out and when the meadows and roadside verges are carpeted in wild flowers. This is also the time for bird song.

There are variations on the theme of peaceful greenness. Normandy's most 'rugged' inland landscapes are in the Suisse Normande (Norman Switzerland). However don't expect ski lifts or cloud-shrouded peaks. This is a landscape very much in the Normandy mould, but with river gorges and steepish hills.

Damp ditches are ideal for opposite-leaved golden saxifrage

There are extensive forests throughout the region, but many of these consist of youngish trees. All are carefully managed, so glades of ancient gnarled trees are few and far between. Often, these forests are on poor, acid soils, so the ground flora is likely to consist of such plants as heathers – good for insects and for reptiles. Normandy still has some areas of open heath and these are well worth seeking out for their bird and insect life. And then, of course, there is the seaside – miles of sandy beaches, often backed by sand dunes. There are also dramatic cliffs, the equal of any on the north European seaboard. Described below are some of Normandy's best areas for scenery and for wildlife, but almost any walk or cycle-ride along quiet, leafy lanes will bring pleasures and rewards.

Vauville Dunes

South of Vauville, on the Cotentin coast due west of Cherbourg, lies an extensive system of west-facing sand dunes, built up by surging Atlantic breakers. This is one of the best areas in Normandy for coastal flowers, with several unusual species. Insects also abound and migrant birds can often be found in the dune slacks (the damp areas in the hollows between the dunes). The pools attract ducks and wildfowl, while in the reedbeds warblers and buntings may be seen. To reach the dunes, head west from Cherbourg and turn south at Beaumont for Vauville. At the village, turn off on the D237 and turn right to park by the campsite. Walk past the nature reserve sign and follow the path southwards.

Exciting and colourful flowers can be found from April until September, although in a dry summer many of the plants may wither by August. One of the most intriguing of the early species is dwarf pansy. The flower is just like a garden pansy, but the whole plant including the flower is minute – often less than one inch (2cm) high. Not surprisingly it can be difficult to locate.

Later in the season, Jersey thrift and spiked speedwell appear among the tussocks of marram grass. Wet, marshy areas harbour marsh orchids and other rare plants. Colourful butterflies abound and great green bush crickets sing loudly. These large, bright green insects can be recognised by their long legs and long antennae. Their colouring, however, gives them good camouflage.

Cap de la Hague

For bracing walks and spectacular views, the stretch of north-facing Cotentin coastline between Urville-Nacqueville and Cap de la Hague is hard to beat. To reach the Cap de la Hague, drive west on the D901 to Auderville and then take the D401 northwards.

Especially in autumn, seabirds often stream past this headland, particularly in northwesterly gales. Look for gannets – large, pure white birds – and several species of gulls and seaducks. Shearwaters, which fly on stiffly

held wings, also fly by in large groups known as 'rafts'.
In the spring and summer, flowers such as gorse, with its colourful yellow flowers and smell of coconut, adorn the scene, and low-growing plants such as spring squill and perennial centaury are found beside the tracks.

Cap de Flamanville
Cap de Flamanville, on the west coast mid-way between Cap de la Hague and Carteret, offers further spectacular walks with a chance to see interesting coastal flowers as well. Park at the *Sémaphore*, signposted off the minor road from Flamanville to Bonnemains. Walk south along the road, then down the path to the cliff edge. The walk southwards is particularly fine. It eventually leads back to the road, from where you can return to your car.
Thrift, also aptly known as sea pink, grows here in the spring and produces a carpet of pink flowers in certain areas. It contrasts with the intense green of clumps of Portland spurge and, in places, gives the effect of a man-made rockery. Later in the season, sea lavender puts on a colourful show on the rock ledges.

Cap de Carteret
This is another part of the Cotentin's west coast that will appeal to anyone interested in coastal flowers. Pass through the village of Carteret and on to Cap de Carteret. The Cap overlooks Havre de Carteret, another good spot for spring flowers, which can be reached from Barneville-Carteret.

Cap Lévy to Phare de Gatteville
The northern Cotentin coastline between Cap Lévy and Gatteville-le-Phare east of Cherbourg is perhaps the most interesting stretch in Normandy for those interested in coastal flowers and seabirds. Almost anywhere can be good and the best approach is to drive along the D116 between Fermanville and Gatteville, taking minor roads north to the coast. There is parking by the shore at the end of most of these roads.
The best areas are north of Renouville and Rethoville. At le Bas de la Rue there are coastal pools and marshes on the landward side of the shingle beach as you walk towards Gatteville. Wetland birds can

Sea spurge – a typical dune plant

Watch for fan-tailed warblers in the marshes east of Gatteville

be found here and fan-tailed warblers are also common. These tiny birds are most easily recognised by the characteristic display of the male: his song is a continuous 'zip-zip-zip' delivered in a song flight where he looks as though he is suspended on a yo-yo. The shoreline along this stretch grades from shingle to coarse sand, and a wide variety of flowers can be found here. Perhaps the most distinctive is sea holly, with leaves and flowers of purple grey. The leaves are extremely spiny and just like those of their namesake tree. Its close relative, field eryngo, also grows here. It too is a very spiny plant, but the leaves are altogether more slender in appearance. Other botanical specialities of this shoreline include cottonweed, whose stems and leaves are cloaked in downy hairs, and purple spurge. The latter is a prostrate plant with fleshy leaves and a purplish stem. Both purple spurge and cottonweed are declining species in other parts of northern Europe.

Coastal Plants

The Cotentin coast is a superb area to see coastal flowers. Most of the plants that grow by the sea are specially adapted to life in this difficult environment. They must be able to tolerate drying sea breezes and constant exposure to salt-laden air. In addition, many coastal plants live in a shifting environment of sand or shingle. Consequently, they often grow long or spreading root systems to keep them anchored and to reach water. The most characteristic plant of sand dunes is marram grass. In fact, it is among the first plants to colonise shifting sand, encouraging the dunes to become stable. Sea spurge and yellow horned poppy are also colonists of the sand dunes and have extensive root systems.

Rocky Outcrops of la Glacerie

The landscape around la Glacerie and le Mesnil-au-Val, to the south of Cherbourg and Tourlaville, is rolling, with small fields, thick hedges and pockets of rich woodland. Additional interest is provided by the rocky outcrops which can be found in the area. Many support a rich growth of moisture-loving plants including ferns, and some are so covered in vegetation that they have ceased to look like rocks at all. To reach the area, drive south from Cherbourg on the N13 and then turn off east towards la Glacerie after a few miles. From there, several minor roads wind their way to le Mesnil-au-Val and on southwards to the D56. Explore any suitable patches of woodland and rocky outcrops, being careful not to leave gates open and not to disturb livestock.

Plants of particular interest to look out for among the rocky outcrops include Tunbridge filmy fern, a delicate, membranous species that forms quite large patches over rocks where water trickles down. The same habitat is also suitable for Cornish moneywort, so-called because the round leaves resemble coins, and ivy-leaved bellflower, which produces delicate mauve flowers in the early summer.

Woodland Birds

Spring is the season to look and listen for woodland birds in Normandy. From March to June, the woods are alive with song, those of resident species being supplemented by migrant visitors. Tits, warblers, finches and thrushes all vie with each other and it would not be unusual to see or hear 10 or more species in a single location. The warblers are perhaps the best woodland songsters. Listen for wood warblers which have a song with a distinctive trill. Blackcaps, males of which do indeed have black caps, have rich, melodious songs, while that of the nightingale is renowned both for its volume and for its variety and range. In addition, there are less conspicuous species such as short-toed treecreepers and woodpeckers to look out for.

White-letter Hairstreak

Because its foodplant, elm, has declined in northern Europe as a result of Dutch elm disease, the white-letter hairstreak – an attractively marked butterfly – has also suffered. However, in Normandy, many of the elms have survived attack, so this is a very good area to look for hairstreaks. The butterflies are on the wing in July and August and generally remain faithful to the particular tree on which they fed as caterpillars. Look for them flying around the highest branches on sunny days. When brambles are in flower, however, they can be easier to see: they descend to ground level to feed on the rich supply of nectar that the flowers produce.

Spring Hedgerow Flowers
In early spring, the hedgerows are full of colourful flowers. The reasons for the profusion of plant life lie in the lack of intensive farming in the surrounding fields and in the way in which the hedges are cut. In April and May, large yellow patches of primroses can be seen with clumps of early purple orchids and greater stitchwort among them.
Where damp patches and ditches are found, look for the delicate white flowers of meadow saxifrage, a plant that cannot tolerate too much disturbance, and yellow splashes of opposite-leaved golden saxifrage. Cowslips are common, but none the less beautiful for that.

Forêt de St-Sauveur
St-Sauveur-le-Vicomte lies in the centre of the Cotentin Peninsula with the Forêt de St-Sauveur to its west. To reach it, drive west from St-Sauveur-le-Vicomte on the D15 and shortly take the right fork of the D130. This runs along the edge of the forest where you can park and explore the broadleaved woodland edge.

Bois de Limors
This area of woodland lies southeast of St-Sauveur-le-Vicomte and can be reached by taking the D900 south from the town and turning east after a few miles to Varenguebec.The woodland lies north of the road. Look for birds of prey circling overhead and listen for woodland birds in spring.

Lessay
South of Lessay – still in the Cotentin, between St-Sauveur and Coutances – lie some of the most extensive areas of heathland left in the Normandy

Perennial centaury, a coastal plant tolerant of wind and poor soil

Summer lady's tresses is becoming rare throughout Europe

region. To reach them, drive south from Lessay on the D2 for a few miles until you reach the heathland habitat. There are several stopping-off points along the main road as well as side roads. One good area is off the minor road which runs eastwards to La Feuillie. Here you can park the car and explore. Birdlife includes hobbies – small, aerobatic birds of prey – Dartford warblers and stonechats; several interesting species of plants grow here, too. The heaths are dominated by bell heather and ling; heath lobelia – similar to many garden varieties – is still common here, although it is a declining species in many other parts of Europe.

Summer Lady's Tresses
Summer lady's tresses is an intriguing species of orchid that grows on the heathlands of Lessay. It gains its name from the time of year of its appearance – summer – and the resemblance of the flower spike to a woven and twisted braid of hair. It has suffered a dramatic decline in its distribution throughout Europe and has become extinct in many areas. However, small colonies still persist in Normandy, although for how much longer it is difficult to predict. Summer lady's tresses has very precise habitat requirements and any change in land use could mean its certain disappearance.

St-Germain-sur-Ay
The coast to the south of St-Germain-sur-Ay offers good opportunities for observing coastal birds. The village lies to the west of Lessay. Drive on the D650 coast road and turn off south through the village to reach the shore. In the summer months, look for terns and gulls while in autumn and winter brent geese, wigeon and other ducks can be seen.

Baie du Grand Vey
On the eastern side of the Cotentin Peninsula, this large estuary is an excellent place for coastal birds. It can be viewed on the west side from minor roads leading from Pouppeville and on the east side from minor roads off the D514 between Grandcamp-Maisy and Isigny. Autumn and winter are the best seasons, when thousands of wildfowl and waders may be seen.

Parc Regional de Brotonne
This extensive area of forest is sited in the meanders of the River Seine to the west of Rouen. It is criss-crossed with roads and tracks from surrounding towns and villages such as Bourneville, Hauville and Caudebec-en-Caux. Associated with the Forêt de Brotonne are a craft centre in Bourneville and a recreational centre at le Mesnil, near Jumièges. The woodland is good for birds and flowers in spring and early summer. Fungi are abundant in the autumn.

Great green bush cricket

Practical

This section (with the yellow band) includes food, drink, shopping, accommodation, nightlife, tight budget, special events etc

FOOD AND DRINK

If one word could sum up Normandy food, it would be 'rich' – rich in the good sense of abundant and various, but also in the not-so-good one of high in calories, or not easily digestible – for example in the alcoholic cream sauce known as *sauce Normande*. It may well not seem the place to go to improve your waistline, because Normandy is known above all for its butter and cheese, its cider and Calvados liqueur. However, the region deserves to be just as well known for its fish (the *sole Normande*) and shellfish, which are low in calories, and its farms produce yoghurt, *crème fraîche* and skimmed milk as well as thick cream and full-fat cheese.

Traditional Fare

Although in the larger cities more cosmopolitan food – from pizza to Chinese meals – is not hard to find, one of the remarkable things about Normandy restaurants and markets is the way they have stuck to tradition. Even Normandy's first-class, Michelin-starred restaurants seldom subscribe to modern schools of cooking, but prefer to perfect traditional recipes, such as *canard rouennais* (Rouen duck). Also against the modern trend are the many offal dishes favoured in Normandy, from *tripe à la mode de Caen* to the *boudin noir* (black pudding) for which Mortagne-au-Perche is known. The traditionalism is often emphasised by the '*ancienne maison Normande*' (old Norman house) decor, more often genuine than not. The ideal pursued time and again is that of the old-fashioned hostelry or coaching inn; Normandy restaurants are very often true inns, with bedrooms.
Normandy's expanses of green pasturage provide good meat of all cuts and most varieties – pork and chicken, as well as beef (though the French prefer their lamb imported from England), not to mention guinea fowl and lots of game. Meals are square and solid: hence the so called *trou Normand* (Norman hole), originally a bolt of Calvados taken during the

meal to 'bore a hole' in a full stomach so as to take more on board. Nowadays it is a much less gross Calvados-flavoured sorbet, but the principle remains. Plates are piled high.

Fish and Shellfish

For seafood, Brittany is a rival, and the fish available in Normandy is caught in international seas, so can be matched elsewhere. Nevertheless, the fish is everywhere fresh and good, especially turbot, brill, mackerel and sole. The local shellfish, however, is virtually unbeatable. Superb are the pink and grey *crevettes* (shrimps), the several varieties of crab, the *moules* (mussels) especially, also the whelks and other molluscs if they appeal. Then there are the oysters, and the lobsters and crayfish of course. These can be obtained on the promenade beside beaches and on the quay of every port, and they will always be fresh and delicious. A normal 'pub lunch' in Normandy is cheap and wholesome *moule-frite* (mussels and chips). There are several traditional fish soup recipes, and these again can be a meal in themselves.

Normandy's Cheeses

Camembert, the most famous of Normandy cheeses, was invented at the beginning of the 19th century, and sold at the market in Vimoutiers in the Auge (see p. 75). But there is an enormous variety of other Normandy cheeses. Most are of the soft (*matière grasse*) variety, creamy and bland when young, shrunken and smelly when aged. The best known, such as Pont-l'Evêque, are now mass-produced and vary in quality. Rather than pursue any particular type, it is probably best to choose what looks best on the day and is ripe in the way you like it. Incidentally, Petit-Suisse is a Norman cheese, not Swiss – it was first made by an immigrant Swiss in the Bray region.Try it with summer fruit, such as strawberries or peaches, and a sprinkling of sugar.

Cider and Calvados

Cidre fermier is a long way from sweet, fizzy mass-produced cider; true Normandy cider can be a very manly drink. But it is also a very pleasant drink, ideal for a break in a café on a hot day. The same may be said of Pommeau, which is the Norman equivalent of Champagne. *Poiré* – the equivalent of cider made from pears – is common in the *Bocage* region.

Calvados can vary from the ordinary – the working man's breakfast, taken with his coffee – to the very special, aged and prized and very expensive. Both cider and Calvados are commonly drunk in Normandy instead of wine; they are not mere 'tourist' specialities, as the liqueur Bénédictine, invented long ago by the monks of Fécamp, perhaps is.

Restaurants

As already mentioned, the typical Norman restaurant is an inn, offering substantial, local, traditional fare in a half-timbered setting (preferably 500 years old). Generally

speaking these establishments are very good – except sometimes in very heavily visited areas. The restaurants named in this guide are usually of this kind. Many of them are not cheap, but they consistently offer good (or even very good) value, compared with what you might pay in other countries or in other parts of France.

Special notice must be taken of the fish restaurants that abound in Normandy's ports and along their beaches. So often the freshness of the fish or shellfish is more important than the cooking, and in these places you can seldom go wrong. Depending on the kind of fish you eat, some of these restaurants can also be very cheap. There are smarter fish restaurants, of course, including some of the best in France. The very best in quality is generally to be found in Normandy's larger cities, especially Rouen and Caen.

Where to begin?

Recommendations

The restaurants recommended in this guide are in most cases well established and tried and tested. Many of them are above average in quality and in price – the sort of place to go for a special occasion rather than for an ordinary meal. It is definitely advisable to book, or at least to get there early for lunch or dinner, at all of them. French restaurant meal times are generally lunch from 12.00 to 14.00hrs, and dinner from 19.00 to 21.30hrs. Most close one day a week and annually for two or three weeks' holiday, frequently for part of the high season if they are not on the coast (in Rouen, for instance), so that should be checked on the telephone, too. Do not worry if your French is poor; basic English is usually understood in such places. To pick out and list everyday places to eat would be lengthy and largely pointless, since you can eat well at a reasonable price virtually anywhere in Normandy. The region abounds in restaurants; all you have to do is to study the menu displayed outside, and go in. While some are better than others, very few are really bad. Even in the most popular tourist resorts at the height of the season, the food usually remains decent, even though prices rise and getting a table can become a struggle.

In summer, a number of farmers' wives will cook for tourists as well as for their families. An *ad hoc* restaurant of this kind is called a *ferme auberge*. Some are so well frequented that they are open virtually every night; others are discreet, and all you will see is a notice on the gatepost as you speed by. It is well worth stopping, and either telephoning or calling at the farm to make an appointment and decide a menu. The meal will invariably be delicious, and will probably be washed down with the Pommeau or Calvados the farmer makes himself. It will be much more than you can eat, and very good value.

In season the seaside resorts abound with fast-food outlets: these will seldom be branded but local and individual and the *frites* (chips) are often very good – not to mention the pancakes from the *crêperies* and the *gauffres* (waffles) which the French seem to flock to eat about the middle of the afternoon.

Lunch 'al fresco' in Honfleur

SHOPPING

Markets

The best shopping in Normandy is for food, and the markets are irresistible. They are mostly food (especially vegetable) markets, but virtually anything can be sold. Every town and big village in Normandy has its market-day (often more than once a week). It is more exactly half a day, for the stalls are invariably closing up by lunchtime. They are filled not only by professional retailers but by many farmers or farmers' wives who are bringing their own produce for sale. Increasingly, farmers have become more imaginative and competitive. Despite CAP (the EC's farming subsidy), despite the many farms at which the lorries of large companies in the food industry draw up daily to remove the herd's entire output, some Normandy farmers have got the organic message and are making really tasty cheese again. Not so long ago it was beginning to seem that, in the land where Camembert was invented, mass-produced cheese was going to become the only sort available. But you will find home-made cheese at the market, as well as bottles of home-made cider and Calvados, besides a great variety of really fresh and often unusual vegetables. Hardware stalls offer good basic kitchen tools and handy gadgets such as oyster knives, or a screw-funnel you insert into a lemon you wish to squeeze (the juice comes tidily down the funnel while the lemon remains intact and can be used again).
Fish markets are usually specially designated, roofed structures. However, fish can frequently also be bought on the quay, when the boat comes in in the evening. At fish markets, each and every stall seems alive with comatose crabs and tetchy lobsters with their claws in rubber bands. Shellfish can often be bought ready cooked, and oysters will be opened for you. If you do buy fish, the messy preparation will be done while you wait. You will see ice used for packing, but never anything frozen.

Food Shops

The markets are complemented by delicatessens and specialist shops. As elsewhere in France, every town has at least one delicatessen where, if you could afford it, you could buy endless delicious prepared dishes and never have to cook. The *boulangeries* (bread) and *pâtisseries* (cakes) are good in Normandy, too. (*Boulangeries* are open on Sunday mornings, but are closed one day during the week – commonly Monday.) Besides these, you will find specialist cheese shops, excellent fishmongers, and butchers or *traiteurs* – which specialise in cold meats and sausages. Many such shops have a *rôtisserie* outside with chickens revolving on a spit in a greasy glass case: do not despise these, for the chickens will usually have ranged very freely and are delicious.

Shop opening hours are generally from 08.30 or 09.00hrs to 12.00 or 12.30; then from about 14.00 or 14.30hrs until 19.00 or 19.30. For more details, see **Opening Times**, page 121.

Supermarkets and Hypermarkets

Supermarkets (*supermarchés*) can be more convenient and in many cases just as good or nearly as good as traditional shops. In particular, their fruit and vegetables will rival those of the greengrocers, if not the market, and they will have a good delicatessen counter. But be warned that they will seldom be significantly cheaper. If you do not wish to shop every day, then it will be worth driving to a *hypermarché* outside town, where, in theory, everything you could wish to buy is gathered under one aeroplane-hangar roof.

The *hypermarchés* can be cheaper for certain things – in particular wine. Wine is not one of Normandy's native products and the quality of its wine-shops is generally low. Even Calvados and cider are better obtained at the *hypermarchés* or the day-markets than at wine shops. Things like children's clothes and toys, even bicycles, can be found at very competitive prices in the *hypermarchés*. They also sell cheaper petrol, though you usually have to queue. *Hypermarchés* remain open all day, often until 21.00 or 22.00hrs, but are closed on Sunday, and sometimes on Monday mornings too.

Other Shops

There are smart shops and department stores in the capitals, Caen and Rouen, and also – perhaps smartest of all – in Deauville. Otherwise, Normandy is the opposite of fashionable. However, its shops are hard to beat for basic, good-value everyday purchases. There are excellent chandlers and fishing shops, and the

Shop early at the market – most stalls pack up at lunchtime

French *quincaillerie* is a wonderful institution. It is usually translated as ironmonger, but it will sell a much wider range of goods, including tableware, light-bulbs and mosquito-killers.

These shops usually keep the same hours as food shops. Some, especially clothes shops, commonly remain closed on Monday morning.

Many newsagents verge on bookshops, and sell guides and maps, also some of the enormous range of French adult comics, which you will perhaps be glad your children cannot understand. Souvenir shops, usually concentrating on pottery, abound at seaside resorts. A certain type of blue and white lobed bowl, a little too small to be useful, with an individual Christian name, is positively ubiquitous.

ACCOMMODATION

Hotels

French hotels are generally cheap, compared with the rest of Europe, and sometimes real bargains. This is true even of the national or international chains, though their tendency is to force up the prices towards the kind of sum businessmen are used to paying elsewhere. Nevertheless, an independent tourer staying for two weeks in hotels will run up a fearsome bill, one that most families will not begin to afford. Fortunately, there are many other ways of staying in Normandy (see below). But hotels are eminently practicable for a weekend, a stopover or a short stay. If you have children it is always worth asking for a family room, with three or four beds. Payment is by the room, not the person.

Finding accommodation is highly seasonal. Usually it will be little problem finding a room at short notice, but July can be well booked and it gets almost impossible anywhere near the coast as you approach 15 August. After that, pressure gradually declines, then drops considerably in September. So, of course, does the temperature.

The easiest way to find a hotel room is to visit or telephone the local tourist office (see the end of many **What to see** entries in this book for addresses and telephone numbers). If you go to the tourist office in person, they will telephone round to find you a room in the price-band of your choice.

Many Norman restaurants have rooms, and many hotels have an excellent restaurant. The hotels and restaurants mentioned in the **What to see** sections of the book are usually of this kind, especially those in small places in the country. Apart from those mentioned, there are many more, which you are likely to find by chance or inquiry. Having few big towns, Normandy has few chain hotels but hundreds of modest, typical, family-run ones such as those belonging to the **Logis de France** organisation, recognised by the yellow and green 'fireplace' sign outside.

If you are touring, be sure to book your room reasonably early – ideally about 16.00hrs,

As well as rural cottages, Gîtes de France offer Chambres d'Hôtes – good-value bed and breakfast

and certainly by 18.00 or 19.00hrs; these family hotels do not like late arrivals. If you are staying in one place for a few days, ask about *pension* (full-board) or *demi-pension* (half-board) rates. Room rates seldom include breakfast, which may be cheaper in a café.

Apartments and Gîtes

Oddly enough, this way of taking a holiday is not well developed in Normandy, at least for foreigners. Rented summer accommodation, at the seaside at least, is geared to the French, who hire by the calendar month, 1st to 31st. With their long summer holidays, this suits them well – except when it comes to the *rentrée*, and they all try to go home at once – but for foreigners this can be too long and too constraining. Although there are now occasional signs of shorter lets being offered, generally speaking non-French looking for a seaside house or flat to rent will have to take a travel agent's package or, perhaps, rent from a compatriot who owns a holiday house in France. Away from the sea, *gîtes ruraux* (country cottages) are popular holiday homes. Through local tourist offices or through **Gîtes de France** – a national body with offices in each *département* – you can obtain a brochure and book direct to stay in a *gîte* on a farm or in the country. These are the addresses of **Gîtes de France** in each *département*:

Seine-Maritime Chemin de la Bretèque, BP 59, 76232 Bois-Guillaume (tel: 35 60 73 34).

Eure 9 rue de la Petite Cité, BP 882, 27008 Evreux (tel: 32 39 53 38).

Orne 88 rue St-Blaise, BP 50, 61002 Alençon (tel: 33 28 88 71).

Calvados 6 promenade Mme de Sévigné, 14050 Caen (tel: 31 70 25 25).

Manche Maison du Département, 50008 St-Lô (tel: 33 05 98 70).

Gîtes de France also have an office in **England**, at 178 Piccadilly, London W1V 9DB (tel: 071-493 3480).

Chambres d'Hôtes

'Bed and breakfast' is an established tradition in Britain, but the equivalent – Chambres d'Hôtes – is something of an innovation in France. Nevertheless, these days you will often see private houses advertising accommodation, particularly in country

Many farms, cottages and châteaux now take paying guests

areas. Whether in cottage or *château, Chambres d'Hôtes* usually offer good value and a warm welcome, and are a good way to save on hotel bills.

Camping and Caravanning

Every little French municipality feels obliged to run a campsite. There are hundreds of modest campsites throughout Normandy where you can stay without much difficulty even during the crowded summer months – the cows are just shifted on to another field when the first is full. Though they are modest, there are few campsites today that do not have a toilet block with a shower, for which you pay. High-grade, four- or five-star sites may not charge extra for showers, but their daily fee more than covers the cost of unlimited hot water. Certain organisations will arrange camping holidays where you stay only at the very best campsites. One such is Castels et Camping-Caravaning, BP 301, 56007 Vannes (tel: 97 42 55 83). Perhaps in the grounds of a château, such a site may have facilities such as a lake for canoeing, or organised table-tennis and other competitions. You can expect these sites to run rather strict rules like a boarding-house. In them, in an increasingly common arrangement, you can hire the tent or caravan by the week or

Mont-St-Michel – always lively

fortnight ready erected and equipped. Such sites are very popular, especially with the English and Dutch; but the only French you see are the people who run it. The **Château de Martragny**, north of Caen, is perhaps top of them all. The French camp in tents rather seldom; they use caravans and often one that remains on the site all year. As a result they tend to have their own area in every campsite anyway.

Château Stays
Château owners who have not opened a camping site sometimes convert their *château* into a hotel or take in paying guests. A good example is the 17th-century **Château d'Audrieu**, southeast of Bayeux, in beautiful grounds and with a famous kitchen. Others near by are **Le Castel,** and **Vaulaville**, near Tour-en-Bessin, which is more properly a stately home taking house guests. **Fervaques** in the Auge is specially for the disabled (tel: 31 32 33 96). Organisations with information available in Britain are **Château-Accueil** (94 Bell Street, Henley-on-Thames RG9 1XS (tel: 0491-578803)) and **Relais Châteaux** (French Government Tourist Office, 178 Piccadilly, London W1V OAL).

Buying a House
Travelling through Normandy today you will see numerous advertisements in the local banks offering mortgages, and the estate agents are quite used to helping foreigners looking to buy. You will even find in newsagents a magazine published in English for residents and house-owners. Although the age of great bargains, if it ever existed, is over, there remain plenty of empty or abandoned houses in the Normandy countryside, which may be very pretty and cheap to buy when isolated and in poor repair, which is often the case. Selling again may be more difficult, letting is not always simple, and all sorts of bureaucratic and tax problems may arise. Take lots of advice.

CULTURE, ENTERTAINMENT AND NIGHTLIFE

The seaside resorts offer plenty of action in summer. Discos and other evening entertainment will probably be advertised in tourist offices.In Normandy, only Rouen has anything approaching a metropolitan culture or subculture.

At the seaside, especially, there is constant life during the season at the casinos, which usually have two classes of play – for higher stakes in the grandest room and for lower ones in other parts. The casinos are usually the venue for various special evening shows, spectacles, comedy, or other entertainments, put on by the town in the summer, especially during August. (See also **Special Events**, pages 111-12)

WEATHER AND WHEN TO GO

There is no doubt that for most people, Normandy is for summer holidays. Not only its resorts but also many of its *châteaux* and museums close down for the winter, and only slowly struggle into life again with the spring. The two months of the real season are July and August, and the absolute peak is the weekend around 15 August. The resorts empty very rapidly in September, and the season ends on All Saints' Day, 1 November.

One reason for this is that July and August coincide with the French school holidays. They are also the only months when you can be reasonably sure of getting good weather.

Occasionally there is a summer of bad weather – though not for some years now. Usually, even if it does rain for a day or two, the temperature never falls very low and it soon clears up – usually more rapidly on the coast than inland.

Of course, you can get good weather out of season as well. But beware of September and October – there are storms about, the rain is more frequent and harder, and you can have a whole bad week, which is much rarer in the summer. June can be a good month. Earlier in the year everywhere is less crowded, of course, but the weather may be fresh.

If you are touring and visiting places, many of them open from Easter, but with restricted days and times. In July and August you can be confident of just turning up – like everyone else, of course.

Do not write off Normandy in the winter. The food is still good, the churches are open, and you can go for a walk on the beach even if it is a bit melancholic. It can make a refreshing Christmas or New Year break, or a long weekend to liven up the bleak winter months.

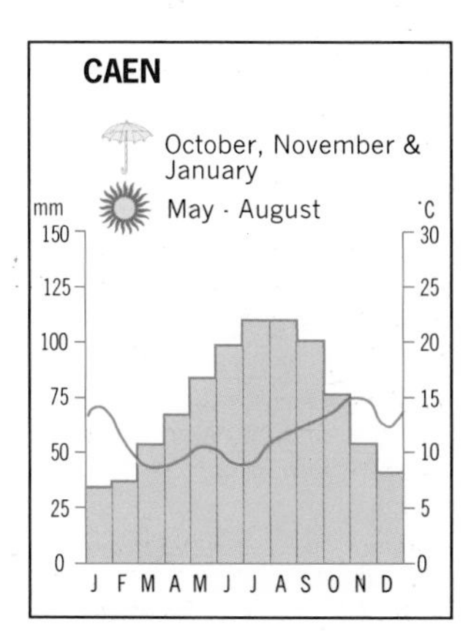

Make time to stand and stare...

HOW TO BE A LOCAL

The Normans, among the French in general, are rather easy-going, content with themselves and their rich land, friendly and relaxed rather than uptight towards foreigners, and not so obsessed as the city-dwellers with elegance, dignity or money. It is not very difficult to blend in, if you are willing to drink what they drink, eat what they eat, and go along with what they think – for a while, at least.

It makes a great deal of difference, there is no denying it, whether or not you speak the language. Despite the influx of foreigners in summer, few shop assistants or bar-keepers speak another language, although if they do it will probably be English. In fact, in the last 10 years or so, the French have generally become less stuffy about speaking anyone else's language or about the way other people speak theirs, and this is still more true in easy-going Normandy. Nonetheless if you can manage the correct French to order a beer, there is a chance you may get a smile, and you should at least get a civil nod; if you can't, the reception will probably be chilly even if the waiter understands perfectly well. A little French makes things much friendlier.

For the rest, though Normandy is a different place it is not a different world. The usual north European conventions tend to apply: people respect queues, they are honest about money transactions, they expect the usual courtesies. However, they greet and expect to be greeted more than some nations, and they are accustomed to using polite appellatives such as *monsieur* and *madame* (sir and madam).

In small Norman towns one finds a lot of respect for the elderly and for the establishment figures of their slightly old-fashioned communities: many people will have lived there all their lives and are reluctant to change their ways readily. They readily accept foreigners, however, as long as they do nothing outrageous or overbearing.

CHILDREN

Normandy is all about family holidays, and it has just about everything children could want, from A to Z – or at least from B for beaches to W for war museums.

Beaches

There is nothing like a beach to keep young children occupied for hours – and Normandy has miles of beaches, with rocks and pools full of shrimps and crabs, and above all superb sand. On many of the most popular beaches, the sea comes in shallow for paddling, and where it becomes deep is watched attentively by lifeguards. They will have a tannoy system for lost children – but if you do have to ask them for help, they will scold you terribly first.

Every municipal beach has a children's play compound or 'Mickey' (many of them take Mickey Mouse as their emblem), where there are organised games, trampolines, often swimming pools, and anyway a host of activities for children up to about 10 years old. The supervisors are generally students, who are usually very good with children. The only disadvantage is that they tend to be a bit expensive. The 'Mickey' has usually closed by about 17.00hrs, and then you will often see other children enter the compound and enjoy the swings and roundabouts for free.

For older children, the larger resorts have equipment you can hire for the various seaside

Carolles-Plage in high season

sports of today such as windsurfing or beach buggying. Many seaside places also have a municipal swimming pool, sometimes covered, with which various other activities are associated, from humble ping-pong to learning how to scuba-dive. Often there is an aquarium. Sports facilities include tennis courts and mini-golf; you can usually hire a bicycle or a horse. If you have money to spend, there is lots to do, but the cost can mount up terribly – not counting the special events in the resorts. These might include castle-building competitions or formula *bille*, a race for model cars round a track built in the sand – you flick a small wooden ball (*la bille*) and move your car as far as you flick it, unless you flick it off the track. But these and similar activities should perhaps be in another category, headed 'Adult children'. Many of the competitors are adults (and take them very seriously), though there will be separate prizes for under-14's as well. Enquire for all these things on the spot or at the local tourist office; and look out for posters.

Formula bille – a game with no age barriers

Inland

Inland, the four- and five-star campsites will have as many facilities as a beach, and will provide all sorts of amusements for children, including special events and competitions. Normandy is rich in forests where children can run about, picnic, cycle or ride horses. Enquire at tourist offices for the many centres for *équitation* (horse-riding). One or two *châteaux* have special entertainments for children, and there are a few zoos.

Museums

The numerous war museums along the D-Day coast, especially the one at Arromanches (see page 50), and the two a little inland, at Caen (page 56) and Bayeux (page 61), are wonderful for children. To them may be added, at Bayeux, the Centre Guillaume le Conquérant with the Bayeux tapestry (page 60) – organised partly with children in mind. Many smaller towns up and down Normandy have little municipal museums with displays of objects, from fishing tackle to firearms, which may capture children's imagination for an hour. A selection of these and others – maritime museums, car museums, lace-making museums, for example – are listed in the **What to See** sections of this book, as are numerous ruined castles and abbeys, some of which have their own museums.

TIGHT BUDGET

In Normandy, like anywhere else, crowds mean higher prices. If you want to pay less, you must go where there are fewer people. The Côte Fleurie in the high season is the most expensive place in Normandy. Life is cheaper, even in July and August, on the west coast of the Cotentin (but well away from Mont-St-Michel). Prices are lower inland: you could stay somewhere outside a main resort and go in during the day. Things are also always cheaper, anywhere, out of high season.

That said, Normandy is definitely, in global terms, a cheap option for a summer holiday. Everyday prices can be as little as half those of the South of France.

- Shop around – not only for meals, hotels and souvenirs but also for expensive essentials like petrol. See **Shopping**, pages 101-3, for the pros and cons of *hypermarchés*, supermarkets and markets. Beware the small supermarket, probably expensive if also convenient (for instance on a campsite).
- Avoid central cafés. The cheaper one round the corner will offer a less attractive view but an equally refreshing drink.
- Study the menus that are always displayed outside restaurants, and look out for 'hidden' charges such as *couverture* (cover charge), drinks and so on, Often, some wine is included in a tourist menu. A fixed menu is often cheaper than *à la carte*.
- Watch the sundries. It is the drinks, ice-creams, tempting-looking cakes and the like – all the treats you buy when abroad and in holiday mood – that can put you over budget.
- Watch your speed! Speeding fines are on the spot and could make a big hole in your budget, For speed limits, see page 115.

SPECIAL EVENTS

During the summer, almost every community will have something on. The tourist office will know all about it, and will have further details on the ones listed below. Travelling fairs are still a constant feature of Norman towns.

February/March *Mardi Gras* (Shrove Tuesday) Granville: carnival
April Bernay: flower festival
May Coutances: jazz festival
May Mont-St-Michel: St Michael's Fair
May (last weekend) Rouen: Joan of Arc festival
May/June (Whit Monday) Bernay: processions
June Caen: antiques fair
June Mortagne-au-Perche: music festival
June St-Pierre-sur-Dives: dressage competition
June Villedieu-les-Poêles: Grand-Sacré procession (every four years: next 1995)
July Bagnoles-de-l'Orne: 'July in Bagnoles'

Canoeing at Clécy

July Cabourg: regatta of '1000 Sails'
July Deauville: bridge (cards) festival
July Forges-les-Eaux: horse fair
July Le Havre: international regatta
July (end) Mont-St-Michel: pilgrimage processions
July (16th, at night) La-Haye-de-Routot: Le Feu de St Clair (bonfire)
July (last Sunday) Granville: blessing of sea
August Deauville: horse-racing, horse sales, polo
August Domfront: medieval festival
August (2nd Sunday) Le Havre: flower festival
August (mid) Barneville-Carteret: 'Fêtes de la Mer'
August (mid) Dieppe: carnival
August (mid) Lisieux: religious procession
August (late) Cabourg/Dives-sur-Mer: William the Conqueror festival
September (early) Deauville: festival of American films
September (early) Lessay: St Cross fair
September Alençon: music festival
September Caen: horse-racing and fair
September Caudebec: cider festival (alternate years)
September Louviers: St Michael's fair
September (end) Mont-St-Michel: St Michael's fair
September (last weekend) Lisieux: festival of Ste Thérèse
October (early) Deauville: vintage car rally, Paris-Deauville
October (mid) Vimoutiers: apple festival
October/November Rouen: St Romain's fair
November Dieppe: herring festival
December St Valéry-en-Caux: herring and cider festival

SPORT

All sorts of beach and countryside sports are available in Normandy: in particular there are numerous golf-courses and horse-riding stables (enquire at the local tourist office or at your hotel). Temporary use or membership of golf-courses, tennis courts, swimming pools and the like is usually possible: the fee will be more than minimal but not outrageous. Equipment such as bicycles, canoes and wind-surfing boards can be hired, though again not cheaply. Apart from these the most common local sport is the very farmerly one of *balltrap* (clay-pigeon shooting). Special competitions, from table-tennis to sandcastle making, are put on in resorts in summer (see **Children**, pages 109-11).

Directory

This section (with the biscuit-coloured band) contains day-to-day information, including travel, health and documentation.

Contents

Arriving

Although there are small airports at Caen, Cherbourg, Deauville, Rouen and Le Havre, most people enter Normandy by land or sea.

Ferries

Ferries from England (Poole, Southampton, Portsmouth and Newhaven) and Ireland (Cork and Rosslare) dock at Cherbourg, Caen, Le Havre and Dieppe. All these crossings take at least four hours, and many British cross to Calais or Boulogne and drive down to Normandy. Especially during August it is wise, and on some dates essential, to book ferries in advance. Trains link up with the ferries, which carry exchange facilities and shops.

Road and Rail

There is a motorway (the A13) between Paris and Caen (with extensions to Le Havre and Deauville), continuing with mostly dual carriageway (N13) up to Cherbourg.
Trains run from Paris (St-Lazare and Montparnasse stations) regularly and quickly to Rouen and some other towns. Getting from place to place within Normandy by train often involves changing.

Entry Formalities
For a stay of up to three months, nationals of Britain, Ireland and other EC countries, the USA, Canada and New Zealand need only a passport. Check, though, with a travel agent or the French Government Tourist Office (for addresses see **Tourist Offices**, page 125), since visa policy is subject to review.

Camping
Normandy is excellent for camping. It is full of campsites of all sorts and sizes, from the basic *camping à la ferme* (farm) or municipal sites to four-star sites, usually taking both tents and caravans, and often hiring tents or caravans ready in place (see **Accommodation,** page 105). Details of sites can be obtained at local tourist offices or, before you travel, in specialist books or agency brochures. In summer, arrive early at the site to be sure of a place. If you do, it is seldom necessary to book.

Cars see **Driving**

Chemist see **Pharmacies**

Crime
This need not be uppermost in your mind in Normandy, but take elementary precautions such as locking the car and not leaving valuables visible.

Customs Regulations
The standard EC regulations apply. See also **Entry Formalities** above.

Disabled Travellers
In most public places these days in Normandy there are ramps as well as steps, and a fair amount has been done to make buildings accessible to wheelchair visitors.

Driving
A certain amount of preparation is required for British and Irish drivers – not least gearing yourself up for driving on the right.

Insurance
Special insurance should be taken out – a current comprehensive car insurance policy will cover you for third-party risks abroad, but for comprehensive insurance you will need a 'green card', which you can arrange through your broker at home. You may also wish to take out special accident, illness, loss or breakdown cover (such as AA Five Star Service), which can be invaluable – especially if you don't speak French or are unfamiliar with the country.

Documents
You should carry with you a valid full driving licence (international permit not required for visitors from the US, UK or Western Europe); a current insurance certificate; the vehicle's registration document, and a letter from the vehicle's owner giving you permission to drive it if the owner is not accompanying the vehicle.

Headlights
Beam deflectors or headlamp converters (available from the AA or car accessory shops) should be fixed to your headlights, for otherwise they will be dipping into oncoming traffic rather than away from it.

A view worth a detour any day – Les Andelys on the Seine

The French like their headlights yellow, and it is possible to stick on a yellow filter or paint the glass with a special yellow lacquer, but this is not so important.

Other Accessories
Your car should display a nationality plate or sticker, usually provided with your ferry ticket. Extras to carry with you include a complete spare-bulb kit for your vehicle and an emergency warning triangle.

Seat-belts
Laws are the same as in Britain.

Speed Limits
Speed limits on French roads are sometimes lower than on the equivalent roads in other countries. They are zealously enforced by the police using radar traps and heavy on-the-spot fines to deter offenders. The speed limit in towns and villages is 50kph (31mph), or sometimes lower – watch for signs. Ordinary roads – even dead straight ones with no traffic – have a limit of 90kph (55mph). On dual carriageways and non-toll motorways you can travel at 110kph (68mph), while on toll motorways the speed limit rises to 130kph (80mph). In rain or other bad weather the speed limits automatically reduce from 90 to 80kph, from 110 to 100kph and from 130 to 110kph. There is also a *minimum* speed limit of 80kph (49mph) for the outside lane of a level stretch of motorway in good daytime visibility.

Drinking and Driving
By far the safest policy is not to drive after drinking alcohol. Apart from increasing the risk of an accident spoiling your holiday, you risk an instant and heavy fine if you are found to be over the limit. French law entitles the police to take random breath tests.

Road Signs

France uses the normal international road signs. *Chaussée déformée* means an uneven road surface. *Chantier* or *Travaux* means roadworks.

Giving Way

This is perhaps the hardest part about driving in France, and it is well worth becoming thoroughly familiar with the necessary road signs.
In towns the rule of *priorité à droite* prevails. Unless a notice says otherwise, you must give way to any vehicle crossing from your right, even from small side-roads. As a corollary, you will often have the right of way when you did not expect it, and you will only annoy French drivers by stopping.
The priority rule at roundabouts no longer applies, which means you give way to traffic already on the roundabout. You are reminded by the signs *Vous n'avez pas la priorité* (You do not have priority), or *Cédez le passage* (Give way).Outside the towns, important main roads have right of way. This is indicated by one of three road signs:
1 A red-bordered triangle surrounding a black cross on a white background with the words *Passage protégé* (You have right of way).
2 A red-bordered triangle with a pointed black upright with a horizontal bar on a white background.
3 A yellow diamond within a white diamond. (The yellow diamond crossed through means 'you no longer have priority'.)
Pay attention to road markings, and do not cross a solid white or yellow line marked on the centre of the road.
Traffic lights also need special care. They can be dim, and are sometimes high above the road. A flashing amber light warns of a particularly dangerous junction.

Accidents

Follow the instructions given by your insurance company. Ask any witnesses to stay in order to make statements, and contact the police. Exchange insurance details with other drivers involved.

Breakdowns

Carry a red warning triangle, and if you break down place it on the road 33 yards (30m) behind the broken-down vehicle. Switch on your hazard warning lights.
France has no nationwide road assistance service such as the AA, so seek help from a local garage in the event of a breakdown. (It is wise to take out emergency breakdown insurance before you leave home. Read the accompanying instructions carefully, and keep them handy in the car in case you break down.) Emergency phones (marked 'SOS'), where they exist, are connected direct to the police, who will contact a garage for you.

Car Rental

This is perfectly possible, though not particularly cheap in France. It may be less expensive to arrange and pay for it before you travel to France.

Fuel
Most petrol stations now take credit cards as well as cash. All except the most old-fashioned pumps in remote villages offer unleaded petrol (*essence sans plomb*). Check the octane rating your car requires.
For a full tank, ask for *le plein, s'il vous plaît*. Expect to pay more than average for petrol on an *autoroute*, less than average at a *hypermarché*.
Some petrol stations now have an unmanned night service with a pump that works like a cash-dispensing machine in requiring a PIN number as well as the credit card. This is a pity for foreigners, for it may not recognise their PIN. Nor will it take cash. If desperate, you could wait for a Frenchman to come along and then offer him cash in exchange for his using his credit card on your behalf.

Electricity
The supply is 220 volts. Plugs have two or sometimes three round pins. Adaptors for French plugs are not easy to find in France, and are best bought before leaving home.

Embassies and Consulates
British Embassy
35 rue du Faubourg-St-Honoré, 75383 Paris (tel: (1) 42 66 91 42), with a consular section at 9 avenue Hoche, 75008 Paris (tel: (1) 42 66 38 10). There are British Consulates with Honorary Consuls in Cherbourg and Le Havre.
US Embassy
2 avenue Gabriel, 75382 Paris (tel: (1) 42 96 12 02)
Canadian Embassy
35 avenue Montaigne, 75008 Paris (tel: (1) 47 23 01 01)
Irish Embassy
4 rue Rude, 75016 Paris (tel: (1) 45 00 20 87)
Australian Embassy
4 rue Jean Rey, 75015 Paris (tel: (1) 40 59 33 07)
New Zealand Embassy
Rue Léonard-da-Vinci, Paris (tel: 45 00 24 11)

Emergency Telephone Numbers
Police 17
Firemen (*Sapeurs pompiers*) 18
Ambulance Number given in telephone call-box; otherwise telephone the Police (17).

Entertainment Information
The local tourist office is the best source of information. See also **Culture, Entertainment and Nightlife**, pages 106-7.

Health
No special precautions or vaccinations are required.
In the event of illness (rather than an emergency requiring an ambulance – see **Emergency Telephone Numbers**, above), doctors

Carriage display at Haras du Pin

(*médecins*) and dentists (*dentistes*) can be found by enquiry at the tourist office (which can also give you a list beforehand) or in the telephone directory.
You will have to pay for treatment, but, under a reciprocal health agreement between Britain and France, the British can reclaim most of the doctor's fee and also prescription charges.
To do this, you need to take with you to France a form E111, obtainable from post offices on completion of the form contained in booklet 'T2'.
Obtain a form (*feuille de soins*) from the French doctor and send it and the receipts of payment to the local *Caisse Primaires d'Assurance-Maladie*. Check with the doctor or the tourist office which *Caisse* to send them to. The Irish can obtain a similar dispensation by applying to their Regional Health Board at home for a form E111.
Normandy is not free from that bane of the summer holiday, the mosquito, but insect repellents of all kinds are available from pharmacies or *quincailleries* (ironmongers). Wasps may also be a problem for picnickers.
If you are on the beach, be very careful about sunburn and sunstroke. Take special care with young children, ensuring they wear sunhats and a sun-screening cream. Acclimatise yourselves to the sun gradually, and do not underestimate the burning power of hazy sunshine, especially if there is a sea breeze.

Holidays
French public and religious holidays are:
New Year's Day (1 January)
Easter Sunday and Monday
Labour Day (1 May)
VE Day (8 May)
Ascension Day (40 days after Easter)
Whitsun or Pentecost – Sunday and Monday
Bastille Day (14 July)
Assumption (15 August)
All Saints' Day (1 November)
Remembrance Day (11 November)
Christmas Day (25 December)

Lost Property
In Normandy, it will be worth returning to the place where you lost anything – a restaurant, shop, hotel, place on the beach – and enquiring, because people are usually honest and glad to help. The police are perhaps less interested in finding lost property than they might be – but inform them if documents such as a passport, credit cards or cheques are involved. For passports, also inform your embassy (see **Embassies and Consulates**, page 117). Make sure you have kept a note of what to do if you lose your credit cards or travellers' cheques (see **Credit Cards**, page 120).

Media
All kinds of brochures and leaflets are available at the tourist office, and local papers will advertise everything going on. In well-frequented towns in summer you can be sure to find a newsagent carrying a good stock of foreign as well as French newspapers (the local

Something for everyone – this bakery sells many different breads

one is *Ouest-France*), also a range of local maps and guides, informing about everything from walks to restaurants.

Radio and Television
You should be able to receive most BBC radio stations in Normandy. *Radio France Normandie* can be heard on 102.6 MHz and there are a number of local stations. French hotels are rather behind other European countries in providing a range of national channels for the television in your room.

Money

The French franc (FF) is the unit of currency. There are silver coins for 50 centimes (1/2 franc), 1 franc, 2 francs and 5 francs. The 10 and 20-franc coins are brass with a silver centre, and there are brass coins for 20, 10 and 5 centimes. Banknotes start at 20 francs, then 50, 100 and 200.

For UK visitors, conversion is very simple: 10 francs is a little more than £1. There is no limit to the currency that may be imported or, in practice, exported.

Exchange
On balance, to get the best rate most conveniently, it is advisable to change money into French francs before you travel to France. If you don't want to take all your money in cash, or need a standby in case of emergency or overspending, then Eurocheques (obtainable from your bank at home) are the next best thing. However, it is often cheapest (in terms of exchange rates and commission) and most convenient to pay at hotels, shops, petrol-stations and restaurants with a credit card where possible – which is

most places.
Eurocheques, travellers' cheques and cash can be changed at most banks, which often have a special desk for exchange. Fortunately the old system where you did the paper transaction at one desk and then went to the *caisse* to get the cash, is becoming extinct. Bank opening hours are 09.00 (or sometimes earlier) to 12.00hrs, then 14.00 (or 14.45) to 16.00 (or 16.45) hrs. Banks are closed on Sunday and either Saturday or Monday. However, in small towns inland you may well find that some banks are only part-time, opening on alternate days, for instance, or only in the mornings. The only way to be sure is to check on the spot.
If a bank is impracticable, then ports, airports, ferries and main railway stations have exchange facilities, but rates are poor. It is usually said that hotels also give poor rates, but if you are staying or eating there they are often happy, these days, to give you the bank rate or even better. Nowadays, especially since ERM (the Exchange Rate Mechanism), the whole business is much less fraught than it used to be.

Credit Cards
Even shops that don't advertise the fact often take credit cards these days. However, some *hypermarchés* don't. Many cash dispensers will now recognise foreign Personal Identification Numbers with credit cards, and this can be a handy method of obtaining cash quickly. The French *Carte Bleue* is the equivalent of Visa; Access or Mastercard is also called Eurocard. Nowadays credit card insurance, which is still comparatively cheap, is well worth having, above all because it reduces the complications of informing the necessary offices of loss or theft.

Eurocheques
Virtually every hotel or shop, including *hypermarchés*, will accept a Eurocheque with its accompanying card. You can also draw money at a bank up to the value of FF1400 per cheque. Be warned that if you make out a cheque for more than this amount, even though it

Colourful shelters, Deauville beach

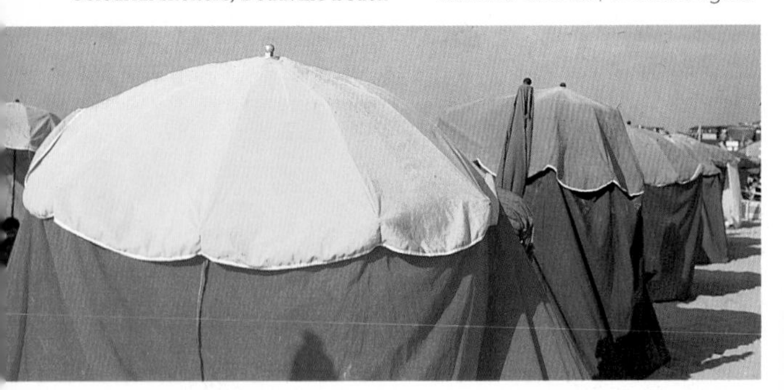

is legitimate (though not guaranteed), you become liable for a much steeper commission with your bank at home. The payee also often has to pay charges, which is the reason why Eurocheques may occasionally be refused.

Opening Times

Banks see **Money**, above.

Bars Times vary, but there are no compulsory closure times. Most are open all day except on one day (*jour de repos*) a week.

Museums, châteaux, etc Tuesday is the usual day on which state museums shut, and many municipal and private institutions follow suit. But not necessarily: Monday is another common closing day, next followed by Wednesday or Friday.

Most institutions close altogether in mid-winter. Many open every day during July and August. Some close on public holidays, others open specially for them. Indications are given in the individual entries in the **What to See** sections of this book. Many places close for lunch – usually from 12.00 to 14.00hrs. Few stay open after 17.00hrs, though some close at 18.00hrs in high season.

Post Offices see **Post Office,** page 122

Restaurants Most close at least one day a week, sometimes one and a half days. Many of the smartest take their holidays during high season, not off season. They vary enormously, so enquire by telephone.

Shops The usual times are from about 09.00hrs (dry goods shops are often later, *boulangeries* earlier) to 12.00hrs, or 12.30hrs in the case of food shops. Lunchtime closing is normal. Shops re-open between 14.00 and 15.00hrs, and stay open (and this is really useful) till 19.00, 19.30 or even 20.00hrs (often depending on business). In Normandy, there are seasonal exceptions: in high season shops will usually open longer and more often (*boulangeries* often forego their weekly closing day), and in low season they will close more readily. Quite a lot of shops, especially *boulangeries* and *pâtisseries*, open on Sunday morning, closing on Monday morning instead. Many shops do not open, or open late after stock-taking, on Monday morning. *Hypermarchés* often stay open during the lunch-hour (they have cafés and restaurants), and until 21.00 or 22.00hrs. They are closed on Sunday and sometimes also on Monday morning.

Tourist Offices The usual hours are 9.00 to 19.00hrs, either closing for lunch or operating with minimal staff. Tourist offices very often close down as such during the winter; or rather, in many places, they are set up for the summer. In smaller places, even in the season, their opening hours are erratic and they may open only on certain days, though they are usually open in the morning.

Personal Safety

Normandy being mostly rural, or at least free from most of the evils of the big city, personal safety is not something requiring special care.

Pharmacies
French pharmacies, identifiable by the green cross suspended outside, emanate a wonderful air of cleanliness and efficiency, and usually manage to be friendly as well as clinical. They frequently offer a bewildering range of beauty products in their window, besides the drugs and medicines which the pharmacist is empowered to prescribe, if necessary, for minor ailments. Often they will speak some English.
In case of emergency, the prescribing doctor will tell you which pharmacies will be open outside normal hours. The rota of *pharmacies de garde*, as they are called, is listed in tourist office handouts, in local newspapers, at the police station, or on the door even of closed pharmacies.

Places of Worship
For anything other than a Catholic mass in French, enquire at the tourist office. Masses are listed on church doors, and sometimes still on signs as you enter towns or villages.

Police
There is a distinction between the *police municipale*, or local police, who also fulfil the functions of various kinds of 'wardens', and the *gendarmes*, who deal with crime and also traffic offences (usually on the open road rather than in a town). *Gendarmes* carry guns. You are most likely to get involved with either sort as a result of traffic offences. You will find them strict, inclined neither to discuss the case nor to let you go; on the other hand they won't moralise tediously, they will just fine you (often on the spot). See also **Driving**, pages 114-17.
An important figure on the beaches is not a policeman (indeed, he is often little more than a student), but the lifeguard. He is responsible for order and safety on the beach and in the sea, and his word is law.

Post Office
Central or branch post offices, or PTT (*Poste et Télécommunications*), are usually open from 08.00 to 19.00hrs on weekdays and from 08.00 to 12.00hrs on Saturdays (branch offices may well close at lunchtime). They will send a telex or fax, also telegrams. They should also – like most hotels and many private subscribers – have a 'minitel', or computerised telephone book: it is better than a telephone book in doing many more kinds of searches.
All towns and districts are now post-coded. When addressing a letter, write the code before the name of the town.
Poste restante only operates in main post offices in major towns. Address the letter: Poste Restante, Poste Centrale, followed by the town name.
Stamps are sold in post offices but can also be bought in a *tabac* (tobacconist's). Letter boxes are yellow.

Public Transport
Getting about between towns and villages in Normandy is not very easy. The railways tend to radiate from Paris, so getting

across Normandy can involve one or often more changes, with long intervals. The local bus service may well be more direct; enquire locally.
Within large towns, such as Rouen or Caen, buses again can be used; in most cases you need to buy the ticket beforehand. Taxis are not very expensive, if you can find them at the taxi rank (you can usually obtain a taxi call number at a hotel, restaurant or shop).
For air and ferries, see **Arriving**, page 113.

Senior Citizens
Normandy is full of locals who have lived there all their lives, or families who have been holidaying in Normandy for generations. People also like to retire to some of the resorts. Given the traditionalism of manners and mores, Normandy is an excellent place for senior citizens, who will be welcomed and respected.
Reductions are available for nationals of EC countries on rail travel and on other communal charges: enquire at the Department of Social Security, at railway station enquiry offices at home, and at tourist offices both at home and in Normandy.

Student and Youth Travel
For reductions on travel into and around Normandy, enquire at student or youth travel organisations at home for qualifications.
The French National Youth Hostel Association (*Fédération Unie des Auberges de Jeunesse – FUJA*) is at 27 rue Pajol, 75018 Paris (tel: (1) 46 07 00 01).
Normandy is full of campsites (see **Camping**). It is quite possible to go on a walking, cycling or driving tour of Normandy and camp and eat very cheaply if you are hardy.

Telephones
The dialling tone is a long, sharp hum. The ringing tone is a long slow burr, followed by a pause and more long slow burrs. The engaged tone (*occupé*) consists of more rapid burrs. To telephone into Normandy from abroad, dial the international code (010 from Britain), then 33, then the eight figures of the number required.
To telephone within Normandy or to the rest of France, dial just the eight figures. To dial Paris, prefix the eight figures with 161. To dial Normandy from Paris, dial 16 then the eight-figure number.
To dial out of France from Normandy, dial 19 and wait for a new tone. Then dial the international code of the country you want (for example

Capturing the view, Mont-St-Michel

Formal gardens at Thury Harcourt

1 for the United States and Canada; 44 for Britain; 353 for Ireland; 61 for Australia; 64 for New Zealand), then the local code (omitting the initial zero) and number. A series of rapid pips means you are being connected.
For directory enquiries, dial 12. Cheap rate (50 per cent cheaper) is on weekdays between 21.30 and 08.00hrs, and weekends after 14.00hrs on Saturday.

Public Telephones
Public call boxes are quite frequent. More and more take a phone card (*télécarte*), which can be obtained in post offices, *tabacs*, newsagents and other outlets that advertise the fact. Put the card in and close the flap before dialling.

Time
France follows Greenwich Mean Time plus one hour, except during summer time (late March to late September) which is plus two hours. French time is the same time as the rest of Europe except Britain and Ireland, which are one hour behind all year (except for a short interval in October, when they are the same).

Tipping
Service is nearly always *compris* (included) these days in hotel, bar and restaurant bills. However, it remains a friendly gesture to leave small change in the waiter's saucer in bars and restaurants. Some people still tip taxi drivers, but it is not expected. Hotel maids may deserve to be tipped with money left in the room.

Toilets
The usual international symbols are used for Ladies, Gents and Disabled toilets. You will still sometimes see *Dames* (Women) and *Messieurs* (Gentlemen) or *Hommes* (Men). You will still find 'squat' toilets, said to be much better for you, in many places, but they make up a diminishing percentage, well under half. You will also find, in places like Deauville, high-tech toilets that do not just flush the bowl but clean the seat

as well. Children love them as much as they hate the 'squat' toilets, if they are not used to them, but you have to pay at least two francs.
Public toilets exist (often, very usefully for children, on beaches) but for these, too, you will have to pay the *concierge*. Otherwise you may ask to use the toilet in a bar, a request that will surely be granted, but do leave a tip or buy a drink.

Tourist Offices
The telephone numbers and addresses of the invaluable local *Offices de Tourisme* or *Syndicats d'Initiative* are given under town entries in the **What to See** sections of this book. These tourist offices provide plenty of information, leaflets or brochures, ranging from entertainment to street maps.
There are also regional and *département* tourist offices, but they tend to provide only much broader information:
For All Normandy Comité Régional de Tourisme de Normandie, 14 rue Charles-Corbeau, 27000 Evreux (tel: 32 33 79 00)
Seine-Maritime Comité Départemental de Tourisme (CDT), 2 bis rue du Petit-Salut, BP 680, 76008 Rouen (tel: 35 88 61 32)
Eure CDT, Hôtel du Département, boulevard Georges-Chauvin, 27021 Evreux (tel: 32 31 51 51)
Orne CDT, 88 rue St-Blaise, BP 50, 61002 Alençon (tel: 33 28 88 71)
Calvados CDT, place du Canada, 14000 Caen (tel: 31 86 53 30)
Manche CDT, Maison du Département, route de Villedieu, 50008 St-Lô (tel: 33 05 98 70).
These are perhaps best for information about accommodation or letting. But French Government Tourist Offices abroad will supply this and are probably more attuned to providing individual orientation and travel details for that particular country:
Britain 178 Piccadilly, London W1V OAL, (tel: 071-491 7622; 24-hour recorded information 071-499 6911)
Ireland 35 Lower Abbey Street, Dublin 1 (tel: 01-771 871)
USA 610 Fifth Avenue, New York, NY 10020 (tel: 212 757 1125); or 645 Michigan Avenue, Chicago, Ill 60611 (tel: 312-337 6301); or 9454 Wilshire Boulevard, Suite 314, Beverley Hills, Ca 90212 (tel: 310-271 6665); or 2305 Cedar Springs Boulevard, Dallas, Texas 75201 (tel: 214-720 4010)
Canada 1981 Avenue McGill College, Suite 490, Montréal, Québec H3A 2W9 (tel: 514-288 4264)
Australia BNP Building, 12th Floor, 12 Castelreagh Street, Sydney NSW 2000 (tel: 02-231 5244).
The sort of information tourist offices usually provide includes how to get there; lists and prices of hotels, campsites, restaurants; services; events; information on what to visit .

Travel Agencies in Normandy
These are almost all geared for French use, and international travel; some will provide Intercity railway tickets.

LANGUAGE

French people always appreciate it if you try to speak to them in their own language. Courtesy is all-important: prefix questions to strangers with *s'il vous plaît* or *excusez-moi*, and address people as *monsieur* or *madame*. Here are a few words and phrases which may help those visitors who are not fluent French speakers.

please s'il vous plaît
thank you merci
hello bonjour
good evening/night bonsoir
goodbye au revoir
I'm sorry pardon
yes oui
no non
today aujourd'hui
excuse me excusez-moi
can you direct me to...? pouvez-vous m'indiquer la direction de...?
where is...? où se trouve...?
toilets les toilettes
how much is it? c'est combien?
I want to buy je voudrais acheter
that's too expensive c'est trop cher
do you speak English? parlez-vous anglais?
a room with a bath une chambre avec salle de bains
the bill, please l'addition, s'il vous plaît

Numbers

one un/une
two deux
three trois
four quatre
five cinq
six six
seven sept
eight huit
nine neuf
ten dix

Days of the Week

Monday lundi
Tuesday mardi
Wednesday mercredi
Thursday jeudi
Friday vendredi
Saturday samedi
Sunday dimanche

Shopping

shops les magasins
baker la boulangerie
newsagents, paper shop, stationers la librairie
library la bibliothèque
butcher la boucherie
chemist la pharmacie
delicatessen la charcuterie
food shop l'alimentation
fishmongers la poissonnerie

Acknowledgements
The Automobile Association wishes to thank the following photographers and libraries for their assistance in the preparation of this book.
Clive Sawyer took all the photographs (© AA Photo Library), except the following: **P Holberton** 110 Formula *bille;* **Mary Evans Picture Library** 7 bathing, 14 Jeanne d'Arc, 18 Gustave Flaubert; **Nature Photographers Ltd** 89 golden saxifrage, 91 sea spurge, 94 perennial centaury, 96 bush cricket (all P R Sterry), 92 warbler (M Bolton), 95 lady's tresses (A J Cleave); **Spectrum Colour Library** 30 St Valéry-en-Caux, 32 Varengeville-sur-Mer, 36 St-Maclou Cloisters, 38 Rouen, *cover* Mont-St-Michel.

INDEX

Page numbers in *italic* refer to illustrations

INDEX